MARIANNE AND THE PRIVATEER

Juliette Benzoni was born and educated in Paris, studying at the Collège d'Hulet, then at the Institut Catholique, where she obtained a BA degree in Philosophy, a Licentiate in Law and a Licentiate in Letters. She was married to Dr Maurice Gallois in 1941 and had two children. Widowed in 1950, she moved to Casablanca and lived there for two years. Back in Paris she married Count André Benzoni di Costa in March 1953. She has been in charge of the historical section of the French paper *Confidences* since 1960. Juliette Benzoni is the author of the famous 'Catherine' series of historical romances, set in medieval France, and of the successful 'Marianne' series, set in Napoleonic France.

By the same author in Pan Books

MARIANNE, BOOK 1: The Bride of Selton Hall

MARIANNE, BOOK 2: The Eagle and the Nightingale

MARIANNE AND THE MASKED PRINCE

CATHERINE

ONE LOVE IS ENOUGH

CATHERINE AND A TIME FOR LOVE

BELLE CATHERINE

CATHERINE AND ARNAUD

Marianne and the Privateer

JULIETTE BENZONI

Translated by
Anne Carter

UNABRIDGED

PAN BOOKS LTD : LONDON

First published in French 1971 as *Marianne: Jason des quatre mers* by
Opera Mundi, Paris
First published in Great Britain 1972
by William Heinemann Ltd
This edition published 1974 by Pan Books Ltd,
33 Tothill Street, London SW1

ISBN 0 330 23883 3

Printed in Great Britain by
Cox & Wyman Ltd, London, Reading and Fakenham

Contents

Part One
THE TRAP

Part Two
THE PRISONER

Principal Characters

Marianne Elisabeth d'Asselnat. The daughter of a French marquis and his English wife, both of whom perished in the French Revolution. She was rescued as a baby by her godfather, Gauthier de Chazay, and taken to England to be brought up by her spinster aunt, Ellis Selton. In 1809, she married Francis Cranmere who, on her wedding night, gambled away both her fortune and her virginity. Marianne saved herself and fled to France where, after many adventures, she fell in love with Napoleon and became his mistress. He gave her the Paris mansion which had belonged to her family and the identity of Signorina Maria Stella, an Italian *cantatrice*. The reappearance of her villainous husband and the discovery of her pregnancy led to the annulment of her marriage and the contracting of a second, equally unconsummated, with the mysterious recluse Corrado Sant'Anna. As Princess Sant'Anna, Marianne returns from the prince's haunted domain near Lucca to find herself welcomed as a leader of Parisian society.

Adelaide d'Asselnat. A French cousin of Marianne's, an elderly spinster. Marianne found her living in hiding in the attics of her house and prepared to burn it down rather than see it occupied by an upstart. She became Marianne's companion.

Jason Beaufort. The American sea-captain to whom Francis Cranmere lost Marianne's fortune and virginity at cards. Jason generously failed to claim the second and reappeared later in Paris to become one of the few people Marianne felt prepared to trust, but he had sailed away out of reach when she tried to turn to him before her marriage to Prince Sant'Anna.

Gauthier de Chazay, a French Abbé, later Cardinal San Lorenzo.

Marianne's godfather, who rescued her as a baby from the Revolution and was responsible for arranging her marriage to Prince Sant'Anna.

Count Alexander Ivanovitch Chernychev. A Cossack colonel and officer of the Russian Imperial Guard on an official mission to Paris. A noted womanizer who has been pursuing Marianne with his attentions.

Francis, Lord Cranmere. Marianne's dastardly first husband whom she had left for dead in the burning wreck of Selton Hall after forcing him to fight a duel with her. He reappeared as an English spy in Paris and attempted to blackmail her, was captured but escaped, probably through Fouché's connivance.

Quintin Crawfurd. A friend of Talleyrand with an adventurous past.

Eleonora Crawfurd. His wife; lived as a girl on the Sant'Anna estates.

Matteo Damiani. Agent of the Sant'Anna estates. One of the few people close to the prince, but with a sinister history connected with the dead witch-princess Lucinda, Corrado's grandmother. Marianne crossed swords with him at the Villa dei Cavalli.

Fanchon Fleur-de-Lis, alias the Dame Désormeaux. A hideous old woman in whose hands Marianne was once a prisoner. At the time of the action, a figure in the Paris underworld and fiercely anti-Revolutionary.

Joseph Fouché, Duke of Otranto. Formerly Napoleon's chief of police, now discredited and exiled.

François Fournier-Sarlovèze. General in Napoleon's army; dedicated duellist, often in disgrace on this account, and lover of Fortunée Hamelin.

Fortunée Hamelin. A Créole lady, and a leading figure in Parisian society. Passionately devoted to the Emperor, she was entrusted by him with the task of introducing Marianne to the polite world and the two women became great friends.

Arcadius, Vicomte de Jolival. A French aristocrat and one of Marianne's staunchest friends; formerly her theatrical manager, now her business agent.

Donna Lavinia. Housekeeper and devoted retainer of Prince Corrado Sant'Anna.

Jean Ledru. One of Surcouf's seamen. Escaped with Marianne from England and was the man to whom she lost her virginity. Their subsequent relations were unfriendly.

Nicolas Mallerousse, alias Black Fish. One of Fouché's secret agents operating in England. Marianne escaped from England in his boat and he developed a deep and fatherly affection for her. She took his name in her first days in Paris. He captured Francis Cranmere and, when the Englishman escaped, vowed to track him down or die in the attempt.

Morvan the Wrecker. Leader of a band of Royalist ship-wreckers: Marianne was once his prisoner when her ship was wrecked on the coast of Brittany.

Gracchus-Hannibal Pioche. A former Paris errand boy, now, at the time of the action, Marianne's devoted coachman.

Savary, Duke of Rovigo. Replaced Fouché as Napoleon's chief of police.

Prince Corrado Sant'Anna. Marianne's second husband. The heir to great Italian estates and scion of a powerful but strangely accursed family. Suffers from some unspecified trouble which makes him live the life of a recluse. He married Marianne because she was pregnant with Napoleon's child.

Baron Surcouf. A sea-captain, famous for his free-lance activities against English shipping off the coast of Brittany.

Charles Maurice de Talleyrand, Prince of Benevento. Formerly Napoleon's Foreign Minister, now somewhat out of favour. Fouché used Marianne as a spy in his household but Talleyrand, who had known her father, recognized her and became her friend and sponsor in Parisian society on her return from Lucca.

Part One

THE TRAP

CHAPTER ONE

Tragedy at the Ball

It was the evening of the first of July and an unending line of carriages stretched all down the rue Mont Blanc and overflowed into the adjoining streets, invading even the courtyard of the big private houses whose double gates had been thrown open to provide more room and to relieve the pressure a little. It was clear, early as it was, that the ball being given by the Austrian ambassador, Prince Schwarzenburg, was a success. The Emperor himself was to be present and, what was more to the point, so was the Empress, in whose honour the party was being held, so that the twelve hundred guests felt themselves highly privileged persons while a good two or three thousand of the uninvited sat at home brooding on this unfeeling neglect.

One after another, at foot-pace, the carriages turned into the short avenue of poplars leading to the colonnaded entrance to the embassy, lit up for the occasion by great cressets of antique design flaring cheerfully in the darkness. The house, which had once belonged to Madame de Montesson, the morganatic wife of the Duc d'Orléans, was not over-large and could not compare for splendour with its opulent neighbour, the Russian embassy, housed by Napoleon in the luxurious Hôtel Thélusson which he had purchased from Murat at the cost of a million francs and the Elysée Palace, but it was exquisitely decorated and possessed extensive grounds in which there was even a miniature farm, as well as a Temple of Apollo.

It was these grounds which had given the ambassador an idea how to provide for the entertainment of all those whom he desired to invite in spite of the comparative limitations of his drawing-rooms. He had commissioned the erection in them of an enormous temporary ballroom made of oilcloth stretched over a light wooden frame, linked to the main reception rooms of the house by a further temporary arcade. This ballroom and its delightful decorations had been the talk of Paris for a week past.

Like everyone else, Marianne had been obliged to sit for an hour or more, wedged in the jam between the house of the banker Perregaux and the embassy, before she could set foot on the acres of red carpet that covered the steps. The carriage in which she rode belonged to Talleyrand who had insisted on escorting her to the ball since, in a way, it marked her official entry into Parisian society.

'The important thing is to be there before the Emperor, eh?' the Prince of Benevento remarked. He was, as ever, a model of restrained elegance, his dark coat relieved only by the ribbons and medals of his Austrian decorations, the grandest of which, the Golden Fleece, nestled unobtrusively in the snowy folds of his cravat. 'Besides, one should always be fairly early if one wants to be noticed, and tonight I trust no one will have eyes for anyone but you.'

Indeed, that night Marianne was breathtakingly beautiful. The pale gold stuff of her dress had been chosen by Leroy, after long thought, to blend perfectly with the warm colour of her skin and the setting of her jewels, the huge, fabulous emeralds which had belonged to the sorceress Lucinda and which Nitot the jeweller had miraculously succeeded in transforming into a parure just in time for this evening. They flashed with green fire as Marianne stepped from the darkness of the carriage into the glittering fairyland of the salons, rousing an answering flash of envy in the eyes of every woman present, and of their male escorts too, although the men's desires were bent as much on the wearer as on her magnificent jewels. She looked like some fantastic, gilded statue and no man watching her as she moved forward slowly to the rustle of her long train could have said whether his admiration was given most to the perfection of her smooth features, the purity of the breast on which the scintillating green tear-drops lay quivering lightly, or to the brilliance of her eyes or the tender, irresistibly touching curve of her smiling lips. Yet not one would have dared give open expression to the feelings she aroused and this not only because she was known to be the Emperor's, but because of something at once remote and detached in the attitude of the dazzling creature herself.

Any daughter of Eve would have burst with pride to wear those fabulous gems. Probaby only Madame de Metternich, newly elevated to the rank of princess, boasted stones of such fine cut. Yet Marianne wore them with an indifference that was almost melancholy and her eyes, below the tiara which so wonderfully matched their deep, uncommon colouring, were strangely absent.

A subdued murmur followed the passage of this oddly-assorted yet impressive pair. The age and austerity of the Limping Devil served as a foil to the Princess Sant'Anna's brilliant beauty. Well aware of the effect they made, Talleyrand smiled to himself behind his bland diplomatic façade. Among those present he could see the most fashionable and admired women of the Empire, women like the Duchess of Ragusa, wearing the diamonds given her by her father, the banker Perregaux, or like Marshal Ney's wife, decked in the sapphires some of which, rumour had it, had belonged to the late queen, Marie-Antoinette. And besides these, there were the great Austrian and Hungarian ladies: Countess Zichy with her famous rubies and Princess Esterhazy whose collection of jewels was accounted the richest in all the Habsburg Empire. Yet not one of them could outshine the young woman leaning so gracefully on his arm who was, he could not help feeling, to some extent his own personal creation. Not even old Prince Kurakin, though he seemed to be dripping with diamonds, or those noble Russian ladies whose massive, barbaric ornaments might have come straight from the legendary realm of Golconda, were more brilliant or more exquisitely regal than the girl at his side. He revelled with an artist's delight in Marianne's unspoken triumph.

Marianne herself neither saw nor heard. Her smile was mechanical, pinned to her face like a mask. She had the curious feeling that the only part of her which was truly alive was her gloved hand resting lightly on the Prince of Benevento's arm. Everything else was blank and dead, an icy façade lit by no inner warmth.

She could not understand what she was doing here in this foreign embassy among all these strangers whom she could feel devouring her with their eager curiosity. What had she come for, beyond a pitiful social triumph over people who had already talked over her strange story to their hearts' content and were now agog to discover more of her secret, of how the daughter of a noble house had descended to treading the boards for love of an emperor, only to rise to yet greater heights by virtue of a marriage that was stranger and more mysterious than anything else in her life?

How they would sneer, she thought bitterly, if they could but know how miserable and lonely was the woman they envied, and how heavy the heart which lay in her breast as silent and dead as a lump of lava. Life, love, passion were all gone. All her charm, her femininity, her perfect beauty, everything in her which asked only to live and flourish in the warmth of love, had been frozen into this effigy of solitary pride. Her eyes dwelt sadly on a little scene being enacted not far away from her: a girl had entered the room, following in the wake of her plumed and impressively bejewelled mama, and a young lieutenant of hussars stepped quickly forward to meet her with an exclamation of delight. The girl was very young and not particularly pretty: she was rather plump with a dull complexion and a shocking air of timidity, besides being dressed in a gown of stiff pink gauze which made her look exactly like a shuttlecock, but the eyes of the young hussar shone like stars at the sight of her, whereas they had scarcely rested on Marianne or any other of the lovely women present. To him, that awkward, insignificant girl was the most beautiful of women because he loved her and with all her heart Marianne envied the child who possessed not a fraction of what she herself had and who was yet so infinitely richer.

The young couple disappeared into the crowd and Marianne sighed as they passed from her view. She turned to greet her host and hostess, who were standing to receive their guests in the doorway of the large drawing-room from which the covered way led into the ballroom.

The ambassador, Prince Carl Philipp von Schwarzenburg, was a man of about forty, dark and stocky, his white uniform strained to bursting-point over powerful muscles. The impression he conveyed was one of strength and obstinacy. Beside him, his sister-in-law Princess Pauline seemed a picture of graceful fragility in spite of being pregnant and very near her time, a fact which she concealed most artistically beneath a muslin peplum and flowing, gold-threaded draperies. Marianne stared with amazement and considerable respect at this mother of eight children who looked like a young girl and whose whole being breathed total enjoyment of life. Then she found herself greeting this charming creature's husband, Prince Joseph, and reflected, not for the first time, that love was a very strange thing.

She collected her thoughts sufficiently to respond with grace to the Austrians' eager welcome and then allowed Talleyrand to lead her in the direction of the ballroom, still striving to throw off the odd feeling of unreality, the torpor that was enveloping her mind. At all costs, she must find something to interest her, she must try at least to look as if she was enjoying the party, if only to please her friend Talleyrand, now pointing out to her in an undertone those foreign dignitaries who came within his vision. But what did she care for any of these people?

At last, a ringing voice did manage to pierce through the dangerous fog which had wrapped itself around Marianne. In a strong Russian accent, it declared: 'My dear Prince, I claim the first waltz! It is mine by right, for I have paid for it with my blood, and would pay as much again twice over!'

The voice was a gravelly baritone, stony as the Urals themselves, but it did at least bring Marianne back to earth. She saw that the owner of the voice was none other than her impudent pursuer from the Bois de Boulogne, the man she had already privately christened the Cossack. It was that odious Chernychev.

He stood, adroitly blocking their path, and though his words were for Talleyrand, his slanting Mongol eyes were staring boldly at Marianne. She gave a faint, scarcely perceptible shrug, not bothering to hide the contempt in her smile:

'It is yours by right? I do not even know you, Sir.'

'Then why, if you do not know me, did you frown so when you saw me? Say you dislike me, Madame . . . but do not say you do not know me.'

Two green sparks of anger showed briefly beneath Marianne's lowered eyelids:

'You were importunate, Sir. You become impertinent. You are making progress. Must I make myself plainer?'

'You might try, but I should warn you that we are an obstinate race and I am noted for my persistence, even among my own people.'

'Much good may it do you! I am no less determined, I assure you.'

She was about to pass on, fanning herself irritably, when Talleyrand, who had observed this encounter with a smile of silent amusement, restrained her gently.

'Perhaps I should intervene before we have a diplomatic incident on our hands, eh?' he remarked cheerfully. 'I set too much store by my friends to leave them floundering in misunderstandings.'

Marianne regarded him with a look of astonishment that was a masterpiece of gracious arrogance.

'This gentleman is a friend of yours? Oh, Prince – I knew you to be acquainted with all the world, but I had thought you more selective in your friendships.'

Talleyrand laughed. 'Lower your sword, my dear Princess, as a favour to me. I grant that Count Chernychev's manners may smack too much of the camp to satisfy the taste of a pretty woman, but what would you? He is both a brave man and something of a noble savage.'

'And proud of it!' the Russian exclaimed, with an unmistakable glance at Marianne. 'Only savages can speak the truth and are not ashamed of their desires. It is my most ardent desire to obtain a dance with the most beautiful lady I ever beheld and, if I may, a smile! I am ready to beg for them on my knees, here and now if need be.'

This time, Marianne's anger was touched with surprise. She had no doubt that this strange man would do precisely what he said and kneel at her feet right there in the middle of the ballroom, without a thought for the scandal it would cause. She knew that his was one of those wild, fantastic and unpredictable natures of which her instinct had always told her to beware. Talleyrand must have been thinking something similar because he intervened quickly, smiling as ever, but holding a little more firmly to Marianne's arm.

'You shall have your dance, my dear Count – or so I hope, if Princess Sant'Anna will forgive you your Tartar manners, but do not be in such a hurry. Leave her to me for a while longer. There are a host of people here wishing to meet her before she will be free to indulge in dancing.'

Chernychev stepped aside at once and bowed in a way that Marianne could not help but find a trifle menacing.

'I yield,' he said briefly. 'But I shall be back. Until then, Madame.'

As they resumed their way to the ballroom, Marianne permitted herself a faint sigh of relief and the smile she turned on her escort was full of gratitude:

'Thank you, Prince, for rescuing me. That Russian is quite inescapable!'

'So most women appear to think. True, they usually say it rather more languishingly, but who knows, perhaps you too may sigh one day? He has great charm, eh?'

'Don't count on it. I am afraid I prefer people to be civilized.'

There was no mistaking the surprise in the look he directed at her. However, he said merely: 'Hmm . . . I should not have thought it.'

The much-talked-of ballroom which had been erected for this one night was a miracle of beauty and elegance. The blue canvas which formed its fragile walls was hung with shining gauze and swathed in garlands of many-coloured flowers made of fine silk and tulle. A profusion of gilded candelabra carried innumerable candles, lighting up the room like fairyland. The passage leading into it was decorated in the same style. A tall aperture provided a view of the lighted gardens and the ballroom, which had been built over a large, dry pool, was illumined outside by oil lamps in sockets.

When Marianne entered on Talleyrand's arm, the floor was already filled with couples dancing to the strains of a Viennese orchestra: glittering dresses and uniforms whirling delightfully in the waltz which had been sweeping Europe for some years now.

'I shall not offer to dance with you,' Talleyrand said. 'It is not an exercise I am fitted for. But I am sure you will not lack for partners.'

This was true. A crowd of young officers was already forming about Marianne, jostling one another in their eagerness to lead her away in time to that seductive music. She refused them all kindly, fearful of the scene which the Russian was quite capable of enacting, for she could feel his eyes still fixed on her. She had just seen her friend Dorothée de Périgord talking to Countess Zichy and the Duchess of Dalberg and was about to join them when she was prevented by the arrival of Their Majesties, the Emperor and Empress. The orchestra stopped dead and the dancers ranged themselves obediently at either side of the room.

'We were just in time,' Talleyrand observed, smiling. 'A little later and the Emperor would have been before us. I can't imagine he would have been pleased.'

But Marianne was not listening to him. Her attention was riveted suddenly on a man whose head rose above those of most of the crowd of guests standing on the far side of the space left for royalty to pass. For a moment she thought she must be seeing things, suffering from a delusion brought about by some wish of her own, so deeply buried in her heart that not even she was aware of it. But those keen features, that thin, fine-boned face, the taut, bronzed skin, dark almost as an Arab's, with the deepset, twinkling blue eyes and firm lips crooked into a half-smile that was both gay and impudent, the thick, unruly black hair that always looked slightly windblown, the careless set of the dark coat across those broad shoulders . . . surely there could not be another man like that in all the world. And suddenly, quite inexplicably, Marianne's heart gave a joyful leap and cried out his name with certainty long before her lips could bring themselves to frame the word: 'Jason!'

'Eh, so it is, upon my word!' said Talleyrand's voice placidly in her ear. 'Our friend Beaufort, to be sure. I knew he was expected but I had no idea he had already arrived.'

Marianne's eyes unfastened themselves briefly from the American and regarded the diplomat in surprise:

'You knew?'

'Don't I always know everything? I knew that a more or less unofficial envoy from President Madison was due in Paris some time soon, ostensibly on a goodwill mission from the United States government, and I knew who it was to be—'

'Jason! An ambassador? You can't be serious!'

'I did not say ambassador. I said envoy, and a somewhat unofficial one at that. It is not difficult to understand. Now that his brother is King of Spain, the Emperor is eager to get his hands on the Spanish-American colonies and is carrying out a propaganda campaign there which President Madison is very far from disliking. He has no respect for the deposed king, the imbecile Ferdinand VII and besides, he hopes to get Florida as a reward for his benevolent neutrality. It's Spanish territory but Bonaparte sold Louisiana to the Americans in 1803, so it would appear to be a logical move. Ssh now, here comes the Emperor.'

Napoleon, dressed as usual in the green uniform of a colonel of Chasseurs of the Guard, had already entered the ballroom. On his arm, Marie-Louise was in pink satin, shimmering with diamonds. They were followed by a brilliant train which included, as well as the Emperor's sisters and his military staff, the charming Prince Eugène, viceroy of Italy, with his wife Princess Augusta of Bavaria, the Duke of Würtzburg, the Queen of Spain, and a whole galaxy of other highnesses.

Like everyone else, Marianne sank into a stately reverence but her head remained obstinately unbowed, her green eyes still on the tall figure of Jason as he made his bow. He had not seen her. He was not looking in her direction. All his attention was fixed on the doorway through which the royal couple had entered and on the Emperor himself. His direct gaze swept past the new Empress and fastened with a curious intentness on the pale face of the imperial Corsican. He seemed to be seeking something in those Roman features.

Napoleon passed on, smiling now at his young bride, now at his host, Prince Schwarzenburg, speaking to no one, only nodding genially from time to time to one or other of the guests. He appeared to be in a hurry to reach the gardens where a grand firework display had been arranged and did not spare so much as a glance for the throne which had been set for him; but perhaps his haste was not to be wondered at, for the heat inside the canvas pavilion was growing more oppressive every moment, in spite of the fountains playing everywhere in the grounds.

Behind the imperial pair and their suite, the mass of guests flowed together like the Red Sea after the passage of the Jews, inspired in part by the courteous wish to keep as close as possible to their sovereigns and, to a still greater extent, by a purely human anxiety not to miss any of the fun. Within seconds, Marianne was submerged in a sea of silks and laces and separated from her partner by a twittering, shrieking throng which bore her irresistibly outside. Jason had vanished amid the swell and not all her efforts could give her a glimpse of him. Talleyrand, she had forgotten altogether. Doubtless he was somewhere in the tide of people.

Her mind was in a strange, feverish state, raging impatiently against all these people who had come between them just as she was on the point of running to Jason. It did not occur to her until much later to be surprised at the indifference with which she had regarded the Emperor's passing when, not so long before, he had been the centre of all her thoughts. Even Marie-Louise, gazing complacently around the assembled company with her pale eyes brimming with gratified vanity, had failed to irritate as she usually did. Indeed, Marianne had scarcely seen the newly wedded pair, so full was her heart of the new, wholly unexpected and revitalizing joy of seeing Jason once again.

Jason, for whom she had waited for so many days in vain! She was not even angry at the thought that he was here, that he must have had her letter and yet had not come to her. Without being aware of it she was already seeking, and finding, all sorts of excuses for him. She had always known, after all, that Jason Beaufort was not like other people.

She did not catch sight of him again until the first rocket sent a gigantic spray of rose-coloured sparks rushing across the dark sky to fall back softly towards the terraces where the women's jewels rivalled the splendour of the milky way in a shower of light that silhouetted every figure sharply against the massed banks of flowers and shrubs. He was standing with some other people, a little apart, by the balustrade of one of the terraces leading to a grotto illuminated within by a soft, pearly light. He was standing with folded arms, watching the dazzling display as calmly as if he had been watching the courses of the stars from the deck of his own ship. Deftly catching up the long train of her dress over one gloved wrist, Marianne threaded her way between the knots of people, intent on joining him.

It was not easy. The terrace between Marianne and Jason was packed tight with guests, all pressing inward around the carpeted area where chairs had been placed for Napoleon and Marie-Louise. Marianne had to push her way past a number of persons who stood gazing upwards, wholly absorbed in what was, beyond a doubt, a very remarkable spectacle. But she was, almost without realizing it, in the condition of a swimmer who, at the end of her strength, had felt her foot touch on the shifting, sandy bottom. She wanted to reach Jason and to reach him now. She had waited too long already.

At last she climbed the three steps leading up to the grotto and as she did so the sky blazed into golden fire from innumerable rockets, surrounding her with such a halo of bright light that the eyes of the occupants of the little terrace were drawn instinctively to the lovely creature who, in her gown and her fabulous jewels, seemed the very spirit of the ball incarnate.

Jason Beaufort, standing a little apart from the group, leaning against an outsized urn filled with flowers, saw her too. A world of feelings flashed for an instant across his set face: surprise, disbelief, admiration, happiness – but only for an instant. Then he was moving forward very coolly to bow before her:

'How do you do? I confess that, coming to Paris, I had hoped to have the pleasure of seeing you, but I did not think to find you here. Allow me to compliment you – you are exquisite tonight.'

'But I—'

Thrown off her balance, Marianne stared at him uncomprehendingly. His tone, so coldly formal, almost ceremonious – when she had come to meet him with hands outstretched, a heart overflowing with gladness, within an ace of casting herself into his arms? What could have happened to turn Jason – her friend and the only man, apart from Jolival, whom she trusted in this vile world – into this polite, disinterested stranger? What, not even a smile? Nothing but worn-out conventionalities?

Stiffened by pride, she managed with a painful effort to dominate her disappointment and accept the slap which fate had dealt her. Up went her head, while her fan fluttered quickly, hiding the trembling of her fingers as she schooled her features to a smile and her voice to the necessary social lightness.

'I thank you,' she said sweetly. 'For myself, your presence took me wholly by surprise.' She laid the faintest of stresses on the 'your'. 'Have you been in Paris long?'

'Two days.'

'Indeed . . .'

The words were nothing, the merest commonplace such as might have been exchanged by virtual strangers. All of a sudden Marianne found herself wanting to cry. She could not understand it. What had happened to her friend? Could this cold, handsome stranger be the same man who, in the summerhouse at the Hôtel Matignon, had begged her to go with him to America, who had snatched her from the quarries of Chaillot, who had sworn never to forget her and charged Gracchus to watch over her every second of her life?

Even as she sought in vain for something to say that would not be either stupid or inept, she was aware of his eyes scrutinizing every detail of her appearance and she resented it, as if he were doing her an injustice. He had only just reached Paris. He could not have heard yet of her marriage and must be thinking that Napoleon maintained his mistress in extravagant style. His bright eyes went from the emeralds to the gold dress, then back to the emeralds, merciless and accusing.

The silence grew uncomfortable, despite the noise of the fireworks. Marianne dared not raise her eyes to Jason's now, for fear he should see the tears in them. She was about to move away, telling herself wretchedly that there was nothing more to be said between them, when his voice stopped her:

'If you will allow me, Madame—'

Hope welled up, instinctively, released by the half-dozen words. 'Yes?'

'I should like to present my wife . . .'

'Your . . .' Marianne's voice failed her. She felt suddenly weak, lost and helpless. Her fan shut with a click and her fingers tightened on it so viciously that several of the slender ivory sticks snapped suddenly, but Jason did not appear to notice her confusion. He held out his hand and drew towards him a woman of whose presence Marianne, absorbed in her own feelings, had not been aware until that moment. Now she stared with all the horror of one seeing a ghost at the slightly-built young woman, dressed in a robe of black lace over an underdress of silver, who stepped out of the shadows behind the American. She wore her dark hair in the Spanish fashion, with a high comb covered by a mantilla of the same lace as her gown, in which was a white rose, matching those which bloomed at her breast. Below the mantilla, Marianne saw a grave young face with finely moulded features and lips which, for all their delicacy, showed a bitter twist surprising in one so young. Her eyes were large, dark and melancholy, surmounted by slim, arched brows pencilled on pale skin. The general impression was of extreme physical fragility but the face revealed both pride and obstinacy.

Whether she was pretty or not, this woman who had stepped

from the shadows of a summer night to shatter her new-found happiness, Marianne could not for the life of her have said. There was no room for anything in her vision, her heart or her mind but one vast disappointment which, little by little, became an aching pain. It was like waking from a dream of joy and warmth and light to the greyness of a dull November morning and for an instant Marianne found herself wishing she could close her eyes and slip back into the dream. As though out of a fog, she heard Jason speaking to the stranger and was aware, even through her misery, that he was speaking Spanish:

'I want to make you known to a very old friend of mine. You permit?'

'Of course – if she is indeed your friend.'

The tone, lightly contemptuous and at the same time more than a little suspicious, made Marianne's hackles rise. A little surge of anger momentarily diverted her thoughts from her own grief and actually did her good by helping her to regain her self-command. She smiled dangerously and, in a voice no less disdainful, asked in the purest Castilian: 'Why should I not be, indeed?'

The beautiful brows rose slightly but the answer came perfectly gravely:

'It does not seem that the word friendship is treated here as seriously as I have been used to find it at home.'

'At home? You are Spanish, I think?'

With the instinct of all seafaring men for the approach of a squall, even a mild one, Jason possessed himself of his wife's hand and, tucking it securely within his arm, was quick to answer for her:

'Pilar is from Florida,' he said quietly. 'Her father, Don Agostino Hernandez de Quintana, owned great estates at Fernandina, near our frontier. It's a small town, maybe, but a vast country, less than half-civilized, and Pilar is seeing Europe for the first time.'

The girl looked up at him, her expression as gloomy as ever:

'And for the last, I hope! I have no wish to return, or indeed to remain here, for I dislike it heartily. Only Spain I wished to see, but it is impossible to go there, alas, with this terrible war! And now, *querido mio*, perhaps you will inform me of this lady's name?'

Marianne seethed inwardly. The girl was a savage! Stuffed full of pride and religious bigotry! And probably an enemy of the Emperor's into the bargain! Was she to spend the whole night meeting barbarians? First that Mongol and now this creature!

She was so angry that it was all she could do to choke back the temper that was making her whole body tremble. And as Jason, unaware of her marriage, opened his mouth to make the introductions, she forestalled the threatened gaffe by saying coldly: 'Let me spare you the trouble. As you yourself said, Mrs Beaufort is very naturally ignorant of society. Allow me to introduce myself, Madame. I am Princess Carrado Sant'Anna. If we meet again, as I sincerely trust we may, you may address me as Serene Highness!'

Denying herself so much as a glance at the shock in Jason's blue eyes, she bowed slightly and then turned away from them to go in search of Talleyrand. The firework display was already coming to an end in a blaze of glory, with the two imperial eagles, the French and the Austrian, colourfully united by the genius of the Ruggieri brothers. There was a burst of applause but Marianne regarded this remarkable pyrotechnic achievement with a jaundiced eye.

It's absurd! she told herself. Pretentious and absurd! And so am I. Flinging my titles at that stupid child! But it was her own fault entirely. I wish the ground had opened and swallowed her up! I wish, yes, I wish she were dead . . . To think that she is *his* wife, his *wife*! The two short syllables stung Marianne like so many wasps. She was seized afresh by the old longing to run away. It was a primitive urge, a legacy perhaps from some remote, nomadic ancestor, which overcame her whenever she was unhappy. It was not cowardice, she was not afraid to face her troubles, but rather a need to hide her feelings from prying eyes and seek her own cure in silence and solitude.

She went with the crowd, automatically, back into the ballroom where the violins were once again in full swing. She had some idea in her head of going straight out to find her carriage, of going home to the quiet of her own house and her own room. She found herself hating this embassy and all the people in it. Even Napoleon, seated on the red and gold throne which had been prepared for him and for Marie-Louise at the far end of the room, no longer had any power over her. She wanted only to go home. But then she saw, coming straight towards her, a group of ladies which included Dorothée and Countess Kielmansegg and a sound of annoyance broke from her at the sight. Now she would have to stand and chatter inanely when all she wanted was peace and quiet to listen to the odd, unhappy murmurings of her heart and try to understand . . . No, she could not, it was too much . . .

Almost in the same instant, she caught sight of Chernychev, standing close by in his dark green uniform and watching her. Scarcely thinking what she did, she turned to him:

'You asked for a dance, Count. This one is yours if you will have it.'

'Oh cruel! Does one ask the humble votary if he would approach the divinity?'

Cold, green eyes stared into the Russian's. 'I did not invite you to make love to me, merely to dance this waltz,' she said concisely.

This time, his only answer was a bow and a smile which showed a glint of white teeth. As they stepped on to the floor, Marianne let fall her broken fan and, catching up her long train, abandoned her waist to her partner's encircling arm. He swooped on it like a bird of prey and bore her off into the midst of the dancers with such enthusiasm that she could not help a small, sad smile.

She did not love this man but he desired her, unashamedly, and in her present confused state Marianne was ready to find comfort in any kind of positive feeling, even that. He was a perfect dancer with an amazing sense of time and to Marianne, whirling in his arms, it seemed as if she were floating on air. The waltz seemed to free her from the weight of her body. If only her mind could be freed of its burdens as easily!

As she danced, she saw the Emperor seated on his throne,

the Empress at his side, speaking quietly, but her eyes did not linger, and already Chernychev had swept her on, his gloved hand firmly clasping her waist. Next she saw Jason, dancing with his wife. Their eyes met briefly but Marianne looked away hurriedly and moved by some feminine impulse of coquetry, by the need which lurks deep in every woman to deal blow for blow and give back hurt for hurt, she favoured the Russian with her most dazzling smile.

'You are very quiet, my dear Count,' she said, loudly enough to be overheard by the American couple. 'Has joy robbed you of your tongue?'

'You forbade me to make love to you, Princess, and since I cannot think of anything else . . .'

'Do you know so little of women that you always take them so literally? Surely you know we sometimes like to be disobeyed, if it is done gracefully enough?'

The Russian's green eyes darkened very nearly to black. His arm tightened in a way that left no doubt of his delight at this unexpected softening. Marianne's sudden cordiality appeared to stir him to such transports of joy that any moment she expected him to burst into some savage yell of triumph. He restrained himself, however, and merely leaned a little closer, until his cheek was pressed against her forehead and his hot breath was on her neck. Held tight against him, conscious of the hardness of his muscles, Marianne had the momentary fancy that she was dancing with some well-regulated machine.

'Take care how you drive me to disobey you,' he murmured passionately into her ear. 'I might want more than you are ready to grant, and when I want something, I do not give up until I have it.'

'But – surely you have got what you wanted? We are dancing together, and I think I even smiled at you.'

'That's just it! With such a woman, how can a man help wanting more and more?'

'Oh, indeed?' Her smile challenged him.

But she was not fated to learn how far Chernychev's desires might have carried him that night, for suddenly, without warning, he uttered an inarticulate cry, startling the couples closest to them out of their abandonment to the music. Marianne found herself released, so abruptly that she kept her feet only by a miracle. Before she could find her voice to protest, or ask him what he meant by it, she saw the Russian officer thrust his way unceremoniously between the pairs of dancers on the floor and spring for the ballroom wall, both arms outstretched to snatch at one of the flimsy garlands of artificial roses which had caught fire from a sagging candle in one of the gilded holders and was blazing merrily. Heedless of burned hands, Chernychev tore down the garland but already it was too late. The flames had seized on the silvery gauzes draping the canvas walls and were spreading rapidly. Within seconds, the whole wall was ablaze.

With one great gasp of horror, the dancers pressed back to the other side of the room, towards the throne. Carried along with the rest, Marianne found herself standing close to Napoleon as Prince Eugène, who had been chatting to the Minister for Foreign Affairs, Champagny, at a little distance, forced his way urgently to the Emperor's side. She saw the young viceroy say something quietly to the Emperor who turned at once and took Marie-Louise by the arm.

'Come,' he said. 'The room is on fire. We must go.'

But the young Empress remained seated, her eyes riveted on the blazing wall, apparently fascinated by the flames.

'Come, Louise!' the Emperor commanded. Almost dragging her from her chair, he hurried her swiftly in the direction of the passage to the house. Marianne tried to follow them but a movement of panic in the crowd lifted her like a straw and bore her helplessly towards the opening leading into the grounds. Nothing, now, could have halted the terror-stricken throng. In another instant, the oiled canvas roof was alight. The fire ran along the other walls with terrifying speed. One by one, the gilded chandeliers with their loads of lighted candles fell from the ceiling on to the milling crowd below, felling some and setting fire to the clothes of others. A girl's dress of blue tulle became a sheet of flame. Screaming in agony, she hurled herself like a living torch blindly into the crowd which, far from offering her any assistance, only tried frantically to avoid her.

One officer did rip off his jacket and throw it round her in an effort to smother the flames but both were soon swallowed up in the hysterical stampede.

Very soon, the exits, the tall windows in the canvas walls and the passageway by which the Emperor had left, were blocked by the fire. The gallery itself was blazing, carrying the fire straight into the embassy drawing-rooms. Now the only passable way out was by the lofty doorway opening into the gardens and towards this the crowd surged with all the violence of water bursting through a dam. A thick, suffocating black smoke was filling the blazing ballroom, stinging the eyes and lungs.

To escape it, men and women fought their way towards the single exit with a savage fury, thrusting with fists and elbows, trampling one another down, battling for life with no thought for anything beyond the naked, primitive instinct of self-preservation. The women were the first to fall, trodden down by the more powerful males, by the very man perhaps who, only a moment before, had been bowing with exquisite grace over the very fingers he now crushed beneath his heel, or murmuring sweet nothings into ears he would have torn off ruthlessly if it would help him to escape more quickly and win through into the blessed, breathable fresh air outside.

Carried away in the midst of this desperate scramble for life, bruised, half-stifled with smoke and by the pressure of so many human bodies, the train ripped from her dress, Marianne had a horrified vision of glaring eyes and screaming mouths, of faces contorted with terror. The heat was unbearable and the drifts of smoke that filled the room with a thick, grey fog made her feel as if her lungs would burst. Among the press of heads around her, she caught sight of Savary's, bobbing like some absurd ship on an angry sea. The Minister of Police was looking very nearly as green as his braided uniform but, shrieking incomprehensibly, he was making a vain attempt to bring some order into the panic-stricken crowd.

The opening leading into the garden was not far away now but the hangings with which it was draped were already beginning to burn and the pressure of the crowd was growing ever more frantic as each person fought to get across the threshold before the way was barred by the flames. Such was the press of bodies with everyone trying to escape at once that the crowd became jammed tight in the doorway, like the cork of a bottle. It was impossible to move, either forward or backwards. People struggled wildly. Marianne was hit in the chest by a senator's flailing elbow and felt hands grasping her hair. Fortunately for her, there was, not far behind her in the crowd, a giant of a man, a great, bearded, bear-like creature whose massive shoulders were clad in the brilliant uniform of the Russian guard. This man was fighting like a fury, pushing at the crowd in front of him with his great hands. Sparks from a falling chandelier set light to his hair and, uttering an inhuman cry, he gave such a violent thrust that the human stopper burst out into the open amid billows of smoke. Marianne found herself, horribly bruised about the chest but safe, outside the ballroom, on the steps leading to the gardens. But she had hardly drawn a breath of slightly cooler air into her lungs before an anguished cry broke from her. A woman beside her groaned piteously, then another gave a shriek that ended on a choking sob. The lamps which had twinkled so gaily on the outside of the ballroom were tipping over, spilling hot oil on to the bare shoulders and uncovered breasts below, causing fearful injuries. Marianne stumbled forward towards an ornamental pool whose waters glowed redly. Servants were hurrying towards it with buckets and basins: none too soon, for by now the ballroom doorway was ablaze.

From the steps, Marianne saw a piece of burning timber crash down on old Prince Kurakin. The massive, gouty Russian ambassador collapsed with a grunt like a wounded bear, but a man in the tattered uniform of a French general sprang forward instantly to rescue him.

Leaning her bare back gratefully against the cold stone of one of the statues, Marianne stared, wide-eyed with horror, at the spectacle of desolation and death which, all round her in the gardens, had replaced the magical beauty of so short a time before. She was still gasping for breath and her chest hurt her, and her shoulder where the skin was blistered and cracked from her burns. Even here, the air was almost too thick to breathe. The ballroom was now a blazing inferno, shooting roaring flames up into the dark sky, as if in search of something more to feed on. Vague shapes could still be seen emerging from the furnace within, their garments blazing, and rolling themselves screaming on the ground in their efforts to put out the stinging flames.

The injured and dying were everywhere. People were rushing hither and thither in panic, not knowing what they were doing. Marianne saw Prince Metternich run towards the flames, a bucket of water in his hands. She saw another man, also running, carrying a woman in a silver dress and she recognized Jason, oblivious of everything but the need to bear his wife, Pilar, safely out of danger.

I no longer exist for him, Marianne thought bewilderedly. He is thinking only of her. He has not tried to find out if I am even alive . . .

She felt suddenly very weak, and very much alone. Among all these people, there was not one who was her friend, not one whose thoughts were only for her. She felt so desolate that she put her arms round the statue, a little figure of Ceres in white marble, and started to cry bitterly, clinging to the stone which was already growing warm from the fire.

'Antonia! Antonia!'

The piercing shriek close beside her roused Marianne from her agony of self-pity. Looking up, she saw a woman clearly far advanced in pregnancy running desperately towards the blaze. Her tangled hair fell about her shoulders, over the shreds of a white muslin gown, and her arms were stretched out before her. To her horror, Marianne recognized the ambassador's sister-in-law, Princess Schwarzenburg, and darted swiftly in pursuit:

'Madame! Madame! . . . Where are you going? For pity's sake—'

The eyes the young woman turned on her were so dilated with horror and anguish that it was doubtful if they even saw her.

'My daughter!' she said. 'Antonia! She is in there!'

With a sudden movement, she wrenched herself free from Marianne's grasp, leaving her holding nothing but a few strips of tattered muslin, and resumed her blind race. Still shrieking and calling, she had reached the fire when, with a mighty crash, the floor of the ballroom collapsed into the empty pool above which it was built and Marianne saw the wretched woman vanish into the fiery pit below.

Sick with horror, her stomach heaving, Marianne could only double up and vomit. Her head was hammering and she was sweating heavily. When she lifted her eyes it was to see with disgust that the musicians, who had escaped with the rest into the gardens, were busy among the injured, robbing them of their jewels. And they, unhappily, were not the only ones. The people who had swarmed up on to the walls of the embassy garden to watch the fireworks with shouts of delight, had come in for their share of the spoils. Groups of ill-favoured rascals were slipping over the walls into the gardens, eyes gleaming like a pack of hungry wolves, and were going silently about their grisly work.

The efforts of the embassy staff to keep the evil tide at bay were worse than useless. A few men attempted to defend the women victims, but they were too few to offer any effective resistance.

But, Marianne thought, with mounting horror, the firemen should be here, soldiers . . . Where is the Emperor's escort?

But the Emperor had gone and his escort with him. How long would it be before a regiment of troops could be brought in to restore order and drive off the looters? A hand fell on her suddenly, snatching the tiara from her head, and a handful of hair with it, then tugging at the emerald necklace, trying to break the clasp. Marianne screamed in terror:

'Help! Thieves!'

A second hand, rough and evil-smelling, stopped her mouth. Instinctively, she struggled with her attacker, seeing a long, pallid face and cruel eyes, a man dressed in dirty overalls, reeking of sweat. Biting and scratching, she managed to wriggle from his grasp and started to run, her hands gripping her necklace, but he was before her, hurling himself forward to jerk her back. She felt a steel blade pricking her throat.

'Give me those!' said a hoarse voice, 'or I'll cut yer throat!'

He pressed lightly, so that the blade nicked the soft flesh. Petrified with fear, Marianne put up trembling hands to unfasten the necklace and saw the man slip it into his sleeve. Then she took the sparkling drops from her ears. The knife was removed and Marianne thought that now he would let her go, but he did not. Instead, he bent over her, chuckling evilly. She felt his breath on her face, foul with the reek of cheap wine, and gave a choking scream; but moist, cold lips were clamped hard on hers, stifling the cry with a kiss that made her retch. At the same time, the man holding her was thrusting her roughly in the direction of a bed of huge peonies guarding the entrance to a shrubbery.

'This way, my beauty! It's not every day I gets me 'ands on a swell mort like you!'

Marianne was no sooner released from the stinking embrace than she began to scream and struggle again, thin, piercing screams uttered on a high note of hysteria. Failing to muffle them, the man drew back his arm and struck her with such force that she fell to the ground. But even as he bent to drag her in among the bushes, a man's figure sprang from the shadows and grappled with him, flinging him down a yard or two from Marianne. The ruddy glow of the fire enabled her to recognize Chernychev. He was bleeding from a cut across his temple and his uniform was badly charred, but he seemed otherwise unhurt.

'Run!' he snarled. 'By St Vladimir, I mean to gut this *moujik* like a herring!'

He did not look at Marianne. In the unnatural, flickering half-light, she could see his green eyes shining with savage joy at the prospect of a fight. He stood with his hands held low and open, ready to grip, his body tense and perfectly controlled, unarmed and wholly forgetful of his recently-healed wound, confronting the villain with the butcher's knife.

'He stole my jewels,' Marianne whispered, holding her hand to her bruised throat and feeling the raw wound on her neck where the necklace had bitten into it as the man pulled.

'That is all? He did not rape you?'

'He had no time, he—'

'Get yourself to safety. I will recover your jewels. As for this gallows-bird, he may thank Our Lady of Kazan he was not born in Russia! There he would have died under the knout for daring to so much as touch you.'

The man gave a crack of laughter and spat out some vile oath, settling the knife more comfortably in his grimy paw.

'But he is armed!' Marianne wailed. 'He will kill you.'

Now it was the Cossack's turn to laugh, his slanting eyes narrowed to gleaming slits as he surveyed his adversary:

'He? His knife will not save him. I have slain bears and tamed wild horses with these bare hands. I shall have throttled him in two minutes, knife or no!'

Then, with a powerful thrust of steely muscles, Chernychev sprang. Caught off-balance, the other man fell heavily, with a choking gasp, striving to tear away the hands that clutched ferociously at his throat, half-throttling him before he could use his weapon. The knife had fallen from his hand and Marianne bent quickly to seize it, but the man was strong for all his gaunt frame and already he had wrenched his neck free and was making a recovery. Both men rolled over and over on the ground, as closely intertwined as a pair of fighting snakes engaged in a savage struggle on the damp grass of a smoothly-shaven lawn.

The Russian was a skilful wrestler and Marianne was not greatly alarmed for him. She was confident that he would emerge victorious. Then, suddenly, she realized to her horror that two more men in working clothes and three-decker caps were creeping up silently on the struggling pair. She guessed that they were associates of the first bully coming to the rescue and knew that it would be no longer a fair fight. It came to her in a flash that Chernychev would need help and she looked round wildly, in time to see a company of soldiers entering the grounds by way of the walls, carrying stretchers and other rescue apparatus. Gathering up the rags of her dress, she ran towards them and seeing a group of men in green uniforms bending over the injured seized one of them by the arm.

'Count Chernychev!' she gasped out. 'He is in danger. Come quickly! They will kill him!'

The man whose arm she held turned and looked at her and so strong was the atmosphere of unreality which haunted that terrible night that Marianne felt almost no surprise to see it was Napoleon himself. Black with soot, his Chasseur uniform charred and torn, he was supervising the removal of an injured woman who lay moaning softly on a stone bench. It must have been he who, on his way back to the stricken embassy, had called out the rescue parties who were already taking control of the grounds. He spoke briefly:

'Who will kill him?'

'Some men . . . over there, by the bushes! They attacked me and the Count came to my rescue. Hurry, there are three of them, all armed – and he is alone, with nothing but his bare hands—'

'Who are these men?'

'I don't know. Robbers! They came over the wall—'

The Emperor stood up. His grey eyes, set beneath frowning brows, were hard as stone, as he called out: 'Eugène! Duroc! Over here! It seems there is murder being done now.'

With the viceroy of Italy and the Duke of Frioul hard on his heels, the Emperor of the French sped off as fast as his legs would carry him to the assistance of the Russian attaché. Marianne, assured now of Chernychev's safety, wandered back automatically towards the fountains. She did not know what to do now, or where to go. She watched, beyond either surprise or relief, the arrival of the fire brigade at last, or of what passed for the fire brigade, for they numbered only six men in all, and those more than three-parts drunk. She heard Savary's roars of rage:

'Six of you, only! Where are the rest?'

'We – don't know, General.'

'What of your commander, that fool Ledoux? Where is he?'

'I-in the country, General . . .'

'Six!' Savary was beside himself with rage. 'Six out of two hundred and ninety-three! And where are the pumps?'

'Here – but there's no water. The conduits in the Grand Boulevards are locked fast and we have not the key.'

'And where is the key?'

The fireman's answer was an evasive gesture which served to madden the already infuriated Chief of Police still further. Marianne saw him turn and hurry away, dragging the unfortunate fireman with him, while the wretched man fought desperately to keep his feet, knowing that any moment would surely bring him face-to-face with an anger far more terrible than any Minister's.

Yet help was forthcoming. The Imperial Guard, summoned by Napoleon and reinforced by a regiment of *tirailleurs*, was now engaged in attempting to save the embassy and those within. The tall ladder had been fetched from the library in the rue de la Loi and the waters of the fountains had been pressed into service. But Marianne soon lost interest in all that was happening around her. Now that the Emperor had taken charge, everything would be all right. She could hear his ringing tones somewhere in the garden . . .

Her head ached and her mind was a blank. She felt bruised in every inch of her body and yet was unable to summon up the strength to try and get away, to find a carriage to take her home. Something had snapped inside her and she gazed round, with what was almost indifference, at the scene of unbelievable devastation which filled the gardens. The terrible fire which, in a few minutes, had transformed a happy, elegant assembly of people into a scene of carnage was too much like the circumstances of her own life not to have a profound effect on her. This tragic ball had dealt her the final blow, the last, unbearable wound. And she had no one to blame but herself. How could she have been so blind to her real feelings? There had been so many wrong turnings, so much obstinacy in the face of the evidence, of the advice even of her best friends, so many fruitless struggles against nothing, all culminating at last in this cruel ending which resolved itself into a single image, the image of Jason carrying another woman in his arms, and it had taken all this for the truth to break upon her unwilling eyes at last, blindingly but too late: she loved Jason, she had always loved him, even when she believed herself in love with another, even when she thought she hated him. How could she have failed to realize it when, in her bridal chamber at Selton Hall, she had felt herself swooning under his stolen kiss? How could she have failed to understand in the midst of her joy at seeing him in the caverns of Chaillot, her disappointment when he left Paris without seeing her, excitement at finding the camellias in her dressing-room on the night of her one public concert, the impatience and, at last, the bitter disappointment when she had looked for him in vain, along all the roads of Italy, right up to the last moment before she pledged herself to an insensate marriage? She could still hear Adelaide saying with quiet concern: 'You are quite sure you do not love him?'

Yes, she had been sure then, in her folly and pride at having enslaved the giant of Europe in the burning chains of sensual passion. For in that bitterest moment of all, Marianne looked clearly at last at the real nature of the bond between her and the Emperor. She had loved him with pride and with terror, with a delight that carried with it a faint, delicious sense of danger and forbidden fruit; she had loved him with all the ardour of her youth and her eager flesh which, through him, had come to know the magic spell born of the perfect unison of two bodies. But she knew now that her love had been made of wonder and gratitude. She had fallen victim to the curious power of attraction he possessed over other human beings and, even suffering from his neglect, the jealousy she had felt was a fierce, burning thing that was somehow stimulating. It was not this pain, this rending agony, this uncontrollable quivering of her whole being at the thought of Jason and Pilar together. And now that she had lost, lost for ever the happiness which had lain so long within her grasp, Marianne felt that she had lost also the will to live.

Feeling that her life was ruined through her own fault, she felt again, more strongly than ever, the sense of being nothing but an empty doll which had haunted her on her arrival at the ball. In her blind folly and pride, she had allowed Jason to slip through her fingers and, turning to another woman, join his life with hers. Pilar was the one who would live with him in the land where the cotton grew, where the black men sang, she would share each moment of his life and sleep at night in his arms, and bear his children . . .

Around her, the gardens had become a battlefield as the newly arrived troops set themselves to drive out the looters, while medical men were supervising the removal of the injured, many of whom were already past help. More soldiers, armed with buckets of water, were endeavouring to halt the progress of the fire and save the embassy building itself. No one paid any attention to the woman watching from the shelter of a bush.

She was fascinated by the great fire. She could feel the heat of it even where she stood. The trees nearest to it had caught fire and long, greedy tongues of flame were shooting up triumphantly from the mass of timbers and falling tree trunks. There were no more screams now, no more groans, only the loud voice of the fire, filling the night. Marianne listened, her eyes full of tears, as if out of that blazing heart might come the answer to her own searing pain. A line from Shakespeare floated up from the depths of her memory: 'One fire burns out another's burning.' Her love for Jason, so suddenly made clear to her, had quenched her love for the Emperor, leaving only kindness and admiration like glowing gems amid the dying ashes. But what fresh fire would come to put out the love that racked her now, before despair brought her to the verge of madness? Jason was far away by now. He had borne his young bride away from this scene of carnage and at that very moment he was probably at her side, calming her fears with soft caresses and whispered words of love. He had forgotten all about Marianne, and his forgetfulness was death to her. Revelation had come too late. It had destroyed her, as lightning destroys the tree it strikes. Nothing remained for her now but to tiptoe quietly away for ever . . .

She had a sudden recollection of Princess Schwarzenburg, casting herself into the flames in search of her child. She had gone into the fire as though into a shrine, unhesitating, unflinching, with a blind certainty, the certainty of finding there the being whom she sought. And the bitter, fearful gateway to death had been transformed for her into a triumphal arch, a way of sacrifice freely consented to, an entry into eternal peace. All that was needed was a little, so very little courage!

With eyes wide open, Marianne left the shelter of the bushes and walked towards the fire. She did not tremble. Grief is a powerful opiate against fear and her anguish was stronger than the Indian hemp on which Hindu widows were gorged by their priests to make them throw themselves unresisting on their husbands' pyres. She wanted to escape from pain but wished no one to suffer for her death. An accident . . . a simple accident . . . And like the poor princess a little while before, Marianne began to run towards the blaze. She tripped over a stone that lay in her path, but the sharp stab of pain was not enough to break the spell that held her. She picked herself up and ran on. She seemed to hear her own name called above the roaring in her ears but even that could not stop her. Whoever was calling her, it could only be to bring her back to the monotonous round of a life she no longer had any use for, to a long trance, a death-in-life, rotting gently in solitude. The death she had chosen for herself was cruel but swift and led to a longer peace, one free of memories and regrets.

The heat was so great that she halted at the edge of the inferno and recoiled involuntarily, shielding her face from the hot breath of the flames. She was ashamed of herself at once and, murmuring the first words of a prayer, launched herself forward. Flames caught at the torn rags of her dress and a long tongue of fire licked up her body, so that she screamed with the pain of it. But just as she was about to fall into the white-hot abyss, a black shape descended on her, enveloping her in its dense folds, and she felt herself rolled violently on the ground. At the last moment, someone had come between her and her death, condemning her to live.

Conscious of the weight of a body, she struggled wildly in an effort to escape the paralysing grip which had successfully smothered the flames, trying in her fury to bite the hand which held her. The man, whoever he was, released her, got to his knees and slapped her face, deliberately, twice. Her eyes could make out only a black figure silhouetted against the ruddy glow of the fire, but she hurled herself at it blindly, clawing and scratching in a mad desire to fight back. The man grasped her wrists and held her off. At the same time, a voice said icily:

'Keep still or I will do it again. My God, are you mad! Another instant and you would have been incinerated! You damned little fool! Is there no room in that brainless skull of yours for anything but stupid, selfish vanity?'

Marianne collapsed abruptly, like a taut bowstring released suddenly by a weary archer, and listened to the torrent of abuse which Jason vented on her with as much rapture as if it had been heavenly music. She did not attempt to ask herself by what miracle he was there, by what unspeakable marvel he had managed to snatch her from the flames when she had seen him quit the scene so short a time before. It was enough for her that he was there. His anger was nothing, it proved only that somewhere in his heart he still cared a little, and only to have him kneel there beside her, Marianne would gladly have submitted to being abused the whole night long. Even the crushing pain he was inflicting on her wrists was happiness.

She gave a blissful sigh and, regardless of her burns, sank back on to the grass and smiled with all her heart at Jason's dark form.

'Jason!' she murmured. 'You are here . . . you have come back . . .'

Abruptly, he released her wrists and interrupted his tirade to stare with a kind of dazed bewilderment at the graceful figure stretched before him, clad in the tattered shreds of a gold dress through which the flesh showed bruised and torn and streaked with blood. Mechanically, he dragged his sleeve across his sweating brow, pushing back the damp hair, trying to smooth away the mixture of terror and anger which had taken hold of him when he saw that the woman racing madly towards the fire was Marianne. And now she was gazing at him as though at a vision, her great, green eyes sparkling with tears, smiling at him for all the world as if her body were not covered in burns, as if she could not feel them . . . But he too was unaware of the burns he had sustained in smothering the flames with his own body, conscious only that he had come in time. He felt more tired than he had ever felt in all his life. It was as if the last few minutes had drained him of every particle of strength.

Marianne herself was blissfully happy. For her, the sound and fury all about them no longer existed. Nothing remained but the dark figure, silently regarding her, and breathing heavily because of the pounding of his heart against his ribs. She wanted to touch him, to find in his strength the refuge she had so long sought and she held out her arms to draw him to her. But even as she did so, the movement ended in a gasp of pain, a terrible, stabbing pain which made her feel as if she were being torn apart.

Jason was on his feet in a moment, staring, shocked, as Marianne lay writhing in the grass at his feet:

'What is it? Are you hurt?'

'No – I don't know . . . the pain . . . aah!'

He knelt beside her again, bending over her, trying to raise her head which lolled alarmingly, but almost at once a long moan escaped from her blanched lips and her body arched beneath a fresh onslaught of pain. When it had passed, Marianne's face was ashen and she was gasping like a hurt animal. She cast a terrified look at Jason, who was very nearly as white as she. Then she felt something warm and wet between her legs and knew, in a flash, what was happening.

'My – my baby,' she whispered. 'I am losing my baby.'

'What's that? You are – pregnant?'

She nodded, saving her strength for the fresh wave of pain that was building up inside her.

'Of course. You are married. But where is your husband, where is this prince of yours?'

How could he mock her so cruelly when he could see that she was in such pain? She uttered a long moan and clung to his arm with all her strength for support. Then she managed to gasp: 'I don't know. Not here. In Italy! . . . Help me, for pity's sake! . . . The child . . . the Emperor . . . I . . .'

The rest was lost in a scream. Leaping to his feet, Jason swore comprehensively and was off like an arrow, making for the group of people standing by a little temple watching as if in a nightmare as the remains of the ballroom and the passage leading into it burned themselves out. It was possible to see beyond them now, to the blackened walls of the embassy, with their shattered windows and the groups of servants and troops still working to extinguish the fires in several of the rooms. Jason saw the Emperor and ran towards him. Marianne had mentioned the Emperor in the same breath as the child.

A few minutes later, Marianne surfaced from a fresh wave of suffering to see two faces bending over her, Jason's and the Emperor's. She heard the Emperor speaking in a strained voice:

'She is having a miscarriage. Hurry. Bring a stretcher. She must be got away from here. And fetch Corvisart – he must be here somewhere, seeing to the injured. You there! Over here!'

Marianne heard no more, nor did she see to whom the last words were addressed. She was aware only that Jason was leaving her and struggled up to call him back. Napoleon's hand forced her gently back again. Then, stripping off his jacket, he rolled it up and placed it beneath her head:

'Hush, *carissima mia* . . . do not try to move. You will be all right . . . do not be afraid. I am with you . . .'

He groped for her damp fingers and squeezed them gently. She looked up at him gratefully. So he still loved her a little, after all. She was not altogether alone in the world with her broken heart and her pain-racked body. It was good to feel that warm, strong hand holding hers reassuringly. Marianne forgot that she had wanted to die and clung to it, as a frightened child clings to its father. Yet would that handsome officer in the gilded frame have soothed his daughter in her wretchedness with such patient tenderness?

Sunk in another tide of pain, she was yet conscious of being lifted carefully and carried with all possible speed through the ravaged gardens where ashes, still warm, drifted on the night wind. In the intervals of pain she looked eagerly for Jason and not finding him whispered his name. The Emperor's hand tightened on hers. He bent over her:

'I sent him back to his wife. You do not need him now that I am here . . . He is only a friend . . .'

A friend . . . It was the word she would have used herself the day before, and meant it, yet now it tortured her. A friend . . . only a friend, not even that, perhaps, if this Pilar forbade it! A moment ago, she had believed he had come back to her. But no, it was all over. Jason had gone back to his wife and she had nothing left to hope for, except perhaps death which, a moment ago, had rejected her. She was still losing blood, not fast but enough, perhaps, to drain away her life . . .

With a little, quivering sigh, she gave herself up to pain.

CHAPTER TWO

Monsieur Carême's Chocolate

Baron Corvisart rolled down his shirtsleeves, fastened his pleated linen wristbands with care and inserted himself into the coat of blue superfine cloth which Fortunée Hamelin was holding ready for him. Then, after a cursory glance at the glass to assure himself that not a hair of his white head was out of place, he returned unhurriedly to the bed and stood for a moment in silent contemplation of the thin, pale face on the pillow, before transferring his gaze to Marianne's hands, like objects carved out of delicate ivory against the whiteness of the sheets.

'Well, you're out of danger now, young lady,' he said at last. 'All you have to do now is get your strength back. Try to eat a little and get up for a bit. You'll live, not a doubt of it, but I don't like the look of you, all the same. We'll have to do something about that.'

Marianne summoned up a smile and answered him in a weak voice:

'Indeed, I'm truly sorry, doctor. I wish I could please you. You have looked after me so patiently. But I don't want anything . . . food least of all. I feel so tired . . .'

'And if you don't eat, you'll feel a little more tired every day,' the Emperor's doctor scolded her. 'You have lost a great deal of blood, and you have to make it up again. Good gracious, you are a young woman, and a strong one, for all your dainty looks! One does not die at your age from a miscarriage and a few burns. What do you think the Emperor will have to say to me when I tell him you won't do as I tell you?'

'It isn't your fault.'

'Oh ho! If you think His Majesty will believe that! He expects his orders to be obeyed, and we have both had our orders: me to make you better, and you to get better as fast as possible. We've neither of us a particle of choice. I attend the Emperor every morning and he always asks after you, let me tell you.'

Marianne turned her head on the pillow so that he should not see the tears in her eyes.

'The Emperor is very kind . . .' she said in a tight little voice.

'He is to those he cares for,' Corvisart agreed. 'Tomorrow, at all events, I mean to tell him that you are better. So don't you let me down, Princess.'

'I'll try not to, Doctor. I'll try.'

The physician smiled and bent forward on an impulse to pat his patient's cheek affectionately:

'That's better, my child. That's more what I like to hear. Until tomorrow, then. I'll have a word with your people here and I trust I'll find you've been a good girl and done as you're bid. Your servant, Madame Hamelin.'

With a bow to the exquisite Créole, Corvisart trod across the room and the door closed softly behind him. At once, Fortunée rose quietly and came to sit on the edge of her friend's bed, enveloping her in a strong scent of roses. Her dress of simple cotton lawn embroidered with tiny coloured flowers was perfect for the warm, summer day, and made her look like a young girl. A huge sun-bonnet of natural straw swung from one white-mittened hand. Looking at her, Marianne felt strangely old and tired, and the expression on her face was so bleak that Fortunée frowned quickly.

'I don't understand you, Marianne,' she said at last. 'You

have been lying here for a week now and you are behaving just exactly as if wanting to be done with your life for good. It's not like you . . .'

'It was not like me once. But now, it's true. I do not want to live. What is the use?'

'Was it so important . . . the child?'

Once again, Marianne's eyes filled with tears and this time she made no attempt to restrain them, but let them flow freely.

'Of course it was important,' she said. 'It was the only thing that mattered in my whole life, my whole reason for living. I could have lived for him, through him. All my hopes were in him, and not only mine . . .'

Ever since she had recovered consciousness on that terrible night and learned that she had lost the child, Marianne had been blaming herself bitterly, and most of all for forgetting, all through those dreadful hours, that she was soon to be a mother. From the moment she had set eyes on Jason, everything else that had mattered to her before suddenly ceased to exist before the blinding discovery of the love which she had carried with her unwittingly for months. The garden, illumined by the blaze of fireworks, had been her road to Damascus and she had emerged from it, like Saul, blind, blind to everything around her, blind to the whole world, to her own life, to everything except this love, so deep that she could not contemplate it without a feeling of vertigo. And by risking her own life, by seeking to make an end of it, she had wantonly imperilled that of the child! Not for an instant had she thought of it, or of the man, far away in the villa in Tuscany, who would wait now in vain for news of the birth of that child on whom he had pinned every hope of his hermitic existence.

Corrado Sant'Anna had married her for the sake of a child of the imperial blood to inherit his name. And now, through her own fault, she, Marianne, had lost all hope of fulfilling her part of the bargain. The prince had been cheated.

'You are thinking of your mysterious husband, are you?' Fortunée said quietly.

'Yes. I am ashamed, ashamed, do you understand? Because I feel now as if I had stolen the name I bear.'

'Stolen it? But why?'

'I have already told you,' Marianne said wearily. 'Prince Sant'Anna married me only for the sake of the child, because it was the Emperor's and so he was not ashamed to acknowledge it ...'

'So, having lost it, you think yourself unfit to live and, if I understand you correctly, your present plan is simply to go into a decline and die?'

'More or less. But don't imagine I am trying to punish myself. I told you: I just do not wish to live.'

Fortunée got up and walked nervously over to the window, threw it open and then returned to her place by the bed:

'If your will to live depends purely on the existence of a child of Napoleon's, then I should think the answer was obvious. Napoleon will give you another and all will be well.'

'Fortunée!'

Gasping, Marianne turned a shocked face to her friend, but the Créole only grinned:

'You may well say Fortunée! like that! Do I shock you? You don't appear to have been quite so squeamish in practice, do you? And if there's one thing I can't endure, it's hypocrisy. Leave that to the experts, like Madame de Genlis, or Madame Campan and her mealy-mouthed set, unless you mean to ally yourself with those mewling dowagers who come flocking back from abroad wailing about the decline in good manners! I like to call a spade a spade! If you want to do right by your invisible husband, you must give him another child, and a child of Napoleon's. Moral: Napoleon must give you another! To my mind, it's as simple as that! Besides, I hear the Austrian is in high hopes, so he may be easy on that score and will have all the more time for you.'

Marianne regarded her with awe. 'But Fortunée,' she protested, 'don't you know you are immoral?'

'Of course I know!' Madame Hamelin crowed delightedly. 'And you can't imagine how happy I am to be so! What I have seen of morality all around me makes me sick! All for love, my sweet, and a fig for your principles!'

As if in endorsement of this declaration of war on conventional principles, there was a sudden report of cannon fire outside, followed almost immediately by a second and then a third. At the same time, borne on the summer breeze, came a sound of solemn, martial music and the murmur of a crowd.

'What is it?' Marianne asked.

'Of course, you don't know! It's the state funeral of Marshal Lannes. Today is the sixth of July and the Emperor is having the body of his old comrade-in-arms transferred from the Invalides to the Panthéon. The cortège must have just now left the Invalides.'

The guns were now firing almost continuously. The melancholy sound of the trumpets and the muffled roll of drums were coming nearer, filling the garden and penetrating into the quiet room, reinforced by the tolling of every bell in Paris.

'Would you like me to shut the window?' Fortunée asked, impressed by the rumble of these solemn obsequies by which the city paid its tribute, for one day, to one of the greatest soldiers of the age. Marianne made a gesture of refusal. She too was listening, more conscious than she had been perhaps during the contrived gaieties of the marriage celebrations, of the greatness of the man who had taken charge of her fate and who, high as he was, could still find time to watch over her. Her heart stirred as she remembered the hand which had held hers through those first moments of her long agony. He had promised not to leave her and he had kept his word. He always kept his word.

She had learned from Fortunée, and also from Arcadius de Jolival, how he had stayed at the Austrian embassy, working tirelessly, until the fire was altogether extinguished, rescuing even a simple housemaid who was trapped by the fire in an attic room. She had learned, too, how angry he had been the next day, and of the retribution he had meted out: the Prefect of Police, Dubois, dismissed, Savary severely reprimanded, the architect who had thoughtlessly designed the ballroom arrested, the chief of the fire service relieved of his post and measures put in hand without delay for a complete reorganization of the entire force, such as it was. Certainly, it was reassuring to find oneself the object of his solicitude but Marianne knew now that her passion for him had snuffed itself out like a candle, leaving something else in its place, a deeper feeling, perhaps, but how much less ennobling!

When she spoke, it was in answer to this secret thought. 'I shall never give myself to him again, never . . .'

'What?' Fortunée said, startled. 'To whom? To the Emperor? You won't . . .'

'No,' Marianne said. 'I can't. Not now.'

'But – why ever not?'

Before Marianne could reply, there was a tap at the door and Agathe, her maid, appeared, deliciously neat and fresh in striped cotton dress and starched apron:

'Monsieur Beaufort is below, Your Highness. He desires to know if Your Highness is well enough to receive him.'

Marianne's cheeks were suffused with a wave of crimson:

'He is here? Downstairs? No, no, I cannot—'

'I dare say you may not know, my lady, but the gentleman has called every day since the accident and when I told him this morning that you were better—'

Fortunée, who had been a bright-eyed observer of Marianne's abrupt change of colour, judged it time to take a hand in the matter:

'Ask the gentleman to wait a moment, will you, Agathe. And then you may come back and help me to make your mistress presentable. Be off with you now!'

Appalled at the very idea of coming face-to-face with the one man who had figured so persistently in her thoughts ever since the ball, Marianne tried to protest. She looked a fright, she knew she did! She was so pale and thin . . . No normal man could help but be horrified at the spectacle she presented! Madame Hamelin, ignoring all this, refrained from pointing out to her friend that, for a woman so wholly determined on renouncing her existence, she was showing highly interesting symptoms of agitation at the prospect of a visit from a gentleman. She confined herself to ascertaining that the Monsieur Beaufort in question was in fact the American who had vanished from her friend's life so abruptly at about the same time as she herself had entered it. This being confirmed, she set to work.

Quick as a wink, Marianne found herself nestled amid the voluminous folds of an exquisite confection, all pink ribbons and snowy lace, her hair combed out, her face rendered a little less pallid by discreet reference to the rouge-pot and her person so liberally besprinkled with Signor Gian-Maria Farina's excellent Cologne that it made her sneeze. The room began to exhale delicious odours of bergamot, rosemary, lemon and lavender.

'Nothing is more abominable than the smell of a sick-room,' Fotunée declared, arranging a rebellious curl with a flick of one clever finger. 'There. That will do now.'

'But, Fortunée, what are you up to?'

'Oh . . . nothing. Just an idea of mine. Now I shall leave you.'

'No!' Marianne almost shrieked. 'No, you must not!'

Fortunée did not argue but went and seated herself in a chair by the window with an alacrity which suggested that her proposal had been made with no very serious intention. She was, in fact, burning with curiosity and by the time Jason, admitted by Agathe, crossed the threshold of Marianne's room that indefatigable man-hunter was lying in wait for him, securely ensconced behind a book which she had picked up at random, in the posture of the perfect sick-room attendant. But, above the leaves, her black eyes made an instant appraisal of the visitor.

He, after a slight bow to the stranger, directed his steps towards the bed in which Marianne lay watching his advance with an unfamiliar feeling of breathlessness. With his clear eyes, tanned face and energetic movements, Jason seemed to bring the whole wide ocean with him into the sea-green bedchamber.

To Marianne, he seemed to have swept away the four walls of the room and let the sea air blow in in great, sweeping gusts, yet in reality he had done nothing. He had only strolled across the room and bowed and uttered some polite expressions of satisfaction at finding her sufficiently recovered to receive him. Overcoming her feelings with an effort, she managed to force herself to answer audibly:

'I have been wishing to thank you for saving me,' she

whispered, in what she hoped was an ordinary, conversational tone. 'But for you, I do not know what might have happened—'

'Well, I do,' Jason retorted coolly. 'You would have been like Madame de Schwarzenburg and the Princess de le Leyen and a good many more. Just what, may I ask, did you think you were after in that inferno? Not the Emperor, at all events. He was in the garden, helping the rescue work.'

'Is there no one but the Emperor I might have been seeking in the fire? In fact, it was something else, I think.'

'Someone dear to you, I imagine. A member of your new husband's family, perhaps? Which reminds me' – a tiny smile twisted one corner of his mouth although his blue eyes remained unwarmed – 'which reminds me, you must tell me all about this marriage. So unexpected, was it not? Where did you dig up the impressive name and title? Another present from the Emperor? He has certainly been generous this time, though scarcely more than you deserve. It suits you better to be a princess than a singer.'

'The Emperor had nothing to do with it! My marriage was arranged by my family. You may remember my godfather, the Abbé de Chazay, from Selton, he—'

'What? So this time it was he who found you your new name? You know, you are quite the most astonishing woman of my acquaintance. I never know who you will be the next time I meet you . . .'

He paused and glanced significantly at Fortunée. She, her curiosity satisfied, and probably thinking that the conversation seemed to be taking a strange turn, judged it advisable to withdraw. She rose and moved with dignity towards the door. Marianne made a move to restrain her, then changed her mind. If Jason meant to be disagreeable, she preferred to face him alone. Fortunée must have realized, in any case, that in trying to present Marianne to advantage, she had been wasting her time. Jason observed her departure with one eyebrow raised, then turned back to Marianne with a saturnine grin:

'Charming woman. Now, what was I saying . . . Ah, yes, that one never knows what name you will be using next. I met you as Mademoiselle d'Asselnat, then, almost immediately, you became Lady Cranmere. The next time we met, in the Prince of Benevento's house, you were Mademoiselle Mallerousse. Not for long, though. The moment my back was turned, a wave of the imperial wand and you were transformed into that ravishing Italian singer called, what was her name? Maria Stella? Now, you are still Italian, am I right? Only you have become a princess, a – what was it you called yourself? Serene Highness, wasn't it? It's not easy for an American citizen like me to understand these things . . .'

Marianne listened with incredulity to his flow of calculated insult, delivered in a cordial, conversational tone, and asked herself what devious ends her visitor was pursuing. Was he mocking her, or was he trying to show her that the warmth of friendship which had developed in the underground caves of Chaillot had changed into a quiet, amiable contempt? If that was it, she thought she could not bear it, but she had to know. Turning her head wearily on the lace pillow, Marianne closed her eyes and sighed:

'I was told that you had called to inquire of me every morning since the ball and, in my innocence, I thought this a sign of friendship. I see that I was mistaken. You merely wished to assure yourself that I should soon be in a fit state to endure the shafts of your sarcasm. I am afraid you will have to excuse me. Unfortunately, I am not yet sufficiently restored to fight you on equal terms . . .'

There was a short silence. To Marianne, behind her closed eyelids, it seemed to go on for ever. For a moment, she thought that he had gone, and she was on the point of opening her eyes anxiously to see when she heard him laughing. She swung her head round instantly, eyes blazing with indignation:

'You can laugh?'

'I'll say I can! You are a truly remarkable actress, Marianne. You nearly took me in for a moment. But one look at the gleam in your eyes is enough to give you away.'

'But it's true. Baron Corvisart—'

'Has just left. I know. I met him. He told me you were very weak, certainly, but I know now that your weakness is only physical. Praise God, your spirit is unharmed and that was all I wanted to know. Forgive me. I was only trying to get a reaction out of you. Since that night, I have been living with the fear that it might no longer be possible.'

'But why?'

'Because,' he said seriously, 'the woman I saw at the ball and during the fire was not the woman I had known. She was cold, distant, there was nothing in her eyes. It was the look of a woman who goes seeking death. You had everything a human being could ask for: wealth, beauty, honours, the love of a great man – and you were going to have a child. And yet you wanted to die a dreadful death. Why, Marianne?'

A rush of warmth pervaded her whole being, reawakening the nerve centres which had been numbed by despair and physical suffering. So his cruelty and indifference had been a pose? Seeing him there, beside her, with that drawn look on his face which betrayed how deeply he felt, she felt a sudden, keener awareness of her love for him. The feeling was so strong that for an instant she had a wild impulse to tell him the truth, tell him that it was grief at the thought that she had lost him which had made her want to die. She was on the point of confessing at that moment how much she loved him and how wonderful her love seemed to her, but she recollected herself just in time. The man before her was a married man. He no longer possessed the right, or even the will perhaps, to listen to a declaration of her love. What had brought him here was simply friendship. And Marianne was fundamentally too honest not to respect the marriages of others, even if her own experience had proved doubly disastrous.

Even so, she summoned up the courage to smile, unaware that her smile was more heartbreaking than tears, and as he repeated 'Why?', she answered at last: 'Perhaps because of all those very things, or because most of it is only a snare and a delusion. The Emperor is married, Jason, and happy in his marriage . . . I am nothing to him now beyond a loving and devoted friend. I believe he loves his wife. For my part—'

'You still love him, do you?'

'I – am fond of him, more than that, I admire him with all my heart.'

'But the child? Was the child too a snare and a delusion?'

'No. It was the one tie which bound us together irrevocably. Perhaps, after all, it is better so, for him at any rate. For me, it complicates matters considerably ... Prince Sant'Anna—' Marianne broke off suddenly and said impatiently: 'But if you have been coming here every day, you must have seen Arcadius?'

'Of course.'

'Then do not tell me he has told you nothing? Surely he has told you all about my marriage.'

'Yes, he has,' Jason agreed placidly, 'but I wished to hear it from your own lips. The first thing he told me was that there was a letter waiting for me with Patterson in Nantes – where I did not put in because I was being chased by an English privateer and was obliged to run to avoid a fight.'

'You! Avoid a fight?'

'The United States are not at war with England. But I'm sorry now I didn't go about and sink that Englishman and then put in to Nantes. It would have made a world of difference. I'm regretting my law-abiding impulse more than you can think.'

He turned and, like Fortunée a little while before, walked slowly over to the window. His broad shoulders and clear-cut profile were etched against the green, leafy garden outside. Marianne held her breath, overwhelmed by a delicious anguish at the real anger she now heard in his voice.

'You are sorry you did not receive the letter? Does – does that mean you would have done what I asked of you?'

In three steps he was at her side, on his knees by her bed, her two hands locked fast in his.

'And you?' he asked eagerly. 'Would you have honoured your pledge to me? Would you have gone with me? Left everything? You would really have become my wife, meaning it, with no regrets?'

Marianne gazed wonderingly into his eyes, searching for confirmation of the truth of what she already knew yet scarcely dared to believe.

'With no regrets, Jason. With a happiness I have only been fully aware of myself for a little while. You will never know how I waited for you . . . to the last moment, Jason, to the very last moment. And when it was too late—'

'Stop!'

His face was buried in the white sheets and Marianne felt his lips warm on her hand. Gently, half-tremblingly, she laid her free hand on the mariner's thick, black hair, lightly caressing the unruly curls and happy in this sudden display of weakness in him, the iron man, happier still in the knowledge that his confusion was as great as her own.

'You see now,' she said softly, 'why it was I wished to die the other night. When I saw you with— Oh, Jason! Jason! Why did you marry?'

As abruptly as he had come to her, he rose and tore himself away, not looking at her.

'I believed that I had lost you for ever,' he said grimly. 'There is no opposing Napoleon, least of all when he loves. And I knew that he did love you. As for Pilar . . . she needed my help. Her life was in danger. Her father, Don Agostino, made no secret of his American sympathies. When he died, some weeks ago, the Spanish governor of Fernandina immediately turned on Pilar who was his sole heiress. He sequestrated her lands and she was on the point of being thrown into prison with little hope of release. The one way to save her and to keep her safe was to make her an American citizen. I married her.'

'Was it necessary for you to go to such lengths? Surely you could have taken her to your own country and established her respectably there, under your eye?'

Jason shrugged. 'She is a Spaniard. Things would have been rather more awkward than that. And I owed a great deal to her father. When my own parents died, Don Agostino was the one person who came to my assistance. I have known Pilar all her life.'

'And, naturally, she has loved you all her life?'

'I think so . . . yes.'

Marianne was silent. Dazzled by the revelation of her own love, she was only just beginning to discover that she knew hardly anything of Jason Beaufort's life before that autumn afternoon when he had walked into the drawing-room at

Selton Hall. He had lived so many years without her, unaware of her very existence! Until that moment, she had thought of Jason only in relation to herself, to the part he played in her own life but before that, away in that distant, vast and, to Marianne, mysterious and vaguely frightening country of his, he had formed other ties of his own and beaten out a path for himself. His memory was full of scenes in which she, Marianne, had never figured, of faces she had never seen yet which aroused in Jason feelings that might vary from hatred to love. That world, or some of it, was Pilar's also. To her, it was familiar, she was at home there and their common experience must have woven between her and Jason one of those bonds which, derived from the same tastes and the same memories, often proved stronger and more enduring than the flamboyant chains of passion. All these thoughts were in Marianne's mind as she said in a small, unhappy voice: 'I love you, yet I do not know you at all.'

'I feel as if I had known you always,' he answered quickly, devouring her with haggard eyes. 'But what is the use? We let go the moment when fate decreed our paths should cross. Now it is too late.'

'Why should it be too late?' Rebellion jerked Marianne out of her natural reserve. 'You do not love this Pilar. You said so.'

'No more than you love the man whose name you have taken, but the fact remains: you bear his name, just as Pilar bears mine. I am no moralist, God knows, and I must be the last person on earth to preach morality to you, but, Marianne, we have no choice. We cannot abandon those who have trusted us. We have no right to make them suffer.'

'I see,' Marianne said. 'She is jealous . . .'

'She is a Spaniard. She knows I am not in love with her but she does expect respect, some affection, that I will preserve at least the outward appearance of a contented, if not a loving marriage.'

There was silence again, a silence occupied by Marianne in examining what Jason had just said. Her joy of a moment before evaporated before harsh reality. An adventurer Jason might be, equal to any risks, bold enough for anything, but one thing he would not do, and Marianne knew it: he would never deal dishonestly with himself, and he would expect the woman he loved to show the same strength. There was no arguing with such determination. Marianne sighed:

'I see. Then you have come to say goodbye. I suppose you are leaving. Your wife did not appear to care for it here.'

A glint of laughter shone briefly in the American's eyes. 'She finds the women too pretty and too bold. She trusts me, naturally, but when I am not with her, she would rather have me at sea than in a salon. We remain for another fortnight. A friend of my father's, Baguenault, the banker, has offered us the use of a place at Passy – a charming house in the rue de Seine set in extensive grounds. It belonged once to a friend of Queen Marie-Antoinette. Pilar is happy enough there so long as she need not go out and I still have some business to settle. Then we return to America. My ship is waiting at Morlaix . . .'

His tone had resumed its ordinary, conversational level and Marianne, sinking back in her lacy nest, gave a small, regretful sigh. The passionate outburst of a moment ago had been suppressed by the iron force of Jason's will, most probably never to be reborn. That will divided them as surely as all the width of the vast ocean which would soon lie between them. The vessel which had sometimes haunted her dreams would sail with another woman on board. Something was coming to an end before it had even begun and Marianne knew suddenly that she could not long hold back her tears. She closed her eyes for an instant and gritted her teeth, then she took a deep breath and said at last: 'Well then . . . let us say goodbye now, Jason. I wish you . . . every happiness.'

He had risen but still stood, staring fixedly at the floor, without looking at her.

'I do not ask for that,' he said, more harshly than perhaps he meant. 'Wish me peace of mind, that will do very well. And for you—'

'No. For pity's sake wish me nothing.'

He turned and walked to the door. Marianne's eyes followed his tall figure helplessly. He was going, going out of her life, back to the world of Pilar, when the sum of their common memories was still so slight. She was seized by a kind of panic and as he laid his hand on the door handle was powerless to stop herself crying out:

'Jason!'

Slowly, very slowly, the blue eyes came back to her, filled with such weariness that Marianne was deeply shaken. At that moment, Jason seemed to have grown much older.

'Yes?' he said in a controlled voice.

'Won't you – we shall not meet again – won't you kiss me before you go?'

She thought he would have sprung towards her. The impulse was written so clearly, almost palpably on his face. But he controlled himself with an effort which whitened the knuckles of the brown hand still holding the ivory door knob and brought a sudden flash of anger into his eyes.

'Can't you understand?' he said, through clenched teeth. 'What do you think would happen at this moment if I were to lay so much as a finger on you? In another moment, we should be lovers and how could I tear myself away from you then? Before I left this room, I should have lost all respect for myself – and for you, too, perhaps. I should have become your slave . . . and for that I should not forgive you.'

Marianne had raised herself to hold out her hands to him, but now she sank back, defeated, on her pillows:

'Go, then . . . Go, quickly! Because I am going to cry and I would not have you see my tears.'

She looked so piteous, so defenceless, that even as she begged him to go Jason turned and, with the irrationality of love, would have gone back to her.

'Marianne—'

'No! If you have any love for me at all, please go! Can't you see that I can't bear any more? I was stupid, I see that now. I should have realized sooner, I should have understood my own feelings, but since it is all lost now, irrecoverably, it is best to end it quickly. Go back to your wife, since you believe you must be faithful to her, and leave me alone . . .'

And as Jason still hesitated at the door, torn by the misery and anger in her voice, she cried fiercely: 'Go away! What are you waiting for? Do you want me to make a complete fool of myself?'

He did go then, without pausing even to close the door behind him. Marianne heard his boots clatter on the stairs, then die away, and, with a gasp of misery, she closed her eyes and let the tears she had been holding back so desperately stream down her face. Yet even in her wretchedness she was conscious of a feeling of absurdity which shocked and frightened her a little. If she were honest with herself, she had to admit that the elevated moral plane on which Jason appeared to exist seemed to her rather too high. For herself, she would have felt neither shame nor remorse in giving herself to him. Surely, it was absurd to be saying eternal farewells at the very moment they had realized their love for one another? That was how Fortunée would look at it, certainly. To one with her compliant moral code and declared belief in the precept of 'all for love', such a scene as had just taken place between Marianne and Jason would appear the height of the ridiculous. Goodness, how she would laugh, and what mockery she would heap on Marianne! And Marianne could not find it in her heart to blame her. It was this which frightened her, her own instinctive, shameful wish that Jason had united them in body as they were already in their hearts, that he had not chosen flight, however glorious and however much in keeping with his Huguenot blood and American upbringing, in preference to the joys beyond all price two lovers find in each other's arms. Had she, all unknowing, so far adopted Fortunée's outlook on life? Or was she, Marianne, one of those women, so infinitely less complex than she had ever realized, for whom to love a man and to belong to him was one and the same, utterly simple and natural thing?

No doubt it was highly complimentary to be placed on a pedestal in the most secret corner of a man's heart in the enviable position of an untouchable divinity, but Marianne thought she would have preferred rather less worship and more passion. Remembering her abortive wedding night, she told herself that Jason had changed a great deal. At Selton, he had been perfectly willing to make love to a young woman who had been married only hours before, even to take her husband's place in the bridal chamber. What had brought about this extraordinary access of puritanism? It was certainly ill-timed, to say the least. Supposing, as Napoleon was in the habit of claiming, that love's greatest triumph lay in flight, then Jason had indubitably won all along the line but Marianne could have wished that this model victory had not left her with such a dismal feeling of defeat. She found herself wondering if he had fled in order to sublimate his love – or prompted by the instinctive longing of every married man for peace and quiet at home, safe alike from passion and domestic strife. That Pilar was evidently as jealous as a cat and rather than cross her Jason seemed prepared to abandon, like an unwanted parcel, the woman he claimed to adore. And she, Marianne, had accepted it! She had even, for an instant, admired him for his lofty sentiments! She had even allowed him to reject her innocently offered kiss with as much evidence of loathing as if it had been the most insidious of love potions! What did he expect her to do now? Sink back into her pillows and wait for death to earn her a place among the legendary heroines who died for love and a less lasting memorial, like the faint scent of faded flowers, in Jason's own memory? Oh no, it would be too stupid, too—

At this point in her reflections, she was prevented from lashing herself into a further fury by the lighthearted entrance of Madame Hamelin. The Créole smiled coaxingly:

'Well? Happy?'

It was not the most felicitous of words. Marianne scowled:

'No. He loves me too much to deceive his wife! So we said goodbye for ever!'

There was a moment's astonished silence, then Fortunée reacted precisely as Marianne had foreseen she would. She let out a hysterical wail of laughter and collapsed heavily on to a small sofa which groaned under the shock. She went on laughing so helplessly and for so long that in the end Marianne began to feel that she was rather overdoing things.

'You think it's funny?' she said in an aggrieved voice.

'Oh! Oh, my goodness, yes! . . . Oh, dear! . . . It's priceless! . . . And perfectly ridiculous!'

'Ridiculous?'

'Yes, indeed. Quite ridiculous!' Fortunée's hilarity gave way abruptly to the most earnest indignation. 'It's more than ridiculous. It's farcical, grotesque! What are you made of, the two of you? Here is a splendid, charming, fascinating man (and I am allowed to be a judge!) for whom, by all accounts, you represent the One and Only Woman with a capital W, and who longs for you all the more fiercely because he can't bring himself to speak . . . And here are you, head over ears in love with him – for you do love him, don't you?'

'I have only just found it out,' Marianne confessed, 'but it is true. I do love him – more than anything in the world!'

'I could have sworn you did, though it has taken you long enough to discover it! Very well, you love him . . . and all the pair of you can find to do about it is to say – what was your absurd phrase? – Goodbye for Ever! Wasn't that it?'

'That was it.'

'Well, the answer's fairly obvious. Either you aren't so passionately in love as you like to think, or neither of you deserves to live!'

'He has a wife . . . and I have a husband!'

'Well, as to that, so have I a husband. Not much of a one, it's true, but I have. Somewhere, there is a Hamelin, just as somewhere there is a Prince Sant'Anna. But if you—'

'Fortunée, you don't understand. It's not the same thing at all.'

'And why isn't it the same thing?' Fortunée inquired, with deceptive sweetness. 'You think, don't you, that because when I want a man I take him, without any question, I must be a lightskirt, a loose woman? Well, I don't deceive myself and I'm not ashamed of it.' Her expression grew suddenly grave. 'You see, Marianne, youth is a great gift, too wonderful and too short for us to waste it. Love, too, the real, true love that everyone hopes for and yet no one dares to believe in, a love like that is worth something more than just sitting on opposite sides of the ocean dreaming regretfully of what might have been. When we are old, it will be better, believe me, to have memories to live on rather than regrets. And don't tell me you don't agree with me,' Fortunée concluded briskly. 'Your regrets are written all over your face!'

'You're quite right,' Marianne acknowledged honestly. 'Just now, I asked him to kiss me before he went. He would not, because . . . because he believed he could not control himself if he touched me. And it's true, I did regret it, and I still do because in my heart I don't care in the least about Pilar or Sant'Anna. It's him I love and him I want. No one else . . . not even the Emperor. And yet . . . in a fortnight, Jason will be gone. He will have left France with his wife, perhaps for ever.'

'If you go about it the right way, he may still leave but he'll be back . . . and fast! As soon as he's taken his lady wife home, I daresay.'

Marianne shook her head dubiously:

'Jason is not like that. He is sterner, more unbending than I ever thought. And—'

'Love moves mountains, and can turn the wisest heads.'

'What can I do?'

'Get up, for a start!'

Fortunée put out her hand and gave the bell an energetic tug. When Agathe appeared in answer to the summons, she demanded to know if everything was ready. Receiving an answer in the affirmative, she gave the order to 'bring it up immediately'. Then she turned back to Marianne.

'First,' she said firmly, 'you have to get back your strength. And downstairs is just the very thing for you. Talleyrand has seen to that, bless him!'

Before Marianne could open her mouth to ask any questions, a strange procession entered the room. It was led by Agathe, who flung wide the double doors. She was followed by Jeremy, the butler, looking every bit as gloomy as if he were presiding at a funeral, although he was succeeded by nothing more alarming than a pair of footmen bearing between them a large silver tray surmounted by a formidable array of pots, jars and cups, after whom came a third footman carrying a small, portable stove. After these again, came two under-cooks upholding with a more than religious reverence a small, silver-gilt saucepan which was apparently extremely hot. Finally, bringing up the rear with all the majestic gravity of a priest approaching the altar to perform a more than usually sacred rite, appeared the celebrated Antonin Carême, the Prince of Benevento's own cook, and the genius whose services half Europe, including the Emperor, envied him.

Marianne had not the least idea what the famous chef could be doing with all this paraphernalia in her bedchamber, but she had lived long enough in Talleyrand's household to realize that Carême's attendance represented an immense honour of which good manners demanded she should show a proper appreciation, or risk being classed by Carême, who, like all true artists, was dreadfully sensitive, as wholly beyond the pale.

She therefore hastened to respond to the bow bestowed on her by the king of cooks and schooled herself to listen with due attention to the speech which he addressed to her once safely arrived in the middle of the room. From it, she learned that Monsieur de Talleyrand, deeply concerned for the health of Her Serene Highness and discovering to his great distress that she was refusing all sustenance, had taken long counsel with himself, Carême, and that the two of them had concluded that Her Serene Highness must be offered such choice selection of delicacies as would most speedily restore her to health and strength, and that these must be presented to her in such a way as to make refusal an impossibility.

'I informed His Highness that I should personally attend Your Highness's bedside and prepare for you with my own hands an infallible restorative of such powerful recuperative properties that it has revived even the most failing spirits . . . I trust I may prevail upon Your Highness to accept what it is my privilege to offer.'

The implication was clear that, short of provoking some unimaginable cataclysm, refusal was out of the question. Amused by all this polysyllabic eloquence, Marianne indicated graciously, in language very nearly as florid as his own, her delight in the prospect of tasting another of Monsieur Carême's matchless creations. Only then did she inquire politely what it was she was required to consume.

'A chocolate, Madame, a simple chocolate, the recipe for which is in fact an invention of Monsieur Brillat-Savarin, although I have had the honour of perfecting it. I do not hesitate to prophesy that, after a single cup of this magic beverage, Your Highness will feel another woman.'

To feel herself another woman was in fact the very thing that Marianne longed for above all. Especially if by some miracle that other woman could possess a heart wholly free from any attachment. But Carême had interrupted his flow of speech for a moment and, with his rich coat of plum-coloured velvet covered by a huge, stiff, white apron carefully draped about his person by one of his assistants, had commenced his office. The small saucepan was placed upon the stove and the lid solemnly removed, allowing a fragrant steam to escape into the room. Then, with the aid of a golden spoon, Carême embarked on an exploration of the various jars which his acolytes held deferentially open for his inspection, at the same time resuming his discourse:

'I may say that this chocolate, the result of many earnest cogitations by the most distinguished minds, is, in itself, a veritable work of art. The actual chocolate, at present contained in this receptacle, was cooked yesterday, in accordance with the recommendations of that expert judge, Madame d'Austerel, Superior of the Convent of the Visitation at Belley, so that by allowing it to stand for twenty-four hours the required smoothness might be imparted to the texture. It was concocted initially from three varieties of cocoa: Caraque, Sainte-Madeleine and Berbice, but in order to create what Monsieur Brillat-Savarin has so aptly called "invalid chocolate" we must have recourse to the subtle skills of the Chinese, adding to it vanilla, cinnamon, a trifle of mace, pulverized cane sugar and, above all, a few grains of ambergris, which constitute the prime element in the almost magical virtues which this beverage may be said to possess. My own personal contribution is expressed in a little honey of Narbonne, some roasted almonds, finely ground, fresh cream and a few drops of fine Cognac. Now, if Your Highness will oblige me . . .'

As he spoke, Carême had been adding the various ingredients to his chocolate. Then, after letting it simmer for a few moments, he filled a delicate porcelain cup and, still with the most elaborate care, placed it upon a small tray which he bore majestically to Marianne's bedside. The tented canopy of sea-green silk became filled with the fragrant odour of chocolate.

Conscious of taking part in a kind of ritual, and of Carême's stern eye upon her, daring her to find fault with it, Marianne carried the cup to her lips and sipped at the boiling liquid. The taste, in so far as it was possible to taste anything so very hot, was very sweet and not unpleasant, although, in her opinion, the scent of ambergris did nothing to improve it.

'It's very good,' she ventured, after two or three painful sips.

'You must drink it all,' Carême commanded her imperiously. 'It is necessary to imbibe a certain amount before the effects are felt.'

Marianne took her courage in both hands, swallowed heroically and succeeded in getting down the whole scorching cupful. A rush of warmth invaded her body and she felt as if a river of fire were running down inside her. Scarlet as a boiled lobster and beaded with perspiration, yet curiously invigorated, she fell back on her pillows and favoured Carême with what she hoped was a grateful smile:

'I feel better already. You are a wizard, Monsieur Carême.'

'I, no, Princess, but the cooking, yes, indeed! I have prepared enough for three cups and I trust Your Highness will drink them all. I shall return tomorrow at the same time and make you some more. No, no, it is no trouble. A pleasure, I assure you.'

Regal as ever, Carême removed his apron, tossed it magnificently to one of his assistants and, with a bow that would not have disgraced a courtier, departed from the room, followed by his escort in the same order as before.

'Well?' Fortunée demanded, laughing, as soon as she was once more alone with her friend. 'How do you feel?'

'Boiling! But a good deal stronger. All the same, I do feel rather sick.'

Without answering, Fortunée poured a little of Monsieur Carême's chocolate into a cup and drank it with evident enjoyment, closing her eyes, like a cat with a saucer of milk.

'Do you really like it?' Marianne asked. 'Don't you find it a bit too sweet?'

Madame Hamelin laughed. 'Like all Créoles, I love sugar,' she said. 'Besides, I'd drink it if it were as bitter as chicory. Do you know why Brillat-Savarin caled it "invalid chocolate"? Because the amber it contains, my dear, has aphrodisiac properties – and I dine tonight with the most magnificent Russian.'

'Aphrodisiac!' Marianne cried, horrified. 'But I don't need those!'

'Don't you?'

Fortunée strolled over to her friend's dressing-table and, carelessly, from among the litter of jars, bottles and gold and silver toilet articles scattered upon it, picked up a large jewel case and opened it. The emeralds Marianne had worn at the ambassador's ball, and which Chernychev had returned on the following day, gleamed in the last rays of the setting sun. Madame Hamelin took out the necklace, dangling it thoughtfully from her fingers and watching the play of light glinting in flashes of brilliant green fire:

'Talleyrand is an old rogue, Marianne . . . and he knows quite well that the best way to restore your zest for life is to revive your appetite for love.'

'My appetite for love! Well, you have just seen where love has got me . . .'

'Precisely. Weren't you telling me that your handsome sea rover remains with us for another fortnight?'

'That's not very long! What can I do?'

Fortunée did not answer directly but went on playing idly with the necklace, at the same time pursuing her earlier train of thought:

'It's not very difficult, perhaps, to renounce a woman dawdling invalidishly in bed. To turn one's back on a dazzling beauty who can lead one of the most notorious rakes in Europe by the nose, is a very different matter. Why don't you let Sasha Chernychev take you out driving, or to the theatre one of these days? If half of what I hear is true, he has amply deserved it . . . if only for not putting these beauties into his pocket! I'm sure I could never have resisted the temptation! But then, when a man's interest in a woman leads him to incur a sword thrust and a knife wound, all in the space of seven days . . .'

She let the gems slide heavily through her fingers and drop back into their nest of black velvet. Then, as though losing interest in the subject, she sat down at the mirror and began rearranging her dark curls, patting a little powder into her already flawless complexion, touching up the cupid's bow of her lips and finally amusing herself by opening every bottle of scent and sniffing it critically. With her vivacious expression, and the opulent figure so attractively belied by her virginal print gown, Fortunée was such a perfect picture of womanhood at its most glorious that Marianne could not help but be aware of it. Unconsciously, or perhaps not altogether unconsciously, Fortunée was showing her where her real weapons lay, weapons against which the noblest and most determined of men's plans were powerless.

Raising herself on her elbow, Marianne stared for a moment at her friend, watching her dab perfume delicately in the warm hollow of her breasts.

'Fortunée!'

'Yes, darling?'

'I . . . I think I feel like finishing that chocolate.'

CHAPTER THREE

Britannicus

Four days later, dressed in a robe of flame-coloured muslin with a head-dress of feathers dyed to match, Marianne made her appearance in a first-floor box at the Comêdie Française and caused a sensation. Count Chernychev was at her side.

The second act of Racine's *Britannicus* had already begun but the couple strolled to the front of the box and, without a glance for the actors on the stage, stood scanning the audience (which, to be fair, was amply returning their interest) with cool insolence. Without other ornament than a fantastic Chinese lacquered fan, trimmed with feathers the same colour as those in her hair, the unrelieved red bringing out all the golden glow of her skin and the brilliance of her great eyes, Marianne was a superb and altogether arresting sight, like some exotic, tropical flower. Her whole appearance was provocative, from the boldness of her deep décolletage to the forbidden fabric of her dress, a silky, smooth-flowing muslin which Leroy had acquired through his own mysterious channels at extravagant cost and which, contrasting strongly with the satins and brocades of the other women present, rendered full justice to every line of the Princess Sant'Anna's magnificent body.

At her side, in a tight-fitting uniform of green and gold, stiff with decorations, Chernychev surveyed the house arrogantly.

They were a striking couple. Talma, playing Nero, had just reached the lines:

'. . . so fair sight ravished mine eyes,
I tried to speak, but lo, my voice was dumb,
I stood unmoving, held in long amaze . . .'

The actor's voice died away and he stood, motionless in the centre of the stage, staring, while the audience, struck by the coincidence contained in the words, burst into spontaneous applause. Marianne, amused, smiled down at him and Talma stepped forward instantly, hand on the heart, and bowed to the box as if it had contained the Empress herself. Then he turned to resume his interrupted dialogue with the actor playing Narcisse and Marianne and her escort took their seats at last.

But Marianne, who was still not fully recovered, had not come to the theatre that night for the pleasure of seeing the Empire's greatest tragic actor. She was looking round, her face partly screened by her fan, scrutinizing the house attentively in search of the face she had come there to find. The great Talma's performances were always well attended and Marianne had hinted discreetly to her friend Talleyrand that she would like him to invite the Beauforts to share his box for *Britannicus*.

There they were, in fact, in a box almost directly facing that occupied by Marianne herself. Pilar, looking more Spanish than ever in a gown of black lace, was sitting in front, next to the prince, who seemed to be dozing with his chin sunk in his cravat and both hands clasped on the knob of his stick. Jason was standing behind, one hand resting lightly on the back of Pilar's chair. The other occupants of the box were an elderly woman and a man evidently a good deal older still. The woman retained some traces of what must once have been quite remarkable beauty. Her bright, black eyes still held the fire of youth in them and the red bow of her lips revealed both sensuality and firmness. She, too, was dressed, severely but sumptuously, in black. The man, who was bald-headed except for some few remaining red hairs, had the flushed, slightly bloated complexion of one over-fond of the bottle, but despite his bowed shoulders it was clear that this man had once possessed strength and endurance above the average. He looked like nothing so much as an ancient, riven oak tree that still manages somehow to survive.

With the exception of Jason, who appeared absorbed in what was taking place on the stage, they were all looking at Marianne and her companion. Pilar had even invoked the assistance of a pair of lorgnettes, which she wielded with about as much cordiality as if she had been looking down the barrel of a gun. Talleyrand smiled his habitual lazy smile, lifted his hand fractionally in greeting and appeared to fall asleep again, despite the efforts of his other neighbour, the black-eyed woman, who seemed to be bombarding him with questions about the new arrivals. Marianne heard Chernychev, at her side, give a soft, mirthless laugh:

'We would appear to have caused something of a stir . . .'

'It surprises you?'

'Not in the least.'

'You dislike it, then?'

This time, the Russian laughed outright. 'Dislike it? My dear Princess, you must know there is nothing I like better; except, of course, when it would conflict with my duty as an officer. But it's not merely a stir that I should like to make with you, it is a scandal.'

'A scandal! You must be mad!'

'By no means. I say: a scandal – so that you will be bound to me, irrevocably, for ever, with no possibility of escape.'

Underlying the lightness of his words there was a faint suggestion of a threat which shook Marianne. Her fan shut with a click.

'So,' she said slowly. 'This is the great love you have been pouring into my ears ever since our first meeting? You want to chain me to you, make me your private property – and guard me fiercely, I dare say? In other words, you would put me in prison . . .'

Chernychev showed his teeth in a smile which Marianne could not help comparing with that of a wild animal, but his voice, when he answered her, was smooth as silk:

'I am a Tartar, you know . . . Once, on the road to Samarkand, where the grass never grew again after it had been trampled down by the hordes of Genghis Khan, a poor camel-driver found the most beautiful emerald, dropped, probably, from some robber's hoard. He was poor, he was hungry and cold and to him the stone represented a great fortune. Yet, instead of selling it and living in ease and luxury, the poor camel-driver kept the emerald and hid it in the folds of his greasy turban, and from that day forth he neither hungered nor thirsted for he had lost the need for food or drink. All that mattered to him was the emerald. And so, in order to be sure that none should steal it from him, he travelled on, ever farther and farther into the desert, until he came to the deep, inaccessible caverns where there was nothing to look for but death. And death came, very slow and painful, but he watched it coming with a smile because he had the emerald pressed close to his heart . . .'

'A pretty story,' Marianne said coolly, 'and flattering in its implications, but really, my dear Count, I think I shall be very glad to see you go back to St Petersburg. As a friend, you are too dangerous by far!'

'You mistake me, Marianne. I am not your friend. I love you and I want you, that is all. And do not rejoice in my departure too soon – I shall return before long. In any case—'

He broke off. A chorus of indignant 'Sshs' was directed at them from all parts of the house while, from the stage, Talma was regarding them with deep reproach. Concealing a smile behind her fan, Marianne turned her attention to the play and Talma/Nero, satisfied, returned to his passionate scene with Junia:

'Ponder it, lady, weigh within your heart
This choice, meet guerdon for a prince that loves you,
Meet for your beauty, too long held in thrall,
Meet for that part which to the world you owe.'

Suddenly, the Russian chuckled under his breath. 'You hear? The piece could scarcely be more apt! You'd think that Nero must have heard me . . .'

Marianne only shrugged, conscious that the slightest retort would revive the argument and bring the wrath of the audience down on them again. But Racine had no power to interest her tonight and indeed it was not for *Britannicus*, nor even for Talma, that she had come to the theatre. She had come simply in order to see Jason and, more important, for him to see her. Her eyes resumed their discreet study of the house.

The Emperor and Empress had returned to Compiègne, so that few members of the court were present and the imperial box might well have been empty, but in fact it was occupied by Princess Pauline. Napoleon's youngest sister found the festivities at Compiègne little to her taste and much preferred to spend the summer at Neuilly, where her new château was on the point of completion. Tonight, she was radiant with happiness, with Metternich, very handsome in a dark blue coat which suited his slim build and fair hair perfectly, on one side of her and on the other a young German officer, Conrad Friedrich, known to be the latest lover of this most charming of the Bonapartes.

Apart from Marianne, the princess was the only woman present who had dared to disobey the Emperor's command. Her gown of snowy muslin, cut so low in front as to be scarcely decent, seemed to have been designed to reveal more than it concealed of her justly-famous form and to enhance the splendour of a magnificent set of turquoises of a deep and dazzling blue which were Napoleon's most recent gift to one who was not known for nothing as 'Our Lady of the Trinkets'.

Marianne was in no way surprised to see Pauline favour Chernychev with one of her brilliant smiles. The Tsar's dashing courier had long been intimate with the princess's boudoir. However, the smile did not linger but passed on to the stage, where Talma almost forgot a line from sheer rapture. Pauline was another who did not visit the theatre to see the play. She came to be admired and to enjoy the effect, always sufficiently gratifying, which her presence produced on the men in the audience.

Not far from the imperial box, Prince Cambacérès, huge and smothered as usual in gold-braid, slumbered in his seat, sunk in the pleasures of a good digestion, while next to him, Gaudin, Minister of Finance, elegant and old-fashioned at the same time in his coat of the latest cut and bob-wig, seemed to find his snuff-box infinitely more absorbing than what was going forward on the stage. In another, darkened box, Marianne caught sight of Fortunée Hamelin, deep in whispered conversation with an unidentifiable hussar who, in turn, was attracting apparently idle but actually extremely penetrating glances from the exquisite Madame Récamier. Next door, in the quartermaster-general's box, his wife, the beautiful Countess Daru, in a gown of peacock blue satin, was sitting dreamily beside her cousin, a young civil servant by the name of Henri Beyle with a broad, plain face redeemed from the commonplace by a magnificent brow, a bright and piercing eye and a sardonic curve of the lips. Finally, in a large centre box, Marshal Berthier, Prince of Wagram, sat dividing his attentions between his wife, a homely and good-humoured Bavarian princess, and his mistress, the tempestuous, wickedly sharp-tongued and grossly overweight Marchesa Visconti whose long-standing liaison with him was a source of never-failing irritation to Napoleon. Of the remainder of the audience, a great many were strangers to Marianne; Austrians, Poles, Russians and Germans who had come to Paris to attend the wedding celebrations and at least half of whom clearly had not the faintest comprehension of Racine. Among them, the palm of beauty undoubtedly belonged to the dazzling Countess Atocka, handsome Flahaut's latest conquest. These two were sitting in a box discreetly to one side, she radiant, he still a little pale from his recent illness, but neither with eyes for anything but each other.

'Talma does not stand a chance!' Marianne thought, but just then the act came to an end amid thunderous applause as those who had failed to understand or simply failed to listen sought to make amends for their lapse. 'The Emperor has to be here,' she told herself, 'to make them really pay attention. When he is in the audience, no one dares to breathe.'

The curtain came down and at once the auditorium was filled with the noise of laughter and conversation. Good manners demanded that all the men should now become extremely active, paying courtesy calls on the wives of all their friends, who, for their part, sat in their boxes receiving visitors with as much grace and dignity as if they had been in their own homes. Some of the boxes were large enough to have small salons attached to them in which refreshments – sweets, ices and drinks – were served. The theatre was just another excuse for the gossip and idle chat so dear to society's heart.

Marianne was familiar with the custom and as soon as the curtain fell on the bowing actors she found herself waiting feverishly for what would happen. Would Jason come to speak to her, or would he stay in Talleyrand's box with the prince's other guests? She was burning with eagerness to see him close-to, to touch his hand and seek in his eyes for such a look as he had given her during their mad drive to Malmaison. Even supposing that he were to leave the box, would he come to her – or would the precious visit fall to some other woman's share? Perhaps Chernychev's presence at her side would put him off?

Perhaps she ought not to have saddled herself with him, after all? But she need not have worried.

Chernychev, like most other men, had risen and was excusing himself with an air of boredom: he must leave her for a moment. Princess Pauline was beckoning to him with a gesture which brooked no refusal.

'Go, by all means . . .' Marianne spoke absently, her eyes and her thoughts elsewhere, concerned only to conceal her joy as she saw Talleyrand get to his feet with the help of his stick and prepare to leave the box in company with Jason. Marianne's eyes were bright with impatience. If Jason was with Talleyrand, the two of them must be coming to call on the Princess Sant'Anna. She was going to see him!

However, her inattention was not lost on Chernychev. He frowned and said shortly: 'I do not like to leave you alone.'

'I shall not be alone for long. Go now, the princess is waiting.'

It was true. Pauline Borghese was again beckoning to the Russian. Suppressing a movement of irritation, Chernychev made his way to the door of the box but before he could pass through he was obliged to stand aside to permit Fortunée Hamelin to enter. Crisp as a lettuce in a dress of bright green brocade trimmed with tiny crystal beads that made her look as if she had just stepped out from a fountain, Fortunée smiled at him provocatively:

'It seems Her Highness does not care to see her favourite stallions disporting themselves in pastures new,' she said with a chuckle. 'You had better run, my dear Count, or I fear you will get a sad welcome!'

The handsome colonel took her at her word, without pausing to take up the challenge. Fortunée was notorious for the freedom of her language, a freedom which in her was by no means unbecoming. She was smiling brightly as she came forward to greet her friend, and Marianne, turning, forced herself to smile back, hiding her annoyance at this unwanted company. The box was suddenly filled with the scent of roses.

'Well!' Madame Hamelin sank into a chair beside her friend.

'My dear, I simply could not resist coming over to hear all about it. When I saw our American friend in the dear prince's box—'

Marianne glanced at her with somewhat sardonic amusement. 'And what have you done with your hussar?' she inquired.

'Sent him off to drink coffee. He was showing a distinct tendency to fall asleep, and that, I promise you, is more than I can allow! It's a positive insult! But tell me, dearest, is that prune-faced Murillo in the black lace really our fascinating pirate's lawful wedded wife? She reeks of the most Catholic realm of Spain, I grant you that. I should think she probably puts incense behind her ears!'

'Yes . . . That is Señora Pilar. And Jason is not a pirate—'

'The more's the pity! If he were he wouldn't clutter himself up with a lot of worn-out prejudices that are as dusty as the Spanish sierras themselves. But pirate or not, I do sincerely trust he may be on his way here now to call on you?'

'Possibly . . .' Marianne smiled faintly. 'But don't count on it.' It seemed to her that the two men were taking a very long time to pass through the intervening corridor.

'Gracious! Talleyrand is no fool and if he has him in tow we're sure to have them here at any moment. And don't worry—' She patted her friend's knee reassuringly. 'I don't mean to play gooseberry, you know. I've a host of things to say to the dear prince. So you may have your little talk . . .'

'With that pair of black eyes glaring at us? Have you seen how the Señora looks at me!'

'Black eyes, black looks!' the Créole said philosophically. 'Personally, I think I might find it rather amusing. You can't think what fun it is, teasing a jealous wife.'

'Talking of black eyes, who is the woman in black sitting on the Prince of Benevento's other side? Elderly, but still rather striking . . .'

'What? You don't know her?' Fortunée exclaimed, genuinely surprised. 'Why, she and her husband, that gingery old Scot who looks like a heron asleep on one leg, are close friends of Talleyrand's. Have you never heard of Mrs Sullivan? The beautiful Eleonora Sullivan and the Scotsman Quintin Crawfurd?'

'Oh! Is that who she is?'

Marianne remembered now a bitter little confidence she had received from Madame de Talleyrand at the time when she had been acting as her companion. The princess had spoken angrily about a Mrs Sullivan as an adventuress who had been the morganatic wife of the Duke of Würrtemberg and implicated in innumerable conspiracies: she had lived with an English agent, Quintin Crawfurd, whom she had finally married for the sake of his great fortune. Marianne recalled also that the princess's antipathy had been motivated chiefly by the fact that Mrs Sullivan, although very far from young, retained a singular power to fascinate men, and in particular Talleyrand, whose relations with her were a source of anxiety to the princess because they appeared to be compounded of a curious mixture of physical attraction and business dealings. It was the Crawfurds who had sold the magnificent Hôtel Matignon to the prince and they now lived in his old home in the rue d'Anjou.

'I don't like to have that woman here,' Madame de Talleyrand had said. 'She reeks of underhand affairs.'

Madame Hamelin, however, waited patiently while her friend studied Mrs Crawfurd, who seemed to exert a considerable fascination for her. She, like Pilar, was dressed in black but in a heavy, dull black silk which had the austerity of mourning.

'Well?' Fortunée asked quietly. 'What do you think of her?'

'Strange! Still beautiful, to be sure, but she would appear to greater advantage in a less gloomy colour ...'

Fortunée gave a little gurgle of laughter. 'She is in mourning, for her favourite lover. Not quite a month ago, if you remember, the Swedes killed Count Fersen, poor Marie-Antoinette's cavalier.'

'He was that woman's lover?'

'Yes, indeed. The poor queen had a rival, although she did not know it. At one time, let me tell you, they made a very pretty *ménage à trois*: Eleonora, Fersen and Crawfurd, but it was a *ménage* of conspirators and both Quintin and Eleonora were deeply involved in the affair at Varennes. I am sure they did all they could to help the royal family to escape from Paris. So, I need hardly tell you that the Emperor is not very popular in the rue d'Anjou.'

'And he allows it? And that man is English?' Marianne said in horror.

'And a long-standing agent of Pitt's. Yes, my sweet, he allows it. It is part of the magic of our dear prince's personality. He answered for them. It is true, of course, that just at this moment he could do with someone to answer for him, but that is life . . .'

It seemed as if Marianne could not tear her eyes from the box where the two black-clad women sat on either side of the empty chair as if keeping some ominous vigil. At last she said softly: 'How she stares at me, that Mrs Crawfurd. She might be trying to learn my face by heart. Why is she so interested in me?'

'Oh, as to that . . .' Fortunée opened her reticule and took out one of her favourite violet-scented chocolates. 'I think it is the Princess Sant'Anna who interests her. Her maiden name, you know, was Leonora Franchi and she was born at Lucca. She probably knows all about your mysterious husband and his family.'

'Yes, perhaps she may . . .'

All of a sudden, the strange woman seemed to take on a new dimension. Once connected with the irritating aura of secrecy surrounding Corrado Sant'Anna she ceased to appear suspicious to Marianne and became only desperately interesting. Too many times, since losing the child, she had asked herself what Prince Sant'Anna's reaction would be, so that she could not but feel the temptation now to approach anyone who might be able to help her unravel the enigma he represented. There were moments when in spite of the dread which had driven her from the villa, she still blamed herself for cowardice. The terror she had gone through in the little temple had grown blurred with time. Very often, in the long hours while she lay ill, and especially in the endless nights, her mind had gone back to the fantastic figure of the rider in the white mask . . . He meant her no harm, had in fact saved her from the criminal madness of Matteo Damiani. He had carried her back to her own room, tended her, perhaps . . . put her to bed . . . and at the recollection of how she had woken to find her bed strewn with flowers, Marianne's heart beat wildly once again. . . . He loved her, perhaps, and she had run away, like a scared child, instead of remaining there to drag from the masked Prince Sant'Anna the secret of his hermit-like existence. She should have – yes, she should have stayed! She might even have left there a chance to find peace and, who could tell, even a kind of happiness?

'Dreaming?' Fortunée's voice sounded teasingly in her ear. 'What were you thinking of? You were staring at the Sullivan as if you meant to hypnotize her.'

'I'd like to meet her . . .'

'Nothing simpler! Especially as the wish is undoubtedly mutual. But—'

Before she could finish, the door opened and Talleyrand, with Jason at his heels, made his way into the box. There was an interlude of bowing and of dainty fingers raised to masculine lips before the incorrigible Créole, having first favoured Jason with a smile so dazzling that it could not fail to contain a strong element of flirtatiousness, laid her hand compellingly on the prince's arm and guided him inexorably from the box, announcing that she had something of the very greatest secrecy to impart to him. Marianne and Jason were left alone.

Instinctively, Marianne had pushed her chair back into the comparative shadow of the back of the box. Out of the direct light, she felt less vulnerable and it was easier to forget Pilar's black gaze fixed on her. It was so little to ask, a moment alone together in the midst of this great chattering throng, but for Marianne everything to do with Jason, everything that came from him or related to him, had become infinitely precious. Their surroundings vanished in an instant: the red and gold furnishings, the glittering crowd of people with their idiot noises, the refined artificiality of it all. It was as if Jason possessed some strange power of breaking down any setting in which he found himself, however civilized, and substituting for it his own world, made to his own size and with the strong, sea-scent of adventure blowing through it.

Speechless, she sat gazing at him with eyes luminous with joy. She had forgotten everything, even the very presence in the theatre of Chernychev, whom she had nevertheless deliberately chosen as her escort for the evening. Because Jason was here beside her, all was well. Time could stand still, the world come to an end, nothing else mattered.

Looking at him, she was conscious of a deep feeling of happiness and she tried vainly to understand how she could have failed to guess, how she could have missed the impalpable signs by which two beings who love each other are bound together secretly and which would have told her that she could never love any other man. And even the knowledge that he belonged to another woman could not quench that happiness, as if the love she felt for Jason were of a kind that nothing human could touch.

Jason, however, did not appear to share her speechless happiness. His eyes had barely rested on her as he made his bow, and then had slipped away towards the far corner of the auditorium, as if he had indeed nothing to say. He stood with arms folded, his lean face turned in the direction of the royal box as if to find there the answer to the problem that made his fine-drawn face look sterner than ever and brought that dark, brooding look into his eyes . . .

To Marianne, this silence soon became unbearable, unbearable and insulting. Had Jason come to her box for no better reason than to show the world how little he cared for her? When she spoke, it was with unconscious wistfulness:

'Why did you come here, Jason, if you can find nothing to say to me?'

'I came because the prince asked me to go with him.'

'Is that all?' Marianne's heart contracted. 'Do you mean to say that but for Monsieur de Talleyrand you would not have come to see me?'

'Precisely.'

The curtness in his voice stung Marianne and she began to ply her fan with quick, nervous movements.

'Charming!' she said, with a tiny laugh. 'I suppose you are anxious not to offend your wife who, I see, has her eye strictly upon us? Well, I would not wish to detain you. Pray return to her.'

'Don't talk such nonsense,' Jason ground out through his teeth. 'Mrs Beaufort has nothing to say to what I may do or not do, nor would she dream of it. I should not have come because you had no need of my presence. I think you made your feelings abundantly clear tonight.'

'Did I indeed?' Marianne said furiously. 'Is that what you think? And, pray, where am I at fault in appearing in public escorted by a very gallant gentleman to whom I owe my life?'

This time their eyes met, Jason's dark with anger and contempt, Marianne's glittering with rage. He gave a harsh crack of laughter:

'That is something you should ask your husband, my dear! Your latest husband, I mean. This Tuscan prince who seems to fill so negligible a place in your life! You have not been married three months and far from staying at home like any decent woman on your own estates, you flaunt yourself half-naked in that ridiculous costume in the company of the most notorious rake in two hemispheres, a man who boasts that no woman has ever denied him!'

'If I did not know that America was a land of barbarians,' Marianne flung back at him, crimson as the feathers in her hair, 'that would have taught me! Not content with being a pirate, or sea rover or whatever, and then a special, and my goodness what a very special, envoy! Now you must needs turn preacher! The Reverend Beaufort! It sounds very well, to be sure! And I can assure you that with a little practice your sermons will be admirable! But then of course when one numbers among one's forebears—'

'At least I number some respectable women! Women who knew enough to stay at home!'

Jason's face might have been carved out of stone and there was a saturnine twist to his mouth which made Marianne want to hit him.

'To hear you, anyone would think I chose my own fate! As if you didn't know—'

'I know all right. All of it. While you were obliged to struggle for your life or liberty you had right on your side – and I admired you for it. Now, you have one right only: to repay the man who gave you his name by at least showing some respect for that name.'

'And how have I failed to respect it?'

'Not three months ago you were known to be the Emperor's mistress. Now you are generally regarded as the mistress of a Cossack famed more for his valour in the boudoir than on the battlefield.'

'Aren't you exaggerating a little? Let me remind you that the Emperor decorated him with his own hand at Wagram, and Napoleon is not in the habit of handing out decorations to all and sundry.'

'I appreciate the ardour with which you spring to his defence. What better proof of love could he ask.'

'Love! *I* love Chernychev?'

'If you do not love him you are giving a fair imitation of it. But I begin to think imitations are your stock-in-trade. Did you do another for your mysterious husband?'

Marianne sighed wearily. 'I thought I had told you all about my marriage. Must I tell you again? Except in the chapel where the service was performed, and where I saw nothing of him beyond one gloved hand, I have never met Prince Sant'Anna. And let me remind you, if you had received a certain letter in time, there would have been no wedding to the prince . . .'

She broke off as Jason began to laugh, hard, painful laughter, rasping like a false note on a violin:

'After what I have seen here tonight, I may thank heaven that letter did not reach me. Because of it, I have been able to save Pilar from a fate she had done nothing to deserve, while as for you, I think you are best left to a future which does not seem altogether repugnant to you, and which seems to me, considering the ease with which you are able to transfer your affections, to be no more than you deserve.'

'Jason!'

Marianne sprang to her feet. Her face changed from crimson to white and her fingers clenched on the fragile sticks of her costly fan. There was a pathetic little cracking sound as the sticks snapped. She fought with all her strength to keep back the tears which started to her eyes from a heart overflowing with unhappiness. Whatever happened, he must not be allowed to see how deeply he had hurt her . . . For she was too much hurt to see that his words had sprung from a bitter, yet reassuring, jealousy. She groped briefly, but in vain, for a biting reply, to give back blow for blow, hurt for hurt and blood for blood. Before she could speak, a tall, green-clad figure had interposed itself between herself and Jason:

'You have just insulted both Her Serene Highness and myself. It is too much. I regret only that I am unable to kill you more than once.'

Chernychev's accent sounded a little thicker, his manner was a little more dramatic, but he was making a visible effort to control his temper. Jason faced him with a faint, contemptuous smile which only added to the Russian's rage:

'It does not occur to you that I might possibly kill you?'

'Never,' Chernychev said simply. 'Death is a woman. She will do as I wish . . .'

Jason laughed. 'If you rely on a woman, you will be disappointed. Nevertheless, I do not go back on my word. I am at your service, Sir. Although I was not aware it was your habit to listen at keyholes.'

'No!' Marianne stepped quickly between the two men. 'No! Please! I won't let you fight over me!'

Chernychev took the hand which she had laid instinctively on his arm and dropped a swift kiss upon it:

'Permit me to disobey you for once, Madame.'

'And suppose I were to add my entreaties, eh?' Talleyrand had entered the box hard on the Russian's heels and now he continued in his leisurely tones: 'I do not care to have my friends slay one another . . .'

This time, it was Jason who answered:

'Just so. You know us both too well, Prince, not to have

known that this was bound to happen, sooner or later.'

'That may be so, but I should prefer it to be later.' He turned to Marianne as he added: 'Come, Madame, I am sure you cannot wish to remain here. I will escort you to your carriage.'

'Will you wait for me?' the Russian interposed quickly. 'Give me a moment to settle this affair and I will be with you.'

In silence, Marianne allowed him to place the great wrap of dull red velvet which had lain over the back of her chair around her shoulders, then, placing her hand on the Prince of Benevento's arm, she left the box, without a glance for either of the two prospective adversaries. The curtain was just rising on the next act and her exit was therefore accomplished without attracting more than a minimum of attention.

As she made her way slowly down the great staircase, empty except for the footmen standing rigidly between the tall torchères, Marianne gave way to her misery and anger.

'What have I done?' she cried. 'Why is Jason so angry with me? Why does he despise me so? I thought . . .'

'One must be very old or exist in a very rarefied atmosphere to be immune from jealousy. Quite between ourselves, wasn't it really what you wanted? If not, what devil prompted you to show yourself here tonight alone with Sasha?'

'You are quite right,' Marianne admitted. 'I did want to make Jason jealous . . . He is so changed since this senseless marriage to Pilar . . .'

'And changed you, also, it seems. Come, Marianne. Stop tormenting yourself. We have to learn to take the consequences of our actions, eh? In any event, Chernychev may be an experienced duellist, but this time I think that he may well find he has met his match.'

Stop tormenting herself! Talleyrand was an optimist! Alone in the cushioned darkness of her carriage, Marianne abandoned herself to her fury. She loathed them all: Chernychev for, in her view, meddling in what did not concern him; Jason for treating her so unkindly when she had longed for a kind word, a look, such very little things; all those people who must have been following every moment of the quarrel with eyes agog at the prospect of a juicy scandal to relate; but most of all she loathed herself for the childish vanity which had caused so much trouble . . .

'I must have been mad,' she told herself. 'And yet, I did not know then that love could hurt so. And now what if Chernychev should wound Jason or even—' Her mind shied away from the thought. Then it occurred to her that she was even then sitting there like a fool waiting for the Russian when she hated him at that moment with her whole heart, and she leaned forward to give Gracchus the word.

'Home, Gracchus. And hurry!'

As the vehicle began to move, Chernychev emerged from the pillared entrance to the theatre, gained the step with one bound and fell rather than jumped inside.

'You were leaving without me! Why did you do that?'

'Because I did not wish to see you again tonight. Please get out.' She raised her voice: 'Gracchus! Stop!'

Half-kneeling on the floor at her feet, Chernychev looked up at her in surprise:

'You want me to get out? But why? You are angry with me? Yet by challenging the man who dared to insult you I was doing no more than my duty.'

'Your duty did not require you to interfere in a private conversation. I have never needed any assistance in defending myself! But just remember this: if Jason Beaufort is even wounded I shall never forgive you, and I will never see you again as long as I live!'

Chernychev did not stir but Marianne could see his eyes glittering in the dimness of the carriage, narrow green slits, luminous as cats' eyes in the dark. Slowly, he stood up, and it felt to Marianne as if some huge bird of prey were hanging over her, filling the small, scented satin-lined interior with its presence. But already, the Russian had opened the door and sprung down into the road. He stood for a moment with his white-gloved hands gripping the door frame, looking up at her, half-smiling. His voice, when he spoke, was infinitely gentle:

'You were right to warn me, Marianne. I will not wound Monsieur Beaufort, I promise you that . . .' He leapt back and, sweeping off his cocked hat, made an elaborate bow. His voice sank to a caressing murmur: 'Tomorrow morning I shall do myself the honour of killing him.'

'If you dare—'

'Oh, I shall dare . . . since there appears to be no other way of removing him from your thoughts. With him dead, I shall know how to make you love me.'

In spite of the fear and anger that clutched at her heart, Marianne stiffened, flung up her chin and stared very deliberately at Chernychev from the vantage point of the carriage. She succeeded in summoning up an icy smile:

'Do not be too sure. You will have very little time, my dear Count. For if Jason Beaufort dies tomorrow by your hand, believe me, before I make an end of a life which will have ceased to be of any interest to me, I shall make it my business to kill you with my own hands. I should tell you, perhaps, that I am accounted as good a shot as any man . . . Good night to you. Home, Gracchus!'

The youthful coachman cracked his whip and the equipage moved off at a fast trot. As it turned into the rue St-Honoré, the St Roch clock struck one, but Marianne did not hear it. When they reached the Tuileries bridge she was still trying to calm herself sufficiently to think sensibly of a way to save Jason from the Russian's murderous intent. With the boundless generosity of love, she blamed herself entirely for what had taken place. She even went so far as to blame herself for Jason's unkindness, by reason of the magic word, alarming yet so obscurely comforting, which Talleyrand had uttered: jealousy. If Jason were jealous, so jealous that he could insult her publicly, it might mean that, after all, everything was not quite lost.

'What can I do?' she asked herself desperately. 'How can I prevent this duel?'

The rattle of the carriage wheels over the deserted streets of the sleeping city of Paris filled her ears like a vast, threatening roar. She stared out at the passing houses, shuttered and silent now, filled with honest citizens lying peacefully in their beds for whom the tempests of the heart were probably matters of very little importance.

The carriage had almost reached the rue de Lille when an

idea came to Marianne. By now, she was blaming herself further for wounding Chernychev. Like a fool, she had believed her power over him greater than it was. Instead of reasoning with him, making him understand that it would grieve her to see anything happen to a friend, she had allowed him to divine her love for Jason and had inevitably roused the very natural fury of a man who finds that the woman he desires prefers another. She ought, at least, to make another effort in that direction.

She reached out and gave a little pull on the cord whose other end was attached to the coachman's little finger. Gracchus looked back.

'Turn round, Gracchus. We are not going home just yet.'

'Very good, Madame. Where are we going?'

'Chassée d'Antin, the Russian embassy. You know it?'

'Used to be the Hôtel Thélusson? 'Course I know it.'

The carriage was turned neatly and headed back towards the Seine, this time at a gallop. The streets were empty and it was possible to maintain this rapid pace, so that it was not many minutes before the enormous triumphal arch, thirty feet high and as many broad, which served as a gateway to the Russian embassy, loomed up ahead. Beyond lay a glimpse of extensive gardens, dotted with statues and pillars, with the house at the far end, lights blazing as though for a party. But the gate was guarded by a pair of Cossacks in long robes and drooping moustaches who were firm in denying her admittance. In vain did Marianne declare her name and titles and explain that she desired to see the ambassador, Prince Kurakin. The guards remained adamant: no pass, no passage. It was not just anyone who could gain admittance to the Russian embassy, at night especially.

' 'Strewth!' Gracchus exclaimed. 'They certainly guard the place well enough! Makes you wonder what's going on inside to make them so suspicious. It's easier to get to see the Emperor . . . What do we do now, Your Highness?'

'I don't know,' Marianne said miserably. 'I must get in or— Listen, Gracchus. Go and ask them whether Count Chernychev has returned yet. If he has not, we will wait for him. If he has . . .'

'What then?'

'Oh well, go anyway. We will think of that later.'

Obediently, Gracchus clambered down from his box and strolled over to the Cossack on the left, whose face looked rather the less forbidding of the two. There began an animated dialogue in which gestures seemed to play a more important part than words. In spite of her anxious state of mind, Marianne could not help being diverted by the contrast between Gracchus's stocky figure, as broad as it was high in the huge, caped coachman's overcoat, and that of the gigantic Russian, with his huge fur hat and splendid whiskers, bending down towards him. The conversation continued for a minute or two, after which Gracchus came back and informed his mistress that the count had not yet returned.

'Good,' Marianne said. 'Get back on the box. We'll wait for him.'

'Are you sure that's a good idea? Seems to me as you didn't altogether part friends . . .'

'Since when have you been in the habit of questioning my orders? Draw up the carriage by the gate and wait.'

But before Gracchus could carry out this command there was the sound of a vehicle approaching through the embassy grounds. Marianne promptly told her driver to stay where he was, with the carriage blocking the gateway so that nothing could leave the embassy. With luck, the person coming might even be the ambassador himself . . .

In fact, it was Talleyrand. Almost at once, Marianne recognized the livery and the great English Arab horses which were the prince's pride. Talleyrand, for his part, had caught sight of Marianne's carriage and given his coachman the word to draw up alongside. His pale head and sapphire-blue eyes appeared at the window.

'I was going to call on you,' he said with a smile, 'but since you are here, I may go home to my bed with the satisfaction of knowing my duty done – and so may you. I don't think there's much more you can do here now, eh?'

'I don't know. I was going to—'

'See the ambassador? Was that it? Or see Chernychev, at

any rate? Then I was right and you may go home and sleep with no fear of bad dreams. Count Chernychev leaves for Moscow tonight with . . . er . . . urgent despatches.'

'He was to go tomorrow . . .'

'Well now he goes in an hour. Prince Kurakin was very ready to understand that some messages are too urgent to be delayed – or possibly endangered by the turn of a sword. Our friend Beaufort handles his weapon quite as skilfully as the handsome colonel, so the chances were equal. Now it seems that just at present, the Tsar requires his favourite courier's presence urgently . . . You need have no fear. Chernychev will do as he is told.'

'And . . . the duel?'

'Put off for a month of Sundays – or at least until the two gentlemen in question find themselves face-to-face again, which will not be for a very long time, since Beaufort is due to return to America in a week's time.'

Marianne's chilled heart melted in a rush of warmth. So great was her relief that tears started to her eyes. Impulsively, she held out her hand to her old friend, through the open window.

'How can I thank you? You are my good angel.'

But Talleyrand shook his head, his face suddenly grave. 'No, I am afraid not. I fear I must bear a large share of the blame for the troubles which beset you. Today is not the first time I have regretted that I ever introduced you to – to you know who. If it had not been for that ill-conceived idea, you might have been happy today. I ought to have realized – that night when you met Beaufort in my house. Now, it is too late, and both of you are married.'

'I shall never give him up! I, too, should have realized it sooner, but I will not listen when you tell me it is too late. It is never too late for love.'

'Oh yes, my dear . . . when you are my age!'

'Not even then!' Marianne cried so passionately that even the cynical statesman was shaken. 'If you really wanted it, you could still love – really love! Who knows, perhaps it might even be the great love of your life.'

The prince did not answer. Hands clasped on the gold knob of his stick, chin resting on his hands, he appeared to be lost in a kind of daydream. Marianne saw that there was a sparkle in the pale eyes, usually so cold, and wondered if perhaps her words had conjured up for him a figure, a face ... a love, perhaps, which he had not allowed himself to dream of, believing it impossible. Softly, as if he had spoken, but really in answer to her own thoughts, Marianne said: 'Impossible love is the only kind that I believe in, because it is the only kind that gives a savour to live, the only kind worth fighting for ...'

'What do you call an impossible love, Marianne? Your love for Jason – for you do love him, don't you? – is not what one would call impossible. Difficult, merely ...'

'I am afraid not. To me, it seems every bit as impossible as if ...' she groped for a moment and then went on, very fast: '... as if you, for example, were to fall in love with your niece, Dorothée, and wish to make her your mistress—'

Talleyrand's gaze shifted to meet Marianne's. It seemed to have grown colder and more inscrutable than ever.

'You are quite right,' he said gravely. 'That is, to be sure, an excellent example of impossible love. Good night, my dear Princess. I do not know if I have ever told you this, but I am very fond of you, you know.'

The two carriages moved apart and Marianne, with a sigh of content, let herself slide back among the cushions, closing her eyes, the better to enjoy her wonderful relief. She felt suddenly terribly sleepy. The relief from nervous tension had left her feeling drained, longing for nothing but the peace of her own room, her own cool sheets. She could sleep so well now that Talleyrand had averted the results of her stupidity and Jason was no longer in danger.

She was still basking in the same sense of gratitude when she reached her own house, and she was even humming a little as she went lightly up the great stone staircase to her room. When she was able to think more clearly, she would find some way of making Jason listen to reason, so that he would understand that he could not insist that they must part for ever. Perhaps when he saw how much she loved him ...

The first thing she saw when she opened her door was a pair of shoes, gleaming man's shoes, resting on a low stool covered in sea-green silk.

'Arcadius!' she cried, thinking the owner of the shoes must be her old friend Jolival, come home unexpectedly. 'Oh, but I am so sleepy—'

The words died on her lips as the door swung wide open under her hand, revealing the man who sat, very much at his ease in a deep armchair, waiting for her. And all at once, Marianne knew that there would be no sleep for her yet, for the figure which was already rising nonchalantly to greet her with a deep, profoundly mocking bow, was that of Francis Cranmere.

CHAPTER FOUR

Night – and an Open Window

Marianne's nerves had suffered too much that night for the sight of her first husband to awaken any feeling in her other than one of profound boredom. However dangerous he might be, and whatever her own reasons to fear him still, she had reached a degree of indifference where she was wholly beyond fear. It was therefore without the slightest trace of feeling that she closed the door behind her, and, according her untimely visitor no more than a single chilly glance, walked coolly over to her dressing-table, dropped her wrap on to the velvet stool and began stripping off her long gloves. Nevertheless, her eyes continued to survey his reaction in the tall mirror.

She was conscious of a certain satisfaction as she observed that Francis seemed disappointed. No doubt he had expected a movement of recoil, a cry. This cold silence must be disconcerting for him. Deciding to continue the game, she patted her curls idly into place, then picked up one of the many cut-glass bottles cluttering the table and dabbed scent on her neck and shoulders. Only then did she ask: 'How did you get in? My servants cannot have seen you, or I should have been told.'

'Why? Servants can be bribed . . .'

'Not mine. Not one would risk his place for a few coins. So?'

'The window, of course.' Francis settled himself back into the armchair with a sigh. 'Your garden walls are not insurmountable, and, as it happens, I have been your neighbour for some three days past.'

'My neighbour?'

'You did not know you had an English neighbour?'

Yes, Marianne had known that. She was, in fact, on quite good terms with Mrs Atkins who had once provided her cousin Adelaide with a refuge when she was being sought by Fouché's police. She was a former actress from Drury Lane whose stage name had been Charlotte Walpole, and had acquired a reputation and the right of residence in Paris by risking her life and fortune in an attempt to assist in the escape of the royal family from the Temple after the death of Louis XVI. What chiefly astonished Marianne was that a woman so sweet-tempered, ladylike and eminently kind should be on friendly terms with such a man as Francis, and she made no attempt to hide her thoughts. Lord Cranmere laughed:

'I might even say that dear Charlotte has a great affection for me. Do you know, Marianne, you are one of the very few women who do not like me? The majority of your contemporaries find me altogether charming and delightful.'

'Perhaps they have not had the pleasure of being married to you. That is the difference. Now, I should be glad if this conversation could be brief. I am very tired.'

Francis Cranmere placed the tips of his fingers together and studied them attentively:

'To be sure you did not stay long at the theatre. Do you not care for *Britannicus*?'

'You were there?'

'Most certainly, and, as a connoisseur, I greatly admired your entry with that magnificent creature Chernychev. Really, there could hardly be a more perfectly matched couple – unless, perhaps, it were you and Beaufort. But I gather that things are not going too smoothly in that direction. It seems the two of you are still at daggers drawn? Is it still the old business at Selton? Or don't you care for his Spanish bride?'

The deliberately airy flow of talk was beginning to irritate Marianne. Swinging round suddenly to face Francis, she interrupted brusquely:

'That will do! You did not come here tonight for idle gossip. Say what you want and go! What is it? Money?'

Lord Cranmere looked at her with a broad grin, then he laughed outright:

'I know you are not short of it. It means nothing to you now. For me, I must confess, matters are a little different, but that is not what I came to talk about ...' He stopped smiling and, getting to his feet, moved a few steps nearer to Marianne. His beautiful face wore a serious expression unlike anything Marianne had seen there before, for it was unmarred by either pride or menace.

'In fact, Marianne, I have come with an offer of peace, if you are willing to accept it.'

'An offer of peace? You?'

Francis walked slowly over to a small side table on which Agathe had left a small cold collation in case her mistress should happen to feel hungry on her return from the theatre. He helped himself to a glass of champagne, drank about half of it, sighed contentedly and resumed:

'Yes. I think we both stand to gain something. On the occasion of our last meeting I went very badly to work with you. I should have been gentler, more adroit ... It did me no good—'

'No indeed! And to be honest with you, I believed you dead!'

'Again!' Francis looked pained. 'My dear, I do wish you would rid yourself of this habit of continually numbering me among the departed. It becomes a trifle depressing after a while. However, if you mean to allude to the bloodhound whom the police put on my tail, I had better tell you that I lost him without the slightest trouble. But there, even the best hounds may be thrown off the scent when the fox knows what he's about. But where was I? Ah, yes . . . I was saying how much I have regretted my somewhat unsubtle conduct towards you. It would have been infinitely preferable to have reached an understanding.'

'And what kind of understanding had you in mind?' Marianne asked, simultaneously irked and comforted by this reference to her friend Black Fish and his quest: irked because the agent had evidently allowed his quarry to slip through his fingers and comforted because, if Black Fish had merely lost Francis, then at least it meant that he was alive. When she had first recognized the Englishman, she had seemed to hear in her head the Breton's furious voice declaring: 'I swear I will kill him, or die in the attempt,' and her heart had contracted at the thought of what Francis's living presence must mean. Her fears had been groundless. Well, so much the better. Even the best-laid plans could go astray.

Francis, meanwhile, had calmly drunk the rest of his champagne before turning his attention to the small writing desk which stood between the two windows, open on to the dark garden. From among the papers that littered the table top, he picked up a gold and jade seal which Marianne used to seal her letters, and stood for a moment, contemplating the device engraved upon it.

'A cordial understanding, naturally,' he said at last. 'And also something in the nature of a defensive alliance. You have nothing more to fear from me, Marianne. Our marriage is over. You have a new husband and the name you bear now is among the greatest in Europe. I can only congratulate you. To me, fate has proved less generous. I am obliged to live like a hunted man, hidden in the shadows, and all in the service of a country which pays me very ill for my pains. My life is—'

'The usual life of a spy!' Marianne cut him short. This new, mild and strangely generous Francis made her nervous and deeply suspicious. He gave a little smile that did not reach his eyes.

'You are not easily softened, are you? Well, so be it. The life of a spy. But it is one which enables me to find out many things, hear of many secrets which may, I think, be of some interest to you.'

'Politics do not interest me, Francis, and now, more than ever, I intend to keep clear of them. The best thing you can do is to leave this house at once – before I forget that I once bore your name and remember only that you are an enemy of my country and my sovereign.'

Francis flung up his hands. 'Amazing! A proper little Bonapartist! And you, an aristocrat! Although they always say there's nothing like sharing a pillow to smooth away hostile feelings, don't they? Don't worry, I did not come to talk to you about politics of that kind. You are not interested, very well. But are you interested in what touches Beaufort?'

'What makes you think I should be interested in Monsieur Beaufort?' Marianne asked with a shrug.

'Oh no, Marianne, don't play that line with me. I know women, and I know you better than you think. You are not only interested in Beaufort, you are in love with him. And he loves you, for all he thought himself in honour bound to marry that sour-faced shrew. The way the two of you were glaring at each other just now was enough for anyone watching you with their eyes open. So now stop beating about the bush. Tomorrow, Beaufort will be in great danger. All I want to know is, do you want to save him or not?'

'If you are referring to the duel—'

'No, I am not. Good God, should I have put myself out for the sake of a duel? I should think Beaufort is the best swordsman in the whole of America. When I tell you he is in danger, I mean really in danger.'

'Then why not go and tell him so?'

'Because he would not listen to me. And also because he would not pay to find out what danger threatens him. Whereas you will certainly pay . . . won't you, Marianne?'

Marianne said nothing, rendered speechless with anger and stupefaction. At the same time, she was aware of a curious feeling of relief. This new aspect of Francis had worried her.

There was something there which did not go with his real nature. Now she found herself back on familiar ground. He had not changed. It was like him to think of coming to her to bargain for a friend's safety. She could not resist letting him see her thoughts.

'I thought he was your friend?' she said with contempt. 'Not that friendship can mean much to you, of course.'

'My friend? That is a large claim . . . The fact of having lost a fortune to a man does not constitute the greatest bond of affection in the world. And these are no times for sentiment. Now, how much will you give me in return for what I know?'

There was excitement, ill-concealed, behind the words and Marianne eyed him with distaste. He was young, undeniably handsome and, at first sight, extremely prepossessing in his fashionably cut coat of dark green velvet. His fair hair was brushed into the style most becoming to his almost too perfect features and his slender hands were very nearly as white and well shaped as those of Cardinal San Lorenzo himself. The grey eyes might be cold and unemotional but his smile was full of charm. And yet the soul which animated this pretty gentleman was a chilling quagmire, a desperate quicksand of selfishness, cruelty, deceit and wickedness. It was a soul its owner would have sold without hesitation for a handful of gold. 'And to think that I loved him!' Marianne thought, sickened. 'To think that for months he seemed to me the incarnation of every hero of romance, all the knights of the Round Table rolled into one! To think that Aunt Ellis believed him to be the paragon of all virtues! It's laughable . . .'

But at all costs she must keep calm, even, and indeed especially, if she was beginning to feel the creeping onset of real fear. She knew Cranmere too well now not to know that he never uttered idle threats. There was undoubtedly a dreadful truth at the base of this bargain he was trying to drive, and it was Jason who would pay for it if she failed to pay up. And now that Francis had discovered her love for Beaufort, he would not easily let go. Marianne clenched her hands hard behind her back to keep her nerves from betraying her, but her face showed no trace of emotion as she said: 'And what if I decline to pay?'

'Then I shall keep my information to myself. But I do not think that we shall come to that, shall we? Suppose we say . . . twenty-five thousand pounds? A reasonable figure, I think?'

'Reasonable? You have the most astonishing effrontery! Do you take me for the Bank of France?'

'Don't be tiresome, Marianne. I know that you have made a very wealthy marriage and twenty-five thousand pounds is nothing to you. Indeed, if the need for money were less pressing I should have been a little more demanding, but I am obliged to leave Paris at dawn. So, enough of this prevarication. Will you or will you not hear what I have to tell you of the threat to Beaufort? I swear to you that if you do not, tomorrow at this time he will be dead.'

A thrill of horror shot up Marianne's spine. She had a sudden picture of a world without Jason and knew that if that were to be, then nothing should prevent her from joining him in death. What was money beside such a disaster: money which for Francis Cranmere was supreme felicity and for Marianne was less than nothing. It was true that ever since her marriage the Prince Sant'Anna's agents had been holding vast sums at her disposal. She bent on Francis a glance heavy with dislike:

'Wait for me a moment. I will go and fetch the money.'

As she made her way to the door, Cranmere frowned and put out a hand as though to stop her. She gave him an icy smile:

'What are you afraid of? That I shall scream for help and have you arrested? In that event, nothing, I should imagine, could save Jason Beaufort.'

'Nothing, certainly. Go, then. I will wait for you.'

Marianne never kept money in her own apartments. It was Arcadius de Jolival, formerly her impresario, now promoted to her man of business with her elevation to the status of princess, who took care of all such matters. There was a safe built into the wall of his room which always contained a considerable sum in cash, along with Marianne's jewels. Only he and Marianne herself possessed keys to it. Now, having first assured herself that Francis was not, after all, following her, she made her way to Arcadius's room.

Arcadius was away. He had announced his intention of leaving Paris to take the waters at Aix-la-Chapelle, the one-time capital of the Emperor Charlemagne being famed throughout Europe for its warm baths and mineral springs. When Marianne had expressed some surprise at this sudden desire to take a cure and inquired anxiously after his health, Arcadius had promptly declared himself to be racked with rheumatic pains and within an ace of losing his voice most irrecoverably. Whereupon Marianne had immediately expressed complete understanding and had confined herself to wishing him a good journey, adding at the last moment: 'Oh, and give Adelaide a kiss from me. And tell her how much I miss her. If she could come home . . .'

She saw from her old friend's suddenly glowing look that she had guessed right and was touched to discover Arcadius in something remarkably like a secret fondness.

Stepping quickly into Arcadius's room, Marianne shut the door carefully and locked it. Then she sat down to recover her breath. Her heart was beating wildly, as if this were some stranger's room which she had come to burgle. She was afraid, without altogether knowing why. Perhaps it was simply because, wherever he was, Francis Cranmere brought with him an atmosphere of menace. Her one thought, now, was to get rid of him. Then she would be able to run to Jason and warn him of this mysterious peril she had paid so dearly to discover.

When her nerves had steadied a little, Marianne extracted the key to the safe from the tiny hiding place hollowed out of the solid mahogany bedpost and concealed by part of the ormolu decoration which moved on a pivot. Next, making for a particular spot on the wall, she selected one of the palmettes in the plaster moulding and pressed it, whereupon a section of the green silken panelling slid aside to reveal a metal safe. Inside, were stacked a number of jewel cases, several bundles of Bank of France notes and two bags of gold coins. Without hesitation, Marianne took out three bundles of notes, put two aside and counted the third. Then, after returning some of its contents to the safe, she locked the door with care, closed the panel and, putting the key back in its hiding place, left the room, clutching what she could not help thinking of as Jason's ransom money. The house was still utterly quiet. The servants, in their own quarters, and Agathe, in her little room next to that of her mistress, were all fast asleep, quite unconscious of the drama which was being played out under their mistress's roof. But not for anything in the world would Marianne have had the servants know anything about it.

When Francis Cranmere saw the notes in Marianne's hands, he frowned:

'I should have preferred gold.'

'I dare say you might, but I do not keep such a sum in gold about me. And do not tell me you do not know a banker who will change them for you. Your friend Baring in London, for instance.'

'You know about him, then?'

'I know a great many things. Such as how it comes about that you were able to run free in Paris when Fouché was Minister of Police. But Fouché is no longer in power—'

'And I, therefore, cannot afford to linger. Give me the notes. I will manage somehow.'

Marianne whipped both hands swiftly behind her back, laying the notes down on a small table behind her:

'One moment! You shall have them when you go. But first, tell me what you know.'

Her heart missed a beat. Francis's eyes, fixed on the money, had narrowed to thin, grey slits. His face was flushed and she knew that the greed of riches was on him once again. There was nothing to prevent him attacking her, wresting the money from her and escaping with it. Perhaps, after all, he had no information for her . . .

Scarcely knowing what she did, she sprang towards a valuable marquetry cabinet, wrenched open the box which stood upon it and drew out one of the two loaded duelling pistols that lay within upon a bed of crimson plush. Levelling the weapon at Francis, she said grimly: 'If you lay a finger on that money before you have told me what you know, you will never reach that door alive. You know I never miss my aim.'

'What ails you now? I do not mean to rob you. What I have to say can be said in a very few words.'

This was true. The sum of it was that on the following night, Jason was engaged to visit Quintin Crawfurd in the rue d'Anjou, ostensibly to inspect his celebrated collection of paintings, in reality to meet a messenger from Fouché who, although at present in exile, was in no way reconciled to his loss of power and determined to retrieve his position by any means, even including high treason. Two fanatical royalists, the Chevalier de Bruslart – who was already well known to Marianne – and the Baron de Vitrolles, would also be there.

'Savary has been informed,' Cranmere went on, 'and all four men will be quietly apprehended before they even set foot over Crawfurd's threshold, taken to Vincennes and shot before daybreak.'

Marianne started. 'You are out of your mind! Execute four men without trial, without the express command of the Emperor!'

Francis's handsome face twisted into a mocking smile:

'Have you forgotten Savary was the man who assassinated the Duc d'Enghien? Bonaparte is at Compiègne and this time those concerned are enemy agents.'

'Jason an enemy agent? Who do you think will believe that?'

'Why – you, my dear. Like a good many other sensible men, he is of the opinion that peace with England is necessary for a host of reasons, chief of which is the good of trade. This peace will be made with or without Boney. King Louis XVIII is wholly committed to it.'

Sheer, cold rage overcame Marianne. She resented it as a personal insult that anyone should associate Jason, the man she loved, with those devious and unscrupulous politicians who, entirely for their own ends, were ready to overthrow empires and set up no matter what wretched puppet on a still reeking throne:

'There is just one thing you may not be aware of, Jason both likes and admires Napoleon. Have you forgotten that he is here in an official capacity, on behalf of his government?'

'Precisely. A most useful position. And have you forgotten that Beaufort is perennially short of money? I should have thought that we had both of us good cause to know that!'

'He is not the only one—'

'Have you forgotten,' Francis went on, ignoring the interruption, 'the circumstances of your first meeting with him, at Selton in England – as one of the intimates of the Prince of Wales? What better proof do you need? The English privateer which he so opportunely let slip just recently on the excuse that America was not at war with England, that privateer was on her way from Spain carrying important despatches from the Duke of Wellington, which His Lordship had judged it wiser to entrust to a fast vessel. And yet the *Sea Witch* is unusually well armed for a merchantman, far outweighing the *Revenge*, and she is swifter, too. Are you convinced?'

Marianne could not bring herself to answer. She looked away. Naturally, she could not blame Jason for placing his own country's interests before those of France, but the thought that he could come back to France under cover of friendship, be received by the Emperor, treated as an honoured guest, and at the same time conspire with the French ruler's worst enemies, was unbearable to her. But there was no denying there was something in what Francis said. Before meeting with Napoleon, Jason had undoubtedly been on friendly terms with the Prince of Wales, even to the point of making one of his intimate circle.

After revolving the matter in her mind for a moment, she said: 'There is one thing I do not understand. You have come here to sell me information which can save Monsieur Beaufort – but this information does not concern him only. What about Crawfurd – and the others?'

'If Crawfurd has enemies, he will find his own way of dealing with them,' Francis said with a short laugh. 'If Savary has got wind of the matter, the source of his information is not far to seek.'

'You mean . . .'

'That Crawfurd is very agreeably situated in Paris. He is no longer a young man and no doubt values his peace far more than the convictions for which he may well feel, and with good reason, that he has made sufficient sacrifice of his purse and person in the past. You need not worry, Crawfurd can have nothing to fear. As for the others, I will take care of them.'

'It may occur to one of them to warn Beaufort?'

'They will have little enough time to get themselves to safety. Have I earned my reward?'

Marianne nodded. She lowered her hand and laid the pistol back in its case as Francis moved slowly to the table. In silence, he stowed the money away in his capacious pockets then bowed deeply and stepped to the window. Marianne was in haste now to have him gone. The transaction which had taken place between them, if it had not added to her hatred of this man, had at least done away with the fear which he had inspired in her ever since that night at the Théâtre Feydeau, and considerably increased her contempt for him. She knew now that a little money would always make it possible to muzzle Francis Cranmere and render him harmless, and money was the one thing she would not be short of in future. More difficult to digest were his revelations concerning Jason. Despite the facts, Marianne could not bring herself to accept that her friend was a common spy. And yet . . .

The Englishman had one leg over the balustrade, preparatory to letting himself down from the balcony into the garden, when he paused suddenly.

'I nearly forgot. How do you mean to warn Beaufort? Will you write to him?'

'I do not see how that may concern you. I shall do as I think best.'

'You know where he is living?'

'He told me he was at Passy, in a house belonging to a friend of his, Baguenault the banker.'

'That's right. A big house with a terraced garden going down to the river. A beautiful place which used to belong to the Princesse de Lamballe and is still known locally by that name. Well, let me give you a piece of advice.'

'You? *Give?*'

'Why not? You have been generous. I will be so too, and

spare you a piece of foolishness. Do not write. You never know what may happen in matters like this and in the event of Beaufort's house being searched a letter could prove dangerous for you. Where there is no evidence, there is no proof, Marianne, and there are circumstances in which your relations with the Emperor could be damaging to you. It will be best for you to see Beaufort yourself – say, at about nine o'clock tomorrow evening, when he will be at home. The meeting at Crawfurd's is not until eleven.'

'How do you know this? He may not be at home all day—'

'Yes, but I have certain information that he is expecting an important visitor at about eight o'clock tomorrow evening. Consequently, he will be at home.'

Marianne studied Cranmere curiously:

'How is it you are so well informed? One would think Jason made no move without first informing you.'

'In my trade, my dear, it is often a matter of life or death to know as much as possible, about friends or foes. You are at perfect liberty to disbelieve me, after all, and act as you think best – but do not blame me if your actions lead to disaster.'

Marianne made a gesture of impatience. She wanted only one thing now: to get rid of him and then run to Jason without loss of time, go to him that instant and make sure he would not go to that senseless meeting. But her thoughts were written so clearly on her face that Cranmere had no difficulty in reading them. Putting up one hand carelessly to straighten a fold of his neckcloth, he said idly, as if it were a matter of no importance: 'It will not do you much good to go running out to Passy at this hour of night. You would have the devil of a job to get them to admit you. Señora whatshername – Pilar, isn't it? – guards her marital bliss as closely as the original Jason cherished his Golden Fleece. She is the only person you would be likely to see, whereas, tomorrow, I can promise you the lady will be at Mortefontaine, visiting that poor little *bourgeoise* from Marseille whom they have turned into the Queen of Spain. It appears that Queen Julie, as they call her, considers it her duty to surround herself with anything even remotely connected with Spain, although on the face of it it seems highly unlikely that she will ever set foot there. Her noble husband much prefers to leave her where she is. Where was I?'

'You were about to take your leave,' Marianne said tartly.

'Have patience. I am in the process of behaving with remarkable gallantry. That is worth the expenditure of a few moments' time. I was saying ... ah, yes. I was saying that tomorrow the Señora will be away from home and the field, my dear Princess, wide open for you. Assuming that Beaufort is not altogether a fool, I imagine it will be up to you whether you return home before morning.'

Marianne's cheeks flamed but at the same time her heart missed a beat. The meaning behind Cranmere's last words was only too clear, but while she could not repress a thrill of pure joy at the image they conjured up, she was by no means pleased to hear the innuendo in his sardonic tone. That Francis Cranmere should presume to bestow his blessing on it seemed to her to besmirch her love.

'You think of everything,' she said cuttingly. 'One would think your whole object in life was to throw me into Mr Beaufort's arms.'

Cranmere rustled the notes in his pocket.

'Twenty-five thousand pounds is a goodly sum,' he remarked casually. Then, without warning, his attitude changed. He sprang at Marianne and, seizing her wrist in a painful grasp, began to speak in a low, angry voice:

'Hypocrite! Filthy little hypocrite! You haven't even the courage to confess your love! But it was enough to see your face, the way you were looking at him in the theatre tonight, to see that you were dying to fall into his arms! But that would be too mortifying, wouldn't it? Fancy admitting after that farcical episode at Selton, after all your fine airs of outraged virtue, that you had finally fallen in love with him! Tell me, how often have you regretted your silliness that night? How many nights have you lain alone in your bed thinking of it? Tell me? How many times?'

Wrenching her arm free of his grip, Marianne fled to the bed and seized hold of the gilded bell rope that hung beside it:

'Get out of here! You have your money, now go! At once, or I call the servants!'

The anger cleared like a mist from Francis's taut face. He took a deep breath and turned back to the window with a shrug:

'Never mind, I'm going. At any moment you will tell me it is none of my business and you are right, after all. But I cannot help thinking that – things might have been very different if you had been less foolish.'

'And you less vile! Listen to me, Francis. I regret nothing that is past and I have never done so.'

'Why not? Because Napoleon taught you how to make love and made you a princess?'

Ignoring this, Marianne shook her head. 'You did me a great service at Selton. You gave me a taste for liberty. Your only excuse, if any, is ignorance. You knew nothing about me. You thought that I was made of the same stuff as you and your friends and you were mistaken. As for Jason, I love him, and I am willing to cry it from the rooftops, and I have you to thank for that, too. If I had yielded to your horrible bargain, I should not love him now as I do. If there is any one thing I am sorry for, it is that I did not see at once what kind of man he was and go with him that first night as he asked me. But I am young enough, thank God, and love him well enough to wait for my happiness as long as need be. For I know, I know in my heart that one day he will be mine . . .'

'Well – I wish you no worse fate!'

Without another word, he stepped out on to the balcony, climbed over the balustrade and began to let himself down. Marianne reached the window in time to see his white hands cling for a moment to the wrought-iron balcony rails. Then there came the muffled thud of a falling body, followed almost at once by quick, light footsteps making for the wall of the neighbouring house. Half-unconsciously, Marianne followed him out on to the balcony and walked quickly up and down, striving to calm her agitated nerves and at the same time put some order into her confused thoughts.

Her first impulse was to ring for Gracchus to put the horses to and drive her to Passy that instant, but Francis's words had not been without their effect and in spite of all her knowledge of him she could not but grant their plausibility. Who could say how that Spanish woman would react to the sight of Marianne on her doorstep in the middle of the night? Would she even agree to warn her husband? Or would her dislike of Marianne provide her with all the reasons she needed to disbelieve every word of what she had to say? And even supposing that she, Marianne, were to attempt to attract Jason's attention by a scene, the result would only be to create a scandal that would do no one any good. Nor did the idea of sending Gracchus alone with a note make more appeal to her, knowing as she did that she would not rest until she knew for certain that Jason was safe. It might take all her tears and entreaties to make him renounce a meeting on which he might have pinned great hopes. Probably the best thing to do would be to wait until morning and then go to Beaufort.

Despairingly, Marianne brushed her forehead with a trembling hand and took two or three deep breaths in an attempt to still the frenzied beating of her heart. The night was still and warm. The distant heavens were bright with stars and from the garden came the sad, silvery note of the little fountain and a scent of roses and honeysuckle. It was a night made for those in love to be together and Marianne sighed at the strange, persistent twists of fate by which she, whom so many men desired, seemed doomed to everlasting loneliness. A wife without a husband, mistress without a lover, mother robbed prematurely of the child whose fragile form she had so often cradled in imagination. Surely this was a kind of injustice, a mockery on the part of fate? What were they doing now, the men whose influence had helped to shape her life? The one who had just left so swiftly, with that strange expression of weariness in his eyes, what was he doing now, in the house of that quiet, romantic Mrs Atkins whose whole life was spent in a long wait for the return of the child of the Temple, the little Louis XVII whom she was convinced that she had helped to escape from his prison? And the masked horseman of the Villa Sant'Anna whose own dreadful solitude seemed to seek an echo in that of his wife in name only, what was he doing now? As for what Napoleon might be doing, amid the splendours of Compiègne, in the company of his Austrian woman – apart, of course, from nursing his sweet-toothed bride through another of her frequent attacks of indigestion – Marianne could imagine it quite well, but the thought gave her no pain. The warmth and brilliance of the imperial sun had dazzled her for a time, but now the sun had set into an horizon of ordinary domestic bliss and had lost something of his fascination in the process.

Infinitely more heartbreaking was the thought of Jason, threatened with deadly danger yet closeted, even then, alone with Pilar in the beautiful house beside the Seine which Marianne had more than once admired. The big, terraced gardens must be especially lovely at this hour of a summer's night . . . but how could that stiff Pilar who hated France feel the potent spell of its old-world charm? She would most likely be happier shut up in some dim oratory, all alone, praying to her own proud and implacably just God!

Abruptly, Marianne turned her back on the night with its strong evocations of the past, and went crossly back into the room. One of the candles on the chimney-piece was smoking, on the point of going out, and she snuffed the whole lot, leaving the room with no other light than the soft, pink glow shed by the small lamps placed at the bedside. But the room, with its dim, mysterious light and the soft, inviting bed, had no longer any power to attract Marianne. She had just made up her mind to go to Passy at once, whatever might be the consequences. She knew that she would never rest until she had seen Jason, even if she had to rouse the whole district and trample over the body of the odious Pilar to do so. But first, she must get out of that dress . . .

She began to undress, first tugging off the head-dress of flame-coloured feathers which was beginning to make her head ache dreadfully and shaking out her hair with both hands so that it tumbled, like a thick, black snake, down to the small of her back. The muslin dress was more difficult to manage and for a moment, driven to distraction by the innumerable hooks, Marianne was on the point of summoning Agathe, but then she remembered that Jason had disliked the dress and with a sudden spurt of anger she tore the fragile stuff away from the fastenings altogether. She was just sitting down in her brief shift tied at the shoulders with narrow white satin ribbon, preparing to take off her shoe, when she had a strange feeling that someone was watching her and looked up quickly. She had been right. A man was standing quite still at the window with his eyes upon her.

With a gasp of indignation, Marianne sprang towards a green silk bed-gown which lay over the back of a chair and hurriedly wrapped it round her. At first, she could see nothing but a gleam of fair hair in the darkness and she thought that Francis must have come back. A closer look, however, told her that the resemblance ended there and, even before he spoke, she knew him. It was Chernychev. Motionless as some dim statue in his severe, dark green uniform, the Tsar's courier stood and devoured her with his eyes. But there was something in those eyes, such a fixed and unnatural brightness that Marianne felt her throat tighten. Clearly, the Russian was not himself. Perhaps he had been drinking? She knew already that he had the capacity to absorb prodigious amounts of alcohol without losing an iota of his dignity.

'Go away,' she said quietly, her voice a little thickened by nervousness. 'How dare you come here!'

Without answering, he took one step forward, then another, turned and snapped the window shut behind him. Seeing him about to close the other, Marianne sprang forward and gripped the casement.

'I told you to go!' she said furiously. 'Are you deaf? If you do not go away this minute I shall scream.'

Still there was no answer, but Chernychev's hand fell heavily on her shoulder, wrenched her away from the window and sent her sprawling on the carpet to fetch up against the leg of a sofa, uttering an instinctive cry of pain. Meanwhile, the Russian calmly shut the window and then turned back to Marianne. His movements were those of an automaton and left a horrified Marianne in no doubt that he was totally drunk. As he came closer, a powerful smell of spirits assailed her nostrils.

She tried to wriggle underneath the sofa to escape him, but already he was upon her. With the same irresistible strength, he picked her up and carried her over to the bed in spite of her frantic struggles. She made an attempt to cry out but instantly a hand was clamped roughly over her mouth while the Russian's slanting green eyes shone like a cat's in the dim light with such an ominous gleam that Marianne felt a chill of real fear creep through her veins.

He released her but only for a second to pull away the gilded cords that held back the bed curtains of heavy, sea-green silk. The curtains swung forward, enveloping the bed in a greenish shade, through which the lamp at the beside showed like a spot of gold. Before Marianne could make a move to protest, she found her wrists tied, swiftly and efficiently, to the bed-head. She tried to scream but the sound was choked in her throat as a summary hand thrust a rolled-up handkerchief into her mouth.

In spite of her bonds, Marianne continued to twist and turn like a snake in a desperate effort to escape from her tormentor but she only succeeded in making the metallic cords bite deeper into her wrists. She was wasting her time. Immobilizing her legs by the simple method of sitting on them, Chernychev proceeded easily to tie both her ankles to the bedposts. Then, as Marianne lay, spreadeagled and quite unable to move, the Russian stood up and regarded his victim with satisfaction.

'You made a fool of me, Aniushka . . .' he said, so thickly that the words were barely intelligible. 'But that's all over now. You went too far. It was very foolish of you to prevent me killing the man you love, because I have never yet turned my back on a challenge. You touched my honour when you made my duty a means to save your lover, and for that I have to punish you . . .'

He spoke slowly and deliberately, each word following the last as monotonously as a child repeating a well-learned lesson.

'He is mad!' Marianne thought, although it required very little imagination to divine the form that Chernychev's punishment was to take. She guessed that he meant to rape her and just then, as though his intoxicated brain were telling him that he had talked enough, the Russian bent and, setting aside the green robe, ripped open her shift from neck to hem and parted the two sides carefully, yet all without laying so much as a fingertip on Marianne's bare skin. This done, he straightened and without another glance at her began to divest himself of his clothes as calmly as if he had been in his own bedchamber.

Half-throttled by the handkerchief which had been rammed so far down her throat that it made her retch, Marianne watched appalled as he revealed a body as white and well-muscled as a Greek god's but approximately as hairy as a red fox. His body descended, without further preliminaries, upon her own and what followed was unbelievably swift and savage and, to Marianne, as unpleasant as it was unexciting. This drunken Cossack made love with the same furious concentration that he might have given to chastising some insubordinate *moujik* with the knout. Not only did he make no attempt to give the least pleasure to his companion, he seemed to exert himself to cause her the greatest possible discomfort. Fortunately for Marianne, nature came to her rescue and her martyrdom, which she bore without a murmur, was mercifully brief.

Weak and half-stifled, she thought that her release had come at last and that Chernychev would leave her and take the road to Moscow; but her tormentor got up and, far from releasing her, said in the same toneless voice: 'Now I am going to make quite sure that you can never forget me. No other man shall touch you and not know that you belong to me.'

It seemed that he had not finished with her after all. Marianne, watching helplessly, saw him take from his finger a large, gold seal-ring of the kind used for sealing letters, with his arms engraved upon the stone, and hold it to the flame of the lamp. As he did so, his eyes roved over the girl's sweat-streaked body with a calculating expression. But Marianne, guessing his intention, was moaning wildly and writhing against her bonds with such a fierce energy of desperation that the Russian's hand, which was in any case none too steady, missed its aim. He had aimed for the belly but it was on Marianne's hip that the searing hot seal landed . . .

So excruciating was the pain that, despite the gag, a strangled shriek of agony burst from Marianne's throat. The only response was a chuckle of drunken satisfaction, followed almost immediately by the sound of breaking glass. More dead than alive, Marianne heard the window flung open with a crash and then, as though in a dream, she saw the curtains round the bed dragged away and in their place the dark figure of a man in hussar uniform, his right hand holding a naked sword. As he took in the extraordinary spectacle before him, the newcomer uttered a magnificently comprehensive oath.

'Well, well,' he remarked, in a strong Périgord accent which sounded to Marianne like the sweetest music in all the world. 'I've seen a good deal one way and another, in my time, but nothing quite like this.'

Marianne was in too much pain from her burned hip and had been through too much that night already to be capable of further surprise. Not even the sight of Fortunée Hamelin's favourite lover, the effervescent Fournier-Sarlovèze, standing at the foot of her bed with a drawn sword in his hand had any power to amaze her. In any case, after a curt command to the Russian, who was sitting blinking on the bed, a good deal astonished, to get dressed 'sharpish' and be prepared to answer to him for this, the dashing François turned his attention swiftly to Marianne, removing the handkerchief which was all but suffocating her, cutting the gilded cords and folding the torn clothes modestly over her maltreated person, all of this without interrupting the flow of his conversation.

'It seems it was rather a bright idea of mine to go home by way of the rue de l'Université,' he said cheerfully. 'In fact, I was only thinking of you, dear lady, and telling myself it was high time I called on you to thank you for getting me out of prison, when I saw this fellow here just heaving himself over your garden wall. Naturally, my first thought was that he was expected, but then I said to myself that a lady who lives alone has no need to make her lovers ruin their clothes with scrambling over walls. When I visit Fortunée, I go in by the door like everyone else. You're up to something, I thought. Besides, if you must know, I'm not overly fond of Russians, and this chap less than most. So I thought about it for a bit, and finally made up my mind to follow. Once I was in the garden, though, I nearly popped out again. There was nothing to be seen and all the windows, even those with lights in, were closed. Damned if I know what it was made me climb up here – curiosity, perhaps. I never could resist other people's business.'

While Fournier talked, Chernychev had been putting on his clothes, still in the same mechanical way, paying not the slightest attention to what was going on.

He was soon brutally reawakened. No sooner was Marianne released than she leapt up, regardless of the pain in her hip, and rushing at her tormentor dealt him a ringing box on the ears. Then, beside herself with fury, she picked up a large Chinese vase which with its bronze base was no light weight and smashed it over his head.

The vase shattered into a thousand pieces but the Russian remained on his feet. His eyes opened wide in an expression of enormous surprise and he swayed slightly. Then he sat down heavily on the edge of the bed while Fournier-Sarlovèze gave vent to a great shout of laughter that effectively drowned the torrent of abuse which Marianne was heaping on her late attacker. When, however, she made a lunge for a second vase, the twin of the first, with the object of following up her advantage, the hussar general saw fit to intervene:

'Now then, easy does it, young woman! Pretty things like that don't deserve such treatment.'

'And what about me? Did I deserve such treatment as this brutal savage meted out to me?'

'Precisely. So there's no need to add to the injury by destroying your own property. You might use the poker or the fire irons just as well— No!' he added firmly, seeing Marianne's eye light with a gleam on the heavy bronze poker. 'Leave that where it is. All things considered, I'd rather kill him myself.'

With difficulty, because she was still in great pain, Marianne summoned up a smile for her unlooked-for preserver. She wondered how on earth she could ever have disliked François Fournier.

'I don't know how to thank you,' she said shyly.

'Then don't try, or we shall never be done with thanking each other. How do you summon your maid? The girl must be deaf!'

'No, no, don't call her! She does sleep soundly, so soundly that she ties the bell rope to her little finger in case I should wish for her in the night. But for once, I am glad of it. I – I am not precisely proud of what has happened.'

'Don't see why you should be ashamed of it. Call it war-wounds! With his kind, it's always war to some extent. But I intend to rid him of any desire to repeat the experiment.' He turned to the Russian. 'Well, you? Are you ready?'

'One moment,' the Russian said gravely. Then he walked with equal gravity to where a carafe of water stood on a table and emptied its contents straight over his head. Water streamed over the smart green uniform and dripped heavily on to the carpet, but Chernychev's eyes at once lost their dull, fixed expression. He shook himself like a dog and, tossing his soaking wet hair out of his eyes, drew his sword and smiled disdainfully at Fournier.

'When you like,' he said coldly. 'I do not care to be interrupted in my amusements.'

'Funny idea of amusement, you have! But I think, if it is all the same to you, we will settle this affair in the garden. There appears, gesturing with the point of his sword at the torn curtains, the broken window, the shattered vase and the pool of water sinking slowly into the carpet, 'there appears to have been sufficient damage for one night.'

Marianne uttered a small, contemptuous laugh. 'The count is not at liberty to fight,' she said frostily. 'He has a mission to perform and should be already on his way to his own country.'

'I am already behind time,' Chernychev agreed. 'A little more or less . . . I can spare time to kill this interfering fellow – who I take it is another of your lovers?'

'No,' Fournier corrected, with dreadful affability. 'Her best friend's lover. Come, now, Chernychev. Stop playing the fool. You know quite well who I am. The best swordsman in the Empire is not easily forgotten, once you have encountered him on the battlefield,' he added with simple pride. 'Remember Austerlitz.'

'And you,' Marianne broke in, 'remember your present position. I swear on my father's memory that I would give ten years of my life to see this villain lying dead, but have you thought of what will be the outcome if you kill him? You have only just come out of prison. The Emperor will have you back there instantly.'

'With the greatest of pleasure,' Fournier agreed. 'He dislikes me extremely.'

'I can't speak for his pleasure, but he will certainly send you back. And for how long? This man must be covered by diplomatic immunity. It will mean the end of your career ... and I owe you too much to let you do that – however much I may want to.'

Fournier-Sarlovèze made a careless pass that made the air whistle past his naked blade and shrugged:

'I will try not to kill him outright. I dare say a stiff lesson will be enough and, since he too is in the wrong, I should think he will keep quiet. As for yourself, Princess, it is useless to persist. There is no power on earth would prevent me from crossing swords with a Russian when I find one. You must realize that this is a high treat for me. You there, are you coming?' The last words were addressed to Chernychev, but before the Russian could reply, Fournier-Sarlovèze had vaulted swiftly over the edge of the balcony and dropped lightly down into the garden. His opponent, following more slowly, paused for a moment before Marianne where she stood with folded arms, watching him with eyes bright with hatred.

'He will not kill me,' he said, the faint slur of drunkenness still sounding in his voice. 'And I shall return.'

'I do not advise you to.'

'I shall come all the same, and you will go with me. I have set my seal upon you.'

'Burns heal, or may be covered by another.' Marianne's voice grew suddenly fierce. 'And I would tear out my own flesh before I retained the least mark of yours! Go! And never set foot here again! And know that if you should ever dare to, the Emperor shall know of it within the hour, if I have to show him what you have done.'

'What can he do to me? I serve the Tsar.'

'And I serve the Emperor. And it may be that your master may not relish the displeasure of mine.'

Before Chernychev could answer, Fournier's voice came up to them impatiently from the garden:

'Are you coming down, or must I come up and fetch you?'

'Go,' Marianne told him, 'but remember this also: I can use a man's weapons and if you ever dare to enter this house again, should you leave it alive this time, know that I will shoot you like a dog.'

A shrug was Chernychev's only reply, then he turned and made for the garden at such speed that he all but dived over the balcony. The next instant, the two men were facing each other on the small, circular patch of grass in the centre of the garden. Clutching her green silken wrap around her, Marianne stepped out on to the balcony to see the fight. Her feelings had undergone a considerable alteration. She was as anxious as ever to see her late, unworthy attacker spitted without mercy, but gratitude towards the general made her hope that he would not ruin his career irreparably for the sake of chastizing a brutal sadist.

Before stepping outside, Marianne had paused to relight the candles and now the light from the room threw a pale glow over the two duellists, making the naked blades gleam as they met in a shower of sparks. The two men were evidently well matched. The Russian was slightly taller than the Frenchman and looked the more powerful of the two but Fournier's lithe, southern build concealed formidable strength and tremendous agility. He was everywhere at once, encircling his adversary in a dance of death and weaving a flashing spider web all about him.

Wholly intent, caught in spite of herself by the odd, boyish fascination which the formidable art of swordplay had always held for her, Marianne was eagerly following every step of the duel when suddenly a head appeared above the wall at the bottom of the garden, adjoining the rue de l'Université, the same wall which Chernychev and Fournier had both climbed in their turn. The head was surmounted, somewhat alarmingly, by a cocked hat. Another head appeared, followed by a third.

'The law officers!' Marianne thought. 'That was all we needed!'

She leaned over the balcony to tell the two men to put away their swords but she was too late. A gruff voice announced: 'Duelling, gentlemen, is against the law. You ought to know that. I arrest you in the name of the Emperor.'

Unperturbed, Fournier laid his sword across his arm and presented it to the officer who was engaged in climbing over the wall, presumably by dint of standing on his horse's back, then smiled disarmingly:

'A duel? Why, officer, whatever gave you such an idea? My friend and I were merely trying a few passes, nothing more.'

'At four o'clock in the morning? And with a lady looking on, and not as if she was enjoying it much, either,' the officer said, looking up at Marianne's troubled face.

It had not taken her very long to realize that the arrival of the officers of the law upon the scene was quite the worst of the night's disasters. After what had occurred at the theatre that evening, a duel at her house in the middle of the night between Chernychev and Fournier was bound to cause a scandal: it meant the wrath of the Emperor, who had grown extremely sensitive in the matter of the respectability of those about him since his marriage to his archduchess, and there would be severe penalties for the culprits as well as the dreadful blow to Marianne's own reputation. Add to that Chernychev's position as a Russian engaged on diplomatic service, and the affair could even develop into an international incident. Something must be done to stop it, and at once! Seeing that the officer, having succeeded in scaling the wall, was now warning the late adversaries that it was his duty to escort them to the nearest police station, Marianne leaned hastily over the parapet:

'Wait, officer! I am coming down. We can talk this over more comfortably indoors.'

'There is nothing to talk about, Madame, as far as I can see. Duelling is against the law. Unfortunately for these two gentlemen, we heard the clash of swords as we were going our rounds. It's a clear case.'

'Not quite as clear as you think perhaps. Do, please, be good enough to wait for me. It will in any case be necessary for me to have the gates opened – unless of course you wish to take these gentlemen out over the wall?'

Hurrying down the great marble staircase as fast as her injured hip allowed, Marianne forced herself to think. The officer had quite obviously not believed in Fournier's rather unlikely explanation. They must think of something else, but unfortunately Marianne's mind, still wholly taken up with Jason and the danger threatening him, was not finding it easy to adjust to this new demand. She was burning to run to Passy and warn Jason and now this stupid duel had come to prevent her and to hold her up for goodness knew how long.

When she emerged into the garden the darkness was already growing perceptibly less thick. A pale band of light showed in the east, revealing a scene of total confusion among the law officers and their prisoners. Fournier was defending himself vigorously against the efforts of two men to apprehend him, while the officer in charge was engaged in gallant but futile attempts to scale the wall from inside which, in the absence of the horse which had assisted him in his entry, was proving an altogether impossible task for a man of unathletic build and hampered, moreover, by a pair of outsize boots. Of Chernychev there was no sign, but from the other side of the wall came the sound of receding hoofbeats.

Realizing the futility of his endeavours, the officer abandoned his assault on the wall and returned to where Fournier was still putting up a spirited defence. He was by this time thoroughly out of temper:

'You are wasting your efforts. Your accomplice has got away, but we shall catch him and meanwhile you shall pay for both, my lad.'

'I am not your lad!' Fournier exploded furiously. 'I am General Fournier-Sarlovèze and I will thank you, officer, not to forget it!'

At this, the other drew himself up and gave a military salute:

'Pardon me, General. I had no means of knowing! Nevertheless, you are my prisoner – I am sorry to say. Not but what I'd rather have kept a hold of the other fellow. It passes me why you should have helped him as you did by hurling yourself on my men like that.'

Fournier gave a shrug, and favoured the officer with a mocking smile:

'I told you. He's a friend of mine. Don't you believe me?'

'How can I, General, when you would not give me your word that you were not engaged in fighting a duel?'

Fournier was silent. Deciding that it was time for her to intervene, Marianne laid her hand, at once soothing and cajoling, on the officer's arm.

'And if I were to ask you to close your eyes for once, Officer? I am Princess Sant'Anna – a close friend of the Emperor.' A timely recollection of the invitations she had received from Savary prompted her to add: 'The Duke of Rovigo is well disposed towards me, I believe, and no one, after all, has been killed or injured. We might—'

'A thousand regrets, Princess, but I must do my duty. Setting aside any questions my men might ask and the awkwardness of explaining matters to them, I should not care to put myself in the position of a colleague in a similar situation. He was lenient, the matter was found out and it broke him. His Grace of Rovigo is very strict in matters of discipline. But then, you know him, Highness, and must surely know this? Now, General, if you please . . .'

Unwilling to admit defeat, Marianne would have gone on pleading and in her distress at the thought that Fournier would be imprisoned again because he had defended her she might well have committed the folly of offering the man money, had not Fournier himself intervened: 'I am coming,' he said; then, turning to Marianne, went on more quietly: 'Do not worry about me, Princess. This is not the first duel I have fought and the Emperor knows me well enough. It seemed better to let the Cossack escape. The thing might have proved more serious for him. The worst I can expect is a few days in prison and a little holiday at home at Sarlat.'

Marianne's sensitive ear did not miss the little note of regret in the hussar's voice. Sarlat might hold for him all the sweetness of home but it also meant inaction, idling away his time away from the battlefields which were his life and, but for this stupid affair, he would soon have been on his way back to Spain. To be sure, she also remembered what Jean Ledru had told her of the horrors of war in that God-forsaken country but she knew that no such considerations weighed with the finest swordsman in the Empire and, indeed, would probably only whet his appetite for the fray.

She held out both hands impulsively. 'I will go to the Emperor,' she promised. 'I will tell him all that has passed and what I owe to you. He will understand. I will tell Fortunée, too. Though I doubt if she will be as ready to understand.'

'Not if it were anyone but you!' Fournier said, laughing. 'But for you she will not only understand, she will even approve. Thank you for your promise. I may well stand in need of it.'

'It is I who should thank you, General.'

Not many minutes later, Fournier-Sarlovèze was swaggering, hands in pockets, out of the front door of the Hôtel d'Asselnat under the bewildered and faintly shocked gaze of Jeremy, the butler, who, still only half-awake, regarded the officers of the law with a kind of scandalized disapproval. One of the men recovered the horse which Fournier, like the rest, had left outside the wall in the rue de l'Université and the general sprang into the saddle as lightly as if about to go on parade, then, turning, blew a kiss to Marianne who was standing on the steps:

'Au revoir, Princess Marianne. And do not let this worry you. You can't think how exhilarating it is to go to prison for the sake of a woman as lovely as you!'

The little cavalcade moved away into the dawn which was already beginning to touch the white stone face of the house with tones of rosy pink, while from the gardens all around came a faint freshness of rising mist and the first notes of birdsong. Marianne was deathly tired and her hip was hurting her atrociously. Behind her, her nightcapped servants, blinking sleepily, preserved a respectful silence. Only Gracchus, the last on the scene, barefooted and barechested, dared to ask his mistress: 'What is it? What has been happening, Miss M – Your Highness?'

'Nothing, Gracchus. Go and get dressed and put the horses to. I must go out. And you, Jeremy, you need not stand there gaping at me as if I were about to sentence you to death. Go and wake Agathe. If the house fell down about her ears that girl would sleep through it!'

'Wh – what shall I tell her?'

'Tell her you're a blockhead, Jeremy!' Marianne exclaimed exasperatedly. 'And that I shall dismiss you from my service if she is not in my room inside five minutes!'

Back in her own room once more, she anointed her burn with Balm of Peru and swallowed a large glass of cold water, without sparing a glance for the desolation of her once-charming bedchamber with its torn hangings and shattered porcelain. When the flustered Agathe came running in, she told her to go at once and make her some strong coffee but, instead of obeying, the girl stood in the doorway staring at the spectacle which met her eyes.

'Well?' Marianne said impatiently. 'Did you hear me?'

'Oh M-Madame!' Agathe managed to say at last. 'Who was it did this? It l-looks as if the d-devil himself had been here!'

Marianne gave a small, mirthless laugh and went to the wardrobe. 'You may well say so,' she remarked as she took down a dress at random. 'The devil in person – or rather in three persons! Now, my coffee, and hurry.'

Agathe departed precipitately.

CHAPTER FIVE

The House of the Gentle Shade

Sunset was lighting blood-red fires behind the hill of Chaillot as once again Marianne's chaise crossed the Pont de la Concorde en route for Passy. The coming darkness, brought on faster by the heavy clouds which had invaded the sky over Paris as the day wore on, seemed to be smothering the last red glow of the dying sun beneath a heavy grey blanket. The air was unbearably hot, clammy and oppressive, and little enough of it made its way through the open windows of the chaise to where Marianne sat stifling among the warm velvet cushions, scarcely able to breathe for the heat and the strain on her overstretched nerves.

This was her second journey to Passy. When she had reached the house that morning, determined to see Jason, even if only for a moment, at the cost of whatever scene might be necessary, in order to warn him, she had found the house shuttered and closed. A Swiss porter in carpet slippers, grumpy and half-asleep, had appeared eventually in response to Gracchus's repeated summons on the bell and told them in his heavily accented French that there was no one at home. Mr and Mrs Beaufort were at Mortefontaine, having gone there straight from the theatre.* The sight of a gold coin did however induce the man to admit that the American was to return that evening. Marianne turned back, disappointed, sorry for once that she had not taken Francis's advice. But then, she had to admit, it was unlike him to be telling the truth.

Tired though she was as a result of her sleepless night and the pain of her injured side, which was making her slightly

* Performances in the Paris theatres began and ended much earlier in those days, enabling patrons to return home to outlying districts.

feverish, she was unable to rest. She had wandered about like a lost soul between her own room and the garden, and running into the salon a hundred times to look at the exquisitely decorated bronze enamelled clock there. The only event which occurred in the whole of that endless day was a visit from the police inspector who came to ask some embarrassed but persistent and distinctly leading questions concerning that morning's duel. Marianne had stuck to Fournier's story, that it had not been a duel, but the man had gone away visibly dissatisfied.

The chaise had now passed out of the Cours la Reine and was travelling at a smart pace along the tree-shaded length of the Grand Chemin de Versailles, following the river Seine in the direction of the Barrière de la Conférence. There was a slight hold-up as they came to the massive building works around the Pont d'Iéna, now nearing completion, on account of a load of stone which had been overturned at some time during the day and which was still partly blocking the road. But Gracchus, swearing like a trooper, had succeeded in circumventing the obstacle, coming perilously near overturning the chaise in the process, and, touching up the horses with a quick flourish of his whip, set them speeding towards the barrier.

It was quite dark by the time they reached the first houses of the village of Passy, a darkness rendered thicker and more menacing by the storm clouds still rolling up like billows of black smoke. No lights showed through the dense mass of bushes which overhung every gateway except for a dim, yellow glimmer from a small house tucked in beside a pair of double gates, which indicated that the porter of the sugar-beet refinery owned by the banker Benjamin Delessert was at his post. A little bit farther on, the old spring gardens of Passy, once filled with noise and animation, presented a blank, dark front, a heavy stillness in which even the trees seemed petrified.

Gracchus took a right-hand turning and edged his horses into a road ascending in a gentle slope between the Jardin des Eaux and the wall of some large property. At the far end, elegant gilt lanterns hung from black iron stanchions illumined the tall gates and twin lodges guarding the entrance to the Hôtel de Lamballe. Marianne, however, stopped her chaise halfway up the slope and told Gracchus to wait with it where he would be as far out of sight as possible. In answer to his surprised question, she said: 'I want to try and get into the house without being seen.'

'But, this morning . . .'

'This morning it was broad daylight and it would have been folly to attempt secrecy. It is dark now, and late, and I wish my presence in the house to remain unknown, if that is at all possible. To have it known would only result in awkwardness for everyone, and especially for Mr Beaufort.' She thought as she spoke of the jealous Pilar's reaction should she ever hear that Jason had been visited by a woman at night, in her absence, and that woman Marianne.

She saw Gracchus shift uncomfortably, not meeting her eyes, and realized that he was thinking of something quite different and believed that this was a lovers' assignation. She lost no time in explaining matters:

'Jason is in great danger tonight, Gracchus, a danger from which I alone can save him. That is why I have to go in there. Will you help me?'

'Help you save Monsieur Jason? I should just think I will!' The eagerness in his voice gave Marianne the measure of his relief. 'But it'll not be easy. The walls are high and the gates pretty stout. There is an entrance giving on to the Versailles road but . . .'

'I noticed this morning that there is a little door somewhere about here. Do you think you could open it?'

'What with? I've only my bare hands, an' if I try to force it—'

'With this.' As she spoke, Marianne produced a picklock from the soft, dark green silken folds of her cloak and put it into her coachman's hand. Gracchus, feeling the shape of the tool in his palm, gave vent to a muffled exclamation:

'Ah! That's the ticket. But where—'

'Hush. Never you mind,' said Marianne, who had found the implement in Jolival's little collection. Like the late king, Louis

XVI, the Vicomte Arcadius had always been something of an amateur locksmith and kept a pretty little bag of tools in his room which might have laid a less respectable man open to some suspicion. 'Do you think you could open the door with that?'

'It'll be child's play – so long as it's not barred on the inside,' Gracchus assured her. 'Just you wait and see.'

'Wait! Go up to the gate quietly first and see if there are any lights in the house. And see if you can see a carriage or horses in the drive. I know Mr Beaufort was expecting a visitor at about eight, he may still be there.'

Gracchus nodded by way of an answer and taking off his hat and livery coat laid both articles inside the chaise, which he then moved to a position alongside the spa gardens where it was overhung by the branches of a huge tree. Having once made sure that the chaise was more or less invisible to anyone not actually looking for it, he turned and made his way up the road to the gates, making no more noise than a cat.

Marianne's eyes had grown sufficiently accustomed to the darkness by this time to enable her to make out the little side door. She went towards it and, having made sure that it was indeed locked, settled down in the angle of the wall to wait for Gracchus.

It was still stiflingly hot but the storm was on its way. There was a dull rumble of thunder away to the south and once a flash of still distant lightning illumined for an instant the watery ribbon of the Seine. Somewhere not far off, probably in the little church of Notre-Dame des Grâces, a clock struck nine and Marianne's heart thudded in her breast in agonized counterpoint. She was beset by vague and terrible fears. What if Jason had not returned to Mortefontaine before going to Crawfurd's house? Suppose the meeting Francis had spoken of had been cancelled – or Jason had already set out, against all expectation, contrary to all Cranmere's supposed information? Suppose that tomorrow in the ditch at Vincennes . . .

The picture which Marianne's imagination conjured up was so real and so hideous that it was all she could do to bite back a groan. She leaned against the wall, shivering and trying to cool her burning forehead by pressing it to the cool stone. She was not yet fully recovered from her recent illness and the brutal treatment to which Chernychev had subjected her the night before had not improved matters, but at the thought of the man whom she now hated with all her heart she felt her courage revive and, fumbling for her handkerchief, began automatically wiping away the sweat which poured down her face. The cool freshness of the eau-de-Cologne which she had sprinkled liberally over it before she came out did her good, and then Gracchus was coming back.

'Well?'

'There are lights in the house,' whispered the lad. 'And there is a coach at the door, as if it's about ready to go. I caught a glimpse of someone come quickly out of the house and jump in. Listen—'

There was indeed a sound of wheels approaching. Then the creak of the gate, the hollow clop of horses' hooves and finally the dark outline of a big berline coming down the hill. Marianne and Gracchus stepped back hastily into the shelter of the doorway, although it was so dark that the driver of the berline never suspected the existence of the small door in the wall and of the two people hidden there. The coach came to the end of the road away in the direction of Versailles.

'I think all's clear now,' Gracchus murmured. 'Let's see what that tool of yours will do.'

He felt about for the lock and inserted the wire hook. There was a scrape of metal on metal, it stuck for a moment and then yielded. The bolt slid back quite easily but the door, which seemed to have been long out of use, remained firmly closed. Gracchus had to set his shoulder to it before it finally gave way, revealing a corner of the grounds. Beyond the ivy-covered tree trunks which occupied the immediate foreground, a pale blur and tall, lighted windows giving on to a row of three stone balconies showed the position of a large white house. From the centre windows, which were also the largest and most ornately decorated, a shallow stone stairway, railed with a tracery of delicate ironwork, descended in graceful twin curves to where marble nymphs reclined at ease.

Marianne's heart leapt in her breast, even before her feet had taken the first steps towards the lighted windows which told her, more clearly than any words, that Jason was at home. Thunder, closer than before, rolled overhead and Gracchus cast a quick look up at the thick roof of leaves:

'Storm's coming. It's going to rain any moment and—'

'Wait here,' Marianne commanded. 'I shall not need you. Or, better still, wait for me in the chaise. But take care to leave this door slightly ajar.'

'Sure I hadn't better come with you?'

'No. Find yourself some shelter, especially if it should come on to rain. I am in no danger here . . . or if I am,' she added, smiling involuntarily into the darkness, 'there will be nothing you can do to help me. Goodbye for the present.'

Without further ado, she picked up her skirts to keep them from getting caught up in the undergrowth and made her way with a light step towards the house. As she came nearer, she was able to appreciate more fully the perfect proportions and restrained elegance of the building. It was certainly a fit dwelling for a delicate and lovely lady, one of the many who had perished in the carnage of the Terror. The shallow steps, as Marianne climbed them with no more sound than a sigh, seemed made for the subtle whisper of full taffeta skirts and satin panniers . . .

Reaching the top of the stairs, Marianne was obliged to stop, pressing her hand to her breast to still the fluttering of her heart, which was pounding as though after a stiff climb. The middle one of the row of tall french windows was open slightly and enabled her to see into a large room, lit by branches of candles in gilt sconces set against walls hung with grey brocade. The fact that all the pictures and hangings within her field of vision seemed to be quite new suggested to Marianne that the house must have suffered during the upheavals of the Revolution. So far as she was able to see, the furniture consisted of a number of chairs, a tall bookcase filled with faded bindings and a harpsichord with old cracked varnish . . .

She put out her hand and gave the window a light, nervous push, afraid in her heart that she would find the room empty and the lights burning only in anticipation of someone's return. Then, suddenly, she saw Jason and a wave of happiness swept over her, driving out fatigue, anxiety, fever and pain.

He was seated a little sideways at a writing desk, writing intently. A silver candlestick stood on the desk and the long goose quill moved steadily over the paper. In the candlelight his strange, hawk-like profile took on a curiously softer look, the high bridge of his nose and firmly jutting chin were thrown into relief while deeper shadows lurked around the thin mouth and the deep-set eyes, now hidden by the lowered lids. The light fell, too, on his strong, slender, strikingly beautiful hands, one of which held the pen as firmly as if it had been a weapon, the other spread upon the desk to anchor the paper on which he was writing.

He had discarded his coat, waistcoat and neckcloth on account of the heat and above his breeches and topboots was wearing only a fine white linen shirt, open at the neck to reveal a firm, strongly muscled throat. The arms that showed below his rolled-up shirt-sleeves might have been carved from old mahogany. In this elegant drawing-room, with its dainty knick-knacks of silver and precious porcelain and the feminine touch of the harpsichord, Jason looked as out of place as a boarding cutlass on a lady's work table. Yet Marianne stood breathlessly in the window staring at him, forgetful of the reasons which had brought her there, sure now that he could never leave her for his perilous assignation, and conscious of a funny little feeling of tenderness at the sight of the lock of black hair which would keep on falling forward over his forehead.

She might have stood there for hours without moving if some animal instinct of Jason's had not made him sense someone's presence. He looked up and round and sprang to his feet so suddenly that he knocked over his chair and it fell noisily. Frowning, Jason peered at the dark figure standing in the darkness by the window and knew her at once:

'Marianne! What are you doing here?'

There was nothing in the least lover-like in his tone and Marianne, brought down abruptly from the dreaming heights of a moment before, could not suppress a sigh.

'If I had any hope that you might be pleased to see me, that would have taught me,' she said bitterly.

'That is beside the point. You appear there in the doorway, without any warning, without anyone being in the least aware of your presence, and then you are surprised when I ask you what you are doing here? Don't you know that if one of the servants had chanced to come in just then they would most probably have fled screaming?'

'I fail to see why.'

'Because they would certainly have taken you for the ghost of the Princesse de Lamballe who is supposed to haunt this house – or so they say, for I myself have never seen her. But the people here are very sensitive about her. They sent so many to the guillotine that now they see ghosts everywhere!'

'I trust, however, that I did not frighten *you*?'

Beyond a slight shrug, Jason made no answer to this but walked towards his visitor who was still standing as though rooted to the spot:

'Very well, and now I am asking you again, what are you doing here? Have you come to find out if your Russian killed me? The duel did not take place. Prince Kurakin compelled your champion to abandon it for the present. Considerably to my regret.'

'Why? Were you so eager to die?'

'What a poor creature you must think me,' Jason observed, with a faint, crooked smile. 'But your Cossack was in much greater danger, let me tell you, for I should have done everything in my power to kill him. I suppose, by the way, we have not got you to thank, have we, for this – er – postponement? I should not put it past you to drag Kurakin out of his bed in the middle of the night and implore him to put a stop to it!'

Marianne reddened. The idea had occurred to her, certainly, and but for Talleyrand it was precisely what she would have done if at all possible. The Prince of Benevento's intervention had saved her, however, from the necessity of confessing her intentions in going to the Hôtel Thélusson. Heaven only knew what construction he would have put upon it! She shook her head:

'No. Not me. You have my word for that.'

'Very well. I believe you. Now, for the third time—'

'What am I doing here? I will tell you. I came to save you from an infinitely greater danger than anything which could have threatened you at Chernychev's hands.'

'Good God, what danger is this?'

The last words were drowned in a violent clap of thunder, so close that it seemed to be right above the house. At the the same time, a fierce gust of wind swirled in through the open windows, lifting the curtains and the papers on the desk. The window banged to behind Marianne. Jason sprang to shut everything tight, then moved about, picking up the scattered sheets of paper and relighting various candles which had been blown out by the wind. At last he turned back to Marianne who meanwhile had come a few steps farther into the room. It seemed to her to have grown suddenly stifling and she took off the light silken wrap which she had flung over her simple, almost girlish dress of white linen sewn with daisies but which now felt unbearably hot, and laid it over a chair. Looking up again, she saw that Jason was observing her curiously and was conscious of a sudden feeling of embarrassment.

'Why do you look at me like that?' she asked, unable to meet his eyes.

'I don't know. Or rather . . . yes. In that dress, with the ribbon in your hair, you reminded me of the kid I met at Selton for the first time less than a year ago. So little time for all that has happened to you! To think that you have had two husbands, that Napoleon is your lover – and not, perhaps the only one – it seems incredible!'

'Bearing in mind that neither of my husbands has been so more than in name, is it so hard to believe?' Marianne asked bitterly.

'I know. By your own account, the Emperor would appear to have coped adequately with the practical side of things.'

He spoke sarcastically, with a kind of cold contempt in his voice. Anger welled up suddenly in Marianne's heart, flushing her cheeks and bringing a sparkle to her eyes. She had come to him in desperate anxiety, half out of her mind with the fear that he might die before dawn before a firing squad, she had come to him crying out that he was in danger, and all he could offer was sarcastic hints and innuendoes about how she had come to lose her virginity!

'I never said that!' she burst out in a voice quivering with anger. 'If you must know, the Emperor was only the second of my lovers. The first was a Breton sailor, a fugitive from the hulks at Plymouth, who was with me when I escaped from England. He saved my life when we were shipwrecked and captured by wreckers and he was the first man I lay with – on a heap of straw in a barn! And I let him do it because he wanted to – and because I still needed his help! Would you like me to tell you his name? He was called—'

A smack which made her catch her breath cut off her anger in mid-flight. She put her hand to her burning cheek and stared up at Jason out of big, tear-filled eyes, like a hurt child. The look of sheer, blazing fury on his face made her flinch. He was so frighteningly angry that she would have turned and fled had he not caught and swung her round, dealing her another ringing slap:

'You grubby little whore! And how many have there been since? How many more men have you given yourself to, eh? . . . And to think that I loved you! Loved you, did I say? I worshipped you . . . I was besotted – so besotted that I dared not even touch you! So besotted that there was a time when I could have killed the man who possessed you, although he was a man I admired with all my heart! And him, how often have you deceived him? And with whom? With this Russian, to be sure—'

All the fury of the storm outside seemed concentrated in that thickened, hideously distorted voice. Half-mad with terror and despair at the outcome of her senseless burst of temper, Marianne realized that she had unleashed in him all the hidden forces of a passionate nature, all the more terrible because the inflexible will of the man made him normally able to master them. In a frantic effort to soothe him, she clung to the iron hands which had her by the shoulders and were shaking her mercilessly to and fro, like a plum tree in August.

'Jason!' she implored him. 'Be calm! At least, listen to me—' But he only shook her harder.

'Yes, I'll listen to you all right! I'll make you tell me. This Russian, now? Can you swear by your mother's memory that you have never been his?'

Hideous recollections of the events of the previous night flitted through Marianne's mind, dragging a groan of anguish from her lips.

'No! No, not that!'

'Will you answer me? Answer me, I tell you! . . . I will be answered.'

This time a strangled shriek was his answer. In his rage, Jason had fastened his hands round Marianne's throat and was squeezing it tighter, and tighter . . . She shut her eyes and ceased to struggle. She was going to die . . . to die at his hands! How much simpler that would make everything! There was nothing for her to do, nothing she need say . . . and tomorrow Savary's men would unite the two of them in death.

Already she was beginning to lose consciousness. Red lights danced before her eyes. Her body went limp in his throttling hands and all at once Jason seemed to realize that he was killing her. He let go of her so suddenly that she would have fallen to the ground but for the chair which happened to be standing directly behind her. For a moment she lay there, helplessly, among the cushions, gasping for the air which was slowly filtering back into her lungs. Her hand went gingerly to her bruised throat, and she gave a sob which felt as if she had swallowed a ball of fire. Outside, the storm had reached its height, but the hellish fury of the elements all about them was no worse than the inferno within. Painfully, she forced herself to utter a few despairing words:

'I love you . . . As God hears me, I swear to you I love you and I belong to no other man.'

'Get out!'

Opening her eyes, she saw that he was standing with his back to her and the whole length of the room between them. But she saw too that he was shaking and that the sweat was making his shirt stick to his brown skin. She stood up, shakily, but was forced to cling to the chair for support. She felt hot and feverish and the room seemed to be spinning around her but she could not go away without telling him what she had come to say, without warning him . . . Since he had not killed her, she did not want him to die either. He must live, live! Even if the rest of her days were one slow death because she had lost him. It was her own blind rage which had made her commit an ineffable blunder: it was right that she should pay for it.

At the cost of a violent effort of will, she made herself walk towards him, over the hundreds of miles of empty desert which the room seemed to have become.

'I can't,' she croaked. 'Not yet . . . I must tell you—'

'You can tell me nothing that I want to hear! I do not want to see you again – ever!'

The words were harsh, but the fury had gone out of Jason's voice. It was flat and heavy – strangely similar, all at once, to a voice Marianne had heard once before, one night, in a mirror . . .

'No – listen! You must not go out tonight. That is what I came to tell you. If you go to Quintin Crawfurd's house, you are lost . . . you will be dead by morning.'

Jason turned abruptly and regarded Marianne with genuine astonishment.

'To Crawfurd's? What are you talking about?'

'I knew you would deny it, but you are wasting your time. I know that he is expecting you at eleven o'clock, with some other men, for reasons which I do not wish to know, because that is your own business and because – because in my eyes you cannot be altogether wrong.'

'Who are these other men?'

Marianne hung her head, hating even to be forced to speak the names. 'The Baron de Vitrolles . . . the Chevalier de Bruslart.'

Against all probability, Jason had begun to laugh:

'I have never heard of Monsieur de Vitrolles, but the Chevalier de Bruslart I do know, and so do you, if I remember rightly. Are you seriously trying to tell me that I have anything to do with these conspirators? Do you expect me to believe that you are doing me the honour to count me one of them?'

'How can I help it? It is true, isn't it, that you are going to Crawfurd's house in the rue de Clichy?' Marianne insisted, a trifle disconcerted by this unalarmed, not to say hilarious, manner of receiving her news.

'Quite true. As it happens I am to visit Crawfurd in the rue de Clichy – tomorrow morning. I am to take a luncheon with him and inspect his very fine collection of pictures. But your idea seems to be that I am to go there tonight, to meet these very dubious-sounding gentlemen. Do you mind telling me the motive?'

'How should I know? All I know is that you are involved in a royalist plot aimed at bringing about peace with England at any cost, that there was to be a meeting at Crawfurd's house tonight, and incidentally that this Crawfurd is playing something of a double game, and that Savary is preparing to arrest you all on the spot and have you taken to Vincennes and shot out of hand. That was my reason for coming here – to beg you not to go . . . to keep you alive, even if your life belongs to another woman.'

Jason sank into a chair, where he sat with his elbows on his knees looking at Marianne. Amusement struggled with amazement in his face:

'I'd like to know where you got this cock and bull story? I can assure you that I am involved in no conspiracy. I, join with royalists, with the men who saved their own skins while they left their king to mount the scaffold and the child Louis XVII to waste away in the Temple? I, plot with the English?'

'Why not? It was in England that I met you first. Weren't you a friend of the Prince of Wales?'

Jason shrugged, got to his feet and wandered over to the book-case. 'It is not hard to become one of Prinny's friends. All it takes is a certain originality, something a little out of the ordinary. He made me welcome, in fact, because I was a friend of Orlando Bridgeman, who is one of his intimate circle. It was Orlando who came to my rescue, dusted me down and put me back in the saddle, after my ship was wrecked off the Cornish coast. We have known each other for ever. Very well. I have one English friend. I imagine that does not mean that I must take all England to my bosom? More especially when, although my country is not yet at war with England, relations are becoming every day more strained and war cannot be all that far off.'

While he was talking, he had opened one of the cupboards at the bottom of the bookcase and extracted from it a decanter and a tray with two glasses, both of which he proceeded to fill. Outside, the noise of the storm was moving away. It was now only a distant mutter underlying the din of the torrential rain which had followed in its wake and which was now scourging the trees and battering furiously against the roofs and windows of the little town. Filled with an unutterable sense of relief, Marianne subsided on to the harpsichord stool and waited for the pounding of her heart to slow down a little. The only thing that made sense to her in the whole of that night's idiotic adventure was that Jason was not in danger, he had never been in danger – neither had he ever had any thoughts of plotting against Napoleon. It crossed her mind, also, that his attitude to herself had softened remarkably . . . Her throat felt stiff and tight and her head ached feverishly. She had never felt so tired in all her life, and yet, obstinately, she was still trying to piece together the fragments of the ridiculous puzzle of all that had been happening to her, trying to understand.

'But,' she said at last, slowly, thinking aloud more than addressing herself directly to Jason, 'but you were at Mortefontaine with your – with Señora Pilar and you came back without her?'

'Correct. I was there and I returned this evening.'

'You returned . . . because someone was coming to see you – someone I saw leave this house . . .'

'Right again,' Jason said. 'Your information up to that point is quite correct but, I repeat, only up to that point. This Crawfurd business is the product of a brilliant imagination and I think it is my turn to ask some questions on that subject. Here, drink this. You must need it.'

'This' was one of the two glasses of sherry he had been

pouring. Marianne accepted it automatically and drank a little. It burned her throat but it did her good.

'Thank you,' she said, putting the glass down on the corner of the harpsichord. 'Ask what you like. I will answer.'

Prepared for a fresh tirade when she mentioned the name of her informant, Marianne resigned herself with a little sigh and sat looking down at her clasped hands. A short silence followed during which Marianne dared not raise her eyes, thinking that Jason was choosing his questions. However, he merely gazed at her.

'Very well,' he said at last. 'In that case, I have only one thing to ask you, and that is the name of the person who told you this extraordinary story. I must try and get to the bottom of this nonsensical affair. You did not think it up for yourself. Who told you I was going to Crawfurd's to meet these conspirators?'

'Francis . . .'

'Francis? You mean Cranmere? Your husband?'

'My *first* husband,' Marianne corrected acidly.

'Never mind that now,' Jason said impatiently. 'Where the devil did he spring from? Where and when did you see him?'

'Last night, at my house. He was waiting for me in my room when I got back from the theatre. He had got in by climbing over the garden wall and up to my balcony.'

'This is fantastic! Insane! Go on. I want to know everything. Where he is concerned, all things are possible.'

All trace of amusement had vanished from Beaufort's expression. His face was very tense and he was leaning against the harpsichord, his tall figure dominating Marianne as she sat and his eyes fixed compellingly on her sweet, downcast features. His voice was stern as he added: 'And look at me, for a start. I must know if you are telling me the whole truth.'

Still that suggestion of contempt, the same hint of distrust. What must I do, Marianne asked herself despairingly, to make him understand that I love him, that he is the only person in the world for me? But she looked up as he bade her and her green eyes met those of the man leaning over her with a gaze that was wholly candid and direct.

'I will tell you everything,' she said simply. 'You shall judge ...'

Few words were needed to describe the scene which had taken place on the previous night between herself and Francis Cranmere. As she spoke, Marianne was able to follow the swift succession of emotions reflected on the keen face before her: surprise, anger, indignation, contempt, even pity. But all the time the story took to tell Jason did not utter a single word, not even the smallest exclamation. Even so, when Marianne came to the end, she saw with joy that nearly all the hardness had vanished from the sea rover's blue eyes.

He remained where he was for a moment, watching her in silence, then, with a shrug and a sigh, he turned and walked away a little.

'And you paid!' he said roughly. 'Knowing him as you do, you paid, blindly! It did not occur to you that he could have been lying, that it was simply an excuse to get money out of you?'

And you, Marianne thought sadly, it does not occur to you that I love you so much I lost my head, that to save your life I would have given him everything I possess? But she did not utter these bitter thoughts aloud. Instead, she merely answered miserably: 'He had it all so pat that I was forced to believe him. It was he who told me that you would be at Mortefontaine all day today, and that you would be alone when you returned, and he told me, too, that you would have an important visitor this evening – and it was all quite true because I came straight here first thing this morning and had it all from the man at your gate. It was all true – except the one, most important thing, but how was I to guess?'

'A conspirator! I!' Jason flung at her. 'And you believed it? Surely you knew me well enough?'

'No,' Marianne said seriously, 'no – I don't really know you at all. Remember I saw you first as an enemy, and then as a friend and a saviour, and then at last as someone – someone indifferent.' The word was not easy to say, but Marianne did say it firmly. Then she went on, very gently: 'Which of these men is the real one, Jason? For from indifference you seem to have come to dislike, even to hate me?'

'Don't talk such rubbish,' Jason retorted sharply. 'What man could be indifferent to a woman like you? There is something about you which drives a man to commit the wildest follies. One must either love you to distraction – or want to wring your neck! There can be no half-measures.'

'You – you seem to have chosen the second alternative. I can't blame you. But before I go, there is one thing I should like to know—'

He was standing with his back to her, staring out, unseeingly, at the rain streaming down the windows and at the blackness of the garden beyond.

'What?'

'This visitor – who was so important as to bring you back from the Queen of Spain. I should like to know – forgive me – I should like to know if it was a woman?'

He turned and looked at her again, but this time there was in his eyes something like an involuntary tenderness:

'Does it matter so much?'

'More than you could ever believe. I – I will never ask you anything else. You will never hear of me again . . .'

It was said in a tone of such doleful resignation, and with such humility, that it found the chink in his armour. A force which he could not control brought the privateer to his knees beside her, imprisoning both her hands in his:

'Little fool! That visit was important only from a business point of view. And the visitor was a man, another American, a boyhood friend of mine, Thomas Sumter, who has just gone off to supervise the loading of my ship. You probably don't know, but on account of the blockade a number of major French exporters are using American vessels to transport their goods. One of these is a delightful lady at Rheims, Madame Veuve Nicole Cliquot-Ponsardin, the head of great champagne *caves*, who has done me the honour to entrust her wares to me. Thomas has just been settling our latest agreement and has driven off to Morlaix tonight to arrange for the cargo's conveyance to – well, to somewhere outside the Empire. That is all my conspiracy. Are you satisfied?'

'Champagne!' Marianne cried, laughing and crying at once. 'It was all about champagne! And I thought— Oh dear, it's too much, it's really too wonderful . . . too funny! I was right when I said I did not know you at all!'

But Jason had only smiled perfunctorily at her relief, and there was no laughter in his eyes as he searched her radiant face with painful eagerness:

'Marianne, Marianne! Who are you yourself with your child-like innocence and the artfulness of a woman of the world? Sometimes you are as clear as day, and at others full of strange shadows, and it may be I shall never know the truth about you.'

'I love you – that is all the truth.'

'You have the power to make my life a hell, and to turn me into a devil. Are you a woman or a witch?'

'I love you – I am only a woman who loves you.'

'And I almost killed you. I wanted to kill you . . .'

'I love you. I have forgotten it already.'

The strong, brown hands had moved steadily up Marianne's arms and folded round her, drawing her close to a hard, warm chest, and Jason's lips were on her eyes, her cheeks, were seeking her mouth. Trembling with a joy so great that for an instant it seemed that she would die, Marianne abandoned herself to the arms that now held her fast, pressing herself close to Jason and closing her eyes which were so full of tears that they overflowed and her cheeks were wet with them. Their kiss tasted of salt and fire, bitter-sweet, with all the passion and tenderness of a thing long awaited, long desired, long prayed for without real hope of that prayer being answered. It was eternity in a few seconds, broken off only to begin again, more passionately still. It was as if neither Jason nor Marianne could ever quench their grievous, burning thirst for each other, as if both were trying to cram into this fleeting moment of happiness all their share of paradise on earth.

When at last they drew apart a little, Jason took Marianne's chin between his fingers and pushed her head up a little until the candlelight shone in the marine deeps of her eyes.

'What a fool I've been,' he murmured. 'How could I ever have imagined for a moment that I could live the rest of my life away from you? You are a part of myself, my flesh and blood! . . . Now what are we going to do? I cannot keep you with me, and you have no right to stay. There is—'

'I know,' Marianne said quickly, laying her hand on his lips to keep him from uttering the names that would have broken the spell. 'But these few hours belong to us. Surely we can forget the real world for a few moments more?'

'Like you, I wish we could – oh, how I wish we could!' he said desperately. 'But Marianne, there is this peculiar behaviour of Cranmere's, this false information – and all that it cost you—'

'The money is nothing. I have more than I know what to do with.'

'Nevertheless, I will repay you. But it was not the money I was thinking of. Why did he spin you this yarn?'

Marianne laughed. 'Just for the sake of the money, of course. You said so yourself, he was undoubtedly in need of it and he found a perfect means. The only thing to do now is to forget it.'

She slid her arms tenderly round his neck and tried to draw him to her once again but Jason unfastened her encircling arms very gently and got to his feet:

'Can you hear? There is a window banging in the next room.'

'Call one of the servants.'

'I sent them all to bed before Thomas came. My business affairs are my own concern.'

He moved towards the door which led to the adjoining room and Marianne followed him automatically. Now that the rain had stopped and everywhere was quiet, she sensed a strangeness in the atmosphere of the house, as if it were full of the rustle of skirts, faint whisperings which were probably nothing more than lingering drops of water dripping from the trees on to the gravel paths outside. The room where the window was banging, a large, almost empty salon, was dark but, glancing out of the windows, Marianne thought she saw lights flitting among the shadows in the grounds that ran down to the Versailles road. There was something ominous about them in the thick dark out there, and she hurried after Jason, who was making the window fast.

'I thought I saw lights in the garden. You saw nothing?'

'Nothing at all. Your eyes have been playing tricks on you.'

'And the noises? . . . Did you hear nothing? As it were a rustle of silk, a sighing?'

It might have been the effects of darkness, for it was almost completely dark, the lights in the next room casting only a feeble shaft through the half-open door, but Marianne found that her hearing and her mind seemed attuned to a host of faint, disquieting sounds. It was as if every board, every panel, every piece of furniture in the house had taken on a life of its own – a frightening feeling.

Startled by the odd note in her voice, Jason folded her once more in his arms, clasping her to him gently, like some fragile, precious object, then, as he realized that she was burning hot, he began to worry:

'You're feverish! It is that which makes you see and hear things. Come, I can feel you shivering . . . You need care. Oh, my God, and to think I . . .' He tried to urge her forward but she hung back, staring wide-eyed into the darkness, which now began to seem less black.

'No. Listen! It is like someone crying. A woman . . . she is crying to warn us . . .'

'Any moment you will tell me you are another who has seen the poor princess's ghost! Enough of this, Marianne. You are doing yourself no good and I am afraid that I have made matters worse. We must not stay here.'

Without further argument, he picked her up in his arms and carried her through into the other room and shut the door carefully behind them before depositing his burden on a small sofa. Having first wrapped Marianne in her silken cloak and placed a cushion underneath her head, he announced his intention of rousing the cook to bring her some hot milk. Walking over to the corner of the bookcase, he pulled the bell rope which had been concealed there. Muffled to her chin in the green silk, Marianne followed him with her eyes.

'It's no good,' she said unhappily. 'The best thing is for me to go home. But – I didn't see the ghost, you know. I heard it. I know I did.'

'Don't be so silly. There is no ghost outside your own imagination.'

'There is . . . it was trying to warn us—'

Quite suddenly, the house seemed to be wide awake. Doors opened and shut noisily and there was a sound of hurried footsteps. Even before Jason could reach the door to inquire what was afoot, it was flung open to admit a bewildered-looking footman bearing all the signs of one who had dressed in great haste:

'The police! It is the police, Monsieur!'

'Here? At this hour? What do they want?'

'I – I do not know. They made the lodge keeper open the gate and they are already in the grounds.'

Seized with a horrible foreboding, Marianne sat up and began feverishly putting on her cloak, tying the silken strings with trembling hands. She stared up at Jason with frightened eyes. The thought in her mind was that Francis might have cheated her and, without the least shadow of proof, have informed on Jason as a conspirator.

'What are you going to do?' she asked in an anguished undertone. 'You see, I was right to be afraid . . .'

'There is nothing to be afraid of,' Jason said stoutly. 'I have done nothing I need be ashamed of and I have no reason to suppose that I have enemies.' He turned to the footman, who was still trembling in the doorway. 'You may tell whoever is in charge that I am ready to see them. No doubt it is all a mistake. But ask them to wait a moment . . .'

He was buttoning his shirt as he spoke, winding his neckcloth deftly about his throat and reaching for the coat which he had taken off earlier for the sake of coolness and laid over the back of a chair. This done, he came back to Marianne and helped her to her feet.

'How did you get in?'

'By the little door in the wall in the rue de Seine. Gracchus is waiting for me there, with the chaise hidden close by.'

'Then you must go to him at once . . . I hope you may still be able to get out without being seen. Fortunately it has stopped raining. Come! They will still be at the front of the house.'

But Marianne clung to him desperately:

'I don't want to leave you! If there is any danger to you, I want to share it.'

'Now you are being childish. I am in no danger. But you, or your reputation at least, will be horribly compromised if these policemen find you here. No one must know—'

'I don't care!' Marianne cried wildly. 'You want to keep it from Pilar, that is all—'

'For heaven's sake, Marianne! Stop this foolishness! I give you my word that in asking you to leave now I am thinking only of you—' He broke off suddenly and his arms, which had been holding her, fell to his sides. It was too late. The door had opened and a man was already in the room. He was a big man, very solidly-built, dressed all in black, buttoned high to the chin below a long, drooping moustache. In his hand he held a high-crowned velours hat, black likewise, and his eyes, Marianne saw in the light of the candles, were the hardest and coldest she had ever seen.

The newcomer sketched a brief salute, 'Inspector Pâques. I'm sorry to disturb you, Monsieur, but we have received information to the effect that there has been a crime committed in this house and that we should find a body here.'

'A crime?' echoed Jason and Marianne together. But while Jason advanced to meet the policeman, Marianne stayed where she was, leaning heavily on a chair. She felt as if she were about to faint. The absurd, yet horrifying menace which had hung over her life since that fateful evening at the theatre seemed to have come home to roost. What was all this about crimes and dead bodies? It was like some dreadful farce in rather bad taste, the police bursting in in the middle of her love scene . . . Then she heard Jason's voice, calm and even a little amused:

'Are you sure your information was correct, Monsieur? I

knew this house was supposed to be haunted, but this talk of corpses lying about . . . I would not cast doubts on your informant but I confess I find it all very surprising.'

His level, courteous tone must have impressed the police officer because he gave a small, rigid bow before replying:

'I am very willing to admit, Monsieur, the information in question reached us anonymously, but it was so definite – and so serious – that I did not hesitate to act.'

'So serious? Does that mean you know whose body you expect to find here?'

'No. We know only that the man is a loyal servant of the Emperor and – and that he is a special agent. I could no more ignore the matter than if a political assassination had been involved.'

It was Jason's turn to bow. 'Very true. Although I am amazed as I am intrigued! My dear Sir, the house is yours. Pray search. I shall be most interested to accompany you. But first, if you will excuse me, I will escort this lady to her carriage. This business is not suitable for her.'

Inspector Pâques was already halfway to the door but he turned at this and came back to the young couple:

'I regret that will not be possible, Monsieur. I must ask you not to leave this room until the search has been made. This lady is the Princess Sant'Anna, I believe?'

This time it was Marianne who answered. She had listened with mounting alarm to the polite exchange between Jason and his unexpected visitor but now at the mention of her own name her fears, although still nameless, took on a new edge of horror. All the same, it was with dignity and a fair assumption of coolness that she said: 'That is so. May I ask how you know me?'

'I have not that honour, Madame,' Pâques replied chillingly. 'But our information stated that you would be found with Monsieur Beaufort – whose mistress you are.'

Before Marianne could say a word, Jason had stepped between her and the policeman. The muscles of his jaw were taut with a rage barely under control and his eyes were very bright.

'That will do!' he said sharply. 'Do what you came to do, since the word of an anonymous informant is enough to make you invade a respectable household, but do not insult people!'

'I was not insulting anyone. I speak as I read—'

'If you believe everything you read, I am sorry for you. Moreover, no accusations have so far been made against either myself or the lady, I think. For myself, it makes no difference, but let me advise you to behave more courteously towards one who is a personal friend of the Emperor, unless you wish me to register a complaint against you. I am, after all, an American citizen, as you may know.'

'Very good,' the inspector cut him short. 'If I have made a mistake in coming here, Monsieur, I'll engage to apologize, but for the present I must ask you not to leave this room.'

He went out and Marianne and Jason were left alone. They looked at each other, he with a faint shrug and a quick, reassuring smile that yet did not reach his eyes and she with an anxiety she no longer made any attempt to hide.

'This is ridiculous,' Jason said. But Marianne shook her head:

'No – I am afraid it may be somehow the work of Lord Cranmere. And there is nothing ridiculous there, unfortunately.'

Jason gave a start and frowned. 'You think this police fellow's letter may have come from him? It's possible – but from what he said, I seem to be the principal target and I cannot see why Cranmere should wish me harm . . .'

'Because he knows quite well that the best way to hurt me is to strike at you!' Marianne's voice held all the passionate urgency of her need to convince her friend of what was growing every moment clearer to herself. Everything pointed to it, even the strange noises in the house which only she, with her extremely delicate sensitivity and an ear which, perhaps owing to the English side of her nature, seemed unusually attuned to anything connected with the supernatural, had heard.

'Think, Jason! You yourself were struck by the coincidence of all that has happened since last night, when I found that man in my house. This curious mixture of truth and falsehood which keeps recurring . . .'

'Truth?' the American said with sudden ferocity. 'What truth do you see in that damned anonymous note, apart from the reference to your presence here tonight?'

'Lord Cranmere was the only person who knew that I was coming—'

'That's as may be. But that is as far as it goes. You are not my mistress, are you? While as for this fictitious crime, this wholly imaginary corpse—'

He stopped short, becoming aware of the sudden reappearance of Inspector Pâques, this time through the french window by which Marianne had entered earlier, and looking, if possible, even chillier than at his first entry.

'Will you be good enough to come with me, Monsieur? And you also, Madame.'

'Where to?' Jason said.

'To the billiard-room in the small pavilion in the grounds.'

Marianne's presentiment of some imminent catastrophe had become a certainty. She read disaster in the set face of the policeman and she was sure that his eyes held a threat. Jason, too, had scanned Pâques's uncommunicative features with surprise, but he gave no sign beyond a slight shrug as he held out his hand to Marianne, saying on a note of exasperated resignation: 'Oh, very well! Since you insist.'

They went out into the garden. The heat which had made the earlier part of the evening so unpleasant had given way to a cool freshness and from the drenched earth and dripping trees there came a reviving smell of new-washed leaves and wet grass. But the dark figures of the police were stationed grimly among the roses on the three terraces and Marianne shivered, thinking that there were enough of them to surround a whole village and wondering at the extravagance which could employ so many men to check on a single house. It was possible, of course, that Inspector Pâques had been expecting a gang of criminals and had been determined at all costs to prevent an escape, which must always be reckoned a possibility in a garden of such size. The men stood quite still. One or two held shaded lanterns in their hands to throw a light on the path, but altogether they gave the impression of some ominous guard. Marianne must have trembled perceptibly because she felt Jason's fingers tighten on hers and drew some comfort from the warmth of the contact.

The little pavilion which had once been used as a billiard-room at some time in the past stood slightly to the right of the house. The light inside gave it the air of a big, yellow lantern standing there in the dark. Two men were standing guard at the door, leaning heavily on the knotted cudgels which were formidable weapons in their hands. They stood, silent and ominous, like two black attendants at the mouth of a tomb, and Marianne's hand clutched Jason's nervously. Pâques opened the door and stood aside to allow the couple to enter:

'Go in and see.'

Jason entered first and after a quick start moved instinctively to block his companion's view, and at the same time to keep her from stepping in the blood which covered the room. But it was already too late. She had seen what lay within.

She gave a single horrified shriek, then turned, her knees giving way beneath her, to escape the nightmare vision, only to come full against the inspector's large chest, blocking the doorway.

In the middle of the room, the legs half-hidden under the billiard-table with its torn cloth, lay a gigantic corpse, with gaping throat and eyes wide open on eternity. Yet for all the bloodless pallor of the face, for all the terrifying fixity of the expression, rigid in a look of horrible surprise, there was no mistaking the identity of the man who lay there, in that place which had once been built for amusement and was now so dreadfully transformed into a scene of carnage. It was Nicolas Mallerousse, Marianne's adoptive uncle, alias the seaman Black Fish, the friend of prisoners escaping from the English hulks and the man who had sworn to destroy Francis Cranmere or die in the attempt.

'Who is this man?' Jason asked tonelessly. 'I have never seen him before.'

'Ah! Is that so, indeed?' the inspector said, making vain attempts to disengage himself from Marianne who was clinging to him, sobbing convulsively, in the first stage of hysteria. 'And yet your initials were found on the razor which killed Nicolas Mallerousse. Now then, lady, now then, if you please! I've better things to do than stand here supporting you.'

'Leave her alone!' Jason cried fiercely, snatching Marianne away from the inspector who had started to shake her in his efforts to get free. 'No one looks to a policeman for compassion! If this poor fellow is indeed Nicolas Mallerousse, as you claim, then this young woman has just received a terrible shock. Get her out of this slaughterhouse, I implore you, or the Emperor shall hear of it, I swear to you! Come, Marianne, come with me . . .'

Still talking, he lifted her shuddering form and carried her outside. Pâques let them go and merely indicated a stone bench which stood beside the path, backed by a bed of tall white lilies whose heady scent filled all that part of the garden. Jason laid down his burden and asked for someone to be sent to find Gracchus-Hannibal Pioche and tell him to bring the carriage for his mistress. Inspector Pâques, however, had his own views:

'Not so fast. I haven't finished with this lady yet. You told me it came as a shock to her that the body was that of Nicolas Mallerousse? Why should that be, now?'

'Because he was a good friend to her. She was very fond of him.'

'Do you expect me to believe that? The shock was caused by the sight of the blood and maybe because she had not thought to be confronted with your handiwork.'

'My handiwork! Are you accusing me of this disgusting piece of butchery? Simply because you found a razor with my initials on it? Razors can be stolen—'

'But motives can't. And you had two, two very good ones.'

'Two motives? How should I have two motives for murdering a man I'd never even met?'

'At least two,' Pâques amended, 'each better than the last. Mallerousse had been on your tail ever since you came to

France, trying to get proof of important smuggling ventures you were involved in. You killed him because he was about to arrest you just as you were leaving France with your holds full of—'

'Champagne and burgundy!' Jason cried exasperatedly. 'You don't kill a man for the sake of a few bottles of wine!'

'If what that letter has to say is true we shall find something else besides that will give us all the proof we need. As for the second motive. The lady herself supplies that. You killed him to save her!'

'To save her? Save her from what? I tell you she—'

'From this! We found it on the body. I don't doubt she knew Mallerousse well enough, or that he, poor devil, knew a good deal more about her than she liked. But I can't imagine her being so very fond of the man who was carrying this paper. Here, Germain, fetch a lantern over here!'

One of the policemen came over to them. The light from his lantern fell on a scrap of yellow paper, the sight of which was enough to rouse Marianne from the depths of horror and grief that had overwhelmed her. Still shaken by sobs, she had heard what was said without being able to gain sufficient control of herself to respond to the inspector's accusations and Jason's angry replies. But this piece of paper, the yellow paper she had seen once before on that day in the Place de la Concorde, in the hands of her worst enemy, acted on her as a counter-irritant because it gave her clear proof; it was the signature added to the nightmare in which she and Jason were caught.

She held out her hand and, taking the paper from the inspector, unfolded it and read it quickly. Yes, it was the same as the one she had already seen, except that it had been brought up to date and the name 'Princess Marianne Sant'Anna' substituted for that of 'Maria-Stella'. But the contents, the accusation that the Emperor's mistress was a spy and a murderess still being sought by the law in England, were the same as ever, still characteristically vile.

Holding it distastefully between finger and thumb, Marianne returned the yellow broadsheet to the inspector:

'You were quite right to keep me here, Monsieur. No one is

better able to give you the full story of that abominable piece of libel. I have seen it before. I will tell you, too, how it was I came to know Nicolas Mallerousse, of the kindness I received from him and why I had good cause to love him, whatever ideas you may have formed on the strength of one anonymous letter and another, equally anonymous pamphlet.'

'Madame—' the police officer began impatiently.

Marianne held up her hand. She looked proudly at the inspector with an expression at once so haughty and so candid that his eyes fell before hers:

'Allow me, Monsieur! When I have done, you will see the impossibility of further accusations against Monsieur Beaufort because what I have to tell you will reveal the names of the real perpetrators of this – this hideous crime.'

Her voice failed her as once again her memory set before her every detail of the scene she had just beheld. Her friend Nicolas, so kind and brave, basely slaughtered by the very ones he should have brought to justice. How it came to pass that this should have happened in this house, the house in which Jason was living, a house which belonged to a man of the utmost respectability, Marianne did not know, but she knew with all the infallible insight of her grief and anger, and her hatred also, who had done this. If she had to cry it aloud to the whole of Paris, if it cost her the last shred of her reputation, she would bring the real culprits to justice!

Inspector Pâques, meanwhile, began to lose some of his assurance in the face of a woman who spoke with such firmness and certainty:

'All this is all very well, Princess, but the fact remains that someone committed the crime and the body has been found here . . .'

'Someone committed the crime but it was not Monsieur Beaufort! The real murderer is the author of that pamphlet,' Marianne cried, pointing to the yellow paper which Pâques still held in his hand. 'He is the man who has hounded me ever since the evil day I married him. He is my first husband, Lord Francis Cranmere, an Englishman – and a spy.'

Marianne could feel, suddenly, that Pâques did not believe.

He was looking alternately at the yellow paper and at Marianne with an odd expression on his face. At last he shook the paper softly under her nose:

'In other words, the man you killed? Do you take me for an imbecile, Madame?'

'But he is not dead! He is in France, he goes by the name of the Vicomte—'

'Think of another story, Madame,' the inspector interrupted her roughly, 'and do not try to divert me with these taradiddles! It is easy enough to accuse a ghost. This house is supposed to be haunted, let me remind you. Perhaps that may provide you with a further exercise for your imagination. For myself, I believe in facts.'

In her indignation, Marianne might have continued to plead, reminding this suspicious policeman of her position in society, her influence with the Emperor, her connections, even, despite the shame evoked by the recollection of those dark hours in her life, of her past record as one of Fouché's most trusted agents. But four more policemen came down the path at that moment. Two carried lanterns while the other two were maintaining a firm grip on a burly individual dressed in a seaman's rough woollen jersey which had seen better days.

'Here, Chief!' one of the men said. 'We found this fellow skulking in the bushes, down by the wall on the Versailles road. He was trying to climb over and make off.'

'Who is he?' growled Pâques.

The answer to his question came from an unexpected quarter. It was Jason who spoke. He had taken the lantern from the hands of one of the policemen and held it up so that the light fell on the prisoner. The face emerging from the shadows and from the filthy collar of the seaman's jersey was bony and unprepossessing, with a broken nose and eyes like black coals.

'Perez! What are you doing here?'

The man appeared to be labouring under all the effects of considerable terror. Strong as he looked, he was shaking so that only the grip of the two policemen kept him on his feet.

'You know this man?' Pâques asked, frowning.

'He is one of my men. Or rather, he was, for I discharged him from my ship when we docked at Morlaix. He is an unmitigated rogue,' Jason said sternly. 'I have no idea what can have brought him here.'

The man uttered a howl like a stuck pig, and before the two surprised policemen could stop him he had sunk to his knees on the ground and was crawling to Jason, clutching at his arms, weeping and groaning all at once.

'No, boss! . . . No, don't do it! Don't give me up! . . . Mercy! . . . No my fault . . . no help it, boss! We go move him, Jones and me, but no time, boss . . . they here already . . . police, boss!'

Marianne listened, stupefied, to the frenzied outpouring of disjointed words, spoken in bad French with a strong Spanish accent, without apparent rhyme or reason, yet terrible to her. She knew now that fate was against her and that Inspector Pâques would never listen to her now that he had what seemed to be a real, live witness. Jason, however, losing his temper at last, had the man by the neck of his grimy jersey and was lifting him bodily from the ground:

'Move him? Who? What?'

'B-but – the b-body, b-boss! That dead man!' the wretched creature gasped out, half-throttled. 'Jones say run and he run fast . . . but I was afraid to run . . . when I get there . . . find the gate shut . . . then I try to climb the wall . . . Mercy! Don't kill me, boss!'

The last word ended in a strangled choke. Beside himself with anger, Jason had his strong fingers clamped so tightly round the man's windpipe that he all but choked the life out of him. He thrust his keen face hard into the other's congested one. 'Liar!' he spat out. 'What orders have I ever given you except to have you flogged off my ship for a sneaking thief? Say it, you snivelling pickpocket! Admit that everything you've said is lies before I—'

'That's enough!' the inspector cried sharply, springing to the rescue of the unfortunate Perez. 'Let that man go! By trying to kill him you admit the truth of what he says. Here, men!'

The four policemen had not waited to be told. They converged upon Jason, and Perez, abruptly released, dropped heavily to the ground and began fondling his bruised throat and whining. 'Tries to kill me . . . after all I've done for him . . . there's ingratitude . . .'

Seeing that Jason was firmly held, the wretched creature dragged himself slowly to his feet, shaking his head, more in sorrow than in anger, as it seemed:

'Always it is the same, with the fine gentlemen . . . When things go wrong, they blame the poor wretch who only obeys orders . . .'

'But this man is lying!' Marianne burst out. She had been watching with a mixture of horror and disgust as this stranger played out his terrible part, for a part it must surely be, just one more act in this fiendish comedy which Francis had devised to ruin Jason, and to ruin her with him. How? By what means was it to be done? She did not know but all her thoroughbred instincts, all the heightened sensitivity of a woman deeply in love cried out to her that this was all part of a plan, lovingly and skilfully prepared.

'Of course he is lying,' Jason said icily. 'But tonight seems to be the night for liars. I don't know what this scoundrel is doing here but he has certainly been bribed.'

'That will have to be gone into,' the inspector said sternly, 'at the trial. In the meanwhile, Monsieur, I arrest you in the name of His Majesty the Emperor and King!'

'No!' Marianne screamed desperately. 'No! You can't do that! He is innocent! . . . I know he is! I know everything! Everything, I tell you . . .' She flung herself after Jason who was already being led away by the men. 'Let him go! You have no right!'

Like a fury, she turned on Pâques, who was busy putting handcuffs on Perez and giving him into the care of one of his men. 'You have no right, do you hear? Tomorrow I shall go to the Emperor! He shall know everything! He will listen to me.'

The inspector's hand reached out and caught her arm in a grip of such brutal hardness that she gasped with pain:

'That's enough of that. Be quiet, now, unless you want me to take you along as well! It is not proved that you were an accessory to the crime and I am letting you go free for the present. But you will be watched . . . and you are free only so long as you keep quiet. One of my men will see you to your coach and escort you home, after which you will not go out again on any pretext whatever. And remember, I shall have my eye on you.'

Marianne's sorely-tried nerves gave way all at once. She sank down on to the stone seat and, laying her head in her hands, began to cry hopelessly, using up what little strength she had left. Two men came out of the billiard-room carrying a stretcher on which lay a large form covered with a cloth which was already showing sinister dark stains here and there. Marianne watched in a kind of daze as it passed by her, her eyes and her mind a blank, beyond knowing even whether her heartbroken tears were for the good, brave man who twice saved her life, whose body they were now taking away, or for the one whom she loved with her whole being and who now stood unjustly accused of a base crime. In her mind, Cranmere's guilt was beyond all doubt. It was he who had engineered all this, he who had woven each of the fine, sticky threads of this deadly spider's web, and he who had murdered Nicolas Mallerousse, killing two birds with one stone, for at the same time he had rid himself of his pursuer and made a bloodbath of the lives of both Marianne and Jason. How could she have been so stupid, so blind as ever for one instant to believe that what he said was true? Her love had made her the tool of a villain and brought about the death of those whom she loved best in the whole world.

She got up slowly, like a sleep-walker, and began to follow the stretcher, a frail ghost in her white dress, its hem still marked with the dreadful traces of the crime. From time to time, a sob burst from her and the sound died away in the quiet, sweet-smelling darkness which had succeeded the storm. After her, a little way behind, not altogether insensitive, perhaps, to the grief of a woman who, only the night before, had had Paris at her feet envying her wealth and beauty, and who now followed this travesty of a funeral procession like a lost and hopeless orphan, Inspector Pâques, too, made his silent way back to the house.

The big white house, a house built for pleasures and happiness, yet where Marianne had seemed to hear the sobbing of a desolate, unhappy shade, emerged through the trees illumined as though for a ball, but Marianne saw nothing but the bloodstained cloth borne before her, heard nothing but the voices of her own grief and despair. At the same mechanical pace she passed the dark groups of policemen on the terraces. She climbed the shallow steps, as though mounting the scaffold, walked through the room where she had known such brief, miraculous happiness and out into the hall, automatically obeying the inspector's voice which came to her from a great distance, telling her that her carriage was waiting at the door.

She was so far away that she did not even flinch when a black figure – another, there had been so many in that last hour! – barred her way. There was no emotion in her eyes as they encountered the burning hatred in Pilar's, she did not even ask herself what Jason's Spanish wife was doing there, and scarcely heard the words which the other woman hissed at her in a passionate fury of denunciation:

'My husband killed for you! But it is not for that he will die! It is for you! Because of you, and the curse of loving you!'

Marianne did not even look at her. She gave a little, weary shrug and moved her arm to put away the importunate figure. The woman was insane! Jason was not going to die. He could not die . . . not without Marianne. From now on, what meaning could there be to that word death which they kept waving in front of her, like flowers at a funeral?

Through the crowd of policemen, servants and curious onlookers, Marianne caught sight of Gracchus, his round face pinched with worry, and behind him the roof of her chaise. Instinct made her reach out to that one friendly face and that familiar refuge.

'Gracchus!' she called weakly.

Instantly Gracchus leapt forward, forging his way ruthlessly through all that separated him from his mistress.

'I'm coming, Mademoiselle Marianne!'

She clung to his arm, whispering: 'Take me away, Gracchus . . . take me home.'

Then the whole world spun round, the white house wheeled above her, leaving her in a lurching maelstrom of faces, trees and turning lights. Driven to the last pitch of nervous exhaustion, Marianne slid mercifully into unconsciousness. She did not hear Gracchus, before he lifted her from the ground, turn, cursing and sobbing at once, and let fly at the stunned Inspector Pâques in the argot of his native slums: 'You bleeding snuffer! If you've killed 'er I'll make sure the Little Corporal 'as the guts out of your stinking carcass, you jest see if I don't . . .'

CHAPTER SIX

The Screw Turns

Beneath a remarkably forbidding exterior, the effect of consorting daily with rogues, thieves, murderers and malefactors of all kinds, Inspector Pâques concealed a considerable degree of subtlety. Jason Beaufort's arrest caused none of the stir which might have been expected. The only witnesses had been a handful of villagers from Passy, attracted by the commotion, and the four newspapers of the day, duly muzzled by the police and by a rigorous censorship, breathed not a word. Moreover, society was for the most part in the process of leaving Paris for its country estates or for a variety of fashionable watering places and consequently did not learn of the affair until a long time afterwards. Apart from the Minister of Police, the Queen of Spain, with whom Pilar found an immediate refuge, Talleyrand, who was told of it by a distraught Marianne first thing the next morning, and, of course, the Emperor, no one was told what had happened.

As far as Marianne herself was concerned, the order for silence had been immediate and categorical. The very next evening, Savary came hurrying round to inform her that his department had received stringent orders from Napoleon that the Princess Sant'Anna's name was in no circumstances to be mentioned in connection with the affair. Marianne found it difficult to be grateful for the favour.

'How can I be kept out of it when there is a horrid anonymous note accusing Mr Beaufort of killing Mallerousse for my sake?'

The Duke of Rovigo coughed discreetly and shifted in his chair, clearly ill-at-ease. He had endured a characteristically unpleasant interview with Napoleon and he could still hear the biting accents of the imperial displeasure ringing in his ears:

'His Majesty is of the opinion that the accused would be quite capable of killing for your sake, Princess, but he has condescended to inform me of the – er – ties of friendship which subsisted between yourself and the deceased and stated his conviction that it would be absurd to associate you in any way with his death.'

Napoleon's actual words had been a good deal more forceful than this but they appeared to Savary, in spite of their august source, to be more suited to the camp than to the drawing-room. Marianne, however, expressed some surprise.

'To inform you? But, my Lord Duke, are you not the Minister of Police? Is it possible that you, as Fouché's successor, can be unaware that when I first came to Paris I occupied the post of *lectrice* to Madame de Talleyrand-Périgord and that the name I went by was Marianne Mallerousse, although my code name in the files at the Quai Malaquais was the Star?'

'Unfortunately, Madame, both you and the Emperor would appear to have forgotten that the Duke of Otranto left me very little of any importance on which to build, that for three days he burned all his papers and files – three days!' he added sighing. 'And the Emperor blames me – as if I could have foreseen it! I have had to start from scratch, patiently finding out who was working for us and on whom I could still count.'

'Not on me, at all events,' Marianne cut him short. She was

not in the least interested in the minister's troubles but she knew Fouché well enough to imagine the perverse pleasure he would have taken in making a clean sweep before his successor took over. 'But all this is beside the point. I must see the Emperor, Duke. It is of the utmost importance. I cannot let him do anything so dreadfully unjust as to allow Mr Beaufort to stand trial. To suspect him of so sordid a crime when he has always behaved as a sincere friend to our country would be a monstrous thing to do! Monsieur de Talleyrand knows him as well as I do, he can tell you . . .'

'No, Madame,' Savary said, shaking his head gloomily. 'His Majesty guessed that you would wish to see him. He charged me to tell you that it is quite out of the question.'

At this blow, delivered in a firm, though not unsympathetic voice, Marianne's colour drained away:

'The Emperor – refuses to see me?'

'Yes, Madame. He told me that he would send for you when he judged that the time was ripe, which it is not at present. There are certain circumstances which make it appear that Monsieur Beaufort may have been less our friend than you imagine.'

'And even if that were true,' Marianne cried passionately, 'even if he hated us, would that be sufficient reason to leave him to face an unjust and ridiculous charge?'

'My dear Princess, this is a serious matter and it is essential that it be cleared up. Leave it to the law to uncover the whole truth about what happened at Passy.'

'Yes indeed – and the law can only benefit from hearing what I have to say. I was with Monsieur Beaufort when the crime was committed and, what is more to the point, I know who is, or rather are, the real murderers of Nicolas Mallerousse. If the Emperor refuses to listen to me, then you, Duke, must hear what I have to say. The man who did this murder and carefully covered up his crime in order to throw the blame for it on to another was—'

But Marianne was not fated to find anyone willing to listen to her. Savary cut her short, laying a hand soothingly on her arm:

'My dear Princess, I have told you the Emperor does not wish to have you involved in the matter. Trust my department to discover the real murderer – if, that is, we have not already discovered him.'

'But won't you listen to me, at least! I was there, I know all about it, you must admit that I am a valuable witness! Even if what I tell you must remain between ourselves, surely it will save you from making a mistake?'

'Valuable, perhaps – but certainly not impartial. No,' Savary went on quickly, forestalling a further protest from Marianne, 'I have not yet done with the Emperor's orders concerning you.'

'Orders?' she echoed, with some alarm.

Ignoring the question in her voice, which might have led him into invidious explanations, the Duke of Rovigo confined himself to expounding the nature of his instructions, taking the trouble to soften them slightly in the process:

'His Majesty desires you to leave Paris within the next few days for some other locality which may be agreeable to you.'

Marianne rose at this, oblivious of the pains the minister had taken to wrap up the harshness of the command, for command it was.

'Let us be frank, Duke. The Emperor is exiling me? Then tell me so plainly, if you please.'

'By no means, Madame,' Savary said, with a suggestion of a sigh which spoke volumes for his longing to be anywhere but where he was. 'It is merely that His Majesty wishes you to spend the summer away from Paris. Anywhere you like – so long as it is at least fifty leagues distant . . . the summer and also possibly the autumn, no more. What could be more natural, indeed, for nearly all our beauties have left Paris for some watering place – my own wife is leaving shortly for the waters at Plombières . . . You will merely be following the general fashion. There could be nothing more natural, after all, when one recalls that you are barely recovered from your illness after the tragedy at the Austrian ambassador's ball. You will return to us fully restored in health and more beautiful than ever, Princess, and no one will be more happy to see you than your humble servant.'

Marianne listened to her visitor's words with an attentive frown. She did not understand this sudden determination to send her off somewhere to take the waters for what was after all, considering that she had incurred the imperial wrath, a comparatively short spell of time. When Napoleon ordered the retirement of one of his subjects who had displeased him it was generally for a much longer period. Because she liked to have an answer to her questions if it were at all possible, she framed this thought aloud:

'I should like the truth, Minister, if you please. Tell me why His Majesty is so anxious for me to take the waters.'

There was authority as well as pleading in the green eyes and with another sigh Savary capitulated.

'The truth is that the Emperor, as I have told you, is anxious to keep your name out of this affair. Now according to the way things go, Monsieur Beaufort may or may not be brought to trial. If it should come to this, the trial will probably take place in October or November . . . The Emperor does not wish to hear that you are in Paris until it is all over.'

'The Emperor wants me to abandon my best friend – more than that – and this is a truth which you may tell him I think, Duke? – the man I love!'

'His Majesty was not unprepared for this reaction. That is why it is a command – and why he will not see you.'

'And suppose I will not obey?' Marianne exclaimed, quivering. 'Suppose I am determined to stay in spite of everything?'

Savary's voice, which had so far been calm and gently resigned, acquired suddenly a new touch of hardness. He was discreetly threatening:

'I should not advise it. It can do you no good to force the Emperor to acknowledge your involvement. Remember that by imposing on you what is, after all, you must admit, a very slight penance, he is moved briefly by the wish to shield you from a scandal which would bring discredit on the name you bear. Must I remind you that, quite apart from Monsieur Beaufort, there is already one man in prison on your account? When a woman of noble family lives apart from her husband, it is bound to cause comment when in the space of forty-eight hours two men find themselves in prison because of her, one for murder, the other for a scandalous duel with an officer of a foreign country who, as it happens, had that very evening called out the first man. Moreover,' the minister concluded, 'any action on your part which compelled us to take sterner steps would not bring you any closer to your friend. It is a long way from St Lazare, the women's prison, to La Force where Monsieur Beaufort is being held. Surely it is better to be free, even fifty leagues away, for both your sakes? Believe me, Madame, by obeying you will be doing the best for yourself and your friend.'

Defeated, Marianne bowed her head. Napoleon was treating her for the first time as a subject, and a recalcitrant subject at that. She would have to obey and go away, just when she longed with all her heart to remain in Paris, as near as possible to the blackened walls of the old prison behind which Jason must lie stifling for so many weeks. She was to be sent into the country, like a troublesome child who must be given a change of air, when the mere idea of Jason as a prisoner made her ill and took away any wish she might have had to enjoy the fine July sunshine. Jason of the seven seas, of the four horizons, as she called him to herself in the warm, tender pride of her love for him, Jason, whom the mighty albatross and the darting swallow could claim as their brother, Jason pining in a filthy prison cell at the mercy of ignorant turnkeys and unspeakable riff-raff of all kinds. To Marianne, it was like mud thrown at the clear blue sky, like blasphemy in the midst of a prayer, like spitting at a star.

'Well?' Savary asked.

'I shall obey,' she said reluctantly.

'Good. You will be gone in – shall we say, two days?'

What good would it do to plead when the master commanded? It might be that the Emperor meant his heavy hand to fall lightly and protectively, but for all that, Marianne felt its grip grinding her bones and crushing the fibres of her being quite as painfully as any medieval instrument of torture. No longer able to endure the minister's solemn face and crocodile sympathy, she gave him a slight bow and left the room, leaving it to the gloomy butler, Jeremy, to escort him to his carriage. She wanted, above all, to be alone to think things out.

Savary was right. It would do no good to rebel openly. Better to seem to bow, even though no force on earth should make her give up the fight!

Two days later Marianne left Paris, accompanied by Agathe and Gracchus, bound for Bourbon-l'Archambault. It had been her first intention to join Arcadius de Jolival at Aix-la-Chapelle, but that great Rhineland spa was very much in fashion that summer and Marianne felt little inclination for society after all that she had been through, and would go through, until Jason Beaufort was proved innocent and finally exonerated. Moreover, Talleyrand, who had arrived at her house on the heels of Savary, had advised her strongly against the historic capital of Charlemagne:

'There is certainly plenty of company to be met with there, but it is company of a very doubtful kind. Every exile and troublemaker is flocking there to the king of Holland now that the Emperor has to some extent set him aside by annexing his kingdom. Louis Bonaparte is the most lachrymose creature of my acquaintance and now he is behaving precisely as if he had been driven from his ancestral acres by some remorseless tyrant. Then there is our Lady Mother, also, with her endless prayers and still more endless economies. To be sure, my dear friend Casimir de Montrond has obtained permission to visit the place but, deeply devoted to him as I am, I cannot but feel he has a talent for courting disaster and God knows you have had enough of those . . . No, you had better come with me.'

For eight years past, it had been the Prince of Benevento's habit to depart each summer with unfailing regularity to drink the waters of Bourbon. His bad leg and his rheumatic pains were, if not greatly eased thereby, at least made no worse and no human strength, no cataclysm in Europe could have prevailed to stop him taking his cure when July came round. He had enumerated the charms of the quiet, pretty little town to his young friend in glowing terms, adding the further persuasions that it was not nearly so far from Paris, that seventy leagues was far more easily covered than a hundred and fifty, that it would be far better to write to Jolival to join her in Bourbon, that it was far easier to sink into a kind of obscurity, and the consequent freedom of action which resulted from it, in a small town than in a city full of people to whom one was known and, finally, that those in disgrace had a duty to stick together:

'You can make up my table at whist and I shall read to you the works of Madame du Deffand. We will reshape Europe between us and talk scandal about all those who talk scandal about us. That ought to keep us busy, eh?'

Marianne had agreed. While Agathe packed her clothes and Gracchus spring-cleaned the big travelling coach, she had sat down to write to her friend Jolival a long letter recounting all that had occurred. She finished by asking him to come back as soon as he was able, with or without Adelaide, and come to her at Bourbon. It made no difference to tell herself that there was certainly nothing the literary Vicomte could do to assist Jason, she was still convinced that, if only he were there, everything would at once seem better. She was perfectly well aware that if he had been there Cranmere's trap would not have worked nearly so well because, being less trusting and a good deal less emotional than Marianne, he would undoubtedly have smelled a rat and acted accordingly.

But the harm had been done and now they could only do everything possible to repair it and to bring the real murderers of Nicolas Mallerousse to justice. In any enterprise of that kind, Arcadius was a priceless ally because he knew far better than Marianne herself those sinister inhabitants of the Parisian underworld among whom the Englishman had found his confederates.

The letter had been entrusted to Fortunée Hamelin, who was even then on the point of setting out hot foot for Aix-la-Chapelle, for she, like her friend Talleyrand, had heard that the irresistible Count Casimir was to take the waters there and no power on earth could have kept her from the man who, with Fournier-Sarlovèze shared her amorous and highly inflammable heart. The fact that Fournier was at that moment in prison in no way deterred her.

'Well, at least he can't run off with anyone else while I'm away,' she had remarked, with her usual airy cynicism, regardless of the fact that she herself was preparing to fly to the arms of the handsome general's rival.

So Fortunée had gone the day before, promising to give the letter to Jolival before she so much as set eyes on Montrond, and reassured on that point, Marianne had set out sedately for the Allier, where she was to meet Talleyrand. It had been his intention, before going to Bourbon, to spend a few days on his estates at Valençay, partly to pay his respects to his permanent though unwilling guests, the Spanish princes, and partly to talk business with his agent, the Prince of Benevento's financial affairs having suffered a grievous blow through the failure of Simons Bank in Brussels.

Marianne left Paris on the fourteenth of July 1810, not without a good deal of regret. Quite apart from the thought that she was leaving Jason in the hands of the police, she found herself hating to leave her own dear house. In spite of Savary's reassuring words, she wondered how long it would be before she saw it again, for she knew in her heart that sooner or later she would disobey the Emperor and that if Jason were brought to trial, if all her own and Jolival's efforts proved vain, then no power on earth could keep her from him at that moment. Sooner or later, she would incur the wrath of Napoleon . . . and God alone could say how far that wrath might go. The Emperor was perfectly capable of ordering the Princess Sant'Anna back to Tuscany and forbidding her to leave it. He might force her to remain shut up in the villa, so beautiful and yet so terrifying, from which she had fled once before after a night of nightmare horror.

The mere thought of it made Marianne's skin prickle with fear. Ever since losing her child, she had been unable to think without apprehension of the moment when the prince in the white mask should learn that the longed-for heir would not be forthcoming, indeed, would never be. She had put off from day to day the moment of writing the fatal letter, so great was her dread of what might be his reaction. Something told her that if the Emperor, in his anger, were to have her returned to the palace of Sant'Anna she would never be able to escape from it again. The memory of Matteo Damiani had not yet faded from her mind.

She had often wondered what had happened to him. Donna Lavinia had told her as she was leaving, that Prince Corrado had confined him in the cellars, that no doubt some form of punishment would follow. But how could he punish a man who all his life had served him, and served his family devotedly . . . and one moreover who certainly knew his secret! With death? Marianne could not believe that Matteo Damiani had been killed, for he himself had killed no one.

The horses trotted on towards Fontainebleau and the sun splashed gaily through the moving curtain of leaves, but Marianne paid no attention to the road slipping by outside the windows of her coach. Her mind remained curiously divorced from the present and divided in the strangest way, part of it dwelling on Germany and her friend Jolival, of whom she had such high hopes, and part, the greater and more vulnerable part, roving about the ancient prison of La Force which she knew so well.

There had been a day when Adelaide, in a mood of nostalgia, had taken her to the old quarter of the Marais to show her her old home, a beautiful building made of pink brick and white stone dating from the time of Louis XIII, a neighbour of the Hôtel de Sévigné, but horribly scarred and disfigured by the warehouses and rope-walks which had taken it over during the Revolution. La Force was not far away and Marianne had glanced with revulsion at the squat, blank shape, under the low mansard roof, the stout though leprous walls and the low, heavily barred gate with its two rusty lanterns. It was a sinister gate, indeed, a dirty rusty-red in colour as if it were still soaking up the blood which had washed about it during the massacres of September 1792.

Marianne's elderly cousin had told her about those massacres. She had seen them from her hiding place in a garret of her own house. She had told of the ghastly death of the gentle Princesse de Lamballe. The story returned to Marianne's mind now in all its hideous detail and she could not repress a shudder of superstitious horror at the fate which seemed to be drawing Jason Beaufort inexorably along the same path as that taken by the martyred princess. He had gone so quickly from her house to what had been her prison. And had not Marianne herself heard her ghost weeping in the house where Madame de Lamballe had sought oblivion from a king's ingratitude? To Marianne's impressionable and highly sensitive mind it seemed a warning of disaster. What if Jason, too, were to leave La Force only to go to his death?

Such thoughts as these, combined with her own utter powerlessness to aid her friend and what she thought of as the Emperor's cruelty, did nothing to improve her spirits. By the time she reached Bourbon two days later, Marianne had not slept since she left Paris and had eaten only a little bread sopped in milk. She was in such a state of depression that she had to be put to bed as soon as she arrived.

Bourbon-l'Archambault was, however, a very attractive little city. It stood at the heel of a large lake through which a bustling river ran and its pink and white houses were piled in the shade of a mighty spur of rock on which had once stood the seventeen proud towers – now reduced to three – of the dukes of Bourbon. The town had been rich, powerful and extremely busy in the day of the *Grand Roi*, Louis XIV, when the choice spirits of the court came there to nurse their rheumatic ailments. But here, too, the Terror had passed. The shades of the poet Scarron, of Madame de Sévigné and the Marquise de Montespan who had there made a good end to a dubious life had melted into the mists along the Allier, while the towers of the château fell and house and chapel along with them. But Marianne had no eyes for the three surviving towers, mirrored so prettily in the shimmering waters of the lake, nor for the fair hills cradling the town, nor even for the country folk in their becoming, picturesque costumes who crowded curiously round the elegant berline with its steaming horses.

She was accommodated in the Pavillon Sévigné, in the room which had been that of the irresistible marquise, but neither Agathe's care nor the respectful and benevolent welcome accorded her by the proprietor of the establishment could rouse

Marianne from the black mood into which she had allowed herself to sink. There was only one thing she wanted, and that was to sleep, to sleep for as long as humanly possible, until someone came to her with news of Jason. It was no use to talk to her of the charms of the countryside or of anything else: she was deaf, dumb and blind to everything around her. She simply waited.

A fortnight passed in this way. It was a strange period because it was one which in after days disappeared altogether from Marianne's memory, so intense was her determination to withdraw from life, to make one moment so like another that they would blend into a single unvarying stream. No one was admitted to her presence and the physicians of the place especially were hard put to it to know what to make of this strange visitor.

The spell was broken by the arrival of Talleyrand, which brought a new spate of activity to the little town and an unexpected annoyance to Marianne. She had been expecting the prince to bring with him only a small suite, consisting perhaps of a secretary and his valet, Courtiade. However, when the house next door began filling up with large numbers of people, she was obliged to admit that she and Talleyrand held widely differing ideas on the subject of what constituted a suitably princely retinue. Whereas the Princess Sant'Anna was content with her maid and her coachman, the Prince of Benevento brought with him an army of indoor and outdoor servants, his cook, his secretaries, his adopted daughter Charlotte with her tutor, Monsieur Fercoc, as short-sighted as ever, his brother Boson, ten years his junior but deaf as a post, and lastly his wife. From time to time, also, there were guests in addition.

It was the princess's arrival which gave Marianne the greatest astonishment. Although at the Hôtel Matignon, Talleyrand endeavoured to be as little as possible in his wife's company, and although with the arrival of fine weather he generally packed her off to rusticate in her own little château at Pont-de-Seine, in which he himself never set foot, greatly preferring the society of the Duchess of Courland and the pleasures of her summer residence at Saint-Germain, he regularly, without fail, brought his wife to Bourbon.

She was to learn that this was a tradition instituted by Talleyrand in the belief that the least he could do was to spend three weeks in the summer in the by no means exclusive company of his wife. Marianne was touched, also, by the welcome she received from her one-time employer, who kissed her warmly as soon as she set eyes on her and showed a genuine delight in seeing her again.

'I have heard of your troubles, child,' she told her, 'and I want to assure you that you have my full sympathy and support.'

'You are much too good, Princess, and this is not the first time I have had cause to know it. It is a great comfort to know that one has friends.'

'In this hole, of all places,' the princess agreed with a sigh. 'It is enough to make one die of boredom, but the prince insists that these three weeks do an immense amount of good to the whole household. Ah, when shall we be able to return to our summers at Valençay!' The last words were uttered in an undertone, to keep them from her husband's ears.

Residence at Valençay had in fact been strictly forbidden ever since the château and the romantic setting, having been made the enforced home of the Infants of Spain, had encouraged an idyllic affair between the mistress of the house and the good-looking Duke of San Carlos. Matters might have gone no further had Napoleon not seen fit to advise Talleyrand personally of his misfortune, and in terms of such coarseness that they had provided a gold mine for unkind tongues. Talleyrand had been obliged to act and the poor princess was inconsolable at the loss of her private paradise.

Leaving the princess to settle in, amid a great banging of doors, bumping of boxes, clattering of feet and calling for servants, all of which proceeded under the interested gaze of about fifty of the local inhabitants, who had assembled about the big travelling coaches, Talleyrand accompanied Marianne back to her own house on the excuse of assuring himself that she was comfortably installed there. But scarcely was the rustic door of her little sitting-room closed behind them than the carefree smile faded from the prince's face and Marianne noted with alarm the lines of worry on his forehead and the way his shoulders suddenly seemed to sag wearily.

'Is it – is it so bad?'

'Worse than you can imagine. That is what caused my delay in joining you here. I wanted to learn all I could and for that reason I barely stopped at Valençay. To tell you the truth, my dear, the news is so bad that I scarcely know where to begin.'

He dropped heavily into a chair with a tired sigh and stretched out his bad leg, which was still stiff from travelling. Then he laid his stick against his knee and passed one long, white hand over his grey face. To Marianne, watching in growing horror, it seemed that the hand trembled a little.

'For God's sake! Tell me! Tell me just as it comes! Do not spare me. Any torture is better than ignorance. I have been dying by inches here for two whole weeks, knowing nothing! Is it possible that Jason's innocence is still not proved?'

'His innocence?' Talleyrand said bitterly. 'Each day that passes only serves to plunge him deeper in guilt. If this goes on, we shall have only one course open to us if we are to save him from . . .' He hesitated.

'From what?'

'From the scaffold.'

Uttering a choking cry, Marianne leapt from her chair as if it had grown suddenly red-hot. Carrying both icy hands to her burning face, she walked up and down the room several times before returning to fall on her knees at the prince's side.

'There can be nothing worse to say,' she said dully. 'Tell me the whole, now, I beg of you, unless you want me to run mad.'

Talleyrand put out his hand and gently stroked the girl's smooth hair. He shook his head. The light eyes, in general so cold and mocking, held a look of deep compassion:

'I know your courage, Marianne. I will tell you, but you must not stay there. Come, sit here, close by me, on this little sofa, eh?'

When they were seated side by side on the rush-bottomed

sofa by the window looking out on to the gardens, hand in hand, like father and daughter, the Prince of Benevento began his tale.

The accusation of murder against Jason Beaufort, which had originally been based on the anonymous letter handed to the police and on the testimony of the seaman Perez, who persisted in his story that he had received orders from Jason to remove the body of Nicolas Mallerousse from the billiard-room and throw it into the Seine, was now reinforced by a good deal of further evidence. First, the seaman Jones, whom Perez asserted was to have assisted him in the removal of the murdered man, had been fished out of a backwater at St Cloud two days later. He had been drowned and as there were no marks of violence on his body the police had concluded that in making his escape from Passy Jones had slipped in the darkness on the river bank, rendered unusually greasy by the night's storm, and fallen into the Seine to his death.

'But that is absurd!' Marianne protested. 'No sailor who fell into the Seine, even in the middle of the night, could fail to swim to safety – especially in summer!'

'Perez says that his companion could not swim. Jason, on the other hand, insists that Jones was one of his best men and swam like a fish.'

'And this wretch Perez is believed?'

'It is apt to go hard with the accused,' Talleyrand said with a sigh, 'and it is all the more unfortunate because by contradicting Perez's lying statements, this Jones might have given the evidence which would have saved our friend. If you ask me, Jones was never in league with this man Perez, whom Beaufort states that he had discharged with a flogging. But whoever arranged our little death trap was not inclined to quibble over one corpse more or less. Besides, I have not come to the end of it. The excise men at Morlaix have searched the holds of the *Sea Witch* and the cargo they found there has helped to aggravate the case against Jason.'

Marianne made a little movement of irritation. 'A cargo of champagne and burgundy! There's wickedness for you! Enough to cost a man his head, I'm sure! As for their sacred blockade—'

'Enough to cost a man his head, indeed,' the diplomat continued quietly, 'when they also find counterfeit money.'

'C-counterfeit? No – it is not true!'

'That Jason put it there, no, I don't think that. But that it was discovered is, I am afraid, beyond any doubt. They found about a hundred thousand pounds sterling in Bank of England notes. The notes were, unfortunately, brand new. I tell you, the plot has been well thought out.'

'Well then, it must be shown up for what it is!' Marianne cried hotly. 'We know, you and I, we know for certain that the crime and everything that has followed is the work of a gang of people well known to the police. Surely, they are the only ones who possess the means to have manufactured these notes, and that is what we have to find: whoever made those notes! Oh, the police must be blind and stone deaf! When I tried to tell the truth to that Inspector Pâques he treated me as if I were practically an idiot, and the Duke of Rovigo refused to listen to me at all.'

'The Duke of Rovigo is the world's biggest and most obstinate blockhead,' Talleyrand remarked, 'with the possible exception of Monsieur Savary – eh?' However dire the circumstances, he could not, it seemed, resist a witticism, even one that was not altogether new, for he had already made the same comment on the Duke of Bassano. 'Our policeman lives in constant terror of displeasing his idol, the Emperor. But for once, I cannot altogether blame him. Think, my child, of all the weight of evidence against Beaufort, while on your side you have only your private convictions and your word – not the least shadow of proof.'

'What more have they?' Marianne asked bitterly. 'All their evidence is mere slander, uttered by creatures so wretched that they should be beneath contempt. Besides, I fail to understand why Lord Cranmere and his associates should have gone to all this trouble merely to be revenged on me for getting him arrested. Especially as I am not directly involved in this. The real victim is Jason Beaufort. But why?'

'Because he is an American.' Talleyrand gave a little sigh. 'My dear child, it desolates me to be obliged to shatter your illusions but your differences with Lord Cranmere are altogether minor matters in this business. They would not, as you so rightly say, have gone to all this trouble merely to be revenged on you. But to bring about a diplomatic incident involving the United States, to tip a situation which had been rendered delicate by the Continental Blockade but which had recently shown some signs of improvement, now that is something which an English spy might find extremely worth while, something which could justify a little trouble.

This was the last thing Marianne had expected. It had not before occurred to her that her own affairs might have become involved with international politics. She turned on her companion a look of such total bewilderment and incomprehension that he smiled indulgently and continued: 'Let me explain. In spite of political differences, trade between England and the United States has been resumed since last year. The United States were deeply shocked by the decrees of Berlin and Milan, especially that of Milan by which Napoleon declared all foreign vessels calling at English ports, or even making contact with English vessels, to be lawful prizes. Lord Wellesley has taken advantage of American resentment and early this year huge quantities of English merchandise began entering the United States, greatly to the good of British trade, which had been suffering something of a recession. However President Madison is friendly to France and anxious to see the resumption of good relations with the country of La Fayette, and he would be glad to see the Milan decree repealed, at least so far as the United States is concerned. He has instructed his ambassador in Paris accordingly and John Armstrong has been working along these lines for some weeks past. I know for a fact that he has recently written to Champagny, who replaced me in Foreign Affairs, asking him to name the terms on which the Berlin and Milan decrees might be annulled in relation to the United States. This affair of murder and contraband is aimed much more at nullifying their efforts than at any idea of revenge for Francis Cranmere. You are an excuse, Marianne, and Beaufort a tool.'

Marianne bowed her head. Cranmere's web had been artistically woven. He had performed his function as a spy for

England to admiration and at the same time exercised his remarkable criminal talents by actually extorting money from his victim. Marianne had paid to join Jason in the trap which the Englishman had dug before their feet. She understood now the scale of the means which had been employed and also the curious behaviour of the man Perez in allowing himself to be caught (having been amply paid for his services, no doubt, and given assurances of his personal safety) in order to make quite sure of his former captain's conviction. Now that international interests were involved, Jason's chances had grown very much slimmer.

'But you mentioned the American ambassador,' she said. 'Can he do nothing for Jason?'

'Be sure that John Armstrong has already done everything possible but if Beaufort is convicted of espionage and coining, as well as murder, then he can only seek the Emperor's clemency.'

'The Emperor!' Marianne broke out. 'Yes, what of the Emperor? Why will he not see me, at least? A few moments' audience and he should have known all and Jason would be free!'

'I am not altogether sure why, Marianne. In such a case as this, the Emperor cannot act until all has been made clear. The matters at stake are too grave. Moreover, he cannot be wholly sorry to teach you a lesson – punish you a little for finding consolation so easily – he is a man, after all, you know. Finally, there is one witness against Beaufort whom Napoleon is forced to consider seriously, if only in the name of common morality, and you know how he cherishes the respectability of his court. The author of the anonymous letter and the seaman Perez may well be scoundrels, but can you say the same of Señora Beaufort?'

There was a deathly silence in the little room. In her mind, Marianne was echoing Talleyrand's last words, seeking some sense in them other than the immediate, horrifying implication. She found none, and at last she found her voice to ask hoarsely, still trying not to believe what she had heard: 'Are you telling me that—'

'That Jason's wife has turned against him? Unfortunately, yes. The poor creature is crazed with jealousy and she believes unalterably that you are her husband's mistress. She admits no doubt of her husband's guilt. According to her, and no fury was ever more vehement, Beaufort would be capable of anything where you are concerned, even murder!'

'But – she is mad! Stark mad! Insane . . . this is the most criminal folly. After this, dare you look me in the face and tell me that she loves Jason?'

Talleyrand sighed again as he answered, in his old, cynical tone: 'Perhaps. You see, Marianne, she comes of a fierce and passionate race to whom a betrayal of love can be paid for only in blood, and an injured woman may deliver up her unfaithful lover unflinchingly to execution – and then wall herself up alive in some unrelenting nunnery to spend the remainder of her life in expiation. Yes, Pilar is a dangerous woman and, as ill luck will have it, she knows that Jason loves you. She knew you at the first glance.'

'Knew me? How could she? She had never seen me.'

'You think not? I gather the figurehead of the *Sea Witch* is more than a little like you. Some of these wood-carvers are very skilful, you know – and some husbands remarkably obtuse! But it may be that, knowing their stay was to be a brief one, Jason hoped that Pilar might never have occasion to meet you – or, if she did, might fail to recognize the resemblance.'

For a moment, Marianne stared at her old friend. She was wholly overcome by this unexpected proof of love and hardly knew whether to be glad or sorry, but in her heart she knew that she had never doubted Jason's love for her. She had always known that he loved her, even when she had driven him away from her that night at Selton, but this simple, almost childlike proof of it touched the deepest and most sensitive chord in her. To think that she had hated that ship, had thrown it at Jason's head continually that he had purchased it from the sale of Selton! And all the time he had made it, as it were, this unexpected extension of Marianne herself . . .

She rose quietly and Talleyrand made no move to stop her.

He was not looking at her. He was sitting with his chin sunk in the immaculate folds of his neckcloth, absently tracing with the tip of his cane the primitive design of roses decorating the carpet.

A board creaked as Marianne moved to the window which opened on to a tiny balcony. She had picked up a blue shawl from a chair and hugged it round her shoulders. She felt chilled to the soul, despite the August heat of the sun, but when she leaned on the worn iron balcony rail she was not conscious of any warmth.

Outside, everything rejoiced in the tranquil beauty of a fine summer's day. From next door, young Charlotte's voice could be heard chanting in clear tones one of the rhyming games that children love. Farther off, by the pump, three women in blue skirts and flowered petticoats were chattering away to one another in the local *patois*, now and then bursting into shrieks of laughter. They wore the charming costume of the region with easy grace and their rosy faces glowed with happiness under their complicated double-headdresses made up of a frilled cap surmounted by a coquettish little hat cocked up before and behind and known delightfully as '*à deux bonjours*'. Some children were playing at quoits under a tree and the Prince of Benevento's grooms were leading the coach horses away to the stables, while in the distance could be seen a rather touchingly old-fashioned sedan chair with drawn curtains, conveying some invisible *curiste* to or from the baths. On all these things the sun poured down his golden beams. Only Marianne seemed excluded, and she wondered why, even in this scene of rural peace where everyone was happy, she should have to bear such a weight of grief and suffering. She had believed that she was pitted only against a handful of villains, the stupidity of the police and Napoleon's displeasure. Instead, she found herself at the centre of a vast and dangerous political intrigue in which neither she nor Jason counted for anything. It was rather as if she had been condemned to imprisonment for eternity and could look out at the world of the living only through the bars of a dungeon. Perhaps the truth was that she was not fashioned for such a world. The world to which she belonged was one of fury and violence that would not allow her to live in peace. It was to that world she must return.

She turned from the balcony and went quickly back to Talleyrand, who had been watching her attentively through half-closed eyes. She met his light blue gaze steadily:

'I am going back. I must see this woman, speak to her. I have to make you understand—'

'What? That you love her husband as much as he loves you? Do you really think that will make her change her mind? This Pilar is like a rock. Besides, you will not get near her. She has the whole of the Queen of Spain's guard to protect her, and if I know Julie Clary she will be only too delighted to play the queen for the benefit of the only one of her subjects who has ever asked for her assistance. At Mortefontaine, Pilar is surrounded, hemmed in by ladies- and gentlemen-in-waiting who are more effective than any castle walls. She has asked never to be left alone and her request has been granted. No visitors. No messages even, unless they are addressed to the queen. Do you think,' Talleyrand said wearily, 'do you think I have not tried? I was politely shown the door. What chance would you have? Your reputation is, to say the least, unlikely to recommend you to those pious ladies!'

'Never mind. I shall go just the same . . . at night, in disguise . . . I'll climb the walls if I have to. But I must see Pilar! It is unthinkable that no one should try and make her see reason, make her realize that her attitude is sheer wickedness.'

'I believe her to be quite aware of that. She simply does not care. When Jason has paid for his crime, then she will expiate her own, that is all.'

'To her, the worst crime is to betray herself.' It was a new voice, speaking from the doorway. Marianne and the prince both turned at once and for the first time for many days, Marianne uttered a cry of pure joy:

'Jolival! At last!'

In her delight at seeing her faithful friend once again, she ran to him impulsively and flung both her arms round his neck and kissed him resoundingly on both cheeks like a little girl, heedless of the fact that the said cheeks had not seen a razor for two days and that Arcadius himself was quite dreadfully dirty.

'Eh, well!' The prince extended a hand to the new arrival. 'You could certainly not have come at a better moment. I was very nearly out of arguments to dissuade this young lady from indulging in the most precipitate piece of foolishness. She wishes to go back to Paris.'

'I know. I heard,' Jolival said gloomily, flinging himself down without ceremony in a chair which groaned under the shock. 'But she must not go back to Paris, for two reasons. The first is that her house is being closely watched. The Emperor knows her very well and he would rather make it impossible for her to disobey him than be obliged to punish her. The second is that her absence is the one thing which might serve to calm that Spanish woman's temper a little. Queen Julie must have put it to her that by sending his former favourite away, Napoleon is paying tribute to the virtue of Beaufort's wronged spouse.'

'Nothing—!' Marianne muttered grittily.

'Possibly. But your return, my dear, would unleash a pack of troubles. Monsieur Beaufort may be in prison but even there he is under close watch by his wife's friends, and in particular by one Don Alonzo Vasquez who seems to have heard something of the estates in Florida and to have ambitions to restore them to the Spanish flag.'

'Good heavens, Arcadius!' Marianne exclaimed. 'Wherever did you learn all this?'

'At Mortefontaine, my love, at Mortefontaine where I have been spying quite unblushingly on your foe while ostensibly engaged in pruning Queen Julie's roses, after a fashion. Yes, for your sake I have been the Queen of Spain's gardener for three whole days!'

Talleyrand smiled slightly. 'I suppose it did not occur to you that one does not prune roses in July, eh?'

'That was why I stayed no more than three days. The head gardener tired of my efforts and suggested I take my talents elsewhere for employment. But if you want to hear any more, for pity's sake give me a bath and a meal! I'm choked with heat and dust, and half-dead of hunger and thirst as well. I can't decide which to die of first.'

'I'll leave you,' Talleyrand said, getting to his feet, while Marianne hurried from the room to give orders. 'In any case, I have said all I came to say and I must go home.' He paused and added in a lowered tone: 'Have you any further news?'

Arcadius de Jolival shook his head sadly:

'Not much. The real murderers seem to have vanished into thin air. Not that I'm surprised at that. Fanchon is an old hand. She and her people must have done their work and gone to earth somewhere. As for the Englishman, he has disappeared so completely, whether to become the Vicomte d'Aubécourt or to assume some other identity, that it is easy to believe – as unfortunately it *is* believed – that he never existed outside our friend's imagination.' He sighed. 'Things are going badly . . . very badly.'

'Quiet. Here she comes. She is sufficiently unhappy as it is. Until later then . . .'

An hour later, adequately washed and refreshed, Jolival was answering Marianne's questions. He told her that he had left Aix-la-Chapelle the moment he had received the letter which Fortunée Hamelin had pledged herself to deliver. Before the hour was out, he and Adelaide d'Asselnat were posting back to Paris.

'Adelaide came back with you?' Marianne said in surprise. 'Then why isn't she here?'

Then Jolival explained how, hearing of the troubles which had beset her young cousin, that elderly spinster had not hesitated for a moment. 'She needs me,' she had declared generously. 'I will go to her.' It seemed, also, that the fascination with the life of the mountebank which had led her to share for a while the existence of the clown Bobèche, was beginning to wear off. Aside from the somewhat doubtful charms of a career as a street player combined with that of a secret agent, Adelaide had finally come to recognize that a difference in age of more than ten years between herself and the object of her affections was a considerable handicap. It may well have been that a budding romance between Bobèche and a blooming flower-girl in the spa gardens at Aix had something to do with her new-found wisdom.

'Naturally,' Jolival said, 'she has returned a little disappointed, rather disenchanted and inclined to melancholy, but at heart I think she is quite pleased to get back to her own life again . . . and to French cooking. She was very fond of Bobèche but she does dislike sauerkraut! Besides, when you are in trouble, she thinks her place is with you. She is vastly proud of the fact that you are now a princess, by the way, although she would be torn in pieces before she admitted it.'

'But then, why did she not come with you?'

'Because she thinks she will be more useful to you in Paris than coming here to sympathize. Your people know about your exile and it is just as well that someone should be there to mind the house. That is something Mademoiselle Adelaide can do perfectly and everything is running quite smoothly there.'

The two friends talked on far into the night. There was so much they had to tell. Arcadius did not mean to make a long stay at Bourbon. It was his intention to return to Paris the next day and his visit was chiefly to inform Marianne of his return and assure her of his practical help. At the same time, he wanted to hear from her own lips a complete account of all that had happened, so that he could draw his own conclusions.

'I gather then,' he said, settling himself with half-closed eyes to the enjoyment of a glass of the old Armagnac which Talleyrand had sent round in the course of the evening, 'that neither Inspector Pâques nor Savary would listen to you when you tried to put the blame on your – on Lord Cranmere?'

'No. One thought I was mad, the other simply refused to listen.'

'The fact that no trace of his presence has been discovered does rather strengthen their belief. The gentleman would appear remarkably adept at concealing his tracks. All the same, he is still in Paris. Somewhere, there must be someone who has seen him.'

'I've an idea,' Marianne said suddenly. 'Has anyone been to our neighbour, Mrs Atkins? Adelaide was very friendly with her and Francis stayed there. She should be able to tell us at least whether or not he is still there, and if he is not, how long he was in her house.'

'Wonderful!' Jolival exclaimed. 'This is just what I came for. You said nothing about Mrs Atkins in your letter. She once hid your cousin in her house, and Adelaide will easily persuade her to tell everything. Her evidence might be all the more valuable precisely because she is herself English.'

'We do not know yet,' Marianne said soberly, 'if she will agree to give evidence against a fellow countryman.'

'If Mademoiselle Adelaide cannot persuade her, then no one can. In any case, we can only try. Another thing is that Lord Cranmere was briefly at Vincennes, when Nicolas Mallerousse arrested him in the Boulevard du Temple. It may be possible to trace him from the prison records.'

'Do you think so? He escaped so easily. He may never have been entered at all.'

'Not entered? When Nicolas Mallerousse handed him over in person? I'll wager he was. And that entry in the register is incontrovertible proof of the connection between Lord Cranmere and your poor friend. If we can get the register examined, then we have a chance of getting first the police and then the court to listen to us. And if necessary we will go to the Emperor. You have been forbidden to seek an audience, my dear, but I have not! And I shall demand an audience, and he will hear me. And then we shall win!'

As he spoke, Arcadius became more and more carried away by the new hope which had risen in him with these two new suggestions, put forward by Marianne and himself. His little bright eyes sparkled and the funny crumpled face which a moment before had been drawn with worry wrinkled into something approaching a smile. To Marianne, his infectious enthusiasm was like a breath of joy and hope. She hugged him warmly, her whole being quite transformed.

'Arcadius! You are a marvel! I knew that as soon as you were here again I should be able to hope and to fight again! Thanks to you, I know now that all is not lost. We may save him yet!'

'May? What is all this *may*?' retorted Jolival, on whom the effects of the prince's brandy were working to increase his natural enthusiasm. 'You must say that we *shall* save him!'

'Yes, you are right. We shall save him. At all costs,' Marianne echoed, in a tone of such ferocious determination that Arcadius returned her hug, so delighted was he to find her showing a touch of her old spirit.

That night, for the first time since she had left Paris, Marianne went to bed free from the overriding feeling of hopeless impotence which had haunted her every night, growing sharper and more agonizing as darkness fell. She had recovered her confidence, at least, and she knew that even if she were exiled, far from Paris, she could still act through others and do something to help Jason. The thought was a comforting one.

When Jolival set out again for Paris the next morning, with a readiness which did honour both to his horsemanship and to his powers of endurance, he carried with him, besides a letter to Adelaide from Marianne, all his young friend's renewed hopes. He left behind him a woman who had rediscovered the will to live.

To Marianne, the next few days provided a much-needed period of relief. Trusting in Arcadius and Adelaide to do what was necessary, she allowed herself to be seduced by the charms of the little spa and the hours passed leisurely, marked by the clock in the Quinquengrogne Tower. She even found a certain amount of entertainment in watching Talleyrand's household relax in conditions of greater freedom than those it enjoyed in Paris.

All day long, she could hear little Charlotte laughing and singing. The child seemed to be making it her business to rejuvenate her staid preceptor, Monsieur Fercoc, and was succeeding for once in encouraging him in a regime in which expeditions into the surrounding countryside played a much larger part than Latin and mathematics.

Every morning, Marianne derived a good deal of amusement from watching from her window the prince's departure for the baths. Having first bundled himself up in such an incredible assortment of shawls, blankets, flannel waistcoats and woollies of every description that he resembled nothing so much as a huge and hilarious cocoon, he inserted himself, according to local custom, in a sedan chair with the blinds drawn down. None of this prevented him from dressing and behaving perfectly normally once the various stages of the ritual had been performed, nor was there any indication of a special diet when the whole company sat down to dinner (Marianne took all her meals with her friends) to do justice to the marvels which Carême managed to produce – from a kitchen of such modest resources that it threw him into a permanent state of nerves each summer until he was able to return to the splendidly appointed nether regions of Valençay or the Hôtel Matignon.

There was also the deaf brother, Boson, who paid shy court to Marianne in a manner both archaic and almost wholly incomprehensible, since he was unable to understand more than half of what was said to him. However, his advances were somewhat interrupted owing to the fact that he passed the greater part of his time with his head immersed in water in the hope, apparently, of achieving a cure for his deafness.

The afternoons were passed either out driving with the princess or reading with the prince. They went to Souvigny, the St Denis of the dukes of Bourbon, to admire the abbey church and its tombs, driving through the wooded Bourbonnais landscape of hedgerows and tree-shaded meadows dotted with big, white oxen. The warm, perfect weather showed the rich farmland in the full flush of peaceful beauty and even Madame de Talleyrand's aimless chatter seemed to Marianne sane and restful in this interlude from the dark plots which surrounded her.

With Talleyrand, Marianne read, as he had promised, Madame du Deffand's *Letters* which the prince enjoyed very much because they reminded him of 'his youth, his first entry into the world and all the people who mattered at the time'. And in his company Marianne found herself plunged to her surprise and delight into the charming, frivolous eighteenth century which had been the setting for her parents' courtship. Often, too, their reading would end in talk and the prince would find pleasure in reviving for his young friend his own recollections of 'the handsomest and most perfectly matched pair' that he had known, but of whom she, their daughter, knew so little. Through his words, which could be strikingly tender and affectionate, Marianne seemed to see her mother, a golden beauty in a white muslin dress, a tall, be-ribboned cane in her hand, moving about the alleys of the Trianon or seated in an armchair by the fire in her own drawing-room, graciously entertaining the guests who flocked to her house to drink 'English tea' and managing somehow to create an intimate and delightful occasion for as many as fifty people at once. Next, Talleyrand would momentarily bring to life again the idealistic Pierre d'Asselnat, his whole life devoted to his two great loves, the monarchy and his wife. Then it would be the big, military portrait in the rue de Lille which came to life in Marianne's imagination as she listened, dazzled and yet oddly envious.

Oh for a love like that! she thought, hearing her friend talk. To love and be loved like them . . . and then if need be, to die together as they did amid the blood and horror of the scaffold. But before that, a few years . . . a few months even, of irreclaimable happiness!

Oh, how readily she could understand her mother's gesture when, seeing her husband taken, she had proudly claimed her right to follow him to his death, rejecting all thoughts of the child she left behind her, in order to live out her love to the end. She herself had thought many times during the long nights through which she had suffered since that terrible night at Passy that she would not outlive Jason. She had pictured a hundred tragic ends to her own, unhappy story, had seen herself breaking from the crowd and casting herself in front of the guns of the firing squad as the command was given to fire or, if he were not given the right to a soldier's death, stabbing herself to the heart at the foot of the scaffold, supposing he were treated like a common criminal. But now that Jolival had given her fresh hope her whole will was directed towards the achievement, against all odds, of that happiness which still seemed so obstinately to elude her. Let her only live with Jason and then let the whole world perish, only so long as they had drunk the cup of happiness together to the last drop.

And so, all in all, the days passed not unpleasantly, yet with each new morning Marianne felt her fears returning. She took to watching for the post and studying Talleyrand's expression closely to see if, in the news which reached him from Paris, there might not have been some hint about the Beaufort affair.

One morning, Marianne and the prince walked out a little way along the tree-lined road beside the lake near the château. Talleyrand's walks were invariably brief, because of his lame leg, but the weather was so fine, the morning so clear and fresh that both had found the urge to take a turn on foot quite irresistible. The countryside was filled with the scents of hay and wild thyme, the sky was white with doves playing tag around the three grey towers of the château and the calm waters of the lake shimmered with iridescent blue and silver, fit to make a fairy's gown.

The man and girl were strolling peaceably along beside the water's edge, throwing bread to the ducks and laughing at the harassed quacking of a mother-duck in her efforts to control a particularly unruly brood of ducklings, when one of the prince's manservants came hurrying towards them holding something white in his gloved hand.

'Post, eh?' Talleyrand remarked with just the faintest shade of irritation. 'It must be urgent to set them running after us.'

There were two letters, one for Talleyrand, the other for Marianne. The prince raised his eyebrows at his own, which was sealed with the Emperor's arms, but Marianne fell on hers eagerly, recognizing the extravagant curlicues which passed for handwriting with Jolival. She tore open the wafer with Arcadius's martlets arrayed upon it and scanned the few lines within. A despairing cry broke from her. Arcadius wrote to tell her that Mrs Atkins had quitted her house in the rue de Lille 'for the country' but that there was no means of finding out whereabouts in the country she might be. This had happened on the very day Adelaide d'Asselnat had returned home. As for the records of the prison at Vincennes, they contained no reference to any political prisoner by the name of Francis Cranmere – only the traces where a page had been torn out of the book. Whoever they were who had dedicated themselves to the ruin of Jason Beaufort and the disruption of relations between France and America, they appeared to have left nothing to chance.

Marianne's eyes filled with tears as she crumpled Jolival's letter nervously between her fingers. At the same time, she heard her companion saying testily: 'Why does he need me to unveil his confounded column! This means that I shall be obliged to interrupt my treatment. And I have not the least desire to return to Paris, eh?'

But Marianne was conscious only of the last words. 'Return to Paris? You are returning?'

'I must. I have to be there for the Emperor's birthday on the fifteenth of August. This year, to add to the magnificence of the occasion, His Majesty has decided to hold the unveiling of the bronze column he has set up in the Place Vendôme in honour of the Grand Army, made from the metal of twelve hundred and fifty cannon captured at Austerlitz. I am not at all sure it is such a brilliant idea. It can scarcely be very agreeable to the new Empress, seeing that a good half of the cannon in question belonged to Austria. But the Emperor is so delighted with the figure of himself as a Roman emperor which is to surmount the column that I suppose he wants all Europe to have an opportunity of admiring it.'

But Marianne's thoughts were very far from the column in the Place Vendôme, so far indeed as to make her forget even her manners and break in on the prince unceremoniously:

'If you are going back to Paris, take me with you!'

'Take you, eh? What for?'

By way of a reply, Marianne held out Jolival's letter. Talleyrand read it carefully and slowly. By the time he reached the end there was a deep furrow between his brows, but he returned the letter without comment.

'I must go back,' Marianne said again after a moment, in a choking voice. 'I cannot stay here, safe in the sunshine, while Jason is in this dreadful danger. I – I think I should go mad. Let me come with you.'

'You know that you are forbidden to go – or I to take you. Don't you think you will only make matters worse for Beaufort if the Emperor hears that you have disobeyed him?'

'He will not hear. I shall leave my baggage and my servants here with orders to admit no one to my room and to say that I am ill in bed and will see no one at all. It will cause no surprise. I did very much the same before you arrived. The people here probably think I am mad anyway. With Gracchus and Agathe here, I know that no one will enter my room and find out the deception. Meanwhile, I will go back to Paris disguised as – let me see – yes, disguised as a boy. I shall be one of your secretaries.'

'Where will you go to in Paris?' the prince objected, looking not at all relieved. 'Your house is being watched, you know that. If the police were to see you going in you would be arrested on the spot.'

'I thought ...' Marianne began, sounding suddenly rather shy.

'That I would take you in? Yes, well, I thought of it myself for a moment, but it would not do. You are known to everyone in the rue de Varennes and I do not think everyone is to be trusted. There is a likelihood that you would be betrayed and that would not help matters, either for you or for myself. I am not, you will recall, on the best of terms with His Majesty ... even if he has asked me to go and unveil his column!'

'Then it can't be helped. I will go somewhere else – to a hotel perhaps.'

'Where your disguise would be seen through in a moment. No, you are being altogether foolish, my child. But I believe I have a better idea. Go and make what arrangements you need. We are leaving Bourbon this evening. I will see that you have some man's clothes and you can pass as a young secretary of mine until we reach Paris. Once there, I will take you to – but you will see. No need to speak of that now. You are set on this piece of folly?'

'I am,' Marianne said firmly, flushed with joy at a degree of assistance she had scarcely dared to hope for. 'I feel that if I am near him, I shall find some way to help him.'

'He is a lucky man,' the prince said with a faint, rather wistful smile, 'to have such a love. Ah, well, I seem to be fated to refuse you nothing, Marianne! And perhaps after all, it may be best to be within reach. An opportunity may occur, and if it should, you will be there to take advantage of it. For the present, let us go in. Good heavens, child! What are you doing?' The last words were accompanied by a vain attempt to draw back his hand which Marianne had carried gratefully to her lips. 'Haven't I chosen you for my daughter, after all? I am merely trying to prove myself a tolerable father, that is all. Though I can't help wondering what your own father would say to all this!'

Arm in arm, the lame prince and the young girl made their way slowly back to the village, leaving the lake to the company of the ducks.

Eleven o'clock was striking from the Quinquengrogne Tower when Talleyrand's coachman set his team bowling along the road to Paris. As the coach began to move, Marianne looked up to the window of her room and saw, behind the closed shutters, the glimmer of the lamplight showing through, just as it had done every night since her arrival. No one would ever think that it shone on an empty bed, in an empty room. Gracchus and Agathe had received strict orders, although Gracchus, especially, had proved hard to convince. He had been deeply shocked to think that his beloved mistress could consider setting out on such a perilous adventure without his stalwart support. Marianne had been obliged to promise that she would send for him as soon as possible, and certainly at the first hint of danger.

The darkened countryside sped past the windows of the coach and very soon the motion lulled her and she slept, with her head on Talleyrand's shoulder, and dreamed that she was going to fling wide the gates of Jason's prison all by herself with her bare hands.

Part Two

THE PRISONER

CHAPTER SEVEN

The Queen's Lover

The house, when Marianne entered it with Talleyrand, was dark and silent. An expressionless servant in staid, brown livery bearing a branch of candles preceded them up a broad, black marble staircase adorned with a handsome, gilded rail of wrought iron to the first-floor landing off which, in addition to a number of darkened salons, there opened a room like a large bookroom but so filled with furniture, pictures, books and works of art of all kinds that, if he had not come to meet them, Marianne and her companion might have had some difficulty in distinguishing the bald head and heavy, stooping figure of the Englishman, or rather Scotsman, Crawfurd.

'When I lived in this house,' the prince had observed with a rather forced lightness of tone, 'this was my library. Crawfurd has made it a shrine of a somewhat different order . . .'

By the dim light of a few, scattered candles, Marianne saw to her astonishment that all the pictures and other objects, or nearly all, were of the same person. In bronze, in marble and on canvas, everywhere the proud, lovely face of Queen Marie-Antoinette stared down at the newcomers. Even the furnishings had come from the Petit Trianon and nearly everything in the crowded room, fans, snuff-boxes, handkerchiefs, books, bore either the queen's arms or her monogram. On the walls, which were hung with grey silk, were many gilt frames in which the occasional note in her own handwriting alternated with portraits and miniatures.

While Talleyrand shook hands with Crawfurd in the American fashion. Quintin Crawfurd himself was watching with a melancholy smile the obvious astonishment with which

Marianne's eyes took in the room. At last he said, in the gruff voice which still retained some traces of a highland accent: 'From the first day on which it was my privilege to be presented to her, I vowed to devote my life to the service of the martyred queen. I did all that I could to snatch her from the hands of her enemies and restore her to happiness. Now I honour her memory.'

Then, as Marianne was silent, awed by the strange passion which throbbed in the old man's voice, he went on: 'Your own parents died for her, and furthermore your mother was an Englishwoman. My house shall shelter you against all your foes, and any that may try to tear you from it, or harm you in any way, shall not live to boast of it.'

He gestured towards a pair of massive pistols which lay on a table and, on a chair near by, an ancient, heavy claymore whose glittering steel blade spoke of the assiduous care which kept it ready for instant use. Yet in spite of the somewhat theatrical drama of his welcome, Marianne could not help finding Crawfurd rather impressive, and he was undeniably sincere in what he said: he was a man who would kill rather than betray his guest. Somehow, startled as she was, she managed to utter some polite words of thanks, but he cut her short at once:

'Not at all. The blood of your family and the prince's friendship make you doubly welcome here. Come, my wife is waiting to meet you.'

If the truth were known, Marianne's feelings when, as they drew near to Paris, Talleyrand had told her that he planned to ask for the Crawfurds' hospitality on her behalf, had been less than enthusiastic. Her recollection of the odd couple she had glimpsed only once, in the Prince of Benevento's box at the theatre, was strange and rather disturbing. The woman, in particular, had both intrigued and frightened her a little. She knew that before her marriages, first, morganatically, to the Duke of Württemberg, then to the Englishman Sullivan, and then to Crawfurd, she had passed the early years of her life with the Sant'Annas and must therefore be familiar with them. But more than this, she had been conscious of Eleonora Crawfurd's dark gaze resting on her for a long time across the width of the house that night. There was admiration in the look, certainly, and a good deal of curiosity, but there was also something else, a kind of detached irony which did not suggest very friendly feelings. On the strength of this look, she had felt a peculiar reluctance when Talleyrand's coach had turned into the rue d'Anjou-St-Honoré on that evening of the fourteenth of August and drawn up at the door of what had formerly been the Hôtel de Créqui. It was a pretty, eighteenth-century house which, two years earlier, had been the home of Talleyrand himself, while the wealthy Crawfurd had lived, since 1806, in the Hôtel Matignon. The exchange had been made partly as a matter of private convenience, for Matignon was far too big for Crawfurd's household, and partly in obedience to the Emperor's desire to see his Minister for Foreign Affairs installed in a suitably grand establishment, to which, be it said, the minister in question had been by no means averse.

But Talleyrand had retained a certain affection for his old home in the rue d'Anjou and he would not have understood if Marianne had expressed any unwillingness to stay there in the care of people whom he counted among his oldest and most trusted friends. He maintained that Eleonora, who had been his mistress before becoming attached to the unfortunate Count Fersen, was the quintessence of all that was most charming in the previous century, a period which, for him, represented an achievement in the art of living which was now gone for ever. And this despite the fact that she had begun her career as an opera dancer – but then Talleyrand had always had a weakness for dancers.

Meekly, forcing herself to think of nothing but the bed which she was offered and which she longed for with all her heart, Marianne followed her host into a near-by sitting-room where Mrs Crawfurd was seated, a branch of tall pink candles at her side, working at a piece of tapestry. In her dress of black watered silk, its folds catching the light, with a white muslin cap and a scarf of the same material crossed in the old fashion over a breast that was still lovely, and her silver hair dressed high with one or two long, flowing curls stressing the line of her neck, the mistress of the house bore such a startling resemblance to the portrait of the late queen in the Temple that

Marianne paused in the doorway and stared at the apparition as if she had found herself suddenly looking at a ghost.

But the resemblance stopped short at the first impression. The black eyes which looked up, sharp and inquisitive, at the visitor and the red, rather hard curve of the mouth, did not belong to Marie-Antoinette, any more than the figure, which was much shorter and slimmer, or the hands, which were seen to be thin and bony, in spite of the black lace mittens and the splendid diamonds which adorned them.

'So this is our fugitive,' Eleonora Crawfurd said, getting up and coming forward to meet them. 'I am very happy to welcome you, my dear, and I hope you will look on this house as your own. You may come and go as you please in it, for although we have few servants, those few are all people we can trust.'

The voice was a splendid contralto, very deep and warm, retaining some musical echoes of its native Tuscany, and extremely attractive. Eleonora knew how to use it, too, like a real artist.

'You are very kind, Madame,' Marianne said, wondering vaguely if she ought to bow and compromising with a smile and a little bob of her head. In her boy's clothes, a curtsy would have been ridiculous and she did not place much confidence in her ability to make a leg with credit. 'I am only sorry to impose upon you in this way, and perhaps put you at some risk—'

'Tut! Who talks of risks in this house? Quintin and I have run risks all our lives and this, supposing it to be one, is very small by comparison. Besides, I trust your troubles will not be of long duration and that you will soon be able to return to your own house. You were only to spend the summer months – er – taking the waters, were you not? You will be home again in the autumn. Until then, you must feel quite at home here, and to start with, you and our dear prince must take a little supper. You must be in need of it. Afterwards, I will show you your room.'

Supper, at that late hour, was brought to the sitting-room and consisted of some magnificent peaches and some light creams and pastries, as well as a superb Brie of which Talleyrand was known to be particularly fond, washed down with an unusually fine old burgundy.

Conversation soon languished, however, owing to the manifest weariness of the guests. It revived only slightly when Crawfurd remarked, as though announcing a fact of no great importance: 'It appears that Champagny has sent a note to ambassador Armstrong.'

Talleyrand raised one eyebrow, while Marianne roused abruptly from her sleepy doze at the mere mention of the American diplomat's name.

A note eh?' the prince said. 'And what does it say?'

'How should I know? All I can tell you is that there was a note from the Ministry of Foreign Affairs – and that the ambassador's expression has been a trifle less harassed ever since the – the fifth of August, I think it was, when the note arrived.'

'Less harassed? What do you think, Crawfurd? Does it mean the Emperor has decided to treat the Beaufort business leniently? It would be quite easy, of course, simply to let him go ...'

'Don't you believe it. The matter is past hushing up now. The seaman, Perez, who, quite between ourselves, seems singularly well-informed as regards political affairs for an ignorant seaman, declares that Beaufort intended to put in at Portsmouth to unload some of his cargo of champagne and is demanding a third of the value as a reward for his evidence, by virtue of the Milan decree. Which reminds me, it's a curious thing how, although the affair was to be kept a deadly secret, every interested department seems to have got wind of it. I wonder what the Emperor thinks ...'

'That,' Talleyrand said energetically, rising to his feet and striking the table with the flat of his hand, 'is what we have to find out. The whole business seems to have got thoroughly out of hand, and we are hearing a great deal too much about this seaman, Perez. Don't be alarmed, Marianne,' he added, seeing her pale face and widening eyes suddenly bright with tears, 'I will try to see the Emperor, and if I fail there I will write to him. It is time a few honest voices made themselves heard. But go and get some sleep now, my child. You can scarcely keep your eyes open. Your hostess will take good care of you and I will tell your friends where you are first thing in the morning.'

This was true. Marianne was wholly exhausted. While the Prince of Benevento sought his coach for the remainder of his journey to the Hôtel Matignon, she suffered herself to be led meekly away by Eleonora Crawfurd to a pretty bedchamber hung with rose-coloured chintz on the second floor of the house. The room had two windows which looked out on to a quiet garden not unlike Marianne's own.

Mrs Crawfurd turned down the bed with deft hands and then turned to light the lamp under a *tisanière* which stood on the table by the bed.

'A little camomile will do you good,' she said. 'It is a sovereign remedy for the nerves. Shall I help you to undress?'

Marianne shook her head with a tired smile of thanks. She was impatient, now, to be left alone but her hostess seemed in no hurry to depart. She was walking about the room, altering the position of a flower in a vase, checking that the curtains ran smoothly in their rings, shifting a chair slightly, as if she were trying to prolong their *tête à tête* indefinitely. Marianne, her nerves on edge, was on the point of committing the ultimate rudeness of asking point-blank to be left alone when Mrs Crawfurd turned suddenly and regarded her guest with an expression half perplexed and half compassionate.

'You poor, poor child,' she said in a tone whose sympathy did not, to Marianne's ears, ring altogether true. 'I had so hoped that you, at least, might have found happiness!'

'Why me at least?'

'Because you are so sweet and fresh and lovely, so – oh, I swear to God that when I heard of your marriage I prayed, I prayed with all my heart that the curse which seems to haunt the princesses of Sant'Anna might spare you!'

'Th-the curse?' Marianne gasped with difficulty, for even in her present state of anxiety the idea of a curse seemed to be going rather too far. 'What curse? If you mean Donna Lucinda—'

'Oh, your unfortunate husband's grandmother was no more

than – than an instance of the dreadful state of affairs which goes back to the fourteenth century. Ever since a Sant'Anna brutally murdered his wife in revenge for adultery all the women of the family – or nearly all, have died violent deaths. It takes courage, or a great love, to marry any of that illustrious name – but you did not know this?'

'No. I did not know,' Marianne said, wide awake now and wondering very much what her hostess could be at. It seemed to her extremely odd that the Cardinal de Chazay should have kept such a tragic legend as this from her, unless, with his fanatical hatred of all superstition, he had simply dismissed it as a horrible, childish tale.

Deciding that this last theory was probably correct, Marianne added: 'But it would have made no difference had I known. I believe in ghosts – but not in curses which attach themselves to innocent people. Besides,' she went on, ruthlessly editing the truth, 'I did not even meet a ghost at the Villa dei Cavalli!' This whole conversation, coming out of the blue at a time when all she wanted was to go to sleep, struck her as fantastic, and that seemed as good a way as any of putting an end to it. But Mrs Crawfurd was not a woman to be easily put off, although it was not easy to see what her object might be in introducing the subject of the Sant'Annas.

'No ghosts?' she said now, with a sceptical smile. 'I am surprised! Even if it were only—'

'Only who?'

'Oh, no one,' Eleonora said suddenly. She came to Marianne and kissed her lightly on the forehead. 'We will talk about all this another time. For the moment, you are asleep on your feet.'

'No, no!' Marianne protested, quite sincerely now, for she was dying to hear more. 'I can sleep later. Tell me—'

'Nothing at all, child. It is a long story and – well, I too am sleepy. It would be a mistake to begin. But don't tell me that you did not know that when your husband, Prince Corrado, was born his father, Don Ugolino, killed his mother . . .'

With that, Eleonora left the room, as softly as one of the ghosts in which she, too, appeared to believe and closed the door behind her, leaving Marianne wide awake and thoroughly confused. She understood this woman less and less. Why had she introduced the subject if she did not wish to explain fully? If it had been to distract Marianne's thoughts from their constant, agonized preoccupation with Jason's fate, she had only partly succeeded because there was no story, however exciting, which could have distracted her from her fears for the man she loved. But if she had meant to give her a sense of uneasiness and insecurity, then she had achieved her object to perfection. How could she help thinking that this curse which had attached itself to the women of her name might extend to those she loved? And what connection was there between the murder of Corrado's mother, Donna Adriana, and the prince's own tragic destiny?

Unable to sleep, she lay turning the problem over and over in her overexcited brain, looking at it from every direction yet without reaching any satisfactory conclusion. The murder seemed to give substance to the theory that Corrado was a monster, yet when she recalled the lithe, powerful figure of the nocturnal horseman the idea became unthinkable. Then was it the face, perhaps, which was repulsive? But a man did not kill his wife on account of a face, however hideous. He might kill in anger – or brutality – or for jealousy. Suppose the child Corrado had borne some striking likeness to another man? But Marianne did not on the whole place much faith in striking resemblances applied to new-born babies. With the exercise of a little imagination, a baby could be made to look like almost anybody. And besides, in that case, why the sequestered existence, why the mask? To preserve for ever from the least breath of scandal the memory of a mother whom the prince had never known and whose memory he could therefore hardly be expected to cherish? No, it was quite impossible . . .

When it began to get light, at about four o'clock, Marianne, seated in a chair by the open window, had still not closed her eyes, nor had she found any answer to her questions. Her head ached and she was deadly tired. Dragging herself up, she leaned out. All was very quiet. Only the first birds were beginning to sing and tiny forms flitted from branch to branch, without stirring a leaf. The sky was pink and orange with streaks of coral and gold which told that the sun would soon be up. Out in the street, the metal-shod wheels of a cart clanked over the cobblestones and a charcoal-vendor's cry echoed nostalgically. Then, from across the Seine, came the sound of a cannon being fired and at that precise moment up came the sun into a sky filled with belfries chiming the first notes of the Angelus.

This glorious din, which was to last all morning, announced to the good people of Paris that on that day their Emperor was forty-one years old and that today was a holiday and everyone should behave accordingly.

But there was no holiday for Marianne and so as to be sure of hearing nothing of the general celebrations which would gradually take possession of the capital, she carefully closed and shuttered the windows, drew the curtains and, utterly exhausted, flung herself at last fully dressed on her bed and fell instantly asleep.

Marianne's meeting with Arcadius on the evening of the fifteenth of August, while all over Paris people were drinking in the streets and squares and dancing under the street lamps to Napoleon's good health, was almost tragic. His face drawn from the fatigue of several sleepless nights spent haunting every locality where he hoped to find some trace of Lord Cranmere, Jolival reproached Marianne with a good deal of bitterness for what he called her lack of confidence in him:

'Why did you have to come back? What do you hope to do? Bury yourself in this house along with an old fool surrounded by memories of his dead queen and that scheming old woman, still mourning for her murdered lover and her own vanished youth? What are you afraid of? That I won't do all that is humanly possible? Well, don't worry. I am doing it. I'm searching – desperately. I'm searching for news of Mrs Atkins. I spend my nights roaming about Chaillot and the Boulevard du Temple, haunting the Homme Armé and the Epi-Scié. I spend hours in disguise, in the hope of catching a glimpse of one of Fanchon's men, or of Fanchon herself. But I am wasting my time . . . Do you think I need anything more to worry about – such as knowing that you are here, in hiding, at the mercy of anyone who might denounce you?'

Marianne waited until the storm had blown over. She understood her friend's weariness and discouragement too well to blame him for his outburst, which was prompted purely by his affection for her. To placate him, she was meek, almost humble.

'Please don't be cross with me, Arcadius. I could not stay there, living quietly in the country, while you were working yourself to death here, and while Jason was – was—'

'In prison,' Jolival finished for her tartly. 'A political prisoner. It's not the hulks, you know! And I know he is being treated well.'

'I know. I know all that . . . or suppose so, but I was going mad! And when the prince told me he had to come back to Paris, I couldn't stand it. I begged him to take me with him.'

'He should not have done so. But women can always get round him. Well, what are you going to do now? Spend your days listening to Crawfurd extolling the virtues of Marie-Antoinette, telling you in detail all about the Affair of the Necklace or the horrors of the Temple and the Conciergerie? Unless you prefer to hear his wife's life story?'

'I shall certainly listen to anything that she may be able to tell me, because she was born at Lucca and seems to know the history of the Sant'Annas better than anyone; but my real reason for coming back, Arcadius dear, is so that I shall be able to hear any news there is as soon as it is known, and be able to decide what to do . . . Monsieur de Talleyrand says that things are going very badly and he will tell you—'

'I know. I have just seen him. He told me he was going to seek an audience with the Emperor to try and throw some light on this dreadful business. But I am afraid he won't find it easy to get a hearing. His position is not very encouraging just at present.'

'Why not? He is no longer a minister but he is still Vice-Grand Elector?'

'A grandiose title which is quite meaningless in practical

terms. No, what I meant was that Napoleon has heard rumours of his financial troubles and, what is worse, of the reason for them. Our prince was involved to some extent in the Anglo-French negotiations got up by Fouché, Ouvrard, Labouchère and Wellesley. Then there was the failure of Simons Bank – Simons's wife, who used to be a Demoiselle Lange, is an old friend of his – he lost a million and a half there. Above all, there is the four million he was paid by the city of Hamburg to save it from annexation. If Napoleon carries out his intention and annexes it just the same, then Talleyrand will have to pay back the money. At that rate, I don't see him being in high favour at court . . .'

'Then it's all the more noble of him to try. Besides, if he needs money, I can give it to him.'

'Do you think you have that much? I did not mean to speak of it because I did not want to add to your worries, but this letter came from Lucca five days ago. It came without the quarter's allowance which should normally have been due. You'll forgive me for having read it.'

Foreseeing fresh trouble, Marianne took the letter somewhat reluctantly. She was blaming herself for not having written to the prince herself to tell him of the accident which had resulted in her losing the child. She was afraid of her invisible husband's reaction yet without being very certain what that reaction might be. Something told her now that that was precisely what this letter contained.

In fact, in a brief missive of chilling politeness, Prince Corrado informed Marianne that he had heard of the loss of their mutual hopes, made perfunctory inquiries as to her own health and added that he was in expectation of a visit to Italy on her part in the near future 'so that we may consider the new situation created by this unfortunate occurrence and what steps should be taken . . .'

'A lawyer's letter!' Marianne exploded, screwing the paper into a ball and hurling it into a corner. 'Consider the situation? Take steps? What does he want to do? Divorce me? I am perfectly willing!'

'Italians do not believe in divorce, Marianne,' Arcadius said sternly, 'and least of all a Sant'Anna! Besides, I should have thought you had had enough of changing husbands every five minutes. Now stop this stupid behaviour!'

'What do you want me to do? Go off there while— No! A hundred times no! Not at any price!'

The explosion of anger which shook her was in reality a cover for her tumultuous thoughts, but for the moment she hated him with all her might, this distant stranger whom she had married in the belief that, in spite of all, she would still keep complete freedom of action, yet who now dared, even from a distance, to dictate to her as lord and master and make her feel the curb. Go back to Lucca! To that house full of hidden dangers where a madman worshipped a statue and offered up human sacrifices to it, where another rode out only at night, wearing a mask? Not now, at all events. If she were to do what she had to do here, Marianne had to be free – free! On the other hand, this act of cutting off her supplies was ominous and more than a little awkward. This was not the moment for anything like that, either, when she might need to bribe people, buy men and weapons ... an army, even, to snatch Jason from the unjust condemnation ahead of him. Moreover this letter, the first she had received from Prince Sant'Anna, represented another source of danger. What if it had been opened, by any chance, by the Emperor's Cabinet Noir? A knowledge of its contents might easily give him the idea of removing Marianne definitively from the Beaufort affair by sending her back to her own distant estates. What could she do about it ... Then something else about the letter struck her as alarming. What were these 'steps' the prince considered taking? Did he think he could compel her to return to Napoleon so that, at all costs, he might have the child he wanted? Logically, that was the only solution, since the prince could not divorce her. If he had any idea of attending to the matter himself, he would surely have done so long ago? Then what? Why this letter, this thinly disguised command to return to Lucca? What for?

A fearful thought occurred to Marianne. Perhaps Prince Corrado meant to subject her to the fate which, according to Eleonora Crawfurd, was common to all Princesses of Sant'Anna? A violent death that would revenge him for what he might, not unreasonably, consider a fool's bargain. Was he summoning her to execution – in the tradition of his family?

Putting her thoughts into words, she said tonelessly: 'I don't want to go back there . . . because I am afraid of them all.'

'No one is asking you to. Not at present, at least. I have already written to say that your health is still delicate after your recent accident and that you have retired, at the Emperor's command, to Bourbon, where the waters are beneficial not merely for rheumatic complaints, but also for female disorders. We can only hope, now that you have seen fit to come back, that no one will be sent to make sure that is where you are. But that is beside the point. I merely wished to make it plain to you that you have no money to throw about rashly and that while you are very far from beggary, you must begin to be a little careful and not spend what you have thoughtlessly. That being done, my dear, I will say goodbye to you.'

'Goodbye?' Marianne cried in alarm. 'You are not – not leaving me?'

It could not be true? Her dear old Arcadius could not be so angry with her as to leave her? Surely he could not blame her so much? Her face went so white that Jolival, seeing the tears that gathered in her big green eyes, could not help smiling. Bending, he took her hand gently in his and dropped an affectionate kiss upon it:

'Where is your common sense, Marianne? I am leaving you – but for a few days only, and on your own business. It has occurred to me that, if he will put himself to so much trouble, Citizen Fouché might do a good deal towards clearing the minds of his former colleagues at the Quai Malaquais, always supposing that the Emperor is willing to let him. I dare not trust a letter to the post, so I am going myself.'

'Going where?'

'To Aix-en-Provence where our friend the Duke of Otranto is wearing out his exile. And I am not without hopes, because quite apart from any kindness he has for you he will be delighted to put a rub in Savary's way. So be a good girl and wait for me nicely – and above all, don't do anything foolish!'

'Foolish? Here? I don't see anything I could do.'

'That depends,' Arcadius said and grinned. 'You might try forcing your way in to see the Emperor, for example.'

Marianne shook her head, saying seriously, as she slipped her arm through his to go with him to the door: 'No, that is one piece of folly I can promise you I will not commit – or not just at present. And in return for that, you must promise me to be quick – very quick! I will be very brave, and very patient, because I know you will bring back the evidence we need. I will be good and wait.'

But waiting was harder than even Marianne had foreseen. Almost before Jolival had left Paris, while the sky was still alight with the many-coloured showers of sparks from innumerable firework displays, the old, stealthy fears returned, insidiously, to take possession of her mind, as if only her friend's presence had the power to exorcize the demons and dispel the evil miasma. It grew worse as time went on.

Shut up in the Crawfurds' house with no other distractions than the detailed inspection of her host's collection of paintings, which was certainly very fine, and walks in the garden where she paced up and down wretchedly for hours on end like a prisoner, Marianne found her hopes melting away, little by little, dissolving like smoke in the chill wind of bad news.

First, she learned that the Emperor had refused to see the Vice-Grand Elector, as indeed it had been feared, and that there was nothing to be done but await the outcome of the very diplomatic letter which had followed the rejection of this request. Next, it became known that Jason Beaufort's trial would open on the first of October before the Assize Court in Paris, and the fact that a date should already have been fixed looked ominous indeed.

'Apparently,' the Prince of Benevento observed, 'the judges are anxious to get the matter out of the way before the new Penal Code which was passed on the twelfth of February this year comes into force next January.'

'What you mean is that the trial will be hurried through and Jason is condemned already?'

Talleyrand shrugged. 'Perhaps not ... but, as the English would say, their lordships are certainly a great deal more at home with the old Code. It is always troublesome accustoming oneself to new procedures.'

In these circumstances, it was understandable that Marianne should have begun to sink under the burden of her own gloomy thoughts, especially when the only relief from these thoughts was the conversation of two elderly persons living exclusively in the past. For them, in fact, as Jolival had foreseen, she had become the ideal listener, since her own life was as fraught with drama as theirs had been.

However, if she felt little interest in the doings of Marie-Antoinette, except in so far as they were concerned with that terrible period in which her own father and mother had met their deaths for the queen, Marianne was very willing to listen to Eleonora's tales, which dealt exclusively with Lucca and the strange family into which her own fate had introduced her.

Oddly for a woman whose Italian blood had gifted her with a highly talkative nature, Eleonora maintained a total silence on the subject of her own private life, and especially about the one man who, more than any other, had been the great love of her life, that Count Fersen in whom so many women besides the queen had seen the living image of their dreams. The only sign of emotion which Mrs Crawfurd permitted herself was a small frown and a slight tightening of the muscles round her mouth when her husband, in the course of one of his interminable monologues, evoked the elegant figure of the Swedish count who had died so tragically two months earlier. But on the subject of the Sant'Annas, Eleonora waxed tirelessly eloquent, and so vivid were her powers of description that Marianne, sitting curled up for hours at a time in a deep armchair beside the tapestry frame over which the older woman's hands had fallen still, seemed to see the people of whom she talked conjured up, one by one, by her voice in the shadowy room.

In this way, Marianne learned that Eleonora had been born actually on the Sant'Anna estates. Her father had been the prince's head groom and her mother the princess's personal maid, an office she shared with the mother of Donna Lavinia, the present housekeeper, who was some years older than herself and with whom Marianne was already well acquainted. It was not difficult for her now to recall the sweet, lovely face, with the grey hair and the deep sadness of expression which seemed to carry in it all the latent melancholy of the domain. It did not seem that Lavinia had altered over the years: she had always been quiet, reserved and inclined to melancholy.

Eleonora and Lavinia had, naturally, been childhood friends. It was otherwise with the man whom Marianne had known as the agent, Matteo Damiani, the unnerving worshipper of statues who had tried to kill her once, one dreadful night when she had discovered his secret. Eleonora had been ten when Matteo was born but, maturing young like all southern girls, she had known immediately that the perilous Sant'Anna blood ran in the veins of the new-born baby brought to the villa one winter's night in the folds of her mother's cloak.

'He was the son of your husband's grandfather, Prince Sebastiano, and a poor girl from Bagni di Lucca called Fiorella who no sooner brought the child into the world than she drowned herself in the Serchio. Fiorella was pretty but slightly simple, yet she had seemed happy enough and no one could think what had made her do it – unless it was not entirely her own doing . . .'

'You mean – someone pushed her?'

Mrs Crawfurd made a vague gesture. 'Who can say? Don Sebastiano was a terrible man – and I imagine you must have heard something of his wife, the notorious Lucinda, the Venetian, the witch whose malignant shade still hangs over the house . . .'

The quiet voice had changed suddenly and become filled with such horror and revulsion that for a moment Marianne seemed to see the credulous and superstitious peasant girl she had once been. But she herself could not repress a shudder as she recalled the temple and the sensuous figure which reigned over the ruins. Instinctively dropping her voice, she asked with an eager curiosity unmixed with fear: 'You know her – Lucinda?'

Mrs Crawfurd nodded and closed her eyes briefly, as if the better to remember.

'In fact, she is the only other Princess Sant'Anna I have known. As for forgetting her – I think if I were to live out many lives I could still not wipe her from my memory. You can have no idea what she was like. I myself have never seen such beauty as hers – so strange and yet so perfect – so demoniacally perfect! God knows you are beautiful, my dear, but next to her you would have ceased to exist. When she was there, one saw only her. Venus herself would have looked like a peasant girl beside such splendour.'

'Did you like her?' Marianne breathed, too eaten up with the desire to know to feel the slightest pique at the slighting way in which Eleonora had spoken of her own appearance. The answer came like a cannon shot:

'I hated her! God, how I hated her! And even after so many years I think I hate her still. It was because of her that when I was fifteen I fled from my parents' home with a Neapolitan dancer who, with his company, was performing at the villa. But when I was a little girl, I used to hide behind the bushes in the park to watch her pass by, dressed always in dazzling white, always covered in pearls or diamonds and always followed by her slave, Hassan, carrying her scarf, her parasol or the bag with the bread she used to feed the white peacocks in the park . . .'

'She had a slave?'

'Yes, a gigantic Guinean Don Sebastiano had brought back from Accra on the Slave Coast. Lucinda made him her bodyguard, her dog and, I learned, afterwards, her executioner.'

At this point, Mrs Crawfurd's voice seemed to flicker, like a lamp in need of oil. She felt in the reticule of black silk which hung always by her chair and, taking a pastille from a silver comfit box, sat sucking it with eyes half-closed while Marianne held her breath for fear of disturbing her contemplation. In a moment or two, the older woman resumed more strongly:

'In those days, I did think that I loved her. She dazzled me. But afterwards—'

'What was she like?' The question had been hovering on Marianne's lips for several minutes. 'I have only seen her statue—'

'Ah, that famous statue! Does it still exist? Well, it was certainly very like her as to face and form, but the colours, the subtle shades of life, it gave no idea of those . . . If I told you that Lucinda had red hair, I should be giving you a wrong idea. Her hair was like a flame, like liquid gold, her great eyes were black velvet and glowing coals and her skin ivory and rose petals. Her mouth was like an open wound filled with pearls. No, there was never anyone like her. Nor was there anyone so cruel and depraved. Anything, human or animal, that crossed her was in danger. I have seen her slaughter the finest mare in the stables in cold blood, merely because she fell from her saddle, I have seen her order Hassan to beat an ironing maid until she bled, merely for scorching one of her laces. My mother never went near her without fingering her beads in her apron pocket. Even her husband, Prince Sebastiano, was forced to fly from her to find rest and peace of mind, and he was thirty years older than she and had loved her and still loved her passionately. That was why he used to spend three parts of the year on his travels, far away from Lucca.'

'And yet,' Marianne said, 'there was one child, at least?'

'Yes, and she was prepared for that because she accepted that there must be an heir. But when she found herself with child, her temper grew so ungovernable that her husband went away again, leaving her sole mistress of the estates. And for seven months no one set eyes on her.'

'No one? But – why?'

'Because she could not bear to let anyone see her in less than her usual beauty. All those months she spent shut up in her own apartments, never going out, never letting anyone in except my mother, Anna Franchi, and Maria, Lavinia's mother, who were her waiting women. And she scarcely spoke even to them. I can still remember hearing my mother tell my father, in a whisper, that when darkness came Donna Lucinda ordered all the candles to be lit and made sure all the doors and windows were fast shut, and no one knew what was the reason for this nocturnal illumination, which lasted until the candles guttered out.

'One night, my curiosity got the better of me. I was ten years old and as quick and agile as a cat. I got out of my bedroom window when my parents were asleep and ran in my bare feet all the way to the house. The climbing plants on the walls made it easy for me to climb up to Donna Lucinda's balcony. My heart was thumping in my chest, for I was convinced that if I were caught my father and mother would never see me again alive. But I wanted to find out – and I did.'

'What was she doing?'

'Nothing. I peeped through a crack in the curtains and I saw her. She had the candlesticks placed in a circle on the floor and she was standing in the centre, facing the statue you have seen and stark naked also. The two figures must have been reflected over and over again to infinity in the mirrors, the white and the flesh pink, and Lucinda stood there for hours, comparing herself with her own marble image, searching for the slightest alterations and deformities brought about by her condition, with her hair all tumbled and the tears streaming down her cheeks . . . Believe me, there was something so hauntingly dreadful in the sight that I never went there again. Besides, when it came to the final weeks there was no more light of any kind. By her orders the mirrors were all veiled and the princess's rooms remained in darkness, day and night.'

Marianne, wide-eyed, had listened breathlessly to her hostess's strange tale.

'She must have been mad, surely?' she said at last.

'Mad, yes, about herself, without a doubt. But apart from that, apart from her insensate worship of her own beauty, she behaved more or less normally. The birth of her son, Ugolino, was the occasion for endless celebration. The servants and the local peasants were almost swimming in gold and wine. Donna Lucinda was quite obviously radiant – as much on account of recovering her old beauty as of having gained an heir! For a little while, we all thought that a new era of happiness had begun for the house. But then – three months later, Prince Sebastiano set out again for some distant land and met his death there. The building of the little temple was begun almost immediately after he went away. It was a little more than a year after Matteo Damiani had been brought to the villa.'

'Donna Lucinda did not mind his presence?'

'No, she simply tolerated it. But then, when her own child was born, she began to neglect it almost entirely and showed a curious preference for the little love-child. She would play with him like a puppy, she took an interest in the way he was treated, how he was dressed, but most of all, she seemed to take a kind of perverted pleasure in bringing out all the most savage instincts in the child. She would alternately tease him and caress him, always encouraging him to be cruel and bloodthirsty. Not that that was very difficult. The foundations were already there. By the time he was five years old, when I left the villa, Matteo was already a little devil, I can tell you, a mixture of brutality and cunning. And from what I have been able to discover since, his character has only grown in those respects. Now, if you please, child, be so good as to ring for tea. I am as dry as a bone and if you want me to talk anymore . . .'

'Oh please. You told me just now that Donna Lucinda was the cause of your going away—'

'It is not a story I care to recall, but you stand now in her place. You have a right to know. But – tea first, if you please.'

In a few moments a tray of china tea had been brought in by a soft-footed servant and the two women drank it in pleasurable silence. To Marianne, the fragrant brew, drunk in that comfortable, elegantly appointed sitting-room, brought with it a faint scent of time past. She saw herself as a little girl, and then as a young woman, seated on a stool by her Aunt Ellis's chair sharing in the daily ritual which Lady Selton would not have neglected for anything in the world. Now the old woman in her old-fashioned cap, the furnishings from a previous age, even the scent of roses floating in through the open window, all reminded Marianne of the happy days of her childhood and for the first time for very many days she was conscious of a sense of relaxation and well-being such as she used to feel when, at the height of some childish outburst of grief or rage, her Aunt Ellis had come and stroked her hair and said in her gruff voice: 'Come now, Marianne! You should know that there is nothing in this world that cannot be got over with courage and perseverance . . . oneself most of all.'

It had always worked wonders and it was both strange and comforting to find the same feeling now in a cup of tea in a strange house. Marianne replaced her flowered teacup on the silver tray and found that Mrs Crawfurd was watching her.

'Why do you smile, my dear? I fear the things I have been telling you were sad enough.'

'It was not that, Madame, It was just that, drinking tea like this, with you, I felt as if I were back again as a child in England. But go on, if you please.'

For a moment, the old woman's eyes lingered on her face and Marianne thought that she read in them a softness and sympathy which she had not seen before. But Eleonora Crawfurd said nothing and, turning her head to look out of the window, offered Marianne only the view of a profile half-hidden by the frill of her muslin cap. She resumed her story after a moment but in a voice so low that Marianne was scarcely able to catch the opening words:

'It is strange how the memory of one's first love can remain alive – and painful, in spite of all the years that have passed. It is something you will learn when you are old. When I think of Pietro, I feel as if it were yesterday I was running to meet him by the chapel of San Cristoforo, running through the purple twilight full of the smell of new-mown hay . . . I was fifteen and I loved him. He was seventeen. He was strong and handsome, and he lived in the village of Capanori, alone since the death of his father, who was a tinsmith . . . He wanted to marry me and we used to meet every night . . . until one night he did not come. One night . . . two nights . . . and no one in the village could tell me where he had gone, but all of a sudden I was afraid, although I did not know why – perhaps because he had never had any secrets from me. On the third night I could not sleep. I went out and wandered about the park, just for something to do. It was as hot as an oven, that night. Even the water in the fountains was warm and in the stables the horses were not even stirring . . . It was then, as I passed by the grotto, that I heard singing – if it could be called singing. It was more like a monotonous wailing, in time to a soft, rhythmic beating on a drum, with now and then a kind of cry. I had never heard anything like it before, but to have dared to walk so close to the house, and especially to the grotto, which was out of bounds to servants, I must have been in an unusual state of mind. Even now, I do not know what instinct made me follow the forbidden path to the clearing with the little temple. But go I did, feeling my way, stealthily, holding on to the rock and flattening myself against it as if I meant to make myself part of it. When the light from the temple fell on my face I drew back, instinctively, then, very carefully, I put my head out again – and then I saw!'

Silence fell once again. Marianne sat rigid, scarcely daring to breathe for fear of breaking the spell through which Eleonora's voice had seemed to come. She recalled too well her own terror when she had discovered the ruins, and Matteo Damiani there, embracing the statue. But she guessed that the ordeal which this woman had endured had been far worse than her own and her voice was very gentle as she breathed: 'You saw . . .'

'Hassan first of all. He was the singer. He was crouched on the marble steps with a sort of small drum, like a gourd, between his knees and he was drumming on it with his big black hands to accompany his chanting. He was gazing up at the stars as though lost in some mindless dream, but the torches burning inside the temple made his black skin gleam like bronze and glistened on the gilded loincloth and barbaric jewels he was wearing. His back was to the temple and I could see through the pillars to a great, gilded bed, all hung with black velvet. And on that bed two people were making love . . . The woman was Lucinda . . . and the man was Pietro – my Pietro. I still wonder why I did not drop dead where I stood, how I found the strength to escape. But I do know that was the last time I saw Pietro alive. The next day, they found his body hanging from a tree on the hillside. And three days later, I left with the players.'

This time, it was a long moment before Marianne uttered a word. She knew the place so well, the place whose name she bore, that she almost felt, listening to this terrible story, that she had experienced it herself, or at least been there to see. It did not surprise her when she saw the other woman brush away a tear, furtively, with the tip of one finger. Only when she thought that her companion was a little recovered, did she busy herself again with the tea-tray, and as she handed Eleonora her cup, asked: 'You never went back?'

'Yes, once, in 1784, when my mother was dying. She had never left the estate, but she had long ago forgiven me for my flight. I think, at heart, she was glad that I had got away from that dreadful house, where she had seen so much that was tragic. It was she who brought up Prince Ugolino, and she was there at the time of the fire which burned down the temple and in which Lucinda met her own, terrible, though self-inflicted, end. Yet she had hoped, then, that the future would be better once the familiar demon of the house had gone. And for a time, it seemed as if she were right. A year after Lucinda's death, her son Ugolino married a charming girl, Adriana Malaspina. He was nineteen and she sixteen and it was a long time since anyone in those parts had seen a more perfectly matched pair, or one more in love. For the sake of Adriana, whom he adored, Ugolino mastered his naturally violent and difficult nature. As ill luck would have it, he took very much after his mother but, wolf though he was, he made himself a lamb for his young bride. It seemed to my mother that the evil days were indeed gone for ever . . .

'When, after a little more than a year of marriage, Adriana found herself with child, Ugolino surrounded her with all imaginable attentions, guarding her day and night, even going so far as to have the horses' hooves muffled in case they should disturb her rest. Then the child was born—and the evil returned. When my mother was dying, she wanted to unburden her heart a little and, before sending for the priest, before she received the last sacrament, she told me of the twofold tragedy of that spring of 1782.'

'A twofold tragedy?'

'Yes. Only two women were with Donna Adriana when Prince Corrado was born: my mother and Lavinia. But,' she added, seeing the sudden light in Marianne's eyes, 'do not imagine that my mother revealed to me the secret of his birth. That secret was not hers to tell and she had sworn on the cross never to reveal it, not even under the seal of confession. What she did tell me was that, on the night after the birth, Ugolino strangled his wife. He could not touch the child, however, for Lavinia, fearing for its life, had carried it away and hidden it. Two days after this, Don Ugolino was found lying in one of the stalls in the stables with his skull smashed in. His death was naturally accounted an accident but, in fact, it was murder.'

'Who killed him?'

'Matteo. Ever since her marriage to Ugolino, Matteo had been passionately in love with Adriana. He lived for her and he killed his master to avenge the woman he loved. From that day onwards, he cared for the child with jealous fondness, he and Lavinia.'

The thought crossed Marianne's mind that perhaps, in spite of what Eleonora had said about her love for her husband, Donna Adriana might have returned Matteo's passion? What if the child were his and it was his resemblance which had unleashed her husband's fury? But then, if that were so, why had he not killed Matteo first?

She had no time to ask her final question. The door of the room opened to admit Quintin Crawfurd. Talleyrand was with him and at once the tragic shades of Sant' Anna fell back before the cares of the present. It was true that the Scotsman's appearance, supported on two sticks with his gouty foot swathed in a mountain of bandages, was funny rather than anything else, but the Prince of Benevento's grim expression was enough to dispel any tendency to laughter. It seemed that once again the news was bad.

With a bow to the two women, Talleyrand silently held out an open letter on which, ominously, the scrawled signature of Napoleon was clearly to be seen. Marianne took it.

'Sir,' the Emperor had written, 'I have received your letter which I read with some displeasure. While you were my Foreign Minister I was prepared to overlook many things. It grieves me, therefore, that you should raise matters which it has been my wish to forget.'

* * *

The letter was dated from St Cloud, 29 August 1810. Marianne returned it to Talleyrand without a word.

'You see,' he said bitterly, refolding the sheet. 'I am in such bad odour at court that I am now suspected of attempting to defend one of my foreign friends! I am deeply distressed, Marianne, most deeply and sincerely distressed.'

'He wants to forget!' Marianne said through clenched teeth. 'I dare say he would like to forget me also! But he shall not get away with it so easily. I will not let him destroy Jason. I will see him, whether he likes it or not, I'll force my way in, even if they do put me in prison afterwards! But I swear by my mother's honour that the Emperor will hear me! And before very long—'

She was already half out of the room when Talleyrand stopped her. 'No, Marianne. Not now, at this moment. If I am any judge of the Emperor's mind, you would be as good as condemning Beaufort on the spot!'

'Would you rather I waited – sat here calmly drinking tea, until they kill him?'

'I would rather you waited at least until he has been tried. It will be time enough to act after the verdict. Believe me. You know that I desire our friend's release as much as you. Be calm, then, and wait, I beg you.'

'And what of him? Have you thought what he may be thinking in his prison? Is there anyone who has ever told him to wait, to take heart? He is all alone, or so he believes, at the mercy of this devilish plot. I want him to know at least that while I live I will not abandon him! Very well, I agree not to try and see Napoleon – for the present. But I want to see Jason. I want to get inside La Force.'

'Marianne!' Talleyrand exclaimed, alarmed by her excited state. 'How can you do that?'

'Nothing could be simpler.' It was Crawfurd, coolly intervening. 'For a long time now, I have had turnkeys in every prison in Paris in my pay.'

'You have?' Talleyrand appeared genuinely astonished.

Shrugging his heavy shoulders, Crawfurd eased himself with a sigh of relief into the armchair which Marianne had quitted, and drawing a low stool towards him tenderly placed his gouty foot upon it.

'It is a useful precaution,' he said, with a small chuckle, 'when one has had, and will doubtless continue to have, friends under lock and key. It is a practice I have been familiar with for a long time. My first – er – clients were two of the gaolers in the Temple, and after that at the Conciergerie. Since then, I have maintained the habit. It is not difficult, if one has money. So you want to see your friend, little Princess? Well, I, Crawfurd, promise you that you shall.'

Marianne, trembling with happiness, could scarcely bring herself to believe in the miracle that was being offered her. To have the gates of Jason's prison open to her, to see him, talk to him, touch him, tell him – oh, she had so many things to tell him.

'You would do that for me?' she asked huskily, as though trying to convince herself.

Crawfurd raised a pair of china-blue eyes to her and smiled:

'You have listened to all my stories with such patience, child, that you deserve some reward. Besides, I have not forgotten what my Queen owed to your family. It is one way of paying the debt. Leave it to me. Before a week is out, you shall be inside La Force.'

CHAPTER EIGHT

An Odd Kind of Prisoner

The cab turned out of the rue St-Antoine and entered, at right-angles to it, a short stub of a street no more than thirty yards long and ten broad, blocked at its farther end by a low, grim-looking building on one floor surmounted by a mansard roof nearly as high again, behind which rose another, taller building. In the darkness, the few peeling houses which gave on to this close, which was called the rue des Ballets, had a sinister appearance and a bleary lantern fixed above a fat stone bollard bound with iron at the farthest corner of the street, almost opposite the entrance to the prison, shone on the greasy cobbles, slippery with the mud and filth left by the rain which had fallen in the early part of the evening. A deep gutter running down the middle of the street was intended to drain off both the water and the refuse but in practice constituted only an additional hazard in the uneven surface. The cab lurched and the driver brought his horse to a stop under the lantern, alongside the squat, round bollard, and with a weary, automatic gesture, leaned down and opened the door on Marianne's side.

Crawfurd, with a swift movement of his stick, hooked it shut again.

'No,' he said roughly. 'Get out my side. Let me go first.'

'Why? The bollard will help—'

'That bollard,' the old man cut her short grimly, 'is where the mob dismembered the body of the Princesse de Lamballe. You will soil your gloves.'

Marianne turned with a shudder from the worn stone and took the hand which her companion was holding out to assist her from the cab, taking care as she did so not to put too much weight on it. Crawfurd's gout was better than it had been, but he still walked with difficulty.

Seeing them descend from the cab, the guard who had been dozing in the noisome sentry box beside the gate, his gun between his knees, got up and straightened his shako:

'Who goes there?'

'Now then, soldier,' Crawfurd said in a low voice, instantly, much to Marianne's surprise, slipping into a strong Normandy accent. 'No need to shout. Keeper Ducatel is a countryman of mine and we have come, my daughter Madeleine and myself that is, to have a little supper with him.'

A large silver coin gleamed for a moment in the fitful light of the lamp and roused an answering gleam in the eye of the guard, who uttered a shout of laughter and pocketed the coin:

'You should've said so right away, man. He's a right one, old Ducatel, and been here long enough to make a few friends, eh. I'm one on 'em. In you go, then.'

He banged vigorously on the low door which stood at the top of a pair of worn steps and was surmounted by a heavily barred fanlight.

'Hi there! Ducatel! Someone to see you!'

While the driver of the cab was still engaged in turning his horse in the narrow rue du Roi de Sicile, preparatory to waiting for them by St Paul's, the door opened, revealing an individual in a brown woollen cap holding a candle in one hand. This candle he raised until it was practically under the noses of his visitors and then, having apparently recognized who they were by this time, he exclaimed: 'Ha! Cousin Grouville! You're late! We were just going to eat without you. And here's my little Madeleine. Come you in then. You've grown a fine big girl now!'

Endeavouring to sound as provincial as possible, Marianne managed to utter a word of greeting. Ducatel, still continuing his flow of welcoming chat, assured the guard that 'a nice mug of Calvados' should be sent out to him as a reward for his trouble, and then shut the door behind them. Marianne saw that she was in a narrow entrance passage ending in a turnstile. To the right was the guardroom through the half-open door of which four soldiers could be seen smoking and playing cards by the lights of a couple of lamps. Still talking loudly, Ducatel led his guests up to and through the turnstile, then opened a door into another darkened room at the far end of which was a second turnstile. Here, Ducatel paused.

'My lodging looks on to the rue du Roi de Sicile,' he said in a whisper. 'I'll take you there, M'sieur, and we'll make a little bit of noise so that the guards know we're at supper. I'd've had you in by my private door, but it's always best to look open and above board.'

'I can find my way alone, my good Ducatel,' Crawfurd replied in the same tone, nodding approval as he spoke. 'You take the lady to the prisoner you know of.'

Ducatel nodded his understanding and opened the gate:

'This way, then . . . He's an important prisoner so he's not in the new building. He's been put with the "specials" in the Condé room . . . very nearly by himself.'

As he spoke, Ducatel unlocked a further door and led Marianne across a courtyard. Crawfurd, meanwhile, turned to the left in the direction of the region known as the Kitchen Court, an appellation more than justified by the powerful smell of greasy soup emanating from it, beyond which lay the keeper's quarters.

As she followed the turnkey, Marianne looked about her with distaste at the building surrounding the courtyard and the treeless expanse of cracked paving which was the entrance to the prison itself: high, menacing walls, crumbling and worm-eaten, dotted with barred windows from behind which came an assortment of nightmare groans and shrieks, hideous laughter and the sound of men snoring, and all the other multifarious noises made by the dirty and dangerous portion of humanity penned within by crime and fear. Four floors of rogues, thieves, debtors, convicts escaped and recaptured, murderers, criminals of every kind which the slums of Paris and elsewhere had thrown up into the net of the police. Here was none of the medieval yet not altogether squalid simplicity of Vincennes, for this was not a place for prisoners of state, held for political offences. This was the common gaol, where all the vilest felons were huddled in appallingly overcrowded conditions.

'We had a bit of a job,' Ducatel confided to Marianne, 'to find him a corner that was a bit quiet-like.' He was leading her up a staircase whose wrought-iron handrail betrayed that in the days of the dukes of la Force it had been noble and handsome, though now the treads were cracked and slippery and made the ascent perilous. 'The prison is stuffed as full as it can hold, you know. Never gets much emptier, either. Here we are now . . .' He indicated an iron-studded door which had come into view in the thickness of the wall. The keeper opened a spy-hole in the door and a little yellowish light filtered out into the passage.

'Someone to see you, M'sieur Beaufort!' he said into the opening before drawing the bolts. Then he added in a lower tone to Marianne: 'It's not my fault, M'dame, but I can't let you have more than an hour or so, I'm afraid. I'll be back to fetch you before they do the rounds.'

'Thank you. You are very kind.'

The door opened almost noiselessly and Marianne slipped through the opening and stood looking a little startled at the sight which met her eyes. On either side of a rickety table, two men were seated, playing cards by the light of a candle. Something which might have been another man was lying curled up in a ball in the corner, on one of the three truckle beds, wrapped in an uneasy slumber. One of the two card players was Jason. The other was an individual about thirty-five years old, tall, dark and active-looking with a good-looking face, regular features, a mocking curve to his lips and bright, inquisitive black eyes. Seeing that a woman had entered the room, the second man rose at once while Jason, too surprised to do more than stare, sat still, the cards still in his hand:

'Marianne! You! But I thought—'

'*I* thought,' his companion broke in with heavy irony, 'that you, my friend, were a gentleman. Did no one ever teach you to stand up for a lady?'

Jason rose mechanically and as he did so received Marianne full in his arms, laughing and crying at once.

'Oh, my love, my love! I couldn't bear it! I had to come—'

'This is madness! You should be in exile, they may be looking for you . . .'

But even as he protested, his hands were drawing her face close to his. His blue eyes shone out of a face too deeply weatherbeaten for a few weeks' incarceration to whiten it with a joy which his words tried to deny. His expression, oddly touching in a man of his strength, was like that of a lonely, unhappy child who, expecting nothing, suddenly finds that Father Christmas has come and brought him the most wonderful present. He gazed at Marianne, unable to speak another word, then suddenly crushed her to him and kissed her hungrily, like a starving man. Marianne closed her eyes and abandoned herself to his kiss, feeling as if she could die of happiness. It was nothing to her that the man who held her in his arms was unshaven and filthy dirty, and that the cell smelled anything but sweet. It was obvious that, to her, paradise had nothing more to offer.

From their respective positions by the table and the door, the other prisoner and Ducatel looked on, smiling, and with a degree of awed fascination, at this unexpected love scene. However, when it showed no signs of breaking up, the prisoner gave a shrug and, throwing his cards down on the table, announced: 'Right! I'm not wanted here. Ducatel, will you ask me to supper?'

'With the best will in the world, my lad. You're already expected.'

The effect of this exchange on the two lovers was to bring their embrace to a swift conclusion and they stood looking so shamefaced at the speed with which they had forgotten the existence of everything but themselves that the prisoner burst out laughing:

'It's all right, you needn't look like that, you know! We all know what it is to be in love.'

Marianne gave him a withering glare and turned indignantly to the keeper:

'Is it necessary that Monsieur Beaufort should be forced to endure the company of—'

'Of people like me? Alas, Madame, the prison is overfull and it cannot be helped. But we don't rub along too badly, do we, friend?'

'No,' Jason responded, grinning, in spite of himself, at Marianne's outraged expression, 'it might be a great deal worse! In fact, I'll even introduce you.'

'Spare yourself the trouble,' the other prisoner interrupted him. 'I mean to do that myself. Fair lady, you see before you your genuine gallows bird, not often met with in polite society: François Vidocq of Arras, three times convicted felon and in a fair way to be so again. Deep bow and exits left, as they say in the theatre. Come, Ducatel. I'm hungry.'

'And that?' Marianne said furiously, indicating the black bundle which had continued to jerk and mutter indistinguishably. 'Aren't you taking *that* with you?'

'Who? The abbé? He'll not trouble you. He's half-cracked

and talks nothing but Spanish. Besides, it would be a shame to wake him. He's having such lovely nightmares.'

And escorted almost respectfully by the keeper, the strange prisoner, apparently very much at home, departed from the cell to go and sup with his gaoler as if it were the most natural thing in the world.

'Well!' said Marianne, recovering from her astounded contemplation of this exit. 'Who is that man?'

'He told you,' Jason said, folding her in his arms again. 'He is an habitual felon, always escaping and as often returning, what they call here an old lag.'

'Is he – a murderer?'

'No, a thief merely. I am the murderer here,' Jason said wryly. 'He's a curious fellow, but I owe him my life.'

'You do?'

'Yes, indeed! You don't know this prison. It is a hell inhabited by demons, a sink of all that is base and cruel and ugly, where the law of the strongest prevails. I was a stranger – well dressed, which was enough to make them take me in dislike. I should have been a dead man beyond a doubt if François had not taken me under his protection. He is a great man hereabouts, and he has the trick of taming these ravening beasts. That poor devil sleeping over there has him to thank that he is still alive. It's a grand thing to be a master of escape. Even the turnkeys respect him – as you've seen!'

Marianne understood the danger which had threatened Jason on his first arrival at La Force better than he could have known. She herself retained vivid memories of the one night she had spent in the prison of St Lazare and from time to time in her dreams she still saw the leering face of the woman known as La Tricoteuse who had tried to kill her only because she was young and beautiful. She saw the yellow eyes and evil grin, and the horrible skill with which the creature had wielded her clumsy knife.

Just then, the black bundle which was an abbé stirred suddenly on his pallet bed and sat up with a smothered shriek. Marianne could see a gaunt, raggedly bearded face and eyes that looked at her with staring terror.

'Tranquilo,' Jason murmured quickly. *'Es un'amiga.'*

The abbé's head nodded and with a sigh he turned his back on the young people and lay down again obediently.

'There,' Jason said comfortably. 'He'll not move again. He has very nice manners. Now let's forget him. Come and sit by me, let me look at you. You are so lovely! No, don't speak!'

He led her to a kind of plank bed covered with a moth-eaten rug and made her sit down, all without taking his eyes from her. If the truth were told, there was little in Marianne's modest print gown, made high to the throat, which was the most countrified thing she had been able to find in her wardrobe, to justify his enthusiasm, yet even in her most fairytale dresses, her most fabulous jewels, Jason had never looked at her like this. It was miraculous and yet at the same time oddly disturbing, so disturbing that Marianne found herself withdrawing a little. She kissed his unshaven cheek lightly:

'Yes but I have come to talk, and we have so little time—'

'No. Hush now. I don't want to waste these moments in talk. They may never come again – and I have prayed so hard just to see you again – if only once!'

He buried his head in her neck but, thoroughly alarmed now, she pushed him away.

'What do you mean? Why may we never meet again? Your trial—'

'I have no illusions about my trial,' Jason said, with a degree of patience he was far from feeling. 'I shall be found guilty and condemned—'

'But – oh, no – not to—' She could not bring herself to say the words which, in this prison setting, had acquired a horrible reality. But Jason nodded:

'Very possibly – even probably. No, be quiet.' His hand came quickly over her lips, checking her fierce protest. 'It is always best to look things in the face. All the evidence is against me. Unless the real culprit is found, which is highly unlikely, the judges will find me guilty. I know that.'

'But this is fantastic! Insane! Jason, all is not yet lost! Arcadius has gone to Aix, to make Fouché give evidence. Fouché can tell how matters stood between myself and Black Fish!'

'But he cannot state positively that I did not kill him. Look, this business is the outcome of a political plot. And I am caught in the toils.'

'Then your ambassador must defend you!'

'He will not. He has told me so himself, Marianne, here in this very prison, because to do so would be a sure way of bringing about the ruin of the present negotiations between President Madison and France to get the decrees concerning the Continental Blockade revoked where America is concerned. It is all very complicated—'

'No,' Marianne broke in, desperately. 'I know. Talleyrand told me all about the Berlin and Milan decrees.'

'God bless him, then,' Jason said, with his crooked smile. 'Well, France's conditions are these: that my country must persuade England, with whom we are not on the best of terms, to revoke what are called the "orders in council", in other words, the English retort to the decrees. And the first condition, naturally, is that the United States shall make no move to interfere with the course of justice so far as I am concerned – this affair of the forged notes is too serious. Cadore has said as much in a note to Armstrong. Armstrong is sorry – but there is nothing he can do. He is almost as much a prisoner as I am. Do you see?'

'No,' Marianne persisted stubbornly. 'I shall never see why they have to sacrifice you – because that is what they are doing, isn't it?'

'Yes, it is. But when you think that my country is prepared to go to war with England as a proof of good faith to Napoleon if the orders in council are not rescinded, you can imagine that my own life matters very little. Nor would I wish it to. You see, my love . . . we must all serve as we can – and I love my country above all things.'

'More than me, even?' Marianne said quietly, on the verge of tears.

Jason did not answer. Instead, his arms tightened round her and he sought her lips again. His heart was hammering so hard that Marianne seemed to feel it beating in her own breast. She felt the shuddering of his whole body and she knew that his desires had grown beyond his power to master them, a knowledge only confirmed when, lifting his head briefly from the lips which he had been crushing under his own, he began to plead with her softly: 'My darling, I entreat you . . . this may be our only chance . . . Now I am asking you to let me love you . . .'

Marianne's heart leapt. Gently, she pushed him away once more, and when she heard him groan she murmured softly: 'A moment, my beloved, only a moment . . .'

Then, lifted beyond herself by a love stronger than fear or modesty, Marianne stood up, oblivious of the priest lying a few yards away. He might be asleep or not, he had his back to them at least. Not taking her eyes from Jason who stayed where he was, half-kneeling, his gaze fixed intently on her, she stripped off all her garments one by one and dropped them on the greasy floor. Then, proud and unashamed, she walked into the arms held open to receive her, and the rough and grimy pallet which was Jason's bed became for Marianne a couch softer and more sumptuous than any she had ever lain on, even in that princely palace where she had slept so many nights alone. Yet she blessed the semi-darkness of the prison, for Jason had snuffed the single candle and only a faint moonlight shone into the cell, because it hid the weal, still red and angry, of the burn which Chernychev had given her. She did not want to have to lie to him, nor yet to involve herself in explanations which would have left a scar on Jason's happiness. In that one, irrecoverable moment when Marianne learned at last in joy and wonder what it meant to become one with another person, the past must be blotted out and even the dread future cry a truce.

When the door opened again a little while later, the candle was burning again and Jason was helping Marianne to put her dress to rights. But it was not Ducatel who appeared. The prisoner named François Vidocq stood in the doorway, one shoulder propped nonchalantly against the door jamb, and after a brief glance at the abbé who was now snoring like a grampus, surveyed the lovers with an air of great amusement.

'A woman of substance, indeed, Madame,' he remarked chattily. 'You have brought him the one thing that could do him good.'

'Mind your own business,' Marianne snapped, all the more furious because he had been right. She felt herself blushing to the roots of her hair and, as she always did when threatened with embarrassment, she lost her temper. 'Besides,' she went on hotly, 'you are talking of matters you know nothing about! The only thing that could "do him good", as you put it, would be if they would acknowledge his innocence and set him free.'

'We are all in God's hands,' Vidocq observed with exaggerated piety. 'Who knows what tomorrow may bring? As the poet says, "Patience and time work more than strength and fury".'

'And however often goes the pitcher to the well, in the end it will be broken . . . Do you think I came here to listen to proverbs? Jason,' she cried desperately, turning to him, 'tell him you are lost, that your one hope now is – is to escape! And if he is your friend, as he claims to be, and at the same time a master at escaping the police, then he must see . . .'

A prolonged and obvious yawn brought Marianne's impassioned tirade to an abrupt halt. She glared at Vidocq with a look of sheer murder on her face while he cocked a thumb in the direction of the open door.

'I hate to be a spoil sport, but Ducatel is waiting for you, fair one – and the watch is due in five minutes.'

'You must go, Marianne,' Jason told her seriously as she clung to him by a kind of instinct. 'And you must be sensible. You have made me – so very, very happy. I shall think of you always. But we must say goodbye now.'

'No, not goodbye . . . or only for a little while! I shall come again and—'

'No. I forbid you to. It would not be wise. You are forgetting that you yourself are watched. I must know that you are safe, at least.'

'Don't you want to see me again?' Marianne was almost in tears.

He kissed the tip of her nose lightly, then her eyes and then her lips.

'Silly! I have only to close my eyes to see you. You will never leave me. But I must be wise for two – and now, especially, when your life may be at stake.'

'Only four minutes!' The turnkey's head appeared round the door, looking anxious. 'You'll have to hurry, lady.'

With one last kiss, Marianne tore herself bravely from Jason's side. She was half out of the door when Vidocq caught her arm and spoke to her softly:

'Do you know the Persian poets?'

'N-no, but—'

'One of them has written: "Never lose hope, even in the midst of disaster, for the toughest bone contains the sweetest marrow." Go now.'

She glanced up at him uncertainly before, blowing one last kiss to Jason, she hurried out to join Ducatel who was pacing up and down outside like a caged bear.

'Hurry!' he told her, shutting the door swiftly. 'We've got no more than three minutes! Here, take my hand. We'll have to run for it.'

They raced together for the stairs while from the passages behind them the measured tread of the watchmen on their rounds was already making itself heard. At the same time, at the clatter of heavy, nailed boots, the whole prison seemed to come awake, Oaths, curses and ugly shouts rang out on all sides until it seemed as if each door concealed its own miniature version of hell. The smell which even in Jason's cell had been unpleasant, became frankly unendurable as they passed certain doors and when they emerged at last into the Cour du Greffe Marianne found herself taking in great gulps of fresh air. They had resumed a normal walking pace by now and the keeper remarked as he let go Marianne's hand:

'I dare say a little glass of something wouldn't do either of us any harm, my lady. You looked like a sheet when you came out, and I can't say I feel so hot myself, after that close shave.'

'I'm sorry. But tell me, this man François Vidocq, is he indeed an escaped convict?'

'I'll say he is. The guards can watch him for all they're worth, but they can never keep a hold on him. Every time he slips through their fingers. But he can't keep out of trouble, seemingly. He always comes trotting back again. But don't get me wrong. He's not one of your real desperate ruffians. He's not killed anyone. So back they sends him again to serve his time – Toulon, Rochefort, Brest, he knows them all. They're all the same to him. Just the same this time, it'll be. They'll pack him away, and after a bit he'll be off out of it again as usual. And then the whole round will begin again, until one day one of his guards has had enough and quietly puts him away. And that'll be a pity, because he's not a bad lad . . .'

But Marianne was no longer listening. She was pondering in her heart the words this strange prisoner had said to her. He had mentioned hope, and hope was the one word she had needed to hear, since Jason had not uttered it. More, he seemed resigned, almost indifferent, accepting with what seemed to her a terrifying calmness the possibility of dying for his country's service.

'He shall not die,' she vowed inwardly. 'I shall not let them kill him and he shall not die! Even if his judges condemn him, I will make the Emperor listen to me and he will have to grant me his life . . .'

That was the one thing that mattered. Even if life meant a slow death in penal servitude. Until that day she had always thought of it as a kind of foretaste of hell from which no one ever emerged alive. But this man Vidocq was living proof that it was not so. And she knew that while Jason lived she, Marianne, would devote every moment of her life to saving him from the undeserved penalty awaiting him. Gathering together all her strength, she thrust away her fears, her anguish and all thoughts of farewell. Every atom of her being belonged to Jason Beaufort but she believed too that Jason Beaufort belonged henceforth to her and her alone. And because of this she felt a greater strength and fighting spirit than she had ever known before, even on the night when, sword in hand, she had challenged Francis Cranmere to answer for the slur on her honour. The fire of the ancient blood of Auvergne and the unrelenting tenacity of her English descent united in her to produce all the warlike qualities of those other women from whose line she came who had studded history with their loves, their passions and their vengeances: Agnès de Ventadour who had turned Crusader to be revenged on a faithless lover, Catherine de Montsalvy who had risked death a hundred times for the husband she loved, Isabelle de Montsalvy, her daughter, who had fought her way to happiness through the horrors of the Wars of the Roses, Lucrèce de Gadagne, wielding a sword like a man to win back her castle of Tournoel, Sidonia d'Asselnat who had fought like a man yet loved like ten women during the Fronde, and so many more. Go back as far as she would in the annals of her family, Marianne would find the same story, the same pattern of war and arms, of blood and love. Only fate might change the course of human life, but as she followed the keeper down the damp passage leading to his lodging, Marianne knew that she had at last accepted the crushing weight of that heritage, owned herself daughter and sister to all these women because now she had found her own cause for which to fight and to live. And so, she felt no sadness or grief but rather a sense of happiness and exultation and triumph, drawn from the hour which had just passed, but most of all a vast, inner peace. Everything was suddenly so simple. Henceforth, she and Jason were one heart and one flesh. If one died, then the other would die too . . . and that would be the end.

As she left the prison, she thanked the keeper warmly and slid into his hand a number of gold coins which brought the blood rushing into his cheeks. Then, slipping back into her part of the country girl elated by a good supper and a drop of wine, she hung on Crawfurd's arm as they set out on the short walk to the church of St Paul where the Scotsman had told the cab driver to wait for them, rather than attract attention by lingering outside the prison. The sentry called out a jovial good night to them as they moved slowly away, walking carefully to avoid tripping on the uneven cobbles.

'You're happy, I can tell,' Crawfurd said softly as they turned into the rue St-Antoine. 'Am I right?'

'Yes. It's quite true, I am happy. Not that Jason gave me much encouragement to hope. He expects to be found guilty and, worst of all, he seems to be resigned to it, because the good of his country demands it.'

'That does not surprise me. These Americans are like their own splendid country: simple and big. Pray God they may never change! All the same, he may be resigned, but that is no reason for us all to be so – eh? As our friend Talleyrand would say.'

'I agree. But I wanted to tell you—'

However, Quintin Crawfurd was not destined to hear what Marianne wanted to tell him of her gratitude, because as they approached the little group of elm trees in the miniature square in front of the old Jesuit church, the Scotsman suddenly pressed the arm which lay within his.

'Sssh!' he said . . . 'There is something there . . .'

A light wind had got up, sending the heavy rain clouds scudding across the sky, veiling the moon so that it shone through only as a pale, diffused glow. Against this faint lightening of the darkness, the trees in front of them seemed to have taken on strange, moving shapes, as if men in billowing cloaks might be concealed behind them. The square shape of the cab was clearly to be seen near the church but the driver was not on the box. A whinny made Marianne glance to her right and she made out several horses standing in a side alley. It needed no words, nor the movement made by Crawfurd drawing the hidden pistol very slowly from the inner pocket of his cloak, to make Marianne suspect a trap, but she had no time to wonder any more.

There was a sudden movement, as if the trees had come to life, and in a twinkling the two on foot found themselves the centre of a menacing circle of black, silent shapes of men dressed in full capes and broad-brimmed hats. Crawfurd presented his pistol:

'What do you want? If you mean to rob us, we have no money on us.'

'Put up your weapon, Señor,' said one of the shadowy figures, speaking in a strong Spanish accent. 'We have more powerful ones trained on you. It is not gold that we are after.'

'Then what do you want?'

But the Spaniard, whose face was invisible beneath his wide

hat, disregarded the question, and at a sign from him the Scotsman found himself expertly gagged and bound. Then the man turned to the figure at his side:

'That is the one?'

The person addressed, who was much shorter and slighter than the first speaker, moved a step or two closer and, taking a dark lantern from beneath the enveloping cloak, opened the shutter and held it up so that the light shone on Marianne's face. At the same time, the light fell on the cloaked figure and revealed it to be a woman. It was Pilar.

'It is she!' she proclaimed on a note of triumph. 'Thank you, my good Vasquez, for all the time you have spent watching here. I knew that, sooner or later, she would come to the prison.'

'Do you mean to tell me,' Marianne said scornfully, 'that this man has been watching the prison for all these weeks purely on the chance of procuring for you this delightful encounter?'

'Precisely. For more than a month we have waited. Ever since, in fact, we heard that Prince Talleyrand had returned from Bourbon l'Archambault ... and that the Princess Sant'Anna was too ill to leave her room. Don Alonso took a lodging in the rue des Ballets and kept watch. We knew that you were not in the prince's house, nor your own. You had to be somewhere, and watching the prison was the one way to find out.'

'I congratulate you,' Marianne said. 'I had not known that you were so intelligent ... or so talkative. And now what do you mean to do with us? Kill us?'

Pilar's pale face was thrust close to hers. Hatred gleamed in the black eyes but Marianne stared back coolly into the beautiful features, their purity already ravaged by bitterness and despair. If ever she had seen her death written in a human face it was here, but in the strength of her newly consummated love she felt no fear. Besides, Pilar was speaking:

'That would be too easy! No, we are merely going to take you with us and take good care of you, in case you should do anything foolish. We cannot have any ill-considered action of yours interfering with the course of justice. I had thought at first to hand you over to the police, but it seems that your Napoleon has a fondness for you.'

'If I were you, I would not forget that fondness. He does not take kindly to having his friends kidnapped!'

'He will not know. After all – you are still in exile, are you not? You had better silence the lady, gentlemen, she seems to be about to scream.'

This was true. But before Marianne could do more than open her mouth to alert the people in the near-by houses, she found herself firmly gagged, then bound and bundled into the cab to join Crawfurd. One of the cloaked men jumped on to the box but Pilar and Vasquez got in with their prisoners. Seated, facing her enemy, Pilar frowned:

'Better bandage their eyes as well, my friend. I don't want them to know where they are taken.'

This the Spaniard did and Marianne, robbed of both sight and speech, could only sit and think her own thoughts, which seemed suddenly to have become rather less optimistic. Things had ceased, in fact, to be as simple as she had been inclined to think. Ever since leaving Jason she had been buoying herself up with the comforting illusion that she was going to snatch her lover from death and set him free, a freedom which she naturally intended that he should share with her. Failing this, she had been determined to die with him, or at least at the same time, so that they might embark together, hand in hand, on an eternity of love. She had even got to the point of imagining the letter she would leave for Jolival, so that he might unite both their bodies in a single grave, and, rather like a spoiled child saying 'I'll die and then they'll be sorry', she had even derived a certain satisfaction from the thought of Napoleon's grief and remorse when he should learn that by his harshness he had driven his nightingale to her death. In all of which, she found herself obliged to confess bitterly, she had quite forgotten the disagreeable fact of Pilar . . .

Until then, she had thought of Pilar as a fanatical barbarian, incapable of any normal train of thought, whose main aim in running to seek refuge with the unlikely Queen of Spain at her court at Mortefontaine had simply been to pull her own chestnuts out of the fire. She had believed her proud and unbalanced, and even base because to satisfy her own unworthy longing for revenge she had sided with the police against her husband. But she could never have believed that her hatred could go so wickedly far. What was it the creature had said? That no action of Marianne's must interfere with the course of justice? ... In other words, she was kidnapping Marianne to prevent her from doing anything to rescue Jason!

For a moment, Marianne seemed to hear Talleyrand again. 'Pilar comes of a fierce and passionate race ... an injured woman may deliver up her faithless lover to execution without flinching – and then wall herself up alive in a nunnery to expiate her crime ...'

That was it! They were going to keep Marianne locked up in some dungeon from which she could not escape until Jason had been executed. Perhaps then they might do her the favour of killing her also? No doubt it would all make the path of expiation much easier for the saintly Pilar!

'If I were in her place,' Marianne thought, 'I should probably kill my rival, but not for anything in the world would I harm the man I loved.'

Her bonds were hurting her and the gag was making it hard for her to breathe. She tried to wriggle herself into a more comfortable position.

'Sit still,' came Pilar's voice coldly. 'We shall be changing carriages very soon.'

They had travelled only a short distance in the cab, but already it was slowing down. Several hands seized Marianne none too gently and dragged her out, but scarcely had her feet touched the ground before she was lifted up again and felt herself sat down on a cushioned seat, much softer than the previous one. Her elbows touched silky velvet. But at the same time she knew for certain that the person sitting beside her was no longer Quintin Crawfurd. It was Pilar. Marianne's delicate nostrils had picked up at once the characteristically heavy scent of carnations and jasmine which she used. No one else entered the carriage and the prisoner began to feel seriously anxious on behalf of her companion, whose stifled grunts she could hear coming from some way away. Then someone spoke through the window, in Spanish:

'What shall we do with the other one?'

'I have told you,' Pilar replied. 'Drive him to the place you know of. I can promise you the police will not come looking for him there, supposing that they look for him at all.'

'They'll do that all right, Doña Pilar, you may be sure. When his wife finds he's not come home she'll raise heaven and earth.'

'Not necessarily. It would mean admitting that they had an exile hidden under their roof. The important part, in any case, is that nothing should be known before the date we have settled. We can let him go after that. We have nothing against him. Which reminds me, did you pay the driver of the cab?'

The man Vasquez's reply to this was a low, guttural laugh which made Marianne's blood run cold. Even Pilar was moved to protest:

'You should not have done that. We are not at home now.'

'Bah! Another curst Frenchman the less! Go now. Three of our men will go with you and we will meet again there. And if I may make a suggestion, she had better not be seen. Allow me.'

Marianne was seized again, bundled up in something rough and warm and smelling so strongly of the stables that it must have been a horse blanket, and dumped unceremoniously on the floor of the chaise.

'I had meant to do that before we arrived,' Pilar said.

'You are all goodness! Are you so fond of the harlot who has stolen your husband?'

'How well you understand me, Don Alonso,' Pilar purred. Her voice was so seraphic that it made Marianne immediately long to bite. 'Thank you. Thank you a thousand times. You have made the prospect of the journey very agreeable – to me at all events.'

The prisoner, lying totally helpless on the carpeted floor of the vehicle, was soon made well aware of how agreeable the journey was to be for her by feeling her enemy's feet planted firmly on her chest. Rather than add to Pilar's enjoyment, however, she refrained from any reaction of her outrage.

'You'll pay for this!' she swore inwardly. 'You'll pay a hundred times over, for this and everything else. You single-minded savage! When I get my hands on you, you murderous she-devil, I'll show you what I can do . . .'

Thereafter, the names which Marianne in her impotent fury applied to Pilar were of a sadly descending order of refinement, being almost exclusively borrowed from the vocabulary of old Dobs, the groom at Selton who had taught Marianne to ride. Nor, indeed, was she invariably certain of the precise meaning of the terms she invoked, but she derived a good deal of comfort from the thought that nothing was too base to describe a woman who could permit the cold-blooded murder of an innocent cab driver, to say nothing of the savagery with which she was working to bring Jason to the block.

Angry, bruised and half-stifled, Marianne lay, feeling the chaise move off smartly, travelling at first over the jolting cobbled streets of Paris. Then, still muffled in her rug, she thought she heard the clash of arms and a brief word of command, as if they were passing a guard post of some kind, although the vehicle had not slowed down. She guessed that they had in fact passed out of the city limits when the driver whipped up the horses to a still faster pace over a good road in which the pot-holes were few.

She heard Pilar, above her, give vent to a sigh of relief, and then felt the blanket being moved away from her face.

'I don't wish you to suffocate,' the Señora said, with insulting solicitude. 'That would be much too quick. Besides, you may as well try and sleep, my dear, because we have a good two hours ahead of us.'

The Spaniard's feet resumed their position but Marianne had succeeded in shifting herself round so as no longer to have them immediately under her nose, though it made her slightly more uncomfortable. At least she was spared the sight of her foe's complacent expression, and thus able to devote herself to her own thoughts.

Two hours? At the rate the horses were travelling, and bearing in mind that there would have to be a change somewhere if Pilar intended to keep up this rapid pace, that would mean a distance of about twenty miles. But a knowledge of how far it might be to the place where she was to be held captive did not tell her very much about the place itself, since she had no idea by which gate they had left Paris. Never mind, she knew at least that if she did manage to escape she would have to steal a horse, or else resign herself to the prospect of walking back to Paris – not that the thought frightened her. In order to escape from her captors and fly to Jason's rescue she would gladly have walked to Paris from Marseilles.

Rather than waste her strength to no purpose, Marianne forced herself to relax as far as possible in her cramped position. Old Dobs's advice came back to her now, perhaps because she had been thinking of him before:

'Relax, Miss Marianne. It's one of the secrets of a good fencer – and of a good shot. It saves wear and tear on the nerves and helps to keep you cool. You have to teach your muscles to relax.'

Then the old man had taught her how, systematically, to relax her arms and legs, take deep breaths. Now, in spite of her bonds, Marianne strove to put his lessons into practice. At the same time, she did her best to make her mind a blank, shutting out even the memory of those miraculous moments in La Force because she could not think of them calmly, and in the end she succeeded so well that she fell sound asleep.

She was woken by the soft plop of the blanket landing once more on her face. Almost at once, there was the metallic creak of gates being opened and another clash of arms, as if they had come to a guard post again. Then the chaise was bowling over some soft, smooth surface which might have been the sanded driveway through a private park. They went on for some way but the rug was wrapped so closely round her head that Marianne could hear nothing. Indeed, it was as much as she could do to breathe.

After what seemed an age, they stopped and she thought that now she would be untied and the gag removed, but nothing of the kind occurred. Two pairs of hands hauled her out of the chaise. There was a splashing and the rattle of a chain, then a soft thud like that made by a boat bumping against a jetty. Her bearers' footsteps, too, had a hollow, wooden sound and almost at once she was deposited in the bottom of a lightly swaying boat. They must be going to cross a river – unless – the thought that came into her mind was a nasty one but it lasted only an instant. Pilar had repeated several times since her capture that they had no intention of killing her immediately, she was to be made to suffer first.

Someone took the oars and the boat began to move out smoothly over the water. The surface must be quite calm and waveless. A lake, perhaps, or a pool of some kind? Her nerves at full stretch, Marianne listened for every sound that might tell her more, but apart from the faint splash of oars and the slightly deeper breathing of the man rowing she heard nothing beyond the cry of an owl in the distance.

The boat drove against a soft bottom and stopped. Once again, Marianne was seized but this time the hands hoisted her on to a particularly hard and uncomfortable back, as though she had been a sack of flour. Her arms were gripped firmly by a gloved hand that might have been made of iron and a bony shoulder dug into her stomach as she lay, bent double, with her head hanging forward.

The man carrying her smelled strongly of the stables, with an underlying odour of rancid oil. The combination was a peculiarly unpleasant one but Marianne had little time to reflect upon it before she felt herself being carried up something that seemed to be either a ladder or some very rudimentary staircase. The treads creaked alarmingly and the climb seemed to go on for ever. At last their progress became horizontal once again and at the same time a mixture of dry, country smells, hay and straw and dust, filled Marianne's nostrils, overcoming the human smell. She was dropped suddenly on to what could only be a pile of hay and almost at once her bonds were loosed, the gag taken from her mouth and the blindfold removed from her eyes.

By the light of the dark lantern carried by one of the men, Marianne saw that she was, as she had guessed, in a large loft three parts full of hay. Just in front of her was a tousle-haired giant, puffing like a grampus, who had apparently been the one carrying her. The other man was still wearing his broad-brimmed hat, long cloak and black mask. Last of all, she saw Pilar come through a narrow opening, which had evidently been formed by the removal of two broad planks from the partition wall.

'Well, here you are. Make yourself at home,' the masked man said. 'You'll do well enough. It's quite dry and the hay is better than bare boards.'

'I suppose I ought to thank you,' Marianne said cuttingly. 'I've always liked the smell of fresh hay. But I should like to know how long you mean to keep me here.'

Before the man could answer, Pilar drew him back with a gesture to him to be silent and it was she who answered:

'You know that already. I wish to prevent you from interfering with the course of justice. You will remain here until a certain verdict has been reached and sentence duly carried out.'

'You call yourself a woman!' the prisoner burst out, unable to contain herself any longer. 'You call yourself his wife! You are nothing but a common murderess, a half-crazy, lying fanatic! Is this how you repay Jason for what he did for you? You see, I know why he married you – he wanted to save your life when it was threatened on account of your father's American sympathies!'

'My father's sympathies were not mine. I should have made my countrymen see where my loyalties were. I did not need Señor Beaufort to marry me for that!'

'Then what did you marry him for? Tell me that if you dare! . . . No, you dare not, of course! Well, I will tell you. You made him marry you by pretending to be a poor, helpless, persecuted girl. You threw yourself on him for protection because it was your only chance to get him for yourself! You were mad for him, weren't you? Yet you knew quite well that he was not in love with you!'

Pilar's foot, in its pointed shoe, caught Marianne agonizingly under the ribs, making her bite back a hiss of pain. In an instant she was on her feet, hurling herself at her enemy, only to find herself caught and held by the two men who had sprung forward to catch her. Pilar gave a small, contemptuous laugh:

'I said she was dangerous. Remember, she is a murderess who has already killed one woman. I was right, you see, to provide good, stout fetters. Make her fast, Sanchez.'

The giant grasped Marianne's two wrists in one huge hand and dragged her over the hay to where a brand new chain had been riveted to one of the massive beams. On the end of the chain, which was too short to allow of more than a couple of yards' freedom of movement, was an iron ring which could be fastened by means of a stout padlock. In no time, Marianne's right arm was held fast by the manacle, which fitted tightly round her wrist. The padlock snapped shut.

'There!' Pilar said with satisfaction. 'Now one may talk to you without fear of attack. Your movements will not be unduly restricted and you may await the end of this affair with patience.'

'Talk!' Marianne retorted with scorn. 'Do not hope to hear any talk from me, Señora. All I have to say to you is this: as you so rightly recall, I killed one woman because she insulted me, as I also fought the man who sullied my good name, and won! You have dared to carry me off and treat me like this to stop me from saving a man you know to be innocent – a man you swore before God to be true to—'

'He was the first to break that oath – when he forgot me, his wife, and became your lover! He is forsworn!'

'That is between you and your conscience. And I know of no convent deep and dark enough to shut out the crying of an ill-used conscience. But I will tell you one thing: take care, because I shall escape from you – and I shall have my revenge! Now go away, if you please, and let me go to sleep. I am extremely tired.'

As if she had lost all interest in her captors, Marianne yawned outrageously and, disposing the straw so as to make a comfortable nest for herself, she curled up into a ball, like a cat, with one arm tucked beneath her head, and closed her eyes. After a moment, she heard the man in the hat say quietly in Spanish:

'It is best that we should go back now, Doña Pilar. There might be talk ... Have you anything more to say to this woman?'

'No. Nothing more. You are right. We should go back. But keep a close watch on her.'

'Have no fear. Sanchez will be in the next loft. And fastened like that, I don't see how she could escape.'

Marianne thought that her persecutors were about to leave her at last but just as she was on the point of moving away, Pilar remembered something. She turned to the giant, Sanchez, and indicating the prisoner, who was still feigning sleep, she said: 'Wait. Go and take all the pins out of her hair. There is nothing like a hairpin for opening locks.'

The man in the hat gave an obsequious chuckle. 'You think of everything, Doña Pilar,' he said admiringly. 'It makes me very happy to think that you are now one of us.'

Marianne was obliged to stifle her fury while Sanchez's clumsy paws burrowed in her hair in search of every single pin, but she stuck to her promise not to speak another word to Pilar. It was all over in a minute. Carrying the lantern with them, the three departed through the narrow, boarded door and Marianne heard the sound of bolts being drawn on the other side and a heavy bar of metal thudding into place, as though in a real prison. This was followed by a dry rustling and thumping, as though bales of straw were being dragged across the door. Marianne heard the masked man's voice say on a note of satisfaction:

'That will do. The door is quite hidden. But keep your eyes open, Sanchez, all the same. They told me no one would come here before the winter, but you never know.'

From the depths of her sweet-smelling and, all things considered, extremely comfortable couch, Marianne offered a silent blessing to the memory of her Aunt Ellis, who had insisted on her learning several foreign languages. Her knowledge of Spanish had stood her in especially good stead that night because Pilar seemed to have forgotten that Marianne could speak a Castilian every bit as pure as her own. One thing was certain: she was imprisoned in a place where it appeared no one was likely to discover her, but they seemed to have taken elaborate precautions to keep her presence in the hayloft a secret from everyone except those who had actually taken part in her kidnapping. What she needed to know now was just who 'everyone' in this case was likely to be. An idea was already taking shape in her mind. It had started initially from her observations about the length of the journey, which suggested that her rural prison was some twenty miles from Paris, and from the clatter of muskets as they passed through the gate, combined with the extent of the park through which they had passed before entering the boat, and, most of all, the precautions which were evidently being taken to conceal her presence. Added to the things Talleyrand and Jolival had said about Pilar's reception by the Queen of Spain and about the attention of a certain Alonso Vasquez, the inference was inevitably that she had been taken to Mortefontaine, to the huge estate where Joseph Bonaparte's wife was living while her husband was attempting to reign in Madrid. Turning the residence of a Bonaparte into one's own private prison certainly showed nerve and a good deal of impudence, but Marianne did not think either Pilar or her accomplices lacked nerve. Moreover, as a hiding-place it was ideal. What policeman would be bold enough to start searching in the grounds of Napoleon's elder brother? Only Fouché would have been capable of it, but Fouché was far away and for the first time Marianne was genuinely sorry for it.

Lying there in the thick darkness to which her eyes had not yet grown fully accustomed, Marianne was conscious, amid these useless regrets, of a growing, insidious fear which she did her best to thrust away. She knew she must not think about the increased danger to Jason arising from her abduction. She had to keep a clear head and a cool brain if she was to fight at all, and the first thing was to get some sleep. Her aching body and her eyeballs parched with weariness told her that.

She snuggled further down into the hay and closed her eyes again, forcing herself, as she used to do when she was a little girl and frightened of something, to recall the prayers learned in babyhood to drive away the fearful shadows of the night. But still her mind would keep returning to Jason and to the moments they had spent together, to the fierce pleasure, halfway between ecstasy and pain, which she had felt in his arms and he in hers, the sweetness of their kisses when their first desire was slaked, slaked only to return again with renewed fervour, and to the wrench of their final parting . . . They had had so little time. Free, they could have drowned whole days and nights in love, surfacing only to gaze at each other, dazzled by the glory of their happiness, then sinking back again beneath the waves.

So it was that despite her fetters, despite the peril hanging over her, Marianne was smiling when she fell asleep at last, like a tired but happy child, and her lips still shaped the words: 'Jason, I love you . . . I love you, love you, love you . . .'

CHAPTER NINE

Concerning the Proper Use of Hay and What May be Found Therein

Daylight enabled Marianne to take a more exhaustive look at her restricted domain. The hayloft occupied the upper part of a steep-pitched roof-space and the length of the main beam and the impressive structure of timbers which formed the frame suggested that the whole must be of considerable size. At present it was rather more than three-quarters filled with huge bales of hay, too dry and brittle to have come from this year's harvest. The smallest spark would be enough to set the whole lot blazing and Marianne understood why she had not been left a light the night before.

It was possible to see fairly well during the daytime by

reason of a long, narrow opening, like a loophole in the end wall, which could be seen to be very thick. There was also something like a small skylight in the roof itself but it was too small to offer the least chance of escape. Marianne thought she would be lucky to get her head through – and even that with a strong risk of getting stuck. Her chain was long enough to enable her to reach both the slit-window and the skylight. The glass was extremely dirty and dusty but she was nevertheless able to make out the tall slate roofs, noble chimneys and gilded weathervanes of a great house rising above some large trees. One of the towers was flying the standard of Spain and Marianne knew that her guess had been right. She was at Mortefontaine. Farther away and a little to the right, the smoke from a number of chimneys indicated the presence of a considerable village.

The slit, on the other hand, offered, besides a pleasant draught of cool morning air, a view of a broad, curving expanse of water dotted with small wooded islets already beginning to take on the golden tones of autumn. A light mist was rising from the water, which was opal-coloured in the early light, and the smooth trunks of the whispering poplar trees and the silvery boles of the birches with their crowns of pale gold were like the sentinels guarding some enchanted domain. All around lay wooded hills and gentle valleys, and Marianne, standing with her cheek pressed against the stone, thought to herself that she had rarely seen a lovelier, more idyllic landscape. If this was where Queen Julie lived, she understood why she seemed in no haste to leave it for the sombre magnificence of Madrid and the arid sierras. In this favoured spot, life must pass sweetly. Surely the nature which could bring violence and force into such a setting must be singularly warped and twisted.

The loft itself seemed to be at the top of a fairly high building, a barn perhaps, which also stood on an island, since they had taken a boat to reach it.

Apart from the mountain of hay, the furnishings of Marianne's prison were minimal. In the darkest corner were a metal basin, a chipped earthenware pitcher which probably contained water, a cake of dark soap, a couple of cleanish, though ragged dishcloths, apparently intended to do duty as towels, and a large bucket for slops. Still, the prisoner might think herself lucky that her captors had thought to provide her with any means of washing herself at all.

Round about midday, big Sanchez appeared, bringing her food which consisted of some cold meat, stale bread, a lump of cheese, so hard that it seemed unlikely to yield to attack by anything less than a butcher's cleaver, and some rather elderly fruit. But Marianne was hungry enough to set to with a fair appetite for even this unprepossessing repast. While she ate, Sanchez attended to the chores, emptying the bucket and refilling the water jug. Finally, he glared ferociously at the prisoner and pointing one knobbly finger at the food announced: 'No more today. Me back tomorrow.'

This was one way of warning her to make her provisions last, but all things considered it was rather good news than otherwise. At least Marianne was sure of seeing her gaoler only once a day, which left her more liberty to ponder on a means of escape. It still remained to be seen, though, whether Pilar or any of her associates meant to visit her at all.

The first step towards regaining her freedom was to rid herself of the chain, but in spite of all her efforts to drag the iron ring over her slender hand, including a lavish application of the dark soap to make it slide more easily, she only succeeded in chafing the flesh so much that by nightfall her hand was swollen to twice its normal size. The only hope of release lay in somehow opening the padlock which held the ring fast. But how, and what with?

This lowering realization produced a burst of tears which at least had the advantage of easing her pent-up nervous state and making her begin to look a little on the bright side again. It was now twenty-four hours since she and Crawfurd had been captured. Eleonora would certainly have alerted Talleyrand, if not the police. The two of them would surely make some efforts to trace them, and Talleyrand knew where Pilar had sought refuge. But would it occur to him that her disappearance was in any way connected with that silent, unsmiling young woman whose sole concern seemed to be to keep out of trouble and procure herself powerful protection? He would be more likely to think that Crawfurd had over-estimated the influence of his friends in the prison service and that the two incautious visitors had been recognized, arrested and incarcerated in their turn. Since Marianne had returned to Paris illegally it would be somewhat awkward to go to Savary and ask for her, while any approach to Napoleon was at once ruled out of court by his recent unfriendly note to the Prince of Benevento. There remained Jolival. But he was not due back for days yet and, even supposing he were to set out in search of her the very instant he returned, how long might it be before he came on any trace of her? Finally, even if he did follow her tracks to Mortefontaine, how could he possibly hope to obtain permission to search the Queen of Spain's grounds? Pilar's plans had indeed been well laid and efficiently carried out.

The logic of this train of thought soon overcame Marianne's temporary optimism and she fell asleep at last in a mood of deep depression.

Several days passed in this way, all desperately dull and very much alike. Sanchez appeared regularly to perform his duties as attendant, but he remained only a few minutes and Marianne had no wish for him to stay longer. He seemed to have nothing to say for himself and when she tried to talk to him she elicited nothing beyond a few unintelligible mumbles. Neither Pilar nor her accomplices bothered to come near her, a fact which made the prisoner feel in a curious way both relieved and abandoned.

As time passed, hope declined also. There was no way for her to escape unaided and she could not count on any assistance from her gaoler. At the same time, the workings of her fevered brain brought her little by little to a curious mental state of fatalistic resignation. She felt as if she were already removed from the world of the living, and was very sure that before long Jason would be so also. Then, on the day when Pilar, triumphant under the widow's weeds which would swathe her from head to foot, came to tell her that Jason was dead, there would be nothing left for her but to goad the vindictive Spanish woman to such a pitch of fury that she would not delay

Marianne's own death longer. Her only hope now, in her prison cell, was in a better life hereafter.

Yet in spite of everything, although she herself was not fully aware of it, Marianne's busy brain was hard at work. There was something about that loft which was not quite right, although it had taken her some time to realize what it was. In fact, that something was the size of the huge bales of hay, some of which still retained their osier bindings.

Contemplating first the bales and then the exiguous dimensions of the door through which Sanchez was in the habit of coming, it was borne in on Marianne that the hay could not possibly have entered the loft that way and that there must therefore be another way in, probably through a trap-door in the floor.

It was true that even if she were to succeed in finding the trap-door she would not be much nearer to gaining her freedom. She still had the chain to deal with and the distance was clearly far too great to jump. But the search for it did provide, if not a hope precisely, at least a way of occupying her time, and so she set about clearing the hay from the floor within the limits of her chain, moving it to a heap on one side and then shifting the heap when the first section explored showed no sign of an opening.

The task was a long and painful one which raised a great deal of dust and made her very tired, but on the third day Marianne found two very large hinges set in the woodwork: irrefutable proof that the trap-door existed.

It was almost time for Sanchez to pay his daily visit and so, hurriedly covering up her find, Marianne went and flung herself down in her usual place in the straw and pretended to be asleep. The Spaniard performed his tasks as usual and then withdrew. Marianne devoured a hunk of bread and a piece of meat, drank a mug of water and returned to her excavations. Gradually, the whole trap-door was revealed. It was certainly a very large one, which explained the size of the hay bales, but the prisoner was unable to suppress a groan of dismay when she saw that her chain was too short to allow her to clear it completely.

Bitterly disappointed by this discovery, she dropped down on her knees in the hay and cried with despair at all her wasted labour. It made no difference to know that her chain still held her fast to the beam. She had cherished absurd hopes of that trap-door. Well, she knew now that it was there, and at the same time that it was useless to her . . . Her back ached and her hands were grimed with dirt and rubbed raw with splinters but all the same she began at last, mechanically, to cover up the floor again. It was then she felt it, something hard that moved under her fingers.

After some frantic fumbling in the hay she drew out a long, thin piece of metal, sharpened to a point at one end, and stared at it as if she could not believe her eyes. It was the tine of a pitchfork, which must have broken off when the hay was being stacked and been thought not worth recovering. A tool beyond her wildest dreams.

Marianne shut her eyes and offered up a silent prayer of thankfulness. With this, it must surely be possible to get the better of the padlock, when she recalled that Pilar had been afraid of what she might do with a mere hairpin.

She was on the point of going to work with her metal pick-lock there and then but at that moment she heard footsteps on the other side of the partition wall. Sanchez was coming back, but this time he was not alone. Marianne heard, as usual, the sound of the bales of straw being dragged aside and, hurriedly re-covering the trap-door, turned to hide her new tool by burying it deeply in the hay. Then, to make doubly sure, she sat down on the place where she had hidden it and began nonchalantly chewing a straw, conscious of a beating heart and hoping that the joy she felt did not show too clearly on her face. It was Pilar who entered.

Jason's wife was dressed all in black, although there was nothing out of the ordinary in this since she invariably dressed so or, when she did permit herself a colour, always accompanied it with a sombre veil or other dark accessories. On this occasion, however, she was wearing a bonnet with a deep poke from which fell a veil of very fine Chantilly lace. She walked up to Marianne, who had not turned at her entrance:

'Well, my dear? How do you feel after so many days of reflection?'

Determined not to utter a word, Marianne did not stir. Pilar continued, as if the interview were the most natural thing in the world:

'I hope you have everything you require. You look well enough, to be sure, and Sanchez tells me that your behaviour is perfectly quiet. However, I felt it right to come and bid you farewell . . .'

This time, it took all Marianne's self-control to keep herself from betraying the least start of surprise. Pilar was going away? It might be good news. Was it possible, after all, that today was her lucky day? She continued to chew on her straw as coolly as if Pilar had not existed. All she wanted now was for the woman to go away and let her get on with her preparations for an escape which had suddenly come within the bounds of possibility. Pilar, however, seemed in no hurry. She was taking a jasmine-scented handkerchief from her reticule and holding it to her nose, as if the smell in the loft offended her.

'You know, I suppose, that today is the first of October and that my – that Monsieur Beaufort's trial is to begin this afternoon. Consequently, I am on my way to Paris, where I am to appear tomorrow as a witness.'

Marianne's hand clenched on a fistful of hay. In spite of all her resolution, it was all she could do not to fling herself on this woman who stood there talking of her husband's trial as if it were the most agreeable social occasion. How she longed to plunge the metal tine with which she hoped to gain her freedom deep into that proud and vicious heart. But Sanchez was standing by the door, his arms folded on his chest and his eye alert for trouble. Marianne knew that she would stand little chance in those great hands.

Pilar, meanwhile, was silent, scanning her rival's face, no doubt for some sign of the effect of her words. But Marianne, still keeping her face averted, yawned ostentatiously and perfectly naturally, then turned her back altogether. She had tried the effects of this dumb insolence once before, on the night of her abduction, and she hoped that the results would be the same. It was. Pilar, with a half-checked exclamation of anger, swung round and made quickly for the door.

'Very well, have it as you please!' she said, her voice shaking with rage. 'We shall see how you maintain this fine show of indifference when I come to tell you that your lover's head has fallen to the guillotine and show you a handkerchief dyed with his blood!'

Marianne gritted her teeth and shut her eyes, praying with all her might that anger should not get the better of her will. 'Have pity, Lord, have pity! Make her be quiet . . . make her go away! Be merciful! Give me the strength not to curse her! Help me to hold my tongue! I hate her . . . oh, God, how I hate her! Help me . . .'

Her mind raced desperately to and fro in an effort to find the one, safe refuge. Never had she endured or imagined anything like the strain of listening while this sadistic creature ruthlessly paraded Jason's deadly peril before her. As if she needed to be reminded! As if the dreadful threat had not been haunting her for weeks! She was dying to tell this woman what she thought of her melodramatic speeches, but she was determined to remain true to her vow of silence.

Pilar, however, in her desire to see the effect of her cruel words upon her enemy, had stepped closer. Marianne raised a face of stone and then, quite deliberately, spat in Pilar's face. Pilar stopped short and for a moment it seemed to Marianne that she was going to attack her, so dreadfully contorted was her face, and she waited for the attack with a savage joy, preparing to rend that hateful face in pieces. Then Sanchez spoke heavily from the doorway:

'The Señora will spoil her dress. And the carriage is waiting.'

'I am coming. But tomorrow, Sanchez, and the day after, you will forget to bring her any food or drink. Give her nothing until I return!'

'I understand.'

This time, their departure was final, attended by a scornful shrug from their prisoner. Tomorrow, with God's help, Marianne would be far away.

All the same, she had sense enough not to move until she

had heard the rattle of the chain which told her that the boat had left. Pilar was going away. She was going to Paris to be revenged and Sanchez would not be back for – for two or three days, at least, thanks to Pilar's decree that Marianne should go hungry.

When she was quite sure that she was really alone, Marianne got out her metal spike and set to work on the padlock, hoping that she would be able to pick the lock. If she failed, she would have to attack the beam to which the chain was made fast by a ring, which would have to be gouged out. Forcing herself to be calm so as to keep her hands from trembling, Marianne probed slowly and patiently with her pointed tine in the keyhole of the padlock. It was not easy and for some time she thought that she must fail, for although the chain was new, the padlock was not. For what seemed like an eternity she went on fiddling. Then, at long last, she heard the blessed click and gave a glad little cry. The padlock was open.

Opening the jaws of the manacle round her wrist and taking it off was the work of a moment and Marianne was free. She nursed her painfully swollen wrist for a moment and then flung herself at full length in the hay and rolled about in an ecstasy of joy at the relief of stretching her cramped muscles which had suffered from her restricted movement. She was hot when eventually she sat up, but the blood coursed swiftly through her veins and she was ready for action. Her next task was to open the trap-door and find a way of getting out of the barn while there was still a little light to see by, for autumn was drawing on and the daylight was fading earlier now.

She cleared the trap-door again quickly. It was soon visible, looking very large and stout. It was sure to be heavy but there was a long loop of rope, passed through a pair of rings, to raise it by. Marianne grasped hold of this, gathered all her strength and pulled. The trap resisted but, endowed with a nervous strength made ten times greater by the spur of freedom, she tensed her muscles, set her jaw and went on pulling, regardless of the coarse rope that bit into the soft skin of her palms. Slowly, slowly, the trap came up, rose to a vertical position and fell back with a soft thud on the hay, leaving a gaping hole in the floor. Marianne knelt on the edge and looked down.

Below her stretched a huge barn, so lofty that for a moment she felt faintly dizzy as she looked. She had hoped to find a ladder fixed below the trap-door, which would have made the descent easy; but there was nothing. To jump was out of the question, unless she wanted to risk broken bones.

Marianne's heart beat wildly as she sat back on her heels and cast about feverishly for a rope, or anything that might help her to get down. Unfortunately, the chain which had held her for so long was far too short and the osier bindings of the bales far too weak to bear her weight. But such was her determination to be free of her prison that at last the idea she needed came to her. She could throw down the hay heaped in the loft until it made a mattress thick enough for her to jump on to.

Hurriedly, for already it was growing dark, she began heaving the hay through the open trap, breaking open the osier bindings on the great bales with the tine as she did so. In seconds, the barn was filled with a whirling storm of hay and dust. Some of the bales set others rolling as they were moved and a dozen times Marianne was nearly swept down through the hole, but gradually the floor of the barn began to disappear beneath a mounting heap of hay.

When she thought the pile was high enough, Marianne, feeling as if her throat were on fire, drained the little water remaining in the pitcher and ate her last apple. Then she sat down on the edge of the trap-door and let herself go.

She landed, bouncing like a ball but quite unhurt, and tumbled quickly to the bottom of the heap. She was on the ground at last. The next thing to find out was whether the barn door would open or whether she would have to resort once again to her pitchfork tine which, to be on the safe side, she had thrown down before she jumped. But either because they trusted in the prison they had made ready for her or because they did not wish to alarm any of the peasants of the estate who might be suspicious if they found an all but empty barn carefully locked, Marianne's captors had left the door on the latch.

Cautiously pushing open one side of the big door, which creaked only a very little, Marianne poked her head out and took a careful glance around. As far as she could see in what was now almost total darkness, there was not a soul about, although the great house, buried in the distant trees beyond the lake which stretched almost at her feet, was ablaze with light, to judge from the number of bright sparks twinkling through the intervening vegetation. At the same time, Marianne became aware that it was raining, something she had not perceived before amid the other preoccupations of the day.

It was also very much colder than it had been inside the barn. October had come and the lovely sunshine which had persisted all through September had given way to more wintry weather. Marianne shivered in her cotton dress, but she knew she had to get away from where she was as soon as possible and so, plucking up her courage, she darted out and began a tour of inspection. As she had guessed, the barn was on an island, and a fairly large one at that, and she began to make her way along the shore in search of a boat. It did not take long to discover that apart from the barn itself and a few trees and bushes, there was absolutely nothing at all on the island, least of all a boat.

'I shall have to swim,' she told herself with a shiver. 'The thing to do is to find the narrowest place and hope it is also the side farthest from the house.'

Her first thought had been to go boldly up to the house, tell them who she was and throw herself on Queen Julie's mercy, letting the police claim her later if they would. Pilar had gone to Paris. It might prove the wisest thing to do in the long run.

Then she remembered that most of her kidnappers probably belonged to the royal household and that it would be the easiest thing in the world for them to get her into their power again on pretence of caring for her safety, and next time there would be no hope of escape. Besides, in her present filthy state, with her torn and grubby dress, she would certainly be taken for a lunatic and sent packing by the servants without being allowed so much as a glimpse of the queen. The best course was clearly to go to Paris in her own way, attracting no attention, and keeping out of the way of such persons as law officers and others whose suspicions might be aroused by her vagabond appearance, however difficult that might prove.

Accepting the fact that if she wanted to get off her island she would have to swim for it, Marianne selected her spot with care, where the crossing looked easiest, then, removing her clothes without further hesitation, she made them into a bundle, tied it with her sash and fastened the bundle on top of her head.

Her dress was wet already from the rain but, even so, it would be drier like this than after a session in the water. She knew, too, how awkward it could be trying to swim in one's clothes. In any case, the place was so deserted and the darkness by now so thick that she felt there was very little risk of anyone surprising her in her unconventional attire, and in a very few seconds after removing her clothes she was deep among the reeds which encircled the island, pushing her way through the fleshy tangle of water-lily stems. Her feet sank deeply into a sticky mud which made her shudder but the bottom shelved steeply almost at once and she was soon out of her depth. Launching herself out into the lake she began to swim quietly, making as little noise as possible. The water was cold but not as cold as it had seemed when she first entered it and the feel of it slipping past her naked body was unexpectedly pleasant after so many days in the dusty loft.

It was a long time since Marianne had done any swimming, but her legs and arms performed as if by instinct the easy, flowing movements which old Dobs had taught her. The only really unpleasant thing about this unforeseen exercise was the stagnant smell of the lake itself and the fleeting, underwater contacts with water snakes, which sent a creeping horror over her bare skin. The crossing was not a long one, however, and very soon she felt her feet touch on a hard, sandy bottom. The banks here were fairly high and lined with tall trees, but by grabbing at the thick, flat, water-lily leaves and then at the low branches of a willow, Marianne managed to haul herself dripping on to the bank. At the top, she scrambled quickly into her damp clothes, pulled on her shoes and set off hopefully through the wood.

It was too dark for her to be able to get much idea of her direction but in any case her principal object was to put as much distance between herself and the house as possible. The domain was so large and the woods so wild and overgrown with bushes and brambles which tore at her in her blind progress that she had some hopes at least that she would not be obliged to climb a wall.

By dint of walking straight ahead, now on a spongy carpet of leaves, now through the occasional muddy clearing, she came at last to a path. Her eyes had grown accustomed to the darkness and she was able to make better progress, avoiding the more painful obstacles. It was still raining but it was drier under the trees than out in the open ground. Marianne walked for a long time without being any too clear where she was going but keeping a lookout for some charcoal burner's hut where she might shelter and rest for a little while. She was frozen to the marrow and desperately tired. In the end she found a large, overhanging rock with a deep, dry hollow at its base which could scarcely have been dignified by the name of a cave. It was a mean enough shelter but Marianne crept into it and, curled up, catlike, in the dead leaves, dropped instantly asleep.

She woke with a start to feel something cold and wet licking her face and found herself staring into the slobbering jaws of a large pointer, who was sniffing at her interestedly. Behind the dog was a pair of legs in canvas leggings and stout, hobnailed boots. Following them upwards, Marianne saw that they belonged to a youth with an ancient fowling piece over his shoulder who was standing looking at her in some perplexity. It was broad daylight and the rain had stopped.

Seeing that the sleeper was awake, the youth called off his dog:

'Here, Briquet! Drop it!'

Obediently, the dog withdrew and sat down by his master, who bent forward and held out his hand to Marianne.

'Good morning,' he said pleasantly. 'I'm glad you're awake.

When Briquet found you I thought at first—' He broke off in some embarrassment and it was Marianne who completed the sentence for him.

'That I was dead? Did I look so dreadful?'

'You were so pale.'

'I'm cold.'

This was true. In the sharp morning air, Marianne was shaking like a leaf and the bruises that showed on her pinched arms did nothing to enhance her sorry appearance. The boy hastily removed the short woollen cloak he wore over his own shoulders and put it round Marianne's.

'Come to my house, my grandmother will take care of you. It's quite close – the first roof you can see through the trees, at the edge of the village.'

Marianne saw that she had in fact almost reached the end of the wood and that the smoking chimneys of a village lay only a little way ahead. She felt so ill that she was glad to accept her new friend's offer, merely asking, before she followed him: 'What village is that?'

'Loisy. You don't come from these parts?'

'Is it – is it very far from Mortefontaine?'

'Oh no! Two or three miles east . . . that's all.'

Was that all? Marianne found it hard to conceal her disappointment. She seemed to have walked so far that she had hoped to have come much farther. Most probably, in her ignorance of the district, she had been walking in circles. She turned her head and looked at her companion. He reminded her a little of Gracchus-Hannibal Pioche. He had the same straw-coloured hair and the same steady blue eyes, but his face was rather thinner and his limbs a good deal longer. On the whole, she was pleased with what she saw and made up her mind to trust him:

'I must tell you I have just escaped from the château of Mortefontaine where some people belonging to the Queen of Spain's court have been keeping me prisoner in a barn. But I give you my word I am no criminal, I have not stolen anything—'

The lad grinned at her cheerfully.

'You don't look like it. And if you had done anything like that, they would have put you in prison, not locked you up in a barn! Come on, you can tell it all to my grannie. She's ever so fond of stories.'

As they went along, Marianne learned that her new friend was called Jacques Cochu, that he owned a patch of land in the near-by village and lived all alone with his grandmother at present, but that he was to be married in a few days' time.

'I'd have waited until spring, myself,' he confided, 'but my grannie wants me to be married before then so I shan't be conscripted. I've been lucky so far because the Emperor hasn't raised any troops this year on account of his marriage. So I'm getting married to Etiennette.'

'Don't you want to go and fight?' Marianne asked, a trifle cast down. Her lively imagination had already decked her saviour out in her own, personal colours. Jacques grinned disarmingly:

'Well, I shouldn't mind it. When I hear the old 'uns talk about Valmy and Italy it fair makes my legs itch. Only, if I go, who will look after the farm? And what would become of my grannie – and Etiennette, too, because her parents are both dead since last year. So I've got to stay.'

'Of course,' Marianne said gently. 'You are quite right. Hurry up and get married and be very, very happy!'

Still talking, they came to a small, spotlessly clean farmhouse in the doorway of which a small, very upright old woman stood waiting for them, her arms folded over her woollen shawl, and looking by no means best pleased at the sight of her grandson coming home in the company of a strange, ragged girl. But when Jacques had given her a rapid account of their meeting and of how he had brought Marianne home with him to be warmed and fed, the ready hospitality of the Valois region was instantly forthcoming. The old woman settled her by the fire with a big bowl of hot soup, cut her a large slice of bread and a thick wedge of bacon, and then began to hunt out some dry clothes while Marianne told her story – or rather the edited version of it which she deemed suitable for the occasion. It went very much against the grain with her to lie to these kind people who had welcomed her with such warmth and generosity but she could not see herself reeling off a list of her pompous Italian titles and so for the present it seemed best to become once again Marianne Mallerousse.

'My uncle was killed very recently in the Emperor's service,' she told her new friends, 'and I was kidnapped by his murderers so that I should not betray them. But I must get back to Paris as fast as I can. I want to avenge my – my uncle, and I have important information to give.'

She wondered for a moment if even this watered-down version of her story might not be coming it rather too strong, but neither Madame Cochu nor Jacques appeared in the least surprised. The old woman, indeed, was already nodding agreement:

'I've never thought much of all those sallow-faced foreign folk we've had roaming about here ever since the Emperor made his brother King of Spain. It was a deal more peaceful before. Not that Joseph's a bad man. Always a kind word and very open-handed! He was well enough liked in these parts and folks were sorry to see him go off to all those savages. As for you, child, we'll do what we can to help you get back home again without a stir.'

'But,' Jacques broke in, 'what's wrong with going straight to the police?'

That was a nasty one and Marianne had to think very quickly indeed in order to make her answer appear sufficiently natural.

'I mean to,' she said earnestly. 'But I must see the minister himself. The people who took me prisoner are members of Queen Julie's court and they have great influence. They have set it about that I was responsible for my uncle's death. There is a search for me, but I must be able to produce proof, and the proof I have is in Paris.'

Having produced this explanation, she permitted herself a faint sigh of relief, hoping that she had been adequately convincing. Jacques and his grandmother had withdrawn to the other end of the kitchen and were holding a whispered colloquy which, though animated while it lasted, was over in a few seconds. Jacques came back to Marianne.

'The best thing,' he said, 'is for you to stay here for a bit and rest. You will be quite safe here. Then, this afternoon I'll take you into Dammartin-en-Goele, to my Uncle Cochu. He's the mayor, and he sends a cart of cabbages and turnips to Paris regularly, every three days. There's one going in the morning. Dressed like a peasant girl, you can go back to Paris without being afraid of the police or of the people who kidnapped you. You'll be there by tomorrow night.'

Tomorrow night? Marianne made a mental calculation. Jason's trial had begun the day before, it was probably going on at that very moment, while she stayed talking with these good people. Time was precious.

'I suppose,' she objected timidly, 'it isn't possible to be there any sooner? I am in such a dreadful hurry.'

'Sooner? How? Of course, there is the diligence from Soissons – you might catch that in Dammartin tomorrow . . . but you'd not gain more than a few hours. And you'd not be nearly so safe.'

That was true enough. Naturally, she wished that she could get a horse, but how and where from? She was completely penniless, having left the contents of her purse in Ducatel's hands at the prison. Common sense told her the sensible thing was to accept. The most important thing was to get back and this way she might do so without risk of recapture. It was better to come late than not at all and a trial of such importance was bound to last for several days. In the end, she gave her hosts a grateful smile.

'I agree,' she said, 'and I thank you with all my heart. I hope I may be able to prove my gratitude one day!'

'Don't talk such nonsense,' the grandmother told her gruffly. 'If poor folks don't give one another a hand there's not much good them calling themselves Christians! As for being grateful – well, that's something to keep in your heart. Now you just come and lie down for a bit. There's not much comfort you'll have had sleeping in that nasty wet wood. And while you're having a nap I'll go and see Etiennette, Jacques's promised wife, and borrow a bodice and petticoat from her. The pair of you are much of a size.'

Late that afternoon, dressed in a coarse red woollen skirt and black bodice and bundled up in a black woollen shawl given her by generous Madame Cochu, her feet thrust into a pair of sabots several sizes too large for her and her head enveloped in a huge linen coif, Marianne got up behind Jacques on the crupper of the big cart-horse, used both for riding and on the farm. In front were two big panniers of late apples, fastened to the horse's collar.

It was quite dark when they reached Dammartin, a walled town on a hill, and Jacques handed Marianne into the care of his great-uncle, Pierre Cochu, a fine-looking old man, like an ancient, knotted vine, who took her in with the noble generosity common to tillers of the soil and asked no awkward questions. She was introduced as a cousin of Etiennette's who wanted to go to Paris to work as a laundress in the establishment of a distant relative. Consequently, when the time came for her to say goodbye to Jacques no one thought it anything but perfectly natural that she should throw her arms round his neck and kiss him on both cheeks. But no one there could guess the gratitude which went into that gesture, or why Jacques should have grown so red at being the recipient of this mark of affection. He gave a nervous laugh to hide his embarrassment and said stoutly:

'We'll meet again very soon, Cousin Marie. When we're married, Etiennette and I, we'll come and visit you in Paris. We'll enjoy that . . .'

'And so will I, Jacques! Tell Etiennette that I shall not forget you, any of you.'

She felt a pang at parting from him. Although she had met him and his grandmother so short a time before, they had been so kind and friendly to her that Marianne felt as if she had always known them. They were suddenly very dear to her and she promised herself that if better times ever came for her she would show them that they had not helped one who was ungrateful. All the same, Jacques was hardly out of sight before Marianne's thoughts had turned once again to their constant obsession with Jason's fate, which was being decided even then, as she was making such efforts to be near him.

After a brief night's rest, spent comfortably enough in a tiny chamber smelling sweetly of wax and citronella, Marianne found herself as day was breaking seated on the driver's seat of a big wagon full of cabbages beside a taciturn fellow who did not utter as much as ten words in the whole course of the journey. They lumbered away peacefully along the road to Paris, far too peacefully, indeed, for Marianne, who nearly died of impatience a hundred times during the interminable drive.

Luckily, it was not raining. The weather was cold but dry. The way was flat and monotonous but Marianne did not succeed in imitating her companion, who dozed a good part of the time, much to the annoyance of his passenger. Whenever she saw his big head nodding, it was all Marianne could do to restrain herself from seizing the reins and setting the whole equipage galloping madly down the endless highway, at the risk of losing all the cabbages. But that would have been a poor return to her friends for all their kindness, so she possessed herself in patience.

All the same, when the spires of Paris appeared at last through the autumnal mists she very nearly shouted for joy and when the wagon reached the village of La Villette and crossed over the site of the unfinished canal of St Denis she had to stop herself jumping down from her seat and running ahead, but she knew it was best to keep up the pretence to the end.

The powerful smell emanating from the city's refuse dump, near which they were obliged to pass, seemed to jerk the driver out of his doze. He opened first one eye, then the second, then turned his head to look at Marianne, but so slowly that Marianne wondered if he were animated by some form of very slow clockwork.

'Tha coozen t'laundress,' he asked, 'wheer dost a live? T'mester said t'set thee doon reet by, but ahm f't'market.'

Marianne had had plenty of time on that endless drive to think about what she meant to do when she eventually reached Paris. A return to Crawfurd's house was out of the question and it could prove equally perilous to make for her own. At this point it had occurred to her that by now Fortunée Hamelin might have returned home from Aix-la-Chapelle. The summer season there was over, surely she would be back in her beloved Paris . . . unless she had sacrificed that love in favour of her other ruling passion for Casimir de Montrond who was officially under open arrest in the Flemish town of Anvers. If that proved to be the case, Marianne decided, she would wait until it was quite dark and then try and slip quietly into her own house in the rue de Lille. So she answered the man: 'She lives quite near the Barrière des Porcherons.'

The yokel's dull eye brightened fleetingly:

'T'beant mooch aht't'road. Ah'll set thee doon thar than.'

Upon which decisive utterance he appeared to fall asleep again, while ahead of them, by the side of a broad expanse of fresh water, there loomed up Ledoux's elegant rotunda and the *guingettes* with their red trellises of the Barrière de la Villette.

Safe in her disguise, Marianne did not flinch when the guards made their routine check. Then they were off again, following the wall of the Fermiers Généraux as far as the Barrière de la Chapelle, after which the wagon turned into the Faubourg St Denis. When Marianne's destination was reached they parted without a word spoken and she set out, shaking uncontrollably with the excitement of finding herself in Paris once more, to run to the rue de la Tour d'Auvergne as if her very life depended on it.

It was something of an ordeal because the streets led steeply uphill all the way to the village of Montmartre. To make running easier she had taken off the heavy sabots, which were too big for her and chafed her unaccustomed feet. Consequently, by the time she came to the white house which always in the past offered her such a warm welcome, she was barefoot, red-faced, tousled and panting, but her only fear was that she might find the shutters closed and the house wearing the dismal, unfriendly look common to all houses when the people who live there are away. No, the shutters were open, the chimneys smoking and a vase of flowers could be seen through the hall window.

But when Marianne entered the gate and made to cross the courtyard to the front door, she saw the gatekeeper come running out after her as fast as a pair of very short legs would carry him, holding his arms out wide as if to block her path. With a sinking heart she saw that he was a new man, one she had not seen before.

'Here! You there, girl! Where d'you think you're going?'

Marianne stopped and waited for him, so that he all but cannoned into her.

'To see Madame Hamelin,' she said coolly. 'She is expecting me.'

'Madame does not receive persons of your kind. Besides, she's not at home. Be off with you!'

He was pulling at her arm, trying to drag her away but Marianne shook him off.

'If she is not at home, then fetch Jonas to me. I suppose he is at home?'

'Fetch him to such a hussy as you? Tell me what name I should say if you want me to go, then.'

Marianne hesitated fractionally, but Jonas was a friend and he was used to seeing her in unexpected guises:

'Say: Mademoiselle Marianne.'

'Marianne what?'

'Never you mind. Go and bring him to me at once and take care Jonas is not angry with you for keeping me waiting.'

The gatekeeper departed unwillingly for the house, mumbling under his breath as he went various uncomplimentary things about brazen hussies forcing their way into honest folks' houses. Not many seconds later, Jonas, Fortunée's major-domo, literally burst out of the glazed front door, his good-humoured black face split in two by an enormous smile of welcome:

'Mademoiselle Ma'anne! Mademoiselle Ma'anne! It is you! . . . Come you inside dis minute! My lord, but what you doin' dressed like dat?'

Marianne laughed, feeling her spirits revive miraculously at the warmth of this familiar welcome. Here, at last, she had found a safe harbour.

'Poor Jonas! Nine times out of ten I seem to arrive on the doorstep looking like a complete ragamuffin. Madame is out?'

'Yes, but she's coming back soon. You come inside and rest yourself while you wait.'

Dismissing the gatekeeper with an imperious wave of his hand, Jonas led Marianne straight into the house, telling her as they went of the anxiety his mistress had been in on her account since her return from Aix.

'She thinks you dead! When Monseigneur de Benevento tell her you disappeared, I thought she would run mad, I give you my word . . . Listen! Here she comes now.'

In fact, hardly had Jonas shut the door before Fortunée's brougham entered the courtyard, described a perfect circle round the fountain and drew up at the foot of the steps. Fortunée got out but she looked very grave and Marianne saw that for the first time since she had known her, her friend was dressed in a plain walking dress of a severe dark purple colour. Also unusual for her was an almost total absence of paint on her face and as her veil was drawn up, Marianne could see by her red eyes that she had been crying. But already Jonas had hurried out to her, calling:

'Madame Fortunée! Mademoiselle Ma'anne is here! See!'

Madame Hamelin looked up and a light of joy sprang into her lack-lustre eyes. Without a word she ran up the steps and flung herself into her friend's arms, hugging her and crying at the same time. Marianne had never seen the light-hearted Créole in such a state and while she returned the embrace with equal fervour she pleaded in an undertone:

'Fortunée, for God's sake, tell me what is the matter! Were you truly so afraid for me?'

Fortunée freed herself quickly and stood for a moment holding Marianne at arms' length, her hands resting on the girl's shoulders while she gazed deep into her eyes with such an expression of compassion that a cold trickle of fear ran through Marianne's veins, leaving her unable to speak.

'Marianne, I have just come from the court,' Madame Hamelin said at last in the gentlest possible voice. 'It is all over.'

'What – what do you mean?'

'Jason Beaufort was sentenced to death an hour ago.'

Marianne staggered as if she had been shot. But after so

many days' unconscious expectation of this very thing, she was to some extent prepared, without knowing it, so that the wound had begun to heal over almost as soon as it was made. She had known in her heart that one day she would have to listen to those dreadful words and, as the human body prepares secretly to fight for life against the disease it harbours, so her mind had armed itself against the suffering to come. The danger was too close now, there was no time for weakness, no time for tears or terror.

Fortunée had extended her arms in an automatic gesture, expecting Marianne to fall down in a faint, but she let them drop slowly to her sides as she stared in amazement at the unknown woman who looked back at her out of a face which had turned suddenly to stone. Marianne spoke in a voice of ice:

'Where is the Emperor? At St Cloud?'

'No. The whole court is at Fontainebleau, for the hunting. What are you going to do? You won't—'

'Oh yes I shall. That is precisely what I shall do. Do you think I care for anything in this world if Jason is not in it? I swore by my mother's memory that if they killed him I should stab myself at the foot of the scaffold. What are Napoleon's rages to me? He shall listen to me, whether he likes it or not, whether it suits him or not! Afterwards, he may do to me what he likes. As if it mattered!'

'Don't say that!' Fortunée begged her, crossing herself hurriedly, as if to avert an evil fate. 'Think of all of us who love you.'

'I am thinking of the man I love, and without whom I will not live! There is only one thing I ask of you, Fortunée. Lend me a chaise and some clothes, and a little money, and tell me where I can go in Fontainebleau to avoid being arrested before I have seen the Emperor. You know the place, I think. If you will do this for me, I will bless you to my dying day—'

'Stop!' Fortunée cried distractedly. 'Will you stop talking about dying! Lend you money, my chaise – what are you thinking of?'

'Fortunée!' Marianne protested in accents of hurt surprise,

but before she could say more her friend's arm was folded lovingly about her waist and Fortunée was leading her upstairs, murmuring affectionately in her ear:

'We'll go together, of course, you silly thing. I have a house there, a little retreat of my own by the river, and I know every inch of the forest. We'll find that useful if you don't succeed in getting into the château – much as Napoleon hates to have his hunting interrupted. But if that is the only way . . .'

'I can't let you, Fortunée! You may be dreadfully compromised . . . even banished . . .'

'Well, if I am, I'll go and join Montrond at Anvers and we'll have a lovely time together! Come, my love. I must say I shan't be sorry to learn how the Emperor came to allow such a sentence to be passed on such an extraordinarily attractive man – to say nothing of one who could not possibly have committed the crimes they have accused him of! A foul murder? Coining? A man with his proud bearing, and those eyes, like a sea-eagle's? It's perfectly absurd! . . . Jonas! Tell my woman to prepare a bath for Mademoiselle Marianne at once, and some clean clothes. We'll have a good meal in half an hour and a post-chaise at the door half an hour after that. Is that understood? Off with you, then.'

The major-domo departed speedily in the direction of the stairs, calling loudly for Mademoiselle Clémentine as he went, and Fortunée, following more sedately with Marianne, said confidentially:

'Now, darling, we have plenty of time so you can tell me all about it. Where have you been . . .?'

CHAPTER TEN

The Imperial Hunt

Madame Hamelin reined in her mount beside the worn stone cross, all overgrown with lichens, which stood in the shadow of a broad oak tree at a place where four ways met.

'This is the cross of Souvray,' she said, pointing at the stone with her whip. 'It will be the perfect spot to wait until the hunt begins. I know there is to be a luncheon at the Carrefour de Recloses, about a mile and a half from here, but I do not know which direction the hunt will take.'

As she spoke, she dismounted and, hitching her horse to the trunk of a tall Scots pine, gathered up the long skirts of her leaf-brown habit and strolled leisurely back to seat herself on the steps below the old cross, while Marianne, following her example, tied her own horse to the same tree and joined her friend on the steps.

The cross-roads was quite deserted. The only sounds were the trickle of water somewhere on the other side of a thicket and the rapid scampering feet of a startled hare on the deep, rustling carpet of fallen leaves. A little way to the south, however, the woods were alive with the unmistakable hum of a crowd of people enjoying themselves, punctuated by noises of hound and horn and distant carriages.

'I've never seen an imperial hunt before,' Marianne said, seating herself and settling the ample folds of her dark green habit round her legs. 'What happens?'

'Oh, it's quite simple. All the court is supposed to take part, but in point of fact the Emperor hunts alone, except for his equerry-in-chief General Nansouty, the master of the hunt Monsieur d'Hannecourt, a single huntsman and his Mameluke servant Rustan, who goes with him everywhere. Before Savary was chief of police, he used to be there as well, but now he is obliged to watch over his master at a rather greater distance. As to the formalities – well, everyone, men and women, including the Emperor, set out from the château in a procession of carriages. They drive to a point which has been decided on beforehand and there is a splendid collation. When that is over, the court either hangs about doing nothing in particular, except digest their luncheon, or else goes quietly home, and Napoleon hunts. That is all there is to it!'

'I never knew he was so fond of hunting. He never mentioned it . . .'

Fortunée laughed. 'My dear child, our Emperor is a man with a prodigious talent for creating the right atmosphere, and doing what he feels goes with the part. Privately, he has no great fondness for hunting, very largely because he is an indifferent horseman, and if his horses were not always very well trained he would certainly have a respectable number of falls to his credit. However, he believes that a sovereign of France is obliged to hunt. French kings have always hunted madly – Capets, Valois, Bourbons, were all devoted to the chase. I dare say he feels he owes it to his uncle Louis XVI! And you need not look so downcast about it, either. It gives you all the better chance of finding him more or less alone.'

For Fortunée's sake, Marianne summoned up a wan smile but the fear which clutched at her heart was too great to allow her any pleasure in her friend's witticisms. Jason's life would depend on what took place that afternoon and in the three days since she had arrived at La Madeleine, Fortunée's charming rural retreat, this thought had never left her, day or night.

Almost as soon as they arrived, in fact, Madame Hamelin had hastened to the palace to see Duroc and try, through him, to obtain an audience with the Emperor. The ever-helpful Duc de Frioul had communicated the request to his master but Napoleon had made it known that he did not desire to see Madame Hamelin, intimating that she had better confine herself for the present to her own delightful property and not venture to appear at court. Marianne's heart sank when she heard this.

'Oh, my poor Fortunée! You are involved in my disgrace! He would not see you because he knows you are my friend.'

'Well, if he does it's because he threw us together. Actually, though, I think it is rather my friendship with Josephine which makes him keep me at a distance. They say her new Danubian majesty is horribly jealous of anything even remotely connected with our own dear Empress. Indeed, I never really thought Napoleon would see me – in fact I expected it so little that I went to the trouble of making a few inquiries on my own account. The day after tomorrow the Emperor goes hunting. You may come upon him at some time during that day – and although he may be a little angry at first, I shall be very much surprised if he won't listen to you.'

'He must listen to me! Even if I have to throw myself under his horse's hooves!'

'Which would be a great piece of folly! With his clumsiness, he'd more than likely ride right over you. And your looks, my dear, are still quite your best weapon.'

It was decided, therefore, and Marianne was left to count the hours and minutes that must elapse before their ride into the forest of Fontainebleau. Yet now, as the fatal moment drew near, her eagerness to be up and doing was tempered by nebulous fears. She knew Napoleon's temper of old. What if he refused to let her speak, sent her away without so much as listening to what she had to say?

Fortunée had taken some chocolate from her pocket and was offering it to Marianne:

'Here. You'll need all your strength and it's none too warm here in the woods. But the luncheon can't go on for ever.'

A little biting wind had got up, sweeping the dead leaves over the surface of the Route Ronde which had been made in the days of Louis XIV to encircle Fontainebleau and a large portion of the forest for the vehicles following the hunt. Clouds raced across a sky more pale grey than blue, just failing to keep up with a dark mass of swallows on their way to find the sun. Marianne's throat tightened as she watched the birds, flying so fast and free, thinking of Jason, a sea bird held basely in a cage until such time as the dull hand of a slavish, so-called justice should strike him down, not letting him see the vast, pure ocean again, even for one day.

A horn blowing deep in the forest dragged her from her gloomy thoughts. She had not hunted all her life without knowing the signs that the hunt was moving off. She jumped to her feet, automatically smoothing out the folds of her riding dress.

'Hurry,' she cried. 'They're away!'

'Not so fast,' Fortunée said easily. 'We need to know the direction first.'

The two of them stood for a moment listening, trying to disentangle the confusing echoes of hounds and horns; then Madame Hamelin beamed triumphantly at her friend:

'Excellent! They are going towards the Haute Borne – we shall be able to cut across the line! Come on! I'll show you the way and then drop behind while you go on alone – since His Majesty would rather not see me! Ready?'

With one accord, the two young women sprang into the saddle. Their whips cracked and they were off at full gallop through the forest, guided by the sound of the horn. At first they followed a cross-ride with heavy cover on either side, bending low over their horses' necks to avoid overhanging branches. The going was rough, over stony ground which climbed steeply from time to time only to descend as steeply into deep valley-bottoms thick with heather and high rusty-golden bracken, but both were excellent horsewomen, Marianne especially, and they were able to avoid the many obstacles in their path without slackening their pace. In the normal way, Marianne would have enjoyed enormously the hectic ride through one of the finest forests in Europe, but today the stakes were too high and the risk of failure too tragic. Galloping in a desperate bid to save Jason Beaufort's life, she knew beyond all doubt that her own life, too, hung on the outcome.

They rode for a long time. The quarry seemed to be doubling endlessly and it was nearly an hour before they caught sight of the flash of white between the bare trees that told them the pack was in full cry. Hounds were running fast, giving tongue as they ran. The horn calls had already told Marianne long before this that the quarry was a boar and with her nerves in their present raw state she was glad of it. Deer-hunting had never given her any pleasure: the grace and beauty of the creatures moved her too deeply.

Fortunée had reined to a halt and now her voice came, borne on the wind:

'There they are – you go on alone . . .'

Marianne could see the boar now, crashing through the undergrowth like a great, black, bristly cannon ball, the pack hard on his heels. After them came two red-jacketed huntsmen, both riding greys, blowing for all they were worth. The Emperor could not be far away. She dug in her heels and shot forward, burst through a thicket, jumped a fallen tree trunk and a tangled brake – and landed almost plump on top of Napoleon, who was also going full-tilt.

Both mounts reared wildly to avoid a collision but whereas Marianne, perfect mistress of herself and her horse, remained easily in the saddle, the Emperor of the French, caught off balance, parted company with his stirrups and took a flying toss into the leafy mould.

'Ten thousand thunders! What half-witted—'

But Marianne was already on her knees beside him, overcome with horror at what she had done:

'It's me, Sire! Only me! Oh, in heaven's name, forgive me! I did not mean – oh, good God! You are not hurt?'

Napoleon glared at her and, getting quickly to his feet. snatched from Marianne's hands the hat which he had lost in his fall and which she had picked up.

'I was under the impression, Madame,' he said, in such arctic tones that Marianne felt an involuntary shiver down her spine, 'that I had banished you. What are you doing here?'

She gazed up at him imploringly. It had not even occurred to her to get to her feet.

'I had to see you, Sire! I had to speak to you, at all costs—'

'Even the cost of my back, it would seem,' Napoleon said grimly, adding, with a touch of impatience: 'Well, get up, get up! The appearance we present is already sufficiently ridiculous – and we are not alone.'

They were not. Even as he spoke, three men, whom the Emperor must have outdistanced in the chase, came thundering up to them. The first to arrive wore the splendid uniform of a general of hussars, the second was in the green suit of the imperial huntsmen and the third, the only one of the three known to Marianne, was the Mameluke, Rustan. The general had dismounted in an instant.

'Sire!' he exclaimed in anxious tones. 'Are you all right?'

But it was Marianne who answered, smiling engagingly: 'It is I, General, who do not deserve to be. My horse bolted with me and I reached here at the same moment as His Majesty. Our horses reared and I was thrown. The Emperor was good enough to come to my assistance, for which I am most grateful.'

As she uttered this piece of diplomatic prevarication she saw Napolean's jaw lose something of its set look and the glare go out of his eye.

'It was nothing,' he remarked, carelessly shaking a dead leaf or two from the skirts of his grey redingote. 'Say no more. But enough of this day's sport. I am tired of it. It has been a fruitless day. Call off your huntsmen and your hounds, Monsieur d'Hannecourt. We are going back to the château. You, Madame,' he turned to Marianne, 'will follow us. I wish to speak with you. Rustan will take you in by way of the English Garden.'

'But, Sire, I am not alone in the forest. A friend—'

A gleam appeared in Napoleon's blue-grey eyes, not of anger this time but amusement:

'I see. Then you had better collect your friend, Madame, before you come. Some people,' he added, with an inflection which told Marianne that he was under no illusions as to that friend's identity, 'would appear remarkably hard to lose.'

Marianne bowed quickly and, placing her booted foot in General Nansouty's gallantly proffered hands, vaulted into the saddle with a neatness that made the hussar's lips twitch irrepressibly. He was too experienced a horseman to be taken in by

Marianne's tactful story. If anyone had taken a header, it was certainly not this girl. But Nansouty was a man of the world and so he merely smiled.

It did not take Marianne many minutes to discover Fortunée or many more to put her in possession of the facts about what had taken place and the new hope which had so unexpectedly resulted for Marianne.

'He will see you, that is the main thing,' Madame Hamelin said. 'I dare say he'll give you one of his scolds, but what matters is if he listens to you. You may win yet.'

Then, wasting no more time, the two women gave their horses their heads and hurtled after the Emperor and his suite.

At the first cross-roads, they found Rustan waiting for them underneath a pine tree, looking like some rigid equestrian statue of a sultan. Making a sign to them to follow, he cantered off in the direction of the château, making a slight detour on the way so as to avoid running his charges into the rest of the court.

Half an hour later, Marianne was inside the palace of Fontainebleau, where she had begun to despair of ever being. She had seen no one beyond a few servants on her way from the English Garden, past the Carp Pool and through the Fountain Court. Then, leaving Fortunée in a small, deserted salon on the ground floor, Rustan had thrown open the door into a large room giving on to the garden and, bowing, indicated a chair. Once again, Marianne found herself in Napoleon's private office. It was the fourth she had seen but although this one had modern furniture and decorations in the style of Louis XVI, the usual litter of papers, maps, personal belongings and the ubiquitous red morocco files made it seem instantly familiar. There was the open snuff-box, the goose quill flung down at random, the big map unrolled on the desk and the hat left carelessly on a bracket table, just as at the Tuileries and St Cloud and the Trianon. To Marianne, it was reassuring. The Emperor's powerful personality stamped all his surroundings with his own identity, and feeling slightly more at home now and in a more hopeful frame of mind, she settled down to await his coming.

When he did come, it was in his usual style: a quick step on the tiled floor of the corridor, slam of the door, a rapid march across the room, hands behind back, pause by the big desk with a swift, appreciative eye for the ceremonial court curtsy, then directly into the subject on hand:

'Well, Madame? No doubt you had excellent reasons for pursuing me here importunately in direct defiance of my commands?'

The tone, aggressive and deliberately offensive, would, in the normal way, have provoked Marianne to an equally stinging reply. But she knew that if she wanted to save Jason she must cast off her pride and humble herself to the dust, and with all the more reason now that this same ruler had not long ago bitten the dust himself on her account.

'Sire,' she said with gentle dignity, 'this is the first time Your Majesty has accused me of being importunate. Have you forgotten that I am your loyal, obedient subject?'

'Loyal, I hope. Obedient, by no means! You are a perfect menace, Madame, and if I did not take good care you would disrupt the whole of my Grand Army altogether. If they're not fighting duels over you, they're killing people for you.'

'That's not true!' Marianne cried, stung to an indignation stronger than her resolution to be humble. 'No one ever killed for me, and those that say so—'

'Are not so very far out. Granting that no actual murder was committed on your behalf, I hope you do not mean to deny that on the same night two men challenged each other to fight and two more actually fought on your account.'

'Not two more, Sire. One more. The same man was the cause of both duels.'

Napoleon struck the desk a resounding blow with the flat of his hand:

'Stop splitting hairs, Madame! I don't like it. One thing is certain. My gendarmes caught two men in the act of fighting a duel in your garden. One escaped, the other failed to do so. How long has Fournier-Sarlovèze been your lover?'

'He is not my lover, Sire,' Marianne said wearily. 'Nor has he ever been. As Your Majesty knows full well, being aware of the deep bond of affection which exists between him and my friend, Madame Hamelin. Now let me entreat Your Majesty to forget that unfortunate business. It is not what I have come about.'

'But it is what I wish to talk about. I want the matter cleared up. General Fournier refuses consistently to offer any explanation other than this idiotic tale about a friendly bout with a foreign acquaintance. Which seems hardly likely when Chernychev had already cried off from fighting this damned Beaufort because Prince Kurakin had given him an urgent message for the Tsar. Not quite the moment to get out the foils.'

So the men who had invaded her garden on the night of the duel had recognized the Russian attaché and Fournier's gesture had been in vain. She bowed her head.

'Your Majesty knows the other man was Count Chernychev?'

Napoleon's face took on a sly grin which to Marianne appeared positively satanic:

'I thought so . . . certainly, but now you yourself have told me so.'

'Sire!' Marianne protested, outraged. 'That was unworthy!'

'It is for me, Madame, to be the judge of what is or is not unworthy. And let me advise you to moderate your voice if you wish me to hear you out.' There was a pause, occupied on his side in a close scrutiny of Marianne's crimsoned face. 'And now,' the Emperor went on, 'now I am waiting to hear from you a complete – and truthful – account of what passed in your house that night. Do you understand? I want the truth, and the whole truth! And you would be unwise to attempt a falsehood. I know you too well not to see through it at once.'

Marianne's eyes glazed at the prospect opening in front of her. Tell what had taken place in her room? Describe to this man, who had once been to her of all lovers the most passionate, the humiliating usage she had suffered at Chernychev's hand. It was an ordeal which seemed beyond her strength. But already Napoleon had walked round to the other side of his desk and was standing propped against it with his arms folded, watching her closely:

'Well, Madame. I am waiting.'

At that moment, Marianne had a brainwave. He wanted to know everything that had happened in her room that night? Then surely, this was the perfect, undreamed of opportunity to tell him all about the dreadful bargain which had been the beginning of the evil plot against Jason? Such a consideration made her own scruples of modesty and pride irrelevant.

Bravely, she lifted her head and stared very steadily into Napoleon's eyes:

'You wish to know everything, Sire? Very well, I will tell you everything. And I swear by my mother's memory that it shall be the entire truth . . .'

Then Marianne began her story. She spoke haltingly at first, forced herself to find words that should be simple and convincing. Then, little by little, she warmed to her story. The horror of that July night took hold of her again so that the words came pouring out with their full weight of agony and shame. She told it all: her bargain with Francis Cranmere, his false warning, her fears for Jason's life, then the appearance of the Russian, having drunk himself into a condition of primeval savagery, and the rape and torture he had inflicted on her, followed at last by Fournier-Sarlovèze's almost miraculous intervention, the arrival of the law officers and the general's action in allowing his adversary to escape in order to avoid possible diplomatic complications. During all this time, the Emperor did not once interrupt, but as she talked Marianne saw the tightening of his jaw and the ominous steely glint which came into his blue-grey eyes.

When it was over, she bowed her face into her trembling hands and said exhaustedly: 'You know it all now, Sire. I swear to you that every word of all that I have told you is the simple truth.' She took her hands from her face and added quickly: 'And I say that Lord Cranmere's visit to me was the start of the tragic events which—'

'Wait a moment, we are not there yet,' Napoleon interrupted her curtly. 'You have sworn that all this is the absolute truth.'

'And I will swear it again, Sire!'

'No need. If it was as you say, you must bear the proof upon your person. Let me see.'

Marianne stared at him wildly, scarlet to the roots of her dark hair:

'You mean – the burn? But, Sire, it is – it is on my hip!'

'Well? Take off your clothes.'

'Here?'

'Why not? No one will come in. And I believe I am right in thinking it will not be the first time you have undressed in my presence? Time was, and not so long ago, you even appeared quite glad to do so.'

Marianne's eyes filled with tears at this cool, sardonic reference to a time which would always count amongst her most cherished memories, although it seemed to her now to belong to another life.

'Sire—' she said weakly, 'that time is – is more remote now than – than perhaps Your Majesty realizes . . .'

'I do not see it so. And if you wish me to believe you, Madame, you must prepare yourself to bring proof. If not, you may go. I shall not detain you.'

Slowly, Marianne rose. A lump came and went in her throat, a lump of misery and shame. It was too much. Had he loved her so little, then, that he could demand from her this painful sacrifice of her modesty and of all that had once existed between them? He had been right when he reminded her that once she had gladly offered her body to his gaze, because then his very gaze had been a caress. But he was looking at her now as coldly as a slave merchant inspecting a new piece of goods. And that was not all. There was a gulf between the woman of Butard and Trianon and the woman who, on the hard boards of a prison, had given herself so passionately to the man whose life might now depend on the wreck of her most intimate feelings.

Not looking at him, she began to unfasten her close-fitting green spencer. Her fingers trembled over the black silk frogs but the short jacket dropped to the ground, followed by the long riding skirt, shift and petticoat. Crossing her arms modestly over her breast, she turned so that he could see her injured hip.

'There, Sire,' she said without expression.

Napoleon bent forward. When he straightened once more his eyes were rather grim and he held Marianne's gaze locked in his for a moment in silence.

'You must love him,' he said softly at last.

'Sire!'

'No. Don't speak. It was that I wanted to know, you see. You do not love me any more, do you?'

Her eyes were searching his now:

'I do love you, indeed I do . . . only – differently.'

'That is what I said. You are . . . fond of me.'

'But yourself, Sire? What of your feelings for me – are they still the same? Is the Empress not . . . very close to your heart?'

He gave her one of his rare, very charming smiles:

'Yes. You are quite right. And yet . . . it will be a long time, I think, before I can look at you without a tremor. Put your clothes on.'

While she, trembling now with haste, pulled up her shift and skirts and refastened her spencer, Napoleon turned to rummage among the papers cluttering his desk as if he were searching for something. At last, he unearthed a large sheet of paper covered with fine writing and already sealed with the great imperial seal and held it out to Marianne.

'Here,' he said. 'This is what you came for, isn't it, at the risk of breaking both our necks? Jason Beaufort's pardon? You see, I attended to it before you came. It is all ready.'

'A pardon, Sire? . . . Oh, God! How happy you have made me! . . . Is this nightmare really at an end? He will go free?'

Napoleon frowned and took back the reprieve. The friend had gone, transformed abruptly into the Emperor once more:

'That I did not say, Madame. I have spared your American pirate's life because I know – although I have no formal proof – that he did not kill Nicolas Mallerousse. But the charge of smuggling remains, as does that of the counterfeit English notes. To make matters worse, it is the talk of every chancellery and I cannot ignore an allegation of such seriousness. Beaufort will not lose his head, therefore, but neither can he go free.'

The flame of happiness in Marianne's heart dwindled to a pale glimmer.

'Sire,' she said in a low voice, 'I can assure you that he is innocent of these as of the other.'

'Your word is a frail defence against overwhelming evidence.'

'If you will only let me explain – tell you what I believe happened and how, then I am certain—'

'No! Ask no more, Madame. It is out of my power to grant your request. Be glad that I have spared his head. I do not say the chain gang is a rest cure, far from it, but men survive – some even return.'

Or escape, Marianne thought, her mind going suddenly to the nonchalant figure of Jason's curious fellow-prisoner. But the Emperor was continuing:

'As to yourself, you are naturally perfectly free to return to your own home whenever you so wish. Your cousin awaits you there, together with that odd character whom you seem to have adopted as another of your "uncles". I have to tell you that he returned from his mission to Monsieur Fouché two days ago. So you have no need to remain in hiding . . . where did you go, by the way, when you – er – decided to retire from the world at Bourbon l'Archambault?'

Relieved of her most pressing anxiety, Marianne allowed herself a smile.

'Is there anything you do not know, Sire?' she asked.

'A great deal too much. Particularly since I have been obliged to do without the Duke of Otranto. About you, for example. What refuge did you find?'

'No refuge, Sire. A prison,' Marianne told him, determined to conceal as far as possible the parts played by Crawfurd and his wife, and also by Talleyrand. 'Jason Beaufort's wife, who has taken shelter with the Queen of Spain, had me carried off and kept prisoner in a barn on an island on the Mortefontaine estate. I managed to escape, thank God—'

Napoleon's fist was brought down angrily on a small table which cracked ominously under the shock:

'This is not the first time I have heard it suggested that my sister-in-law's house has become, unknown to herself, an asylum for all kinds of people. She is good-natured to the point of stupidity. Tell her any tale and she throws open her purse and her house! But this is too much. It shall be seen to. Now, Princess,' drawing his watch from his fob and giving it a quick glance, 'you have leave to withdraw. I have an audience with Madame de Montesquiou in a few moments, concerning her appointment as governess to the King of Rome – or the Princess of Venice, as may be. Go and rejoin your friend and, in future, do as I tell you. I hope to see you again very soon.'

The interview was over. Watched approvingly by the master, Marianne sank into the deep, formal curtsy which protocol demanded, so low that she was almost kneeling. Then, again in accordance with court etiquette, she backed her way to the door, while the Emperor rang a bell to summon Rustan.

She had reached the door when he stopped her with a gesture:

'Oh, by the by, your friend Crawfurd is also back in the nest. They had been keeping him in a deserted farmhouse somewhere near Pontoise and released him with no other harm than that resulting from the necessity he was at to walk all the way home. A somewhat painful exercise for a man with a gouty foot.'

For an instant, Marianne was speechless. Napoleon's expression was stern but his eyes were laughing. With another wave of his hand, this time of dismissal, he added suddenly:

'You seem to have a genius for making loyal friends, Madame, even of those like that old rascal Talleyrand who are not renowned for their loyalty. Nor is it any mean feat to have attacked that night-owl Crawfurd. Before you came he lived for nothing but his worship of our unhappy aunt Marie-Antoinette – you have given him a new zest for youthful adventure. Cherish your friends, Madame. One day, they may be of service to us.'

'I will do my best, Sire.'

Again she was waved to the door but that day Napoleon could not be done with Marianne so easily. He called her back once more:

'I nearly forgot. You may inform the encroaching creature at present kicking her heels in the yellow salon that her beloved Fournier has been back for the past month with his regiment in Spain. It may lessen her temptation to spend the winter at Anvers! And finally – as regards Count Chernychev, when he returns to France I shall let him know my opinion of him. You have my word on that . . . I have never permitted anyone to hurt those I love. I do not mean to start with you.'

'Sire,' Marianne stammered, moved almost to tears at this last, utterly unlooked-for proof of affection. 'What can I say—'

'Nothing. Your servant, Princess.'

This time, it was over. The closed door stood between Napoleon and the Princess Sant'Anna, but Marianne carried away with her a great sense of comfort, born, initially, of the knowledge that Jason's life was safe, and also of the assurance that she had been restored not perhaps to the Emperor's love, which she would have found something of an embarrassment as things stood, but to his friendship at least. Once again, she was free to act according to her own will, and she meant to make the most of her freedom.

'Well?' Fortunée Hamelin demanded anxiously when Marianne rejoined her in the little drawing-room where she had been left to kick her heels.

'Jason is already reprieved! The Emperor knows that he is innocent of Black Fish's death, but there is still the affair of the counterfeit money. He – he goes to prison.'

Fortunée frowned, thought for a moment and then shrugged:

'A terrible ordeal, but not one to get the better of a man of his stamina. Do you know where he will be sent, and for how long?'

No, Marianne did not know. In her confusion, she had not even thought to ask these two very fundamental questions. The second, indeed, was of minor importance. It mattered not to her whether Jason were sentenced to ten, twenty or thirty years, even to life, since she was determined to do everything she could to bring about his escape. So she only said: 'Let's go. We can talk more freely at your house . . . I have so much to tell you.'

She took her friend's arm and they followed the footman, who had appeared suddenly as guide, out into the Fountain Court where their horses were waiting.

As they rode back to La Madeleine together, side by side in the gathering dusk, Marianne's mind was already busy with the days ahead. The first thing was to get back to Paris as fast as possible. She was eager now to be at home again, now that she knew that Adelaide and Jolival were waiting for her there. All her trust was in Jolival and in him alone, in his ingenuity and profound knowledge of people of the world, to devise a plan of escape for Jason. Ever since she had been sure that Jason was not to die, she had been looking at things through a rose-coloured haze. Thinking that she was being rather too optimistic, Fortunée set herself to keep her within bounds. Marianne seemed to think that everything would be easy from now on, and that was a dangerous attitude.

'You must not think escape will be a simple matter, Marianne,' she said gently. 'Men sentenced as he is are kept under strong guard. It will need long and careful preparation if the plan is to have the greatest possible chance of success.'

'That man I saw in La Force, François Vidocq, has escaped I don't know how many times. It can't be so very difficult.'

'He escaped, certainly, but he has been recaptured each time, hasn't he? Beaufort's only chance, if you should manage to get him away from his guards, is to embark instantly for his own country. The law officers will have little chance at sea. You must have everything ready, beginning with a boat . . .'

'We can arrange such details as that at the last minute. I am sure anything Vidocq has done, Jason can do too.'

'Marianne! Marianne!' Fortunée sighed. 'You are talking just like a child. I grant that his life is what matters most but take care, remember that the least slip could prove fatal. Vidocq is familiar with the insides of prisons, he knows what he is doing

– Jason's situation will be very different. Take care you do nothing foolish.'

Too happy to be cast down by any such dismal forebodings, Marianne simply shrugged lightly, convinced that a rosy future lay before her and Jason. She was now picturing the penal settlement as a kind of seaside prison where the convicts worked all day outside in the fresh air and where, with the aid of a little money, it would always be possible to obtain special favours from the guards. She had ceased to be greatly concerned even about money. Her far-off husband might cut off supplies but she still had fabulous jewels which she would part from without a pang to win the freedom of the man she loved.

However, the following evening when, after the first joyful greetings were over, she heard Arcadius saying very much the same things, she did begin to feel the faintest suspicion of uneasiness. Arcadius was truly glad to know that Jason was no longer in danger but he did not conceal from Marianne that a sentence of hard labour in a penal colony was very nearly as serious and meant little more than a death sentence somewhat delayed.

'It is hell, Marianne,' he said gravely, 'and the way there a hideous ordeal. Death can strike in a hundred different ways: exhaustion, disease, the ill-will of the other prisoners, punishments, dangerous employment. There is very little mercy in commuting a sentence of death into one of imprisonment and if we mean to attempt an escape we shall have to proceed with infinite caution, and the greatest patience. A prisoner of his kidney will be under stricter guard even than the rest, and failure on our part could lead to his death. You must let me take charge of everything.'

Marianne had noted with amazement how these last weeks had aged Jolival. His usually cheerful face was sunken and silver threads were beginning to show among the black around his temples. He had returned from his journey to Aix with a disappointed heart and a more bitter knowledge of men for, against all his hopes, the Duke of Otranto had refused, stubbornly and categorically, to have anything to do with the Beaufort affair. He had said in coarse but unequivocal terms that it was no longer any concern of his and the Emperor's staff must get along as best they might with his successor. He had even delivered himself of sentiments referring to Marianne which Jolival was careful to keep to himself.

'Princess or no, that woman has a face and a body no man could tire of easily,' he had said. 'While she can make Napoleon want her, she'll get whatever she wants out of him, even now he's shackled himself to a wife. I'll do myself no good by getting mixed up in the business . . .'

And Arcadius had returned to Paris, stricken and grieving, to find Marianne had disappeared. Day after day, with Talleyrand and Eleonora Crawfurd, he had searched every avenue for news of what had become of her and her aged companion. Their inquiries had led them as far as La Force but there they stopped. The people at the prison had seen the supposed Norman and his daughter walk away comfortably arm-in-arm down the rue des Ballets and turn the corner – after which they had vanished as completely as if they had melted into thin air. All that had been found was the body of the cab driver, floating in the Seine with his throat cut.

'We thought you were dead,' Adelaide said, the traces of her grief still visible in her reddened eyes. 'It seemed impossible that you had not been dealt with in the same way. We were afraid – oh, so afraid! Until the day, last Tuesday it was, when Mr Crawfurd came back at last and told us you had been carried off by a woman and a whole lot of Spaniards, all wearing masks. He knew they did not mean to kill you – or not straight away at least – because he heard them say so. They were waiting for the outcome of the trial.'

'After the sentence was delivered we were nearly mad,' Jolival went on. 'I went to Mortefontaine, thinking Pilar might have had the audacity to take you there, and searched, but I found nothing. In fact, of course, you were already gone because all this happened this week.'

Shocked to read on their faces the agonies they had endured on her account, Marianne blamed herself bitterly for having to some extent neglected them. When she reached Paris after her escaped she could have, indeed she ought to have, sent word to

Adelaide at least, but when she heard that Jason had been condemned it had driven every thought out of her head except the one idea of how to snatch him from death. The rest of the world had simply ceased to exist for her.

There was such sweetness and real affection in her attempts to explain all this, that neither Adelaide nor Jolival would allow her to continue. Arcadius summed up their feelings in a few words:

'You are here, in one piece, and we are sure that Beaufort's head is safe. And that is that. After that, any complaints would be base ingratitude! We are going to drink to your return, Marianne!' Smiling, he rang the bell for Jeremy to bring them some champagne.

'Do you think we can start celebrating today?' Marianne said, with some asperity. 'When you told me yourself that Jason's life is still not wholly out of danger?'

'Not celebrate, no, merely enjoy a little respite before plunging back head-first into the fray. I may as well tell you at once. Another letter has arrived from Lucca. Your husband demands your instant return and threatens to complain to the Emperor and appeal to him as a vassal to his suzerain to have you sent back to Lucca.'

Marianne felt the colour drain from her face. She had not been expecting such a brutal set-down and Eleonora Crawfurd's stories came back to her mind, giving to this ultimatum an oddly menacing note. Clearly, the prince took her for an adventuress and meant to make her pay for having taken him in, pay with her blood, perhaps.

'He can do as he likes, I shall not go! The Emperor himself cannot compel me to. Besides, I shall probably have left Paris in a little while.'

'Again?' wailed Mademoiselle d'Asselnat. 'But, Marianne, where are you going? And I thought we were going to settle down to a nice quiet life here, in this house, with all it stands for.'

Marianne smiled, a fond and very understanding smile, and held out her hand to her cousin with impulsive tenderness. That elderly spinster seemed to have changed a little as a result of her little adventure, which had surely cost her some degree of heartache. The irrepressible energy which had seen her through more than forty years of an eventful and far from easy life seemed to be dead, or at least sleeping. What she must want now above all was quiet and peace. Her expression as she looked round the elegant salon with its fine furniture and ornaments, was almost greedily possessive and acquired a hint of an appeal whenever her eye came to rest on the big portrait of the Marquise d'Asselnat over the fireplace.

'You need not come with me, Adelaide. You need rest and tranquillity, and this house needs a mistress who is here rather more permanently than I have been. I am going away again, and you know I am. Jason's prison will not be in Paris, and I want to go with him now wherever he goes.' She turned to Arcadius. 'Is it known yet where he will be taken?'

'Brest, for sure.'

'That is good news. I know the town well. I lived there for several weeks with poor Nicolas Mallerousse, in his little house at Recouvrance. If I cannot manage to arrange his escape on the way, I am sure I shall have a better chance in Brest than at Toulon or Rochefort where I have never been.'

'*We* shall have a better chance,' Jolival corrected her. 'I have already asked you to allow me to take charge of everything.'

'Will you leave me all alone?' wailed Adelaide, sounding like a hurt child. 'What shall I do when all these messengers start arriving from the prince, your husband? What shall I say to them?'

'Anything you please! Say I am away, that will be best. Besides, I am going to write to him myself and say that – that I have to go away – a long way away – on the Emperor's service, let us say, but that on my return I shall not fail to comply with my husband's – er – request,' Marianne said, thinking out her letter aloud as she spoke.

'That is madness! You yourself said not a moment ago that you did not wish to return to Lucca—'

'Nor shall I. You must understand, Adelaide, that I am simply trying to gain time . . . time to rescue Jason. Afterwards, I shall go away with him, away to his own country and live there with him, at his side, in a log cabin if needs must, in poverty, but will never leave him, never, never again.'

Jolival was swift to intervene. His little black eyes held Marianne's huge ones steadily.

'You are deserting us, then?' he asked softly.

'No, no! The choice is yours. Stay here, in this house – I will give it to you – or come with me over there, with all the risks that involves . . .'

'Have you remembered that Beaufort is still married to that harpy? What do you intend doing with her?'

'Arcadius,' Marianne said, with sudden gravity, 'when that woman dared to use me as her footstool, and when, most of all, I heard her tell me coolly and implacably that she was determined to send her husband to his death, I swore that one day I would make her pay for it. If she dares to approach Jason again, I shall get rid of her without a second thought. There is nothing,' her voice shook with the intensity of her feelings, 'nothing I would not do to keep him for myself. I would not even shrink from a murder which, all told, would be no more than a just execution. I fought a duel with one man who debased me, I killed the woman who insulted me . . . I shall not let a wicked wife destroy the one love of my life!'

'You have turned into a terrifying woman, Marianne!' Mademoiselle d'Asselnat exclaimed, with a horror not entirely devoid of admiration.

'I am your cousin, my dear. Can you have forgotten that the night we met you were trying to set fire to this house to punish it for belonging to a creature you had decided was unworthy of it?'

The entrance of Jeremy bearing lighted candles forced them to break off the conversation. Absorbed in their discussion, not one of the three had observed that it was growing dark. Shadows had crept into the farthest corners of the room and crowded thickly about the curtains and hangings and under the lofty ceiling. The only light came from the fire blazing in the hearth.

They sat in silence while the butler disposed branches of candles about the room, clothing everything in it in a golden radiance. When he had departed, with a gloomy pronouncement that dinner would be served shortly, Adelaide, who was sitting bundled up in a vast, white woollen shawl in the armchair by the fire, stretched out her thin hands to the dancing flames and remained for a moment staring into them. Locked each in their own thoughts, Marianne and Arcadius, one seated on a cushion before the fire, the other leaning against the chimney piece, were also silent, as though waiting for the familiar sounds of the house to give them an answer to the questions which filled their hearts but which they dared not utter for fear of influencing, however little, the steps which would decide the others' futures.

At last, Adelaide looked up at Jolival and rubbed her hands together quietly.

'They say America is a wonderful country,' she said placidly and a flicker of the old fire shone for a moment in her grey eyes. 'And I have heard it said that in those southern parts it is never cold. I think that I should like never to be cold. You, Jolival?'

'I too,' the Vicomte returned gravely, 'I believe I too should like—'

The doors were flung wide open.

'Her Serene Highness is served!' Jeremy intoned from the doorway.

Marianne slipped her arms companionably through Jolival's and Adelaide's and smiled with deep gratitude upon them both.

'Indeed I am,' she said, 'I am served far, far better than anything I deserve.'

CHAPTER ELEVEN

The Road to Brest

Day dawned, grey and dirty, a sodden November dawn, soaked through and through with the thin, freezing rain that had been falling on Paris for some days, penetrating everything. Looming through the yellowish fog of early morning, the old hospice of Bicêtre with its soaring roofs, lofty gateway and nicely balanced buildings, recovered some ghost of its former elegance. The mist concealed the cracks in the walls, the chipped gables and the smashed and glassless windows, the dark streaks that mottled the crumbling stonework below gutters cracked by frost and all the unsightly decay of a building which had once been royal, a work dedicated to the loftiest aims of charity, now put to the meanest uses of the law. Ever since 1796, when it had replaced La Tournelle, it had been the last stage before the galleys, the antechamber to hell, whether the road led via the Conciergerie and the scaffold or to penal servitude, which was a death no less certain but more horrible because stripped of the last rags of human dignity.

In the normal way of things, this gloomy edifice, brooding on its hillside with the waste lands all about, stood silent and alone, but on this day, despite the early hour, a swelling, noisy crowd was surging up against the rotting walls, big with a nameless joy, an unwholesome curiosity. It was the crowd which always assembled there, four times a year, to witness the departure of the 'Chain'. The same crowd of milling humanity, alerted by heaven alone knew what mysterious signs, pressed around the scaffold on execution days, no matter how quiet the thing was kept, a gathering of connoisseurs come together to watch a most choice spectacle with undisguised relish. They beat upon the closed doors of the hospice like patrons in a theatre stamping with their feet, impatient for the curtain to go up. Marianne gazed at this grisly mob with loathing.

She was standing, enveloped from head to foot in a great, black, hooded cloak, in the lee of a broken wall which had once belonged to the hovel whose crumbling remains still stood beside the road. She was up to her ankles in mud, her face was wet and her cloak already sodden with rain. Beside her was Arcadius de Jolival, grim-faced, his arms folded on his chest, also waiting, chewing the ends of his moustache.

He had wished to spare Marianne the pitiful sight in store and had tried, right up to the last minute, to dissuade her from coming, but in vain. She clung stubbornly to her pilgrimage of love, determined to follow every step of the cruel journey that lay before the man she loved, only repeating endlessly that some opportunity might occur on the way and that they must not let it slip.

'The chances of an escape while the chain is on the road,' Arcadius had explained tirelessly, 'are non-existent. They are all chained together, in batches of twenty-four at a time, and they are searched at the first halt to make sure that no one has managed to slip them any tool to sever their chains as they set out. After that they are kept under close guard and any man who is fool enough to try and escape is shot down on the spot.'

In the long days which had gone before, Arcadius had acquired minutely detailed information on everything which concerned the penal colony, the life the men led there and the conditions of the journey which took them there. He had penetrated, in ruffianly disguise, into the worst dens of the Cité and the Barrière du Combat, buying many drinks, saying little but listening a great deal, and, as he had told Marianne, his conviction had grown that any escape would need extremely careful preparation down to the minutest details. Nor had he concealed from her his fears regarding her ability to face the brutal facts about what awaited Jason. There had been a time when he had hoped to keep the greater part from her by advising that she should go to Brest and begin to make arrangements there while he followed the convict chain on its journey. But Marianne had refused to hear of any such plan. Nothing would dissuade her from following Jason step by step from the moment of his leaving Bicêtre.

Jolival gazed with a jaundiced eye at the desolate scene about him. Here and there in the waste an occasional chimney was beginning to smoke. On the edge of the crowd a number of dark figures stood in isolated groups of two or three, with the wretched, hopeless air of people in great grief. They were the wives, relatives and friends of those about to be deported. Some were weeping, others simply stood, like Marianne herself, faces strained towards the hospice, eyes wide open, every feature turned to stone by the hard frost of unshed tears.

There came a sudden roar from the crowd. Creaking, grinding, the great gates were swinging open ... Two mounted officers appeared, their bodies hunched against the rain which streamed from the angles of their cocked hats, using their horses and the flat of their swords to beat back the crowd, which was already surging forwards. A shudder ran through Marianne. She took a step forward, but instantly Jolival seized her arm and dragged her back.

'Stay where you are!' he said, with unconscious harshness. 'You need not go any closer. They will pass us here.'

The first wagon had already appeared, to be greeted by a horrid outburst of boos, catcalls and abuse. It was a kind of long cart, supported on two enormous iron-shod wheels and divided along the whole of its length by a two-sided wooden bench on which the prisoners sat back-to-back, twelve to a side, their legs dangling, held in place by a crude rail at waist level. Each man was chained by the neck by means of a solid, three-cornered iron collar attached to a length of chain, too short to allow him to jump from the wagon on to the road. This chain was in turn connected to the much heavier chain which ran the length of the bench, its end lying firmly beneath the foot of the armed guard standing at the end of each wagon.

There were five of these conveyances. There was no protection, not even the most rudimentary piece of sacking, to stand between the prisoners and the rain which was already soaking through their clothes. Their prison uniform of black and grey striped canvas overalls had been taken off them for the journey and their own clothes restored to them, but so mutilated that should any man escape no one who saw him could doubt that he was a convict. Coats were lacking their collars, cuffs were shredded to ribbons, and hats, for those that had them, had been shorn of their brims.

Marianne watched them pass, appalled at the pallid, unshaven faces, hate-filled eyes and open mouths that spewed out blasphemies and obscene songs. They were shivering in the icy rain and some, the youngest, had to bite back tears when in a grieving face that loomed up through the grey drizzle they recognized the features of someone they knew.

In the leading wagon, she caught sight of François Vidocq. He sat wrapped in a scornful silence which in the midst of the cursing and groaning all about him had its own kind of greatness. The eyes that rested on the excited mob held such contempt that they seemed not to see at all, yet they saw Marianne and were instantly transformed. She saw the stubbly jaw relax in a brief smile as Vidocq nodded to the wagon next in line. At the same time, Jolival tightened his hold on Marianne's arm.

'There!' he hissed. 'Fourth from the front.'

But Marianne had already seen Jason. He was sitting very upright among the rest, his eyes half-closed, his mouth set in a thin line. He was quite silent, his arms folded on his chest, and seemed wholly insensible to all that was going on around him. His attitude was that of a man refusing either to see or to hear, his being turned inwards the better to conserve his strength and energy. The rags of his torn cambric shirt and the ripped, collarless coat gave little protection to his broad shoulders and the tanned skin showed through in many places, but he did not appear conscious of the cold or the rain. In the midst of this howling mob, with fists raised in impotent menace, mouths distorted by foul invective, he was as remote as a figure carved in stone. Marianne, her lips already parted to call out his name, fell silent when he passed her unseeingly, realizing quite suddenly that it might only have caused him pain to see her there in the crowd.

One cry of horror she could not repress, when the guards, tiring of the racket kept up by their prisoners, took out their long whips and laid about them impartially, flailing at cringing backs and shoulders, and at the heads they tried to shield with their folded arms. The shouting ceased and the cart rolled on.

'Bastards! Stinking bastards, knockin' about a right'un like him!' muttered an angry voice behind her. Marianne knew the voice and, turning, saw Gracchus, whom she and Arcadius had left with the chaise in the square of Gentilly village, standing bareheaded in the rain with clenched fists and great tears rolling down his cheeks, mingling with the rainwater. He must have left the carriage to take care of itself and come himself to see the chain pass by. His eyes followed Jason's cart until it was out of sight. Then, when it had been swallowed up in the mist, and the other carts had come and gone and the kitchen wagon was clattering by with a great clanging of metal pots and pans, Gracchus looked at his mistress, who was sobbing on Jolival's shoulder.

'We're never goin' to leave him like that?' he asked belligerently.

'You know quite well we're not,' Jolival told him. 'We are going after him and we are going to do our best to free him.'

'Then what are we waiting for? Beggin' your pardon, Mademoiselle Marianne, but you'll not get him out of it by crying. We've got work to do! Where's the first stop?'

'Saint-Cyr.' It was Arcadius who answered. 'That's where the last search is made.'

'We'll be there first. Come on!'

The discreet travelling carriage, with no outward signs of wealth beyond a pair of lively-looking post horses, was waiting with lighted lamps under the trees not far from the Pont de la Bièvre. As the morning advanced, the tanneries which bordered this stretch of the river began to come to life, spreading a powerful stench through what was otherwise a pretty scene, dominated by the square church tower. Marianne and Jolival got into the chaise in silence while Gracchus hoisted himself nimbly on to the box. A click of the tongue as the whip curved gracefully through the air to flick the leader's ear, a faint creak from the axles and they were off. The long journey to Brest had begun.

Marianne leaned her cheek against the rough fabric of the squabs and abandoned herself to her tears. She wept quite silently, with no sobbing, and it did her good. It was as if the hideous sights she had just beheld were being washed from her eyes, and at the same time her own natural courage and will to succeed slowly returned to take possession of her mind. Arcadius, sitting beside her, knew her too well to make any attempt to stem the beneficent flow or offer the least word of comfort. What could he have said? It was necessary for Jason to endure this dreadful journey because it led not to his prison alone, but to the sea, from which he had always drawn his strength.

Marianne left Paris without regret, with no expectation of ever going back there, or with no more regret than the slight pang she felt at parting from her few remaining friends there: Talleyrand, the Crawfurds and, most of all, her dearest Fortunée Hamelin. But Fortunée had refused to give way to sentiment. Even as she embraced her friend for the last time, her eyes full of tears, she had insisted, with all the infectious enthusiasm of her sun-loving nature:

'This is not goodbye, Marianne! When you are an American, I shall come and visit you there, and see if the men are as handsome as they say. Judging by your corsair, it must be true!'

Talleyrand had confined himself to a calm assurance that they were bound to meet again some day, somewhere in this wide world. Eleonora Crawfurd had applauded Marianne's plan to put the width of the ocean between herself and her alarming husband. Adelaide, left to act as mistress of the family mansion, had treated their parting in a philosophical fashion. As far as she herself was concerned, there was little to fear however matters turned out. If Marianne failed in her plans for Jason's escape, then she would of course return to her own place in the household. If she succeeded and she and Jason won their way to the State of Carolina, then there would remain nothing for Adelaide to do but pack up her traps, slip the key under the door and catch the first boat to a new and adventurous life, with the idea of which she was already half in love. All was therefore for the best in the best of all possible worlds!

Before she left Paris, moreover, Marianne had received a communication from her lawyer which, in the circumstances, was extraordinarily welcome. It stated that the unfortunate Nicolas Mallerousse had, during the time when she had stayed with him in Brest, after her escape from Morvan's manor house, constituted her his sole heir. The little house at Recouvrance and the few bits and pieces it contained were henceforth her own property, 'in memory', Nicolas had written in his will, 'of the days when she had made me feel as if I had a daughter once again'.

This legacy had touched Marianne deeply. It was as though her old friend were speaking to her from beyond the grave, assuring her of his affection still. She also saw in it the hand of providence and something very like tacit approval on the part of fate for what she meant to do. There was, in fact, nothing which could possibly have been more useful just then than the little house on the hill, looking out one way to the sea and the other to the buildings of the arsenal and, in the midst of them, the prison.

All these things were in her mind as the horses trotted easily towards the next stage. The day was as grey as ever, but the rain had stopped. As ill luck would have it, its stopping had been the signal for a sharp wind to get up which must have been unpleasant for men out in the open in wet clothes. A hundred times, as they went on, Marianne looked back to see if the chain were yet in sight, but it never was. Even at their present gentle pace, the carriage could outstrip the lumbering wagons with ease.

Just as Jolival had predicted, they reached Saint-Cyr far in advance of the convict chain, giving him time to engage rooms for Marianne and himself in a modest but respectable inn. Even this necessitated a certain amount of argument, since her first concern was to discover where the prisoners were to spend the night. She was directed to a huge barn just outside the town, whereupon she immediately rejected the inn, declaring she could perfectly well sleep in the chaise, or even in an open field. For once, Arcadius lost his temper with her:

'What are you trying to do? Catch your death of cold? That will be a fine help, if we are obliged to put up in some inn for a week to nurse you!'

'Of course I should not stay anywhere – not if I were shivering with ague! If I were at my dying gasp I should still go with him, on foot if I had to!'

'Much good that would do you, if I may say so!' Jolival growled. 'For God's sake, Marianne, stop playing off these tragedy airs! It will not help Jason Beaufort if you catch your death on this damned road. On the contrary. And if your only aim is to mortify your flesh so as to share his sufferings, then you had better shut yourself up in a convent, my dear, the strictest we can find, where you may fast and sleep on the floor and have yourself beaten three times daily if you please! At least you will not be a hindrance when the chance of an escape does arise!'

'Arcadius!' Marianne cried, shaken. 'To talk to me so!'

'I talk to you as you deserve. And, since you will have it, I think this insistence of yours on following the chain is foolish beyond permission!'

'I have told you a hundred times: I cannot be apart from him. If anything were to happen to him—'

'I should be here to see it. You would be a hundred times more useful to us posting on to Brest and settling down in the house you have inherited, establishing yourself in the neighbourhood and getting to know the people. Have you forgotten that we are going to need assistance, a sea-going vessel and a crew? No, you prefer to stay here, weeping at the foot of the Cross! Trailing in the wake of the chain, like some self-dramatizing Magdalen! Or are you going to whip out a veil and mop his fevered brow, like St Veronica? Confound it all, if there had been the slightest chance of saving Jesus, I promise you those women wouldn't have wasted their time trotting about the back streets of Jerusalem! Are you determined the Emperor should hear that you have been defying his commands again? That the Princess Sant'Anna is following the convict chain to Brest?'

'He will not know. We are travelling very quietly. I pass for your niece.'

This was true. For greater safety, Jolival had procured, through Talleyrand, a passport in his own name, including a mention that his niece Marie was travelling with him. But the Vicomte only shrugged irritably:

'And do you think no one will know your face? You little fool, the guards with the column will have found you out within three days! So no dramas, if you please. Do nothing to make yourself conspicuous. Like it or not, you will go to bed like other people – at an inn!'

Overborne, but resentful, Marianne gave in at last, with the stipulation that she need not retire to her inn until the convict chain had halted for the night. She could not bear to give up a single chance of seeing Jason.

'No one will even notice me,' she pleaded. 'There are so many people waiting there already.'

Once again, she spoke the truth. The dates on which the chain came through were always the same and they were known throughout the district. It had a curious fascination for the country people and they would come, often from miles around, together at the place where the wagons halted and sometimes to follow them for part of the way. Some came with charitable intentions, giving the prisoners little gifts of food, or a worn garment, or a few small coins. But for the most part, they came simply for amusement, honest folk finding a powerful relief from their own humdrum troubles in contemplation of the criminals' punishment, and of a wretchedness beyond anything even the poorest there would ever know.

The little town was full of people, although the sharpest, and the better informed, had already taken up their positions near the barn. The fact was that before they were allowed to rest for the night the convicts had to submit to a thorough, detailed search, intended to simplify the task of the guards during the remainder of the journey. At the other halts, there would be nothing more than a check on the shackles and a brief run-over. Marianne wormed her way through the crowd, Jolival, still disapproving, on her heels.

They heard the chain coming long before they saw it. Borne on the wind came a fearsome clangour of voices howling and loud, raucous singing, made louder as it approached Saint-Cyr by the roaring of the worthy townsfolk. Then, just passing the last houses of the town, two mounted officers appeared, their shoulder belts showing up as a white cross on each chest. They stared straight ahead, grim-faced, whereas the prison guards who came after them were grinning at the crowd, like the heroes of a successful play. Behind them, the first wagon lumbered into view.

When all five vehicles had been lined up together in a field, the prisoners were made to get down and the search began. At the same moment, as if in response to some secret signal, the rain came on again.

'Are you really determined to remain here?' Jolival murmured into Marianne's ear. 'I warn you, it is no fit sight for you. You should—'

'Once and for all, Arcadius, I ask you to let me alone. I want to see what they do to him.'

'As you will. You shall see. But don't say I didn't warn you.'

Marianne turned away from him pettishly. A few moments more found her staring very hard at the ground, scarlet with shame. Despite the cold and the rain, the prisoners were being made to strip off every vestige of clothing. Standing there, barefoot in the mud, in nothing but the iron collars round their necks, they were subjected by their guards to a search so thoroughly degrading that it could only have been intended as an additional punishment. While one man inspected suits, shoes and stockings, another examined every orifice of their bodies with minutest care. It was a known fact, however, that the prisoners were adept at concealing a variety of tools, from tiny files to watchsprings which could release a man from his irons in less than three hours.

Marianne, crimson to the roots of her hair, kept her eyes firmly on her own feet and on the clump of trampled grass on which she stood. To everyone around her it seemed to be a high jest. Even the women, honest matrons for the most part, were commenting on the prisoners' persons with a freedom which would not have disgraced a grenadier. Desperate, Marianne tried to turn and beg Jolival to take her away, but a sudden movement among the now wildly excited crowd parted her from him and, without quite knowing how, she found herself carried into the front rank of the onlookers. The hood which she had drawn down over her hair to hide her face had been pushed back in the press and suddenly she saw Jason right in front of her.

The distance between them was not so great that he could help but see her. She saw his face change horribly. His skin turned suddenly grey and the look of anger and shame glaring in his eyes was frightening. He thrust at her violently to drive her away, oblivious of the whip which at that instant thudded into his back.

'Go away! Go away at once!'

Marianne tried to answer, to tell him that she had only wanted to share his sufferings, but already there was an iron hand gripping her arm, dragging her back, irresistibly, regardless of the pain it caused her. There was a moment's agonizing pressure, a quick scuffle and Marianne found herself at the back of the shouting wedge of people staring into the face of Jolival, who was literally green with anger:

'Well? Are you satisfied? You saw him? And you made damned sure that he saw you – at the moment of all moments when he would a hundred times rather have died than be seen by you! Is this what you call sharing his ordeal? Don't you think he has enough to bear?'

Marianne's overstretched nerves snapped all at once and she burst into convulsive sobs:

'I didn't know, Arcadius! I couldn't ever have known, ever imagined anything so vile! I was pushed forward by the crowd – when I only wanted not to look . . .'

'I warned you,' Jolival said ruthlessly. 'But you are worse

than a mule! You will not listen to anyone! One would think you took pleasure in torturing yourself.'

Marianne's only answer was to cast herself into his arms in such desperate floods of tears that he was softened. His hand came up to stroke her rain-sodden hair.

'There, there . . . Hush, now, my baby! I am sorry I was angry – but you make me so when you insist on adding to your own troubles.'

'I know . . . dear friend . . . I know! Oh, I am so ashamed! . . . You can't know how ashamed I am! I have hurt him . . . I wounded him, when I would give my life . . .'

'Now, now – don't begin again!' Jolival besought her, gently removing her clinging form from about his neck. 'I know all about it, always have done, and if you do not calm yourself at once and stop turning the knife in the wound, I swear to you on my honour I will box your ears as if you were my own daughter! Come, now, let us go back to the inn.'

Taking her wrist once more, he led her rapidly back towards the town, ignoring her feeble protests and the sporadic efforts she still made to run back to the barn. Only when they reached the first houses did he release his hold on her at last.

'Now promise me that you will go straight back to the inn at once, and no turning back!'

'Go back – all by myself? But Arcadius—'

'No. No "but Arcadius". Back, I said. I am going back to the field.'

'But – what for?'

'To see if a little payment to the guard won't procure me a few words with him. And to give him this.'

Opening his big cloak, Jolival showed the loaf which he had been carrying all this time, tucked under his left arm. Marianne looked again from the bread to her friend's suspiciously bright eyes. It made her want to cry again but this time her reasons were different and she managed a smile instead. It was a pathetic enough little smile, in all conscience, but it tried hard to be brave:

'I'll go. I promise.'

'About time too. Now you're being a sensible girl.'

'Only—'

'What now?'

'If you do speak to him – ask him to forgive me – and say I love him.'

Jolival shrugged, raised his eyes to heaven as if to call the skies to witness the idiocy of some people, then folding his cloak around him once more, he strode off into the wind. His voice came back to her:

'Do you think that's really necessary?'

Faithful to her promise, Marianne too began to run back towards the inn, where an ostler was already lighting the big oil-lantern hanging over the gateway. It was nearly dark. The rain had stopped again for the present but the clouds piling up on the horizon were more than just the harbingers of night. She forced herself to shut her ears to the savage din which still floated after her and plunged into the inn like someone running for her life. She went straight up to her room. The single public room was too full of people, mostly men drinking mulled wine and talking over what they had just seen, and Marianne had no desire to meet anyone.

When Arcadius came up to her an hour later, she was sitting in a basket chair by the fire, her hands lying in her lap, so still that she seemed scarcely conscious. However, she looked up when she heard him come in, a questioning look in her eyes.

'I was able to get the bread to him,' Arcadius said, with a slight shrug, 'but not to speak to him. The prisoners were too excited. The search had made them nearly mad. None of the guards would have dared to break the chain – not even for gold. I'll try again later on. Now, Marianne, will you listen to what I have to say?'

He drew up a chair to the fire and sat down opposite her, leaning his elbows on his knees, his black eyes looking very steadily into hers:

'Listen – calmly? Like a sensible girl?'

When she nodded, without speaking, he went on: 'You will leave here in the morning, without me, but taking the chaise. Gracchus is more than adequate protection. He'd let himself be torn in pieces for you, that boy. No, let me speak,' he added, seeing Marianne's eyes widen and her mouth half open to protest. 'If you continue to follow the chain, we shall have to conceal your presence not only from the guards, who would not take long to spot you, as I said, but also from Jason himself. Your being here can only increase his sufferings. No man worthy of the name wants the woman he loves to see him reduced to the status of an animal. You will go on ahead, therefore, to begin preparations for his escape, while I follow on horseback.'

Marianne sighed. 'I know. You want me to go to Brest and—'

'No. You are quite wrong. I want you to go to St Malo.'

'To – to St Malo? Good heavens, whatever for?'

Jolival's small answering smile managed to combine pity, doubt and some irony.

'What I find so disheartening about you, Marianne, is the speed with which you contrive to forget the very friends who can be most useful to you. I thought you had a friend named Surcouf – indeed, I had the impression you had actually saved his life?'

'Yes, but—'

'Baron Surcouf, my love, may not be a privateer any longer, but he remains a very powerful shipowner.' Jolival spoke silkily. 'Can you tell me a better way to obtain a sound, seaworthy craft and a reliable crew? Well then, tomorrow morning you will set out post-haste for St Malo and lay siege to the gentleman. What we need is a good ship and a crew willing and able to help us get a prisoner away from Brest.'

Marianne could think of nothing to say. Jolival's words had suddenly opened up an immense perspective, dominated by the vigorous, reassuring figure of the corsair-baron. Surcouf! Why had she not thought of him before? She was trying to rescue a sailor – how could she have forgotten that supreme sailor of them all? If he would agree to help her, then Jason's freedom was assured! But would he?

'It's a good idea, Arcadius,' she said after a pause. 'But don't forget, Surcouf is a loyal subject of the Emperor's – while Jason is simply a condemned criminal. He will never do it.'

'He may not, but it is worth trying all the same. I shall own myself very much surprised if he does not give us some help at least, or else the legend and the man are very different things! At worst, you can offer to pay him for both ship and crew. Always supposing you are not robbed on the way, you have enough in that coffer of yours to buy a kingdom!' The Vicomte pointed with a long finger at one of Marianne's boxes.

Marianne's gaze followed his finger and brightened visibly. When she had left home, she had done so with the Sant'Anna jewels in her possession, fully determined to use them to further her plans should the need arise. If and when she ever reached America with the man she loved, then she meant to send the precious casket, with what remained of its contents, back to Lucca, reserving the right to pay back later anything she might have spent. Whatever happened, it was true that she had the wherewithal to buy not one but a dozen ships.

Jolival had been following the direction of her thoughts as they were reflected in her mobile countenance. When he thought she had pondered his proposal long enough, he said quietly: 'Well? You'll go?'

'Yes. You win, Arcadius. I will go.'

It was blowing a gale when Marianne's chaise clattered on to the Chaussée du Sillon, the narrow strip of dry land which formed the causeway linking St Malo to the mainland, and Gracchus had much ado to hold his horses, frightened as they were by the stinging lash of the salt spray bursting over the sea wall. Even in the sheltered anchorage on the other side, the close-packed masts were bowing before the wind. At the far end of the causeway, wrapped in the circle of its classic fortification, the corsair town loomed like an enormous pie made of grey granite, topped by the blue-tiled roofs of its houses, the tall church spires and the massive towers of its medieval castle.

The sea which pounded against the causeway, throwing up great, snowy bursts of spume from its heaving, greenish surface and sending white horses charging furiously against the city of men, was no stranger to Marianne. It was the same sea which, long months ago now, had caught her up in its wild raging, beaten and tumbled her as it smashed Black Fish's boat to pieces and cast them all up at last, naked and half dead, beside the wreckers' deceitful fires. It was the same sea which battered Morvan's estate, a frenzied and malignant sea, quick to anger and to malice, relying, when the power of a direct assault had failed, on the deadly snares of its deep waters, undersea reefs and treacherous currents. The wind howled round the carriage and crept in through the small crevices around the windows, bringing with it a sharp sea-tang of salt and seaweed.

The streaming horses plunged through the echoing vault of the huge St Vincent gate and instantly their panic ceased. Behind the great ramparts, where the sea could not reach, all was comparative peace and Marianne was a little surprised to find the people going about their business as naturally as in the finest weather. Hardly a soul seemed to take notice of her tempestuous arrival. Only one of the soldiers mounting a somewhat casual guard upon the gate took the clay pipe from his mouth and remarked to Gracchus, who was shaking the water from his dripping hat: 'Bit of a blow like, eh, lad? Nor'wester ... 'orses ever takes agin it.'

'So I noticed,' Gracchus responded amiably. 'And grateful I am to know it's a nor'wester, but if it's all the same to you I'd be gladder still to know where Monsieur Surcouf lives.'

The words had been addressed to the man on the gate but almost before the words were out of his mouth a crowd of people had gathered round the vehicle, all talking at once: women in calico bonnets who set down their baskets and pointed, sailors in hard waxed hats and aged fishermen in red stocking caps so prolific of hair and whisker that there was little of their faces to be seen beyond a red nose and a pipe. Everyone was offering to show the way. Gracchus stood on the box and endeavoured to make sense of the hubbub.

'Not all at once, now ... for pity's sake! Is that the way?' He had gathered that all the arms seemed to be pointing in much the same direction, but still no one would consent to be quiet. He was just going to sit down again and prepare to wait patiently for the rumpus to die down when two men rather more determined than the rest took hold of the horses' bridles and began leading the chaise sedately along the street that ran like a deep cutting in between the wall and tall houses within. Marianne stuck her head out of the window in puzzlement:

'What is happening? Have we been arrested?'

'No, Mademoiselle Marianne, taken over, more like. Seems to me Monsieur Surcouf is something of a king in these parts, all these folks is so eager to serve him.'

They were led for some way, passing two more gates and then, still following the line of the wall, bearing right until at last the procession reached a large, rather grim house built of grey granite whose tall windows and lofty doorway adorned with armorial bearings above and a bronze dolphin below pointed to a residence of some importance. Marianne's willing escort thereupon pronounced unanimously that this was it and all that remained to be done was for Gracchus to distribute a number of small coins with the recommendation that the thirstier among them should go and quench their thirst to the health of Baron Surcouf and his friends.

The various persons then dispersed happily, the old salts setting a course for the nearest tavern for a mug of mulled cider, well known to be the most comforting drink in the world when the nor'wester was blowing. Meanwhile, Gracchus had taken hold of the bronze dolphin door-knocker and was gravely asking the ancient serving man who answered it, and who bore a strong suggestion of the retired seaman about him, whether his master was at home to Mademoiselle d'Asselnat. Of all the many names which Marianne had borne, this was certainly the one the privateer knew best.

He was informed that 'Monsieur Surcouf' was at present down at the dry dock but that he would not be long and if the young lady liked she could 'heave to and come aboard', a mode of expression which confirmed Marianne in her first impression of the old man's earlier profession. She was admitted to an entrance hall with a black and white tiled floor and old oak panelling. There was little furniture beyond a sideboard bearing, between a pair of heavy bronze candelabra, a superb model of a flute in full sail, armed for war, gun-ports open and guns run out. A pair of high-back oak chairs stood guard on either side.

The whole house breathed the smell of new wax, suggesting to the visitor that the Baronne was a proud housewife. Indeed, everything about the house shone with cleanliness: even in white gloves it would have been hard to pick up a grain of dust. The effect was striking, but also slightly chilling.

Surcouf's 'cabin', when she was shown into it, turned out to be panelled in the same dark wood as the hall but was altogether more human. It was the room of a man of action, redolent of adventure and the sea and rumbustious life, a cheerfully untidy room, the desk heaped high with maps and compasses, papers, pipes and quills, in the middle of which was a spirit-lamp and a candlestick with a candle and a few sticks of sealing wax. Barbaric, brightly coloured rugs were scattered on the gleaming, polished floor, on which sprawled a huge map of the world, held down by a sextant and a brass meridian. Exotic weapons and tattered colours still with the stains of battle on them were arranged about a large chart on the wall and every piece of furniture in the room, with the exception of a bookcase stuffed with books, was covered with a clutter of telescopes, cases of pistols and instruments of navigation.

Marianne had scarcely seated herself in the straight-backed chair, as rigid as its fellows in the hall, which the old man had brought forward for her before there was a sound of booted feet. A door slammed somewhere and almost at once the big room seemed to fill with a great gust of sea air, smelling of iodine and spindrift, and Surcouf himself burst into his private domain. His arrival reminded Marianne so strongly of what she felt each time Jason appeared that something seemed to twist inside her. They were strangely alike, these men of the sea, as if they bore the insignia of some secret brotherhood to which all belonged. Just how far, she wondered, would that brotherhood carry him?

'Now, here's a surprise!' the privateer cried thunderously. 'You, here in St Malo? I can't believe my eyes!'

'You may quite safely do so,' Marianne said, submitting to a smacking kiss on both cheeks, country fashion. 'I am really here! I hope my coming is not disagreeable to you.'

'Disagreeable! Never think it! It's not every day I get the chance of kissing a princess! Damned if I don't do it again!'

He suited the action to the word and Marianne felt herself blushing. She had announced herself by her maiden name.

'How – how did you know—?'

Surcouf's great laughter rang out so heartily that all the lustres in the crystal chandelier tinkled softly in answer:

'That you were a princess? My dear girl, I do believe you think we Bretons are so cut-off it takes us three or four years to get the latest news from Paris! Not a bit of it! We are well up in all the news. Especially' – and here his joyous laugh boomed out again – 'especially when one numbers Baron Corvisart among one's friends. He attended you a short while ago and I got news of you from him. That is all there is to it. And now sit down and tell me what fair wind blows you here. But first, a glass of port to celebrate your coming.'

While Marianne resumed her seat and tried to get over her surprise, Surcouf went to a carved wooden chest and took out a decanter of dark red Bohemian glass and a pair of tall glasses which he filled three-quarters full of a golden brown liquid. Feeling better already for his bracing presence, Marianne watched his movements with a smile.

Surcouf was never anything less than himself. His broad face, framed in a pair of handsome sidewhiskers, was still the same coppery brown and his blue eyes as direct as ever. He had put on a little weight, perhaps, and his broad chest had filled out until the everlasting blue redingote was bursting at the seams and dragging at the massive gold buttons which, when she looked closer, Marianne saw in a kind of daze were none other than Spanish gold doubloons, pierced for the purpose.

After a ritual toast to the Emperor, they drank their port in silence, nibbling little airy ginger biscuits which seemed to the traveller the most delicious food on earth. Then Surcouf swung round a chair and, seating himself astride it, regarded his young friend with an encouraging smile.

'I asked what wind blew you here,' he said. 'But by the look of you, I'd say it was more in the nature of a heavy squall. Right?'

'A storm would be nearer the truth. In fact, I am beginning to wish I had not come. I'm afraid I may embarrass you – or make you think the worse of me.'

'You could not. And whatever reason brings you here, I'll tell you right away that you did quite right to come. Your own delicacy forbids you to say straight out that you need something of me, but I have no hesitation in telling you I owe my life to you. So let's hear it, Marianne. You know quite well there is nothing that you cannot ask of me.'

'Not even – if I were to ask you to help me arrange a man's escape from the penal colony at Brest?'

For all his self-control, he could not conceal the slight start of shock which set Marianne's heart fluttering anxiously. When he spoke, it was very slowly and deliberately:

'The penal colony at Brest? You know someone in that clutch of felons?'

'Not yet. The man I want to rescue is still on his way there. He was sentenced for a crime he did not commit – he was condemned to death, but the Emperor granted a reprieve because he was sure he did not kill – and perhaps, too, because he is not French. Oh, it is a terribly complicated story, but I must try and explain . . .'

She was growing muddled and confused already. She could hardly speak for fatigue and emotion and could no longer bring herself to look Surcouf in the face. But he interrupted her, saying roughly: 'Wait a minute! A foreigner? What kind of foreigner?'

'An American. He is a sailor, too . . .'

There was a crack from the chair-back as Surcouf's fist smashed down on to it:

'Jason Beaufort! Thunder of fate! Why didn't you tell me so at once?'

'You know him?'

He got up so suddenly that he knocked over his chair but, ignoring it, he answered: 'It is my business to know every captain of every vessel worth the name both sides of the equator.

Beaufort is a fine sailor and a brave man. His trial was a blot on French justice! In fact, I wrote to the Emperor and told him so.'

'You did?' Marianne exclaimed in a choking voice. 'D-did he answer you?'

'Told me to mind my own business. Or words to that effect. You know he's not one to beat about the bush. But how comes it about that you are acquainted with the fellow? I thought you were – that is, I believed you to be on terms with His Majesty? I even thought of writing to you to ask for your help, but the business of the counterfeit money decided me against it. I feared to cause you embarrassment. Now here you are, come to ask *me* to help you help Beaufort to escape, you—'

'Napoleon's mistress!' Marianne finished for him sadly. 'Things have altered since our last meeting, my friend. I am no longer quite such a favourite at court.'

'Suppose,' Surcouf suggested, reaching for his chair and setting it on its feet once more before turning back to the chest where he kept his port, 'you were to tell me all about it. I'm a true Breton, you know, and we all dearly love a good story.'

Heartened by another glass of wine and a fresh supply of biscuits, Marianne embarked on a somewhat tangled account of her relations with Jason and of her recent dealings with the Emperor. However, the port soon exercised a warming effect and in the end she acquitted herself reasonably well in the ordeal. When she finished, Surcouf's comment was typical of the man:

'Damn fool ought to have married you in the first place, not this bowel-less wench from Florida who must have been got by a wild Indian fed on crocodiles! You, now, you'd make a real sailor's wife! I saw that right away, when that old devil Fouché got you out of St Lazare.'

Marianne took this as a great compliment, and though she refrained from asking him to elaborate on the subject it was with rather more confidence that she inquired: 'So . . . you will help me?'

'Need you ask? A little more port?'

'Need you ask?' Marianne retorted, feeling an unexpected lightening of her heart.

The two friends drank eagerly to the success of a plan which they had yet to work out and Marianne felt a delicious sense of well-being creep over her. However, it took considerably more than three glasses of port to produce any noticeable effect on Surcouf's equilibrium. Draining his glass to the dregs, he announced his intention of escorting his visitor to the best hostelry in the town to take a little well-earned rest while he took care of the 'little matter in hand'.

'You can't stay here,' he explained, 'because I am pretty well alone in the house. My wife and children are at our house at Riancourt, near St Servan . . . and I can scarcely take you all the way there. Besides, Madame Surcouf is a very fine woman but I don't know if the two of you would deal together. She can be a trifle stern – and not overly tender-tongued.'

'A tartar!' Marianne decided mentally, while aloud she assured her friend that she really much preferred to go to an inn. She was anxious to pass unnoticed as far as possible and the fact that she was travelling incognito would make it awkward for her to visit his family. She might have added that she had no desire to figure as a nine days' wonder for the benefit of a pack of children, or to listen to a perfect housewife's comments on the price of grain and the difficulties of procuring foreign goods under the Blockade. A room to herself at a good inn seemed infinitely more attractive.

On this comfortable note, they parted, Surcouf confiding Marianne to the care of his man, the aged Job Goas. Job, who turned out as expected to be a retired seaman, was told to deliver Marianne to the Auberge de la Duchesse Anne – which, besides being the best in the town, was also the regular posting house – and see her suitably accommodated. Surcouf promised to come himself later in the evening, when he had found the man they needed.

It may have been due to the intoxicating qualities of port wine or perhaps somewhat to relief at this swift acquisition of so substantial an ally, but certain it was that Marianne found the inn charming, her room all that was comfortable and the smells which wafted upstairs from the large public room very thoroughly appetizing. For the first time for very many days, life seemed to have something agreeable to offer.

The little town lay snug within its walls but outside the wind was howling with redoubled fury. The night promised to be a stormy one and the riding lights on the tall masts in the harbour were bobbing up and down like so many drunken sailors. In Marianne's room, however, protected by thick walls and thick panes of leaded glass in the windows, all was warmth and safety. The bed, with its piled-up mattresses surmounted by an enormous red eiderdown, smelled pleasantly of linen dried in the sun, spread on the juniper bushes out on the open heath. Tired from her long journey in bad weather, Marianne could have gone straight to bed, but the port and ginger biscuits had given her an appetite. She felt ravenously hungry and her hunger was sharpened by the delicious cooking smells which were seeping through the whole building. Besides, Surcouf had advised her to eat her dinner in the public room so that he would not have to be taken to her bedchamber when he came with the man he had gone to find. The inn itself was a highly respectable one where a lady might eat alone without fear of importunities. Nevertheless, Marianne decided that Gracchus should share her dinner, so as to be on hand in the event of unlikely but still possible trouble while she waited for Surcouf and his friend.

Seated at a small table close to the immense hearth at which a woman in the graceful lace hennin worn by the women of Pléneuf was making pancakes with the aid of a long-handled pan, the Princess Sant'Anna and her coachman applied themselves unashamedly to the enjoyment of Cancale oysters, large crabs of the kind known as 'sleepers' served with salted butter and a vast *cotriade*, the Breton bouillabaisse, pungent with herbs. They ended the meal with the traditional golden pancakes and sparkling cider.

Marianne and Gracchus were sipping their fragrant coffee while all around them pipes were being filled with the fine tobacco of Porto Rico, when the low door flew open at a vigorous push from Surcouf. His entrance was the signal for a chorus of loud and joyful greetings, but Marianne paid no attention to these. All her senses were trained on the man who entered in the privateer's wake. Most of his face was hidden by the upturned collar of his heavy pilot coat, but Marianne knew that face too well to be mistaken in its owner, even if he had been wearing a false beard and a hat pulled over his eyes, which he was not. The 'man they needed' was Jean Ledru.

CHAPTER TWELVE

The Ninth Star

In the little house which had belonged to Nicolas Mallerousse, Marianne settled down to begin her vigil. She was waiting for two things. The first of these was the convict chain which should by this time be nearing the end of the journey begun more than three weeks before. The second was Jean Ledru's lugger, the *Saint-Guénolé*, which was working her way round the coast from St Malo to lie up in the little port of Le Conquet until it was time to move out into Brest roadstead.

Despite the bad weather, Ledru had put to sea with a crew of ten able-bodied seamen on the same morning as Surcouf had handed Marianne into her chaise and sent her on her way with boisterous good wishes.

The previous night, when Jean Ledru had reappeared in her life, Marianne had hesitated for a moment before committing Jason's future to the very person to whom she owed her own first, highly unenjoyable sexual experience, as well as subsequent trials of a very different kind. Surcouf, seeing Marianne's troubled face, had uttered a shout of laughter and given Ledru a cheerful push in her direction:

'He came to me last March, along with a personal letter from the Emperor asking me to take him back. To please you. So between the pair of us we patched things up – and have not ceased to be grateful to you. That Spanish war was no good for Jean. He did well enough, but he's not at home on shore. And I was happy to have a good seaman back.'

Feeling deeply conscious of the explosive nature of their earlier relations, Marianne extended her hand to her one-time comrade in misfortune: 'How do you do, Jean. I am glad to see you again.'

He had taken the proffered hand, unsmiling. The eyes that were like two blue forget-me-nots beneath lashes bleached white by the sea, remained thoughtful in the face whose tanned skin and short fair beard were still as she remembered, and for an instant Marianne was in doubt of his reaction. Was he still angry with her? Then, quite suddenly, the still face came to life and the gap between beard and moustache widened into a candid smile:

'And I'm glad too! I should rather think so after what you did for me – and if I can repay it . . .'

It was all right then. Everything was going to be all right! After that, she had tried to warn him of the risks involved in trying to outwit the law of the Empire but, like Surcouf, he would hear none of it.

'The man we have to rescue is a sailor and Monsieur Surcouf says he's innocent. That's enough for me. I don't want to know any more. What we have to do now is decide how to go about it.'

For two long hours, the three men and the girl sat round the table with a pot of coffee and a pile of pancakes in front of them, working out the broad outline of their plan. It was an audacious one but although Marianne's green eyes were occasionally shadowed with doubt, in the three pairs of blue ones belonging to the three men there was never anything but blazing enthusiasm and the thrill of adventure, so infectious that she soon abandoned every objection, except for one final one when the question of the lugger *Saint-Guénolé* was raised.

'But surely, these luggers are small boats, too small to sail all the way to America? Don't you think a larger vessel—'

She had repeated her proposal, which Surcouf had already turned down with magnificent disdain, to purchase a ship; but once again the corsair king explained to her, quite kindly, that she was talking nonsense.

'This is the ideal type of vessel to pass unnoticed, and to get someone out of Brest in a hurry, especially in the tricky waters of the Fromveur and the Iroise. She holds well in a sea-way and sails close to the wind. Leave what comes after that to me. And don't worry. There'll be a ship for America when it's wanted.'

With this, Marianne was obliged to be content and they parted for the night. All the time they had been talking, Marianne had been observing Jean Ledru, trying to discover from his inexpressive face whether or not he was cured at last of the destructive and ill-fated passion he had felt for her. His face had told her nothing but, just before they parted, he had told her himself, with a little teasing smile on his lips. Rising to put on his pilot jacket he had spoken, ostensibly to Surcouf, but really for the girl's benefit:

'All right if I leave you here, Cap'n? If I'm to sail with the tide I must say goodbye to Marie-Jeanne. There's no knowing how long we may be away, and a man can't put to sea without a last kiss for his girl.'

The glance at Marianne which accompanied this declaration was bright with mischief. It said, as clear as day: 'You needn't worry. It's all over between us. There's another woman in my life now.' And such was Marianne's delight that she smiled beamingly on him and shook his horny hand with real goodwill. So that it was with a quiet mind on the subject of future relations between them that, with Gracchus on the box and under a steady downpour of rain which showed no signs of ever stopping, she took the road to Brest.

Ever since her arrival in that great port, Marianne had made a point of remaining as inconspicuous as possible. Gracchus had driven the chaise straight to the posting house of the Seven Saints and there they had left it. It was a hired vehicle which would return to Paris with the next traveller. Then, modestly dressed with their baggage loaded on a handcart, he and Marianne had gone down to the quay below the castle to take the ferry across to Recouvrance. This way, as Marianne had discovered when she had been staying with Nicolas, was much shorter than going round by the bridge, which meant following the Penfeld as far as the arsenal, passing close to the grim, high walls of the *bagne*, the convict prison, and the rope-walks.

A fisherman in the blue cap of the men of Goulven had laid aside the net he was mending to take them over in his boat. The weather that day was very nearly fine. The wind that swelled the red sails of the fishing boats heading into the Goulet and smacked in the flags that flew from the great, round towers of the castle was cold but not unduly rough. In mid-stream, their boatman had backed water to give way to a long-boat towing-in a frigate, proud in her panoply of war, even with all her canvas stowed. The rowers, straining at their oars in time to the whistle blasts of the *comite*, wore the red caps and jackets of convict labourers. There were even some among them displaying with a kind of pride the green cap of the 'lifer' and all, the green caps and the red, carried the metal plate with their number on it. Marianne, seated on the rough, wooden thwart, had watched them go by with a curious sensation of horror and revulsion. The galleys might exist no longer but these men were still galley slaves of a kind and before long Jason would take his place amongst them. It had been left to Gracchus to rouse her from her gloomy reverie:

'Don't look, then, Mademoiselle Marianne,' he said. 'It'll only make you miserable.'

'Right you are there,' the boatman had agreed, setting his craft in motion once more. 'It's no sight for a young lady. But it's the *chiourme* does everything hereabouts. Those that aren't needed down at the docks work in the rope-walks or the sailmakers'. They collect up the garbage, too, and carry powder and cases of shot. You're for ever bumping into them. After a while, you just stop seeing them.'

Marianne thought this unlikely, even if she remained ten years in the town.

The boatman had been duly recompensed for his trouble and gave them good night, assuring them that if ever they wanted him they had only to give him a shout.

'My name is Conan,' he told them. 'Just stand on that rock there and give a hail and I'll be right over.'

Followed by Gracchus with the big trunk on his shoulder and a small boy humping a pair of carpet bags, Marianne had plunged into the stepped alleys of Recouvrance and headed in the direction of the Tour de la Motte Tanguy. More than a year had passed since she had left Brest on the mail coach but she found her way as easily as if it had been no more than a week before.

As they drew near to the tower, she was able to pick out Nicolas's little house at a glance: the whitewashed walls and granite cornerstones, the high, pointed gable window and the neat little garden, bare now of its summer flowers. Nothing had changed, not even Madame le Guilvinec from next door who for years had kept house for the secret agent without the least suspicion of his real activities.

Warned in advance by letter, the good woman came bustling out of her own house the moment Marianne and her escort had come in sight, arms spread wide and happiness written all over her long, rather masculine face, which was surmounted somewhat disconcertingly by the traditional head-dress of the women of Pont-Croix, in the shape of an erection rather resembling a kind of lace dolmen tied securely under the chin. The two women had clung together for a moment, crying a little as each remembered the sturdy figure of the man who had first brought them together.

It gave Marianne an odd feeling of homecoming to step once again into Nicolas's little house. Everything there was familiar, from the old, well-polished furniture and gleaming brass and copper to the collection of pipes and the tiny figurines of the Seven Saints which stood on a shelf, the well-thumbed books and the little wooden model of a ship which hung from a beam in the low ceiling. She settled into the house more easily even than she had done into the refurbished splendours of the Hôtel d'Asselnat and from then on, whenever the weather permitted, she had spent the best part of her time wrapped in a big, black shawl in the little leafless garden, gazing out at the roadstead and the quays along the Penfeld.

She had nothing to do but wait, now that the matter of a ship had been settled by Surcouf in his decisive fashion. She had introduced Gracchus as her servant, without defining his duties exactly, but there was little for him to do in such a small house and he passed his days exploring the town, roaming endlessly about the neighbourhood of the *bagne* and the poor area called Keravel which lay in a cluster of tumbledown houses and twisted alleyways between the wealthy shopping street, the rue de Siam, and the forbidding walls of the prison itself. For company, therefore, Marianne was limited to Madame le Guilvinec who would pop in for an hour or two and sit, knitting interminably, by the fire, or to the worthy woman's cat which had promptly adopted her and was more often than not to be found sleeping contentedly on the hearthstone.

Time seemed to stand still. Already it was December and even inside the Goulet the grey waters of the roadstead were rough with the great winter storms. On nights when the wind roared with the greatest violence, Madame le Guilvinec would set aside her knitting and quietly take out her beads, to pray for sailors and fishermen out at sea. Then, remembering Jean Ledru's lugger, Marianne, too, would begin to pray.

Then, one evening, as the short-lived winter sun was sinking seawards into the mist, the town became filled with a clamour so loud that it rose even above the usual noises of the port: whistles blew and there were echoes of commands roared into loud-hailers. Marianne reacted to the sounds like a war horse to the sound of a trumpet. She snatched up her great, hooded cloak and was out of the door, without even hearing the words her neighbour called after her. She sped down the narrow streets in between the tiny gardens, skidding and jumping on the stones, and reached the quay just in time to see the first wagon round the corner from the rue de Siam and turn along the quay towards the prison.

Even at that distance she could not mistake the uniforms of the guards and the long carts with their enormous wheels on which the men seemed to be crammed together more wretchedly even than at the start, but already it was getting dark and the miserable cortège was soon invisible through the skeins of mist rising from the river. Marianne shivered and, hugging her thick woollen cloak more closely about her, she turned and made her way home to wait for Arcadius, knowing that now the chain was there the Vicomte could not be far off. She had been tempted for a moment to go on as far as the Pont de Recouvrance and wait for him there by the bridge, but then she recollected that if he took the ferry, as she had done, then she would wait in vain.

He came, guided by Gracchus who had found him at the very gate of the prison, just as Madame le Guilvinec was closing the shutters and Marianne herself was bending over a stewpot suspended over the fire, gently stirring a thick and savoury-smelling soup.

'Ah, here is my uncle arrived from Paris at last, Madame le Guilvinec,' Marianne said simply, while the Breton woman fussed about the new arrival. What a long journey indeed! He must be tired!

Arcadius's face was undoubtedly drawn with fatigue, but there was something else in his expression which alerted Marianne at once. His silence, too, was disquieting. He thanked the goodhearted neighbour for her welcome, then went and seated himself on the edge of the hearth, shifting the cat to make room, and held out his hands to the fire without another word.

Marianne stood watching him anxiously, but without saying anything, while Madame le Guilvinec hurried to set the table. Gracchus stepped forward quickly:

'Never mind that, Madame. I'll do it.'

The Breton people are not talkative and they are highly sensitive to atmosphere. The widow of Pont-Croix was quick to realize that her neighbours wished to be alone and lost no time in bidding them good night, saying that she wanted to go to evening service in the chapel near by. Then, scooping up her cat as she went, she disappeared into the night. Almost before she had gone, Marianne was on her knees beside Jolival, who had let his head droop wearily on his hands.

'Arcadius! What is it? Are you ill?'

He raised his head at that and gave her a wan smile which only added to her fears.

'Something has happened to Jason?' she said, anguish suddenly catching at her throat. 'They have—'

'No, no! He is alive. But he is hurt, Marianne, hurt badly.'

'Hurt? How? Why?'

Then Arcadius told them what had happened. When they halted at Pontorson, one of those on Jason's chain, a young lad of eighteen, had the ague and was calling for water to slake his raging thirst. One of the guards had amused himself by emptying a jug of water over the boy's head and then kicking him in the ribs until he lay still. This had put Jason in a rage. He had sprung at the man and knocked him down. Having done so, he had then knelt on his chest and done his best to choke the life out of him. The guard's fellows had come hurrying to the rescue with their whips and one of the officers had drawn his sword.

'He was wounded in the chest,' Jolival went on. 'The brutes would have killed him but for one of the other convicts, a man called Vidocq, who encouraged the rest to gather round him and protect him. Even so, the remainder of the journey was a nightmare . . .'

'But – wasn't he looked after?'

Jolival shook his head. 'His comrades did their best when the chain stopped, but they were made to walk two stages on foot as punishment. I thought he would not reach here alive.'

'It's horrible!' Marianne said tonelessly. She sat back on her heels, her whole attitude one of despair, and stared unseeingly at the familiar room. Instead, she saw a bleak road, swept by wind and rain, and a wounded man dragging himself along in chains, kept on his feet by other vague, human figures as exhausted as himself.

'They will kill him,' she said. 'He will never survive. Have these poor wretches even a hospital?'

It was Gracchus who answered:

'There is one in the *bagne*. But I thought the chain was supposed to have a medical inspection at Pont-à-Lézen before they even got here?'

'The guards refused to leave him there. It's too easy to escape from the quarantine camp. And the man he attacked was against it, saying he'd have sufficient treatment in the prison to make him able to endure the punishment that was coming to him. That man's nothing but a brute beast. He'll not be satisfied until he has his pound of flesh.'

'Punishment? What punishment?'

'A flogging first, and then the cells, where he may remain for several months, if he survives the flogging! And there's no escaping from there.'

The waiting, buoyed up by the very real hopes which Marianne had brought with her from St Malo, had been a time of comparative peace compared with the horror which now took hold of her. She knew now that Jason was caught in the jaws of a relentless and awful machine from which it would be terribly difficult to free him and which might yet destroy him. In his present state, escape was unthinkable and if he recovered it would only be to fall into a still worse plight.

While she sat lost in these dismal meditations, Gracchus, swearing fluently, had taken up the sailor's pea jacket which he had bought the better to mingle unnoticed with the inhabitants of the great port and was putting it on again. Then, pulling his brown woollen cap down over his ears, he made swiftly for the door.

He paused at the sound of Marianne's voice.

'Where are you going at this time of night?'

'To Keravel. There's a wine-shop by the prison gates where the guards go to drink. I'm known there now and I've struck up an acquaintance with a Sergeant La Violette who's a great one for the bottle. A tot of rum'll be enough to make him tell me anything I want to know – and what I want to know is what's become of Monsieur Jason.'

A light came into Jolival's tired eyes at these words.

'He sounds a useful man to know. Well done. You go alone for tonight, but tomorrow I'll come and assist in the saturation of your sergeant.'

When Gracchus returned, two hours later, Marianne and Jolival were still downstairs, he smoking by the fire in silence, she, incapable of sitting still, trying to calm her fidgets by putting away the crockery. The news which Sergeant La Violette had breathed out, along with the fumes of his rum, confirmed that brought by Jolival in all respects, but with one slightly more encouraging addition. One of the prisoners had been brought in wounded and sent at once to the prison hospital. It was his good fortune that the surgeon in charge of the medical arrangements in the prison was still there at the time the chain arrived. A former escapee being brought back to complete his sentence had managed to inform him and he had examined the injured prisoner at once.

'François Vidocq again,' was Marianne's thought. But the thought of that odd, insouciant individual who had so annoyed her in La Force, now evoked nothing but gratitude. She could almost have remembered him in her prayers, knowing that it was thanks to him that Jason was alive at that moment. But for how long? The enmity of the man he had knocked down was all about him, watching its opportunity, and that thought, in the days ahead, was to breed in Marianne's heart a vague, but ever-present fear.

To an outside observer, those days would have appeared calm and unvaried to the point of monotony, punctuated only by the church bells and the castle gun. The inhabitants of the little house lived a quiet, ordered life, attending to their small domestic affairs or walking out, uncle and niece together strolling sedately arm-in-arm through the streets of the town or along the esplanade by the castle, visiting the harbour and the historic old quarters. The young servant, when he was off duty, loafed about doing nothing in particular, as was to be expected of a lad of his age. He would spend hours on the quays by the Penfeld watching the prisoners loading cases of shot and grenades aboard the warships, coiling the new-made ropes as they emerged from the hands of their comrades, working on vessels undergoing repairs and stacking the great baulks of freshly cut timber, still redolent of their native forests, for use in the shipyards. Yet there was another side to these innocent wanderings, which was to gather the greatest possible amount of information and, most important of all, to watch for the arrival of the *Saint-Guénolé*.

The lugger was taking an inexplicably long time. According to Jolival's calculations, it should have been sighted at least a week before and Marianne found the delay both fretting and alarming. The sea had been so rough of late that who could say whether the little craft would manage to get safely through the Fromveur channel, with its perilous reputation, round the Promontoire de St Mathieu and make the little harbour of Le Conquet without being driven on to the rocks? Even the fishermen mostly stayed at home and they were saying on the quays and in the taverns that no news had come through from the offshore islands for a fortnight or more. As so often in the winter months, Molène and Ushant were cut off from the mainland by the pounding seas.

Once the doors and shutters were safely closed, however, the occupants of the house devoted themselves to less innocent occupations. Jolival spent hours painstakingly cutting in half the big bronze *sous*, in size and thickness more than adequate for the purpose, and just as carefully putting them together again, but with gold coins concealed inside, money being an indispensable tool for the convict. He had also made a copy of the brass numberplate worn by every convict on his cap, with, on it, Jason's number – learned from Sergeant La Violette – only this time in steel with minuscule saw teeth which would enable it to saw through chains. Meanwhile, Marianne had been learning to bake bread and two large loaves had already been dispatched to the *bagne*, again through the good offices of La Violette. Inside each one was a piece of ordinary civilian clothing.

After dark, Jolival and Gracchus would slip out of the house and make their way down to Keravel, to the tavern known as 'The Girl from Jamaica' where they were looked on by now as regular customers. Nor was the news they brought back unencouraging. The injured man was recovering, slowly but surely. His youth and strong constitution had won. The danger of infection was past. Arcadius and the surgeon of the prison were, in fact, agreed on the beneficial effects of sea air on healing wounds; but still Marianne was unable to think without a shudder of the narrow pallet of seaweed and the chains which held the body of the man she loved, for the convicts were never released from their chains.

Christmas was coming and as it fell this year on a Tuesday

and Friday was market day in Brest, Marianne went with Madame le Guilvinec on the Friday before, down to the rue de Siam to make the necessary purchases in preparation for the festival which was probably dearer than any other to Breton hearts. It would have looked suspiciously odd if the new inhabitant of Recouvrance had behaved differently from her neighbours in this.

The weather was mild but misty. The rue de Siam, always at its busiest on market days, was wrapped in a dense yellow fog, making the animation all about appear strangely subdued. The sailors' striped trousers and varnished hats, the rich, colourful costumes of the peasant girls, a different dress for every village, seemed to fade into unreality. The Léon girls, in their tall hennins with long, fringed shawls falling almost to their heels, took on the air of witches from a fairy tale, while those from Plouaré, all smothered in red and gold embroidery, were like so many figures of the Virgin, stepped down from their niches in the church. Everyone, even the old people in their sombre blacks, was transformed into a fantastic being from another world, while the men, with their embroidered waistcoats, wide, pleated trousers and little round hats were as colourful and gay as any.

Marianne was wandering in Madame le Guilvinec's wake from a stall of oysters to another heaped like a small mountain with cabbages, when she saw a cart loaded with refuse coming towards her. It was being pushed and pulled along by a group of four convicts, one of them wearing the green cap of the incorrigible criminal, under the somewhat vague eye of the guard who was following on behind in a bored way, nose in the air and hands clasped behind his back, oblivious of the sabre banging against his calves. No one took any notice of them. Convict labour was an everyday affair to the people of Brest. There were even some who smiled at them, as at old acquaintances.

The man in the green cap seemed especially well known. A ship's chandler, standing smoking his long clay pipe in the doorway of his shop, gave him a friendly wave. The convict waved back and Marianne saw suddenly that it was Vidocq. He was quite close to her by then and, drawn as though by a magnet. Marianne could not withstand the longing to attract his attention. Madame le Guilvinec had paused underneath the awning of a market gardener's stall to gossip with another old soul in a similar dolmen head-dress to her own and had temporarily forgotten her companion. Marianne raised her hand.

The convict's bright eye caught hers at once. He gave a hint of a smile to show that he had recognized her and then nodded at the next street corner where a heap of refuse was waiting to be carted away. Next, he jerked his head back to where the guard was still ambling along behind the refuse cart and tossed a pebble in his hand, as if it had been a coin. Marianne realized that he was telling her to go to the heap of rubbish where, for the price of a coin, she would be able to exchange a few words with him.

Slipping swiftly between two groups of people, without Madame le Guilvinec seeing her, she made her way hurriedly to the corner and waited for the cart to come up with her. Then, taking a silver coin from her purse, she slipped it into the guard's hand, saying under her breath that she would like a word with the man in the green cap.

The man shrugged and uttered a crack of ribald laughter:

'That Vidocq! He's a right one for the girls, he is. Go on, then, sweetheart, but not more than a minute, mind!'

It was dark in the entrance to the alley which was no more than a narrow passage, sucking up the fog. Marianne stepped quickly inside, while the convict, with an unnerving rattle of his chains, stationed himself against the slate-hung wall, half-hidden by a small, wooden shrine adorning the corner of the house.

Still out of breath from her haste, Marianne asked: 'Have you any news?'

'Yes. I saw him this morning. He is better, but still far from well.'

'How much longer?'

'A week, at least, maybe ten days.'

'And after that?'

'After?'

'Yes . . . they told me he . . . was to suffer some punishment . . .'

The convict shrugged with a gesture of fatalism. 'He's certainly earned a flogging. It all depends on the man who administers it . . . If he goes easy with it, he'll survive.'

'But I can't – not even the thought of it! He must escape first. If not, he may be crippled – or worse!'

Quick as a snake, the convict's arm shot out from his jacket pocket and clamped down on Marianne's arm.

'Not so loud!' he growled. 'You talk of it as if it were like going to church! Don't worry, everything's in hand. Have you a vessel?'

'I shall have – or so I hope. It has not arrived yet and . . .'

Vidocq frowned. 'Without a boat, the thing can't be done. As soon as the alarm is given from the *bagne*, everyone for miles round takes up the hunt. It's worth a hundred francs to capture a man on the run . . . and there's a gipsy encampment right by the gates with just that one thought in mind. Real bloodhounds! The moment the gun goes off, it's out with the scythes and pitchforks and away!'

The other convicts had by now finished heaping the refuse somewhat haphazardly on to the cart and the *comite*'s head poked round the corner:

'Ready, Vidocq . . . on your way, now!'

Vidocq dragged himself away from the wall and began to move out into the street:

'When your boat comes, tell Kermeur at the Girl from Jamaica. But try and make it in a week from now – ten days at the latest. So long!'

Without giving a further thought to Madame de Guilvinec, who had in any case disappeared from sight and was probably looking for her at that moment in some other part of the market, Marianne made her way back to the esplanade by the castle, eager to get back to Recouvrance at once and tell Jolival what had occurred. The street sloped steeply and the bumpy cobblestones were slippery with damp but she was almost running, Vidocq's words whirling round and round in her head: in a week – ten days at most . . . and Ledru had not come, might never come! They must do something – find a boat . . . They could not afford to wait any longer. Something must have happened to Ledru and they would have to make other arrangements . . .

As luck would have it, old Conan, the ferryman, was on her side of the river, sitting on a rock, smoking his pipe as placidly as if the sun were shining, and spitting from time to time into the water. Marianne was so excited that had he been on the other bank she might very well have jumped straight into the river in her haste to get across. As it was, she was in the boat before the good man had so much as noticed that he had a customer.

'Hurry!' she ordered. 'Take me across!'

The old man shrugged expressively. 'Bah!' he grunted. 'You young folks, always in a hurry. It's a wonder you take time to breathe!'

All the same, he plied his oars rather more energetically than usual and not many minutes later Marianne was scrambling out on to the rocks, tossing the man a coin as she went, and setting off homewards at a run. When she burst, panting, into the house, Jolival was standing by the table, deep in conversation with a fishermanwho had just set down his basket full of fresh, steel-blue mackerel. The smell of fish mingled with that of the wood fire in the hearth.

'Arcadius!' Marianne began urgently. 'We must find a boat at once. I have seen—'

She broke off for the two men had turned and she saw that the fisherman was none other than Jean Ledru.

'A boat?' he asked in his placid voice. 'What for? Won't mine do for you?'

Feeling her legs give way beneath her, Marianne sank down on to the settle and undid her heavy cloak, which seemed to have grown suddenly too hot. Then she pushed back the linen bonnet which covered her hair and gave a sigh of relief:

'I thought you would never come – that something had happened to you!'

'No, all went well. Only I had to put in to Morlaix for a few days. One of my men was . . . sick.'

He hesitated slightly over this explanation but Marianne was too glad to see him to be conscious of any such detail.

'Never mind,' she said. 'You are here now. And you have your boat?'

'Yes, not far from the Madeleine tower. But I'm off again soon, back to Le Conquet.'

'You're going away?'

Jean Ledru indicated the basket of mackerel:

'I'm an ordinary fisherman, come to sell my catch. That's my only apparent motive for being in Brest. But don't worry. I shall be back tomorrow. Is everything ready, as we decided at St Malo?'

In a few words, Arcadius and Marianne told him all that had happened since she had last seen him: Jason's injury, the impossibility of his being in any condition to attempt an escape before another week was out, and the threat which hung over him as soon as he was in a way to be better which left them so small a margin of time in which to get him out. To all this, Jean Ledru listened, frowning and chewing the ends of his moustache with increasing discontent. When Marianne came to the end of her conversation with Vidocq that morning, he slammed his fist down on the table with such violence that the fish leaped on their bed of seaweed and rushes.

'You are forgetting one thing – one rather important thing. The sea. You can't treat that with impunity. The weather in a week's time will have made the Iroise impassable. Your prisoner must be aboard the vessel coming to pick him up at Le Conquet in five days at the latest.'

'What vessel is this?'

'Never you mind. The one that's to take him across the ocean, of course. It will be off Ushant in three days and it can't lie off the coast for long without the coastguard seeing it. We sail on Christmas Eve.'

Marianne and Jolival stared at each other speechlessly. Had Ledru gone mad, or had he understood not one word of all that they had told him? In the end it was Marianne who spoke first.

'Jean,' she said again, very quietly, 'we told you, a week at least before Jason will be strong enough to climb a rope or scale a wall or do any of the other things he will have to do if he is to escape.'

'I suppose he is strong enough, at least, to saw through the chain fastening him to his bed? You tell me you have managed to get all the tools he needs smuggled in to him, and money to buy himself extra food?'

'Yes, we have done all that,' Jolival said quickly. 'But it is still not enough. What would you do?'

'Carry him off, just like that. I know where the prison hospital is, the end building, almost outside the prison itself. The walls are not so high – easier to climb. I have ten men, all used to going aloft in a full gale. To get into the hospital, get your friend out and over the wall will be child's play. We simply knock out anyone who gets in our way. It'll be all over in a brace of shakes. High tide on Christmas Eve is midnight. We can sail on the turn. The *Saint-Guénolé* will be moored off Keravel. Besides' – he grinned briefly at the two startled faces before him, 'it'll be Christmas Eve – and the guards have their own way of celebrating. They'll be drunk as lords. We'll have no trouble from them. Any other objections?'

Marianne took a deep breath, as if she had just surfaced after swimming for a long time under water. After all these days of doubt and anxiety, Jean Ledru's quiet confidence left her feeling slightly dashed. But, goodness, what a comfort he was! She smiled.

'I'd hardly dare! You wouldn't listen to them if I had, would you?'

'No, I shouldn't,' he agreed seriously, but his eyes twinkled suddenly as he hoisted the fish basket back on to his shoulder, with the crinkling smile which, in this taciturn Breton, was a sign of extravagant mirth:

'Warn the prisoner it's for Monday night. Let him have his chain cut through by eleven o'clock. The rest is up to me. As for yourselves – watch for the boat and when you see her alongside wait until it's dark and then go aboard.'

With a final wave of his hand, the sailor passed out of the house and through the little garden then, with his basket on his shoulder, he set off with great strides in the direction of the harbour. For a little while, the sound of his whistling came floating back to them up the steep, narrow streets, the same, jaunty little tune which Marianne had heard once before, one anguished morning as she stood watching a tiny sailing boat put slowly out to sea, leaving her the captive of Morvan the Wrecker: it was the song of Surcouf's sailors:

> The thirty-first of August,
> With the larboard watch below,
> We spied an English frigate . . .

Left alone, standing looking at each other across the table on which Jean had left them a few fish, Marianne and Jolival said nothing for a moment or two. Finally, Arcadius gave a shrug and went to fetch himself a cigar from the blue Delft jar. He sniffed it gently for a moment before bending and taking a light from the fire. A rich, tobacco smell filled the room, overcoming the smell of fish.

'He's right,' he said at last. 'It pays to be bold in matters like this. Anyway, we have no choice.'

'You think he will be able to do it?' Marianne asked anxiously.

'I hope so! If he can't, my dear child, nothing can save us. We shall all be hanged at the yard-arm – unless they decide to shoot us instead. There will be no quarter, you know, if we are caught? Are you afraid?'

'Afraid? The only thing I fear, Jolival, is a life without Jason. I care for nothing else, rope or a shot is all one to me.'

Arcadius drew luxuriously on his cigar and then considered the glowing tip of it intently.

'I always knew you had the makings of a great tragic heroine,' he said equably. 'Or else a great lunatic! For my own part, I've no complaints about staying alive and since we've seven saints in the house, I'll ask them kindly to make sure this exciting Christmas Eve which our ebullient captain promises us may not be our last.'

With that, Arcadius strolled out to finish his cigar in the

garden while Marianne, left to herself, started unthinkingly to gut the fish.

December the twenty-fourth began badly. When daylight dawned belatedly, it was to reveal dense, yellow fog, thick enough to cut with a knife. Recouvrance, with its grey stone walls and isolated trees, might have been a lost world drifting in some cloudy infinite. Visibility extended no further than the tower of La Motte Tanguy. Everything else, town, port, castle and roadstead, had vanished as utterly and completely as if the hill had loosed its moorings suddenly and sailed away into the sky, like some enormous air balloon.

Marianne, who had not slept a wink all night long, stared out resentfully at the fog. Fate seemed to be taking a malicious pleasure in making things difficult for her. She was angry with fate, angry with nature, angry with herself for her own fidgets, she was even angry with the world for continuing to turn in its ordinary way while she was in such suspense. She was so nervous and complained so many times that they could never see the *Saint-Guénolé* even supposing that she was able to feel her way into the river mouth, that in the end Jolival told Gracchus to go and keep watch from the rocks by the castle point on whatever shipping appeared.

This was at about noon and after that Marianne did make some effort to behave normally for the remainder of the crucial day which was to decide the whole course of her life. Even then, she could not refrain from asking the endlessly patient Jolival a hundred times over if he were quite sure that Jason had been warned to hold himself in readiness and if François Vidocq had also been alerted, as he had requested, so that he could help the American while at the same time seizing a heaven-sent opportunity to escape himself. For Marianne was quite sure that Vidocq was not the man to do anything for nothing.

Madame le Guilvinec, who was spending the festive season with her niece at Portzic, came in during the morning to make sure that her neighbour would want for nothing during her absence and also to bring the traditional yule log which was supposed to be put on the fire to burn slowly up to the time for midnight mass. This one was prettily decorated with red ribbons, golden laurel leaves and sprigs of holly, and Marianne was all the more touched by this mark of friendship because she had been careful to give no hint of her intention to leave Brest that night for the last time and had been inclined to look on the niece's invitation as a stroke of luck.

The good lady was so distressed at the thought of leaving her new friends for this, their first Christmas, that she came back two or three times to ask them if they would not rather she stayed, or would like to come with her to her family. However, in the face of their firm, though smiling refusal, she eventually brought herself, with many expressions of regret, to say goodbye, although not without innumerable injunctions to Marianne regarding local customs: the welcome to be given to the youthful carol singers, not to forget to say a prayer for the dead before going off to midnight mass, to have the hearth cakes and the chicken ready for the modest *reveillon* which should follow and a host of other things, one of the most important of which was a strict injunction to remain fasting until the evening.

'To eat nothing?' Jolival protested. 'When we have enough ado as it is to make her eat like anyone else?'

Madame le Guilvinec raised an admonitory finger to the blackened rafters:

'If she wants to see miracles happen on the holy night, or even if she wants her own wishes to come true, she must take nothing all day long, not until after dark when she can count nine stars in the sky. If she is still fasting when the ninth star comes out, then she can expect to have a gift from heaven.'

Arcadius, being a rational man with a strong aversion to anything that smacked of superstition, might have muttered a little, but Marianne was deeply attracted by this romantic prophecy. It was with eyes suddenly softened that she looked at the widow from Pont-Croix, standing there in her black garments, like some antique sibyl.

'The ninth star,' she said seriously. 'I will wait, then, until it is out. Although in this fog—'

'The fog will go away with the tide. God bless you and keep you, young lady. Nicolas Mallerousse did well to leave his house to you.'

With one last stroke for her cat which she was leaving with her neighbours, she was gone and Marianne, watching her wide, black cloak billowing along the road to the church, felt oddly sad for a moment. Just as Madame le Guilvinec had predicted, the fog was already beginning to clear, blown away by the gusts of wind that had got up, and by the beginning of the afternoon it had gone completely, leaving the countryside restored to all its wild beauty. It was about an hour after this that a lugger with red sails entered the harbour channel below the castle and came on up the Penfeld. The *Saint-Guénolé* had reached the rendezvous. The adventure had begun.

That evening, when it was quite dark, Marianne, Jolival and Gracchus left the house silently. They locked the door behind them, having taken care to leave a window open and unshuttered so that Madame le Guilvinec's cat, left with ample supplies of fish and milk, might come and go at will. Gracchus skipped lightly over the low garden wall and slid the key under the neighbour's door, along with a note explaining that Marianne and her 'uncle' had been obliged to return to Paris unexpectedly.

It was long after the time when the castle gun and the great bell of the prison had announced the end of work for the day and the church bells had rung for evening prayer, yet the town was not going to sleep as it usually did. The ships of war were dressed overall and as the lights went up on the mastheads so the lighted sterncastles showed that those aboard were keeping their own Christmas Eve. From the taverns came the sounds of lusty voices singing everything from the old Christmas carols down to lewd sea shanties, while the streets were full of people, whole families of them, all in their best caps and bonnets, the men carrying in one hand a lantern and in the other the knotted wooden staff called the *pen-bas*, and all hurrying off to spend the evening with friends until the time came round to go to church. There were groups of small boys as well, armed with beribboned branches, going the rounds of the houses knocking on doors and singing carols for all they were worth, for the reward of a few coins or a cake apiece. The whole town basked in the aromatic scents of cider, rum and pancakes.

The three of them attracted little notice, in spite of the small box containing Marianne's few clothes and her jewels which Gracchus carried under his arm, beneath his heavy cloak, and her own carpet bag. There was little to mark them out from other pedestrians that night.

Once they reached the other side of the Pont de Recouvrance, the bridge being the shorter way on this occasion, they began to encounter the occasional drunk. The lights of the taverns at the lower end of the rue de Siam, near the harbour, shone out across the pavement, and now and then gleamed on the dark water beyond. Everywhere there was a holiday feeling in the air and only those few vessels that were putting to sea on the tide showed any signs of activity aboard.

Marianne had taken Arcadius's arm and all the way she kept her eyes glued to the dark sky, counting the rare stars that appeared there. So far, she had reached no more than six and Jolival smiled at her worried face.

'If it clouds over, you're likely to starve to death, my child.'

She only shook her head, without answering, then pointed suddenly to where the seventh star had come out, above the tall masts of a frigate in the bay. As for starving, until she had found Jason again she was oblivious to hunger.

At the same time, she caught sight of the lugger, tied up below Keravel, and the figure of Jean Ledru beckoning on the deck. The *Saint-Guénolé* looked very small alongside the brig *Trident* and the two frigates, *Sirène* and *Armide*, berthed close by, but her very insignificance was a safeguard, as was the single, modest riding light at her masthead.

Seconds later, the fugitives had crossed the plank connecting her with the shore and were aboard. Suddenly, in the yellow light of the ship's lanterns, Marianne found herself the centre of a ring of silent faces which might have been carved out of mahogany, despite the many blond heads and beards among them. Dressed all alike in thick, dark jerseys, their caps pulled well down over their eyes, Jean Ledru's men looked far more like a crew of pirates than of honest seamen, but all their faces wore the same look of grim determination and the muscles beneath the heavy jerseys were certainly like knotty oaks.

'You're just in time,' Ledru grunted. 'You go down below, Marianne, and wait for us. Monsieur, your uncle, will stay with you.'

With one accord, the two persons addressed opened their mouths to protest.

'No!' Arcadius said. 'I'm going with you.'

'Me, too!' echoed Marianne.

It was one of the men, a big, red-headed fellow with something of the look of a large, reddish bear, who voiced immediate opposition to this suggestion:

'It's bad enough, Cap'n, having a woman aboard! If we've got to cart her along with us!'

'You'll not be obliged to *cart* me, as you put it,' Marianne exclaimed indignantly. 'And if I go with you, I shall be the less time aboard your boat. It is my man you are going to rescue and I want to share the risk with you.'

'And climb the wall, in your petticoats?'

'I can wait at the bottom. I'll keep watch. And I know how to use this, as well . . .' she added, putting aside the folds of her cloak and showing one of the pistols Napoleon had given her tucked into her belt.

The red-headed seaman gave a shout of laughter:

'By God! If that's the way of it, come you shall! You're a brave lass, after all, and an extra hand is always welcome.'

Jean Ledru, who had disappeared for a moment during this exchange, now reappeared, closing the cabin door behind him. As he did so, Marianne's sharp eyes caught sight of the length of rope coiled neatly about his chest. He glanced quickly round his crew.

'Is everyone ready? Joël, got the rope? You, Thomas and Goulven, the grapnels?'

Three men, the redhead among them, opened their thick jackets simultaneously. One was wrapped about in hemp, like

Jean himself, the other two, one of whom was the redhead, who seemed to be called Thomas, had stuck into their belts the long grappling irons which were to be thrown up over the wall.

'We'll be on our way then,' the young leader declared. 'In small groups, if you please, and try and look as natural as you can. You three' – once again he addressed the newcomers – 'you three follow at a little distance, as if you were on your way to spend the evening with friends. And try not to get lost.'

'No fear of that,' Gracchus muttered. 'I know Keravel like the back of my hand. I could get about the place with my eyes shut.'

'Better keep them open, all the same! Otherwise you might run into things you don't expect.'

In small groups, two or three at a time, they left the boat, until the only people left on board were an old man, who answered to the name of Nolff and the cabin boy, Nicolas. Marianne and her escort were the last to leave. The girl's fingers tightened nervously on Jolival's arm. In spite of the cold, she felt as if she were stifling. When they plunged into the unsavoury streets of Keravel, she had the impression that the houses, their overhanging upper stories all crooked and reared up at strange angles, were only waiting to spring on her. This was the first time she had ventured into this area of the town, a place forsaken by God but not by men, and the maze of squalid, twisting alleyways where now and then the red light of a tavern shone through greasy curtains, were obscurely terrifying. Far ahead, as though at the end of a tunnel, a lantern hung, creaking, on a chain stretched between two crumbling buildings, but every dark, shadowy hole and corner in between was filled, she saw with a sick feeling of disgust, with a squeaking, scampering colony of rats, scurrying to and fro among the refuse on the ground. The slender ribbon of sky seemed so far away that there was no hope of even the smallest star.

'You ought to have stayed on the boat,' Jolival said, feeling her shiver, but Marianne pulled herself together instantly:

'No, not for anything!'

They were obliged to make a detour to avoid passing directly in front of the big gates of the prison and the guards on duty there but not long afterwards the little band was stretched out in the shelter of the great, dark walls, hearing the steady tramp of the sentry going his rounds on the footway above. One by one, they passed between the prison and the rope-walks, deserted at this late hour, and, rounding a corner to the right, saw before them a series of barred windows on the far side of a wall distinctly lower than the rest. This was the prison hospital. There was light in the windows, a feeble, reddish glow that probably came from a night light.

On a level with the first of these windows, Jean Ledru assembled his party. Taking off his coat, he began unwinding the rope from his middle. Joël did the same, while Thomas and Goulven unfastened their grapnels. Marianne pointed a little timidly at the window:

'There are bars . . . How will you manage?'

'You don't think we'll be going in that way?' the Breton said, on a smothered chuckle. 'There's a door on the other side of the wall. We can jump the sentry from the top and flatten him!'

The grapnels were made fast in a moment. The sailors stood back, drawing Marianne and Jolival with them. Jean Ledru and Thomas measured their distances and then, standing with legs well apart for balance, they began to swing the grapnels with the same easy motion.

They were just about to let go when, suddenly, Jean let his go slack and signed to Thomas to do the same. There had come a sound from above. They heard a noise of running footsteps, then lights sprang up in one window after another. Then, without warning, and so close that it felt to Marianne as if the entire wall had exploded, came the report of a cannon being fired, followed by a second and a third.

Throwing caution to the winds, Jean Ledru swore comprehensively and snatched up his equipment:

'There's been an escape! They'll search the prison, then the town. After that the coast and country around. Back to the boat, all of you, fast as you can make it!'

Marianne's cry came like an echo: 'But we can't! We can't go and leave Jason!'

But already the men had scattered, making their own way through the dismal lanes of the old quarter. Seizing Marianne swiftly by the arm, Jean began dragging her firmly away, ignoring her protests:

'It's all off for the present. If we stay here, we'll only get ourselves caught.'

Marianne made desperate efforts to resist, still looking back frantically at the windows, behind which figures were already moving about. The whole prison was awake now. There were sounds of nailed boots running and the click of weapons being cocked. Someone had got to the bell and was hauling on it like a madman, sending its ominous strokes booming and clanging out over the festive town.

With Ledru on one side of her and Jolival gripping her just as firmly on the other, Marianne was forced to run with them, although her heart was thudding painfully in her chest and her feet were bruised and tender from stubbing them on the slippery cobbles. She raised her tear-filled eyes to the sky and smothered a groan. It was all clouded over and there were no stars at all.

'Faster!' Ledru said gaspingly. 'Faster! They can still see us.'

The black streets of Keravel swallowed them up and, once in darkness, Arcadius halted, still holding Marianne, forcing the younger man to do the same.

'Now what's the matter?' Ledru barked at him. 'We are not there yet.'

'No,' the Vicomte agreed calmly. 'But can you tell me where the danger is now? It is not written on our faces that we have been intending to help a prisoner to escape. Do we look any less like honest folk out to enjoy ourselves than we did on the way here?'

Ledru's panic left him in an instant. He took off his woollen cap and ran his fingers like a comb through his sweat-streaked hair.

'You're quite right. It was the cannon – I think it must have sent me off my head. Of course, we'd much better just walk back quietly. We've had it for tonight, anyway . . .' He paused, seeing Marianne burst into gasping sobs on Jolival's shoulder. 'I'm truly sorry, Marianne. Maybe we'll have more luck next time.'

'Next time! He'll be dead before then. They'll have killed him!'

'Never think that! We may be luckier than you expect. And it's nobody's fault if some other poor devil had the same idea as us and chose Christmas Eve to show a clean pair of heels.'

He was trying, in his clumsy way, to comfort her, but Marianne refused to be comforted. She pictured Jason, lying on his hospital bed with his chains sawn through, waiting for a rescue that never came. What would they do to him tomorrow when they found his fetters loose? Would the man Vidocq, perhaps, manage somehow to prevent the worst?

The little group had moved on again. Jean Ledru went ahead now, hands in his coat pockets, cap pulled down over his eyes and back hunched forward, eager to have the deck of his ship beneath him again. Marianne followed, more slowly, clinging to Jolival's compassionate arm, her mind still searching feverishly for a way to achieve the impossible and rescue Jason after all. She felt as if every step she took was carrying her inexorably farther away not only from the prison, but also from the man she loved. In the privacy of her hood, she wept, in small, hard sobs that hurt her throat.

When they reached the waterfront, Jean hurried straight to his boat, not without an uneasy sidelong glance at the gendarme who was strolling up and down with hands behind his back with every appearance of a man waiting for something. Jolival bent and spoke quietly in Marianne's ear:

'We had better go back to Recouvrance, child. Wait here, while I go and fetch our bags and find out what has become of Gracchus. He must have gone with the sailors.'

Marianne nodded to show that she had understood and while he made his way to the boat she remained where she was, her arms hanging at her sides, drained alike of all her courage and all capacity for thought. Then, without warning, the gendarme who had been walking towards Jolival had rushed up to her instead and grabbed her by the arm, paying not the least attention to her feeble cry of fright.

'Good God! What are you dawdling here for? As if we weren't in enough danger already. For the lord's sake, get on board! We've been sitting here gnawing our fingers' ends for half an hour waiting for you!'

For a second, Marianne very nearly fainted from shock for underneath the gendarme's cocked hat she had recognized the face of Vidocq. It was Vidocq himself, although scarcely recognizable as the same man. Then all other feelings were swept away in a sudden burst of anger:

'You? You were the one who got away? It is you they are looking for – and meanwhile Jason—'

'Jason is already aboard, you brainless idiot! Up with you, now, and get aboard!'

He half-lifted and half-threw her up on to the deck where the crew was already busy about the business of casting off. Then, while she practically fell into Jolival's arms, he vaulted lightly on to the gunwale and strolled forward to the mainmast where he posted himself conspicuously with one foot on a coil of rope, so as to give the port officers the full opportunity of observing his uniform.

All around them, the agitation in the town seemed to have subsided for the present. The bells were ringing for mass and the good people of Brest, in this instance, were putting God before man.

Just then, the figure of another gendarme hoisted itself out of the cabin. The face was thin, haggard and unshaven under the cocked hat but the eyes were full of laughter.

'Marianne!' he called softly. 'Come! I'm over here!'

She tried to speak, tried to express her joy, but her recent alternations of hope and fear, terror, grief and shock had used up all her resistance. She had just strength to tumble headlong into his arms and he, although barely able to stand upright himself, found somehow the strength to hold her to him. For a long moment, they clung to each other in silence, too happy and too deeply moved for speech. Sails flapped around them, climbing rapidly up the mast. Barefooted sailors ran noiselessly about the deck. Jean Ledru at the tiller gave the faintest shrug and turned his eyes away from the couple who seemed to have forgotten that the world existed.

Vidocq, however, remarked from his observation post: 'If I were you, I should go and sit down under the gunwale where you can't be seen. Even a fool of an exciseman or a drunken soldier might think there was something odd about a policeman going hunting escaped convicts with a woman in his arms!'

Without a word, they did as he suggested and found a sheltered corner where they settled like a pair of lovebirds in a nest. Gently, Marianne took off the ridiculous cocked hat and let the salt wind ruffle Jason's hair. As she did so, she glanced up, automatically, at the sky. All the stars were out, and they were many more than nine.

The night of miracles had kept its promise.

CHAPTER THIRTEEN

That Justice be Done

While the *Saint-Guénolé* with Jean Ledru's skilled hand on the tiller ran with the wind on her quarter for Cape St Mathieu and Le Conquet and the coast of Brittany slipped by like a ragged ghost in the darkness, François Vidocq explained:

Late that afternoon, there had been a serious accident in the prison shipyards. A mast which was undergoing repairs in the dry dock had come crashing down on a group of prisoners stacking timber on the quayside. One man had been killed and a number seriously injured. The prison sick bay, somewhat grandly styled the hospital, had been full in a moment, so that Jason Beaufort who was now considered pretty well recovered had been returned at once to the communal dormitories. Fortunately, owing to the haste with which the move was accomplished, the business of chaining him to another prisoner had been put off until the next day and he had merely been fastened to the bail with the rest.

'Knowing what your plans were, I had to get to you fast and warn you that it was all changed and at the same time not let slip the wonderful chance offered by your vessel. Sawing through Beaufort's chain was a matter of minutes – I'm not without experience at that game.' He grinned. 'My own were done already. The next thing we had to do was to find a way of getting out by the front door. Beaufort could walk. He was sufficiently recovered for that, but not to go climbing walls. So I did the only possible thing – knocked out two gendarmes and stole their uniforms, putting them carefully out of harm's way in a nice quiet place, all neatly gagged and bound.'

'Not as quiet as all that,' Jolival commented sourly. 'It didn't take them long to discover them, to judge by how soon they sounded the alarm!'

The Vicomte was suffering from sea sickness. Stretched at full length alongside a heap of ropes, as much to be out of the way of the boom which swept low across the deck at the end of every tack as to spare himself any unnecessary movement, he lay staring in a determined way at the dark sky, knowing full well that the mere sight of the sea would only make matters worse.

'I'm quite sure they've not been discovered yet,' Vidocq stated categorically. 'They are in the rope loft and no one will set foot there until the morning. And, believe me, I know the way to bind and gag a man.'

'Yes, but the alarm was given—'

'Yes . . . but not for us! Someone else must have decided to try Christmas Eve to make his escape. It's not something we thought of' – he paused – 'but then I suppose we can't claim a monopoly where escape's concerned.'

Marianne cried out at that: 'But then, perhaps they may not be looking for you at all?'

'Oh, yes, they will. Even if they've not discovered the gendarmes yet, they're bound to have noticed our absence very soon. Once the alarm had been given, there was no reason for the others to keep mum. Our best hope is in the fact that they'll probably be looking for us along the coast and in the open country. It's practically impossible for a convict to get hold of a boat, especially one like this, even with outside help. Most of them aren't rich, you know . . .'

He continued to expatiate for a little while on his private philosophy of escape, its techniques and the various opportunities which could arise, but Marianne soon ceased to listen. She leaned back against the side of the boat, feeling the wind in her hair, with Jason's head in her lap. He was still very weak, and his weakness touched Marianne and gave her at the same time a secret source of joy, for like this he belonged to her completely, he was hers, a part of her, flesh of her flesh, like the child she had lost, like the children she would give him . . .

Neither of them had spoken very much since leaving Brest, perhaps because they had too much to say and also because from now on they had all of life before them. It stretched ahead, limitless as the ocean which was all around them, leaping and jumping at their heels and making deep, moist panting sounds, like a pet animal whose master had returned after a long absence. At one point Marianne had thought that Jason was asleep, but when she bent over him she saw his eyes wide open and very bright and she knew that he was smiling.

'I had forgotten the sea smelled so good,' he murmured, holding the hand which he had not let go for a moment against his rough, unshaven cheek.

He had spoken very quietly, but Vidocq had heard and laughed:

'Particularly after the reek of the last few weeks. Human dirt and human wretchedness – it's the worst stench I know. Worse even than the stink of corruption because corruption is at least new life beginning. Try and forget – put it out of your mind. For you, it's all done with.'

'For you also, François.'

'Who can tell? I was not made for the wide open spaces but for the small world of men's thoughts and instincts. The elements may do very well for you. For myself, I prefer my fellow men. It's not as beautiful, but a lot more varied.'

'And more dangerous. Don't try to be too independent, François. Freedom is the one thing you have always lived for. You would find it in my country.'

'It depends what you mean by freedom . . .' Changing his tone abruptly, he asked: 'How long before we make Le Conquet?'

Jean Ledru answered him:

'We've a fair wind. In an hour, I'd say. It's not much above fifteen mile.'

They had run up a topsail and a flying jib to the bowsprit and the little craft was now carrying all her canvas, skimming the waves like a gull. On their starboard side, the coast fled past with now and then the squat belfry and roof of a church just visible, or the curious, angular shape of a dolmen. Pointing to one of these, Jean Ledru told Marianne: 'The legend has it that on Christmas Eve, when the clocks strike twelve, the dolmens and the menhirs go down to the sea to drink, leaving all their fabulous treasures uncovered. But woe betide anyone who tries to rob them if he is not quick enough, for on the last stroke they all return to their places, crushing the thief who may be caught inside.'

Marianne laughed, feeling again the pull of a good story which had always formed so strong an aspect of her appetite for life.

'How many legends are there in Brittany, Jean Ledru?'

'As many as the pebbles on the beach, I think.'

The beam of a lighthouse shone out suddenly through the darkness, yellow as an October moon, brooding over the jumbled mass of a huge, rocky promontory nearly a hundred feet high. Their youthful captain jerked his head towards it:

'St Mathieu's light. It is one of the westernmost points of Europe. There used to be a rich and powerful abbey there . . .'

As he spoke, a faint, uncertain shaft of moonlight filtered through the clouds and showed them the skeleton of an immense church and a great range of ruined buildings spreading out before the lighthouse, giving to that bare headland so gloomy and desolate an air that the sailors crossed themselves instinctively.

'Le Conquet is about a mile and a half to the north of here, is it not?' Vidocq asked, but Jean Ledru made no answer. He was searching the sea ahead. Then, just as the vessel rounded the point, her nose pointing out to sea, the shrill voice of the ship's boy rang out from the masthead:

'Sail ho, on the starboard beam!'

Everyone sat up and looked. Not more than a few cables' lengths away was the dainty outline of a brig, beating up wind with all sails flying in these perilous waters as surely as any fishing boat. Jean Ledru's voice rose above the wind: 'It's them! Get out the riding light!'

Marianne, like the rest, was watching the beautiful craft as it bore down on them, knowing that this was the rescue ship Surcouf had promised. Only Jason had not stirred but lay still, staring up at the sky, locked in a dream of sheer exhaustion. At last Ledru spoke impatiently:

'Well, Beaufort, take a look! It's your ship . . .'

A tremor ran through the privateer and he started to his feet then and remained, clinging to the rail, staring wide-eyed at the approaching vessel.

'The *Witch*!' His voice was husky with emotion. 'My *Witch* . . .'

Seeing him get to his feet, Marianne had followed, instinctively, and now standing next to him, she too stared:

'You mean – that ship is your own?'

'Yes . . . she is mine! Ours, Marianne! Tonight has given me back the two things I had thought lost for ever: you, my love . . . and her!'

There was such tenderness in that one short word that for a moment Marianne felt a stab of jealousy. Jason talked of the ship as he might have spoken of his own child. As if, instead of wood and metal, it had been made of his own blood and bone and his joy in looking at it was a father's joy in his child. She tightened the clasp of her hand on his, as though unconsciously trying to regain possession of him, but Jason's whole being was straining towards his ship so that he did not even seem to notice. He turned his head and looked at Jean Ledru, saying sharply:

'Do you know who is sailing her? Whoever he is, he is a master of his trade.'

Jean Ledru uttered a laugh of mingled pride and triumph:

'I'll say he is! A master indeed! It is Surcouf himself! We lifted your ship for you from under the very noses of the excisemen in Morlaix river . . . That's what made me later than we thought getting to Brest.'

'No,' came a quiet voice behind them. 'You did not "lift" it, as you put it. You took it, with the Emperor's knowledge. Hasn't it struck you yet that the excisemen seem unusually heavy sleepers tonight?'

If Vidocq had been striving for theatrical effect, he had certainly achieved his aim. Forgetting the brig, whose anchor chain could be heard running out and splashing into the sea, Marianne, Jason, Jean Ledru and even Jolival, who revived abruptly, turned with one accord to look at him. It was Jason who spoke for them all:

'With the Emperor's knowledge? What do you mean by that?'

Vidocq leaned back against the mainmast and folded his arms, his gaze going in turn to each of the tense faces turned towards him. Then, with the silky softness which his voice was able to assume when he wished it, he replied:

'I mean that he has given me my chance in these last months, and I am his loyal servant. My orders were to help you to escape at all costs. It has not been easy because, with the exception of our young friend here, everything, men and events, has been against me. But I had received my orders before you were even tried!'

For a moment, no one could say a word. They stood, rendered speechless by amazement, while their eyes struggled to take in what it was that had altered in this extraordinary man. Marianne clung to Jason's arm, still trying in vain to understand, and it was perhaps because it was beyond her power to do so that she was the first to recover her voice:

'The Emperor wanted Jason to escape? But then, why was he imprisoned, sent here . . .?'

'That, Madame, he will tell you himself. It is no part of my job to reveal to you reasons of State.'

'How can he tell me? You know that in a little while I shall have left France for good.'

'No.'

Marianne thought she could not have heard aright:

'What did you say?'

Vidocq looked at her and she saw a great compassion in his eyes, as he repeated, if possible still more gently than before: 'No. You are not going, Madame. Or not for the present, at least. As soon as Jason Beaufort has put to sea, I am to escort you back to Paris.'

'No! She stays with me! But it's time we had a few things explained. Just who are you?'

Gripping Marianne by the arm, Jason thrust her behind him, as though to make a shield for her of his own body. Her arms closed about him instinctively to hold him to her while he spoke to Vidocq in a voice made hard by anger. Vidocq sighed:

'You know who I am: François Vidocq and, until tonight, a convicted felon with the law on my tracks. But this escape is my last, once and for all, because I have a new life before me now.'

'A police spy! That's what you are!'

'I thank you, no! I am not a police spy. But a year ago I was given my chance, by Monsieur Henry, head of the Sureté, to work inside at tracking down crimes too sordid ever to come to light in any other way. They knew I was clever – my escapes proved that. And intelligent – my instinct for the guilty party showed that soon enough. I was working inside La Force and when you turned up it didn't need more than a glance to see that you were innocent, or one look at your file to show that it was a put-up job. The Emperor must have thought the same thing because my orders came through straightway to drop everything and concentrate on you. Further instructions followed which I adjusted to the occasion. If it hadn't been for that Quixotic gesture of yours, I should have had you away on the journey.'

'But why? What is it all about? You suffered as I did – the chain – the *bagne*?'

Vidocq's rather hard face lit up in a quick smile:

'I knew it was the last time, for your escape was to be mine also. No one is going to hunt for François Vidocq – or for Jason Beaufort, either. You have earned me the right to stop being an agent who works in secret, hidden behind prison bars and a convict's chains. From this moment, I belong openly to the Imperial police.* Everything that was done for you, was done with my approval. One of my men followed the so-called Mademoiselle de Jolival to Surcouf's house at St Malo and, before he left the town, he made known to the baron the Emperor's wish that he should take the brig *Sea Witch* from Morlaix roads and sail her to a spot chosen by me, but to make it look like a real theft. As you say, I suffered everything with you. Does that look like the action of a police spy?'

Jason's glance moved to Marianne who was still clinging to him. He could feel her whole body shuddering.

'No,' he said dully. 'I don't suppose I shall ever understand Napoleon's reasons, but I owe you my life, and for that I thank you from the bottom of my heart. But, what of her? Why must you take her back to Paris? I love her more—'

'More than life itself, than liberty, than anything in the world,' Vidocq finished for him wearily. 'I know all that – and so does the Emperor, undoubtedly. But she is not free, Jason. She is the Princess Sant'Anna ... She has a husband, even though that husband may be no more than a phantom, for he is a singularly powerful phantom, and his reach is very long. He is asking for his wife and the Emperor is bound to grant his request or his sister, the Grand Duchess of Tuscany, may well find herself with a rebellion on her hands.'

'I won't!' Marianne cried, clinging closer to Jason. 'I won't go back there, ever again! ... Jason, save me ... Take me with you! I am afraid of him, and his rights over me – even though I have never seen him. For pity's sake don't let them take me from you!'

* It is a matter of historical fact that at this period a one-time felon named François Vidocq who had been working secretly as a police agent within the prisons was authorized to escape. From then on, he became a member of the official police force and even lived to become its head.

'Marianne . . . darling! Quiet, my love, hush! No, I won't let you go. I'd go back to prison, back to my chains, anything rather than leave you.'

'I'm afraid you will have to, however,' Vidocq said heavily. 'There is your ship, Jason. The Emperor gives her back to you. Your life is with the sea, not languishing at the feet of another man's wife. For the Princess Sant'Anna a carriage waits by the harbour at Le Conquet.'

'Then it had better stop waiting!' A new voice had spoken, thick with anger. 'Marianne stays here!'

Jean Ledru, a pistol in either hand, stepped quickly in between Vidocq and the other two.

'This is my ship, Vidocq! It may be small, but I am master here after God! We have the sea under us and these men are all mine! There are fourteen of us to one of you. If you value your life, let me advise you to let Marianne go with the man she loves. Or, believe me, the fishes won't know the difference between a secret agent and an escaped convict! Now move, backwards, into the cabin. Once they are both aboard the brig, I'll land you on the coast.'

Vidocq only shook his head and pointed to where the brig was now hove to on their bow. Her tall sides loomed higher above the little lugger at every moment:

'You are reckoning without Surcouf, sailor. He knows this woman is married to another, and that other is demanding her. He is a man of honour and he knows where his duty lies.'

'He proved that when he agreed to assist Marianne, even when he could not have known that I was innocent,' Jason said quickly. 'He will help us now.'

'No. Nor should I ask him, if I were you.' He turned to Marianne, ignoring the pair of black muzzles aimed at his middle. 'I appeal to you, Madame, to your own loyalty and sense of honour. Did you wed the prince under any constraint, or of your own free will?'

Marianne's whole body stiffened in Jason's arms, as she fought with all her might to shake off the burden of doom which was descending on her at the very moment when happiness seemed finally within her grasp. She turned and hid her face against Jason's shoulder, saying in a muffled voice:

'I married him . . . of my own will. But I am afraid of him.'

'You, Jason? Haven't you a wife somewhere?'

'The demon who sought my death and Marianne's? She is nothing to me now.'

'Only your wife in the sight of God and men. Listen to me. If you part now, you may meet again later and be the better for it. For you, Madame, my duty is not to take you to your husband, but to the Emperor who desires your presence.'

'I have nothing to say to him!' Marianne said fiercely.

'But he has. And I cannot believe that you will have nothing to answer him – when he may help you perhaps, both of you, to be free from the ties that hold you. So be sensible. Do not oblige me to use force. Jason cannot be allowed to go unless he goes alone, and on condition that you go with me quietly to Paris.'

Jean Ledru, who had not released his grip on his pistols, laughed shortly and glanced up at the *Sea Witch*'s counter which now towered above them.

'The force is on our side, I think. And I tell you Marianne shall go with Jason and that Surcouf will help me send you to the bottom of the sea if you persist in this . . . Now, do as I say. Get below! There's a heavy sea getting up and we've no time to lose. The Iroise is no place to sit around and talk, and that low island that you see over yonder is Ushant. You know what they say about Ushant? That whoso shall see Ushant, shall see his own blood flow!'

'Force is not on your side, Jean Ledru. Look there!'

Marianne, whose hopes had risen when she saw the Breton's firm stand, gave a despairing groan. Rounding St Mathieu's Head was a frigate, the moonlight gleaming ominously on the muzzles of the guns protruding from her open ports.

'The *Sirène*,' Vidocq said in explanation. 'She is under orders to keep a close watch on what passes here. Emperor's orders, although he may not be precisely aware of them. All her captain knows is that on sighting a pre-arranged signal he is to open fire on the brig.'

Jolival, who had remained silent during these exchanges,

spoke for the first time. 'I congratulate you. You appear to wield considerable influence – for an ex-convict!'

'The power is the Emperor's, Monsieur. I am only the humble instrument. You know that he does not care to be disobeyed, and it seems he has his own reasons for not relying on this lady's blind obedience.'

Jolival shrugged scornfully:

'A warship cleared for action! And all to drag one unhappy woman from the man she loves! Not to mention that if the *Sea Witch* is sent to the bottom, you send your famous Surcouf with her!'

'At any moment, Baron Surcouf will be aboard this vessel. See, here he comes now.'

It was true. A rope ladder had been flung over the brig's side, down which a burly figure was clambering like a monkey on a stick, at a speed that said a good deal for his fitness.

'Moreover,' Vidocq continued, 'Madame here is no unhappy woman but a very great lady whose husband is in a position to cause great trouble. I say nothing of Beaufort's importance – but the Emperor would not have been at such pains to rescue him had he been a person of no account. Our good relations with Washington depend on his reaching his own country intact, and with his ship, whether or not he is supposed to be rotting in the hulks. Well, Madame? What is your decision?'

Surcouf had jumped down on to the deck and was striding lightly towards them.

'What are you about?' he called. 'You must get aboard at once. The wind's getting up and the sea's rising. Your men are waiting for you, Monsieur Beaufort, and you are too good a sailor not to know the dangers of hanging about off Ushant, especially when the wind sits in this quarter.'

'Give them a moment more,' Vidocq interposed. 'Time at least to say goodbye.'

Marianne shut her eyes and a tearing sob broke from her. She clung to Jason with all her strength, as though hoping for some miracle from heaven to make them into a single person. She felt his arms holding her tightly, his breath on her neck and in a moment a tear rolled down her cheek.

'Not goodbye!' she implored desperately. 'Not goodbye for ever. I could not bear it.'

Jason tightened his hold. 'Nor could I. We shall be together again, Marianne, I swear it!' The words were whispered close into her ear. 'They are stronger than we are and we must obey. But they are sure to send you back to Italy, and I will meet you there . . .'

'Meet me?'

In the agony of her grief, the sense of what he said had scarcely penetrated, despite the hope it held.

'Yes. I will meet you, in Venice – in six months. My ship will lie offshore and wait for as long as need be.'

Slowly, he was inspiring her with the same indomitable fighting spirit which he himself had never lost, forcing the words into her ear as if he would have forced them into her mind and, little by little, life seemed to return and her brain began to function once again.

'Why Venice? Leghorn is the nearest port to Lucca.'

'Because Venice is not a French possession. It is Austrian. If your husband will not release you, you must fly there to me. Napoleon cannot touch you in Venice . . . Do you understand? You will come? In six months . . .'

'I shall come, but Jason—'

He stopped her mouth with a kiss, infusing into it all the passion of his love for her. When he let her go at last, his blue eyes looked earnestly into her tear-filled ones as he said in a low, vibrant murmur:

'Before God, Marianne, I will never give you up! I want you and I am going to have you. Even if I must go to the end of the world to find you . . . Jolival, you will take care of her? I have your promise?'

'What else have I ever done?' the Vicomte said gruffly, tenderly receiving on his chest the trembling form given into his care. 'Have no fears on that score.'

Jason turned resolutely and, making his way to Surcouf, bowed gravely.

'I'm no great hand at thanks,' he said, 'but you may command me, Baron, as and where you like. I am your most grateful servant.'

'My name is Robert Surcouf,' the baron retorted. 'Come here and let me embrace you, lad!' And added, for Jason's ear alone: 'Try and come back for her. She's worth it.'

'I have known that for a long time,' Jason said with a fleeting smile, returning the Malouin's vigorous embrace. 'I shall be back.'

Last of all, he turned to Vidocq and offered him his hand, unreservedly.

'We have been through too much together, you and I, François,' he said, 'for us to be aught but brothers. You did your duty, that was all. You had no other choice.'

'Thank you,' Vidocq said simply. 'Don't worry over her. I, too, shall be watching. Come, I'll help you up.'

He indicated the rope ladder, now banging in the rising wind, that climbed the sheer sides of the brig above them. But even as he spoke men were descending on the deck from the American vessel, hoisting up their captain like a parcel. Ledru's men, reaching out to shake Jason's hand in a crushing grip as he was borne past, held the ladder stiff and steady.

Leaning against Jolival, Marianne watched his progress, following him with her eyes until he reached the frieze of human heads and bodies lining the rail above. Jason's arrival on deck was the signal for a rousing cheer which rang like a death knell in Marianne's already breaking heart. To her, it sounded like the voice of that distant country of his, claiming him from her, back again to a place where she was not allowed to follow.

Meanwhile, Vidocq had gone to the lugger's stern and signalled three times by opening and closing the shutter of a lantern, and away beyond the promontory of rocks the frigate was already going about for Brest. Already, the sky above the coast was almost imperceptibly lighter, though the wind was strengthening, filling the sails as they were set once more, and the lugger's crew, armed with long gaffs, fended her off from the brig's side. Jean Ledru was back at the tiller and, slowly, inexorably, the gap of water between the two vessels widened.

The lugger slipped astern of the great sailing ship and lay for a moment in the pool of light cast by her two gilded stern lanterns. And there, high above her as she stood unable any longer to restrain her tears, Marianne saw Jason, his tall figure supported by his own men. He raised one arm in a gesture of farewell, but already he seemed very far away ... so far, indeed, that for a moment Marianne forgot the promise she had made only a moment before, forgot to be brave, forgot that this parting was not goodbye but only *au revoir*. She was only a desperate broken woman, seeing the best part of herself borne away from her on the wind. With a last, terrible effort, she tore herself from Jolival's comforting arms and flung herself at the rail.

'Jason!' she screamed, oblivious of the tossing bow wave which drenched her in spray. 'Jason! ... Come back! ... Come back! ... I love you ...'

She clung with dripping fingers to the slippery wood, tossing back the sodden tangles of her hair in an automatic gesture. The lugger plunged deeply into a trough of the waves, nearly sending her sprawling on the deck, but all the strength that she possessed was in her clinging hands, her whole life in the eyes which still gazed at the fast-dwindling shape of Jason's ship. At last, two strong arms came to encircle her, drawing her back from her desperate watch, and from the peril in which she stood.

'Are you out of your mind?' Vidocq's voice scolded. 'Do you want to fall overboard?'

'I want to see him again ... I want to be with him!'

'And he with you! But it's not a corpse he'd hope to find, it's you, yourself, alive! Good God! Do you want to die before his eyes to prove your love? For the love of heaven, live! Live at least until the time he appointed for your meeting.'

Marianne's eyes widened in amazement. Already the instinct for life was reviving in her, willing her to fight on towards the goal which at this moment had eluded her.

'How did you know?'

'He loves you. He would never have parted from you without something of the kind. Now go and get under cover. You are soaking wet and the dawn mist is rising. It's as easy to die of an inflammation of the lungs as it is by drowning.'

She submitted docilely when he led her to a more sheltered spot on the deck and wrapped a heavy canvas sailcloth about her, but rejected all attempts to make her go below. While Jason's ship was still there to be seen, she was determined not to lose sight of it.

Far out, near the islands with their attendant train of rocky reefs and islets, the *Sea Witch* was heading out to sea, dipping gracefully under the frail, towering white peaks of her crowded sails. In the grey light of dawn, she looked like a gull, gliding among the black rocks. For a moment, as the vessel went about to pass between two jagged islets, she presented herself to Marianne's eyes broadside on and she recalled then what it was that Talleyrand had told her one day about that figure shaped like a woman on the prow. He had said that the figure-head was carved in her own image, that Jason had had it made to adorn the prow of his ship, and Marianne found herself wishing passionately that she could be that woman made of wood whom he had caused to be created, and on whom his eyes must often rest.

A moment later, the American brig had gone about again and nothing more remained to be seen but the stern, with its two lanterns vanishing into the mist.

Sighing, Marianne made her way to where Surcouf and Jolival were sitting, talking quietly together, on some coils of rope while all around them was the slap of the sailors' bare feet as they went about their duties. In a little while now, the carriage would be bearing her back to Paris, as Vidocq had said, back to Paris and the Emperor. She wondered why he should want to see her. Barely recalling now that she had ever loved him, Marianne could think only that she had no desire to see Napoleon.

Three weeks later, as her chaise clattered under the gateway of the château of Vincennes, Marianne glanced up at Vidocq with an expression full of alarm.

'Do your orders say I must be put in prison?' she asked.

'Good heavens, no! It is the Emperor's wish to grant you an audience, that is all. It is not for me to know his reasons. All that I can tell you is that my mission ends here.'

They had completed their journey from Brittany the night before and as he set Marianne down at her own door Vidocq had told her that he would come for her the following evening to take her to the Emperor, adding that court dress was not necessary but that she should be sure to wrap up warmly.

She had been a little mystified by this advice but too tired to ask any questions. Nor had she waited to interrogate Jolival. Instead, she had gone straight to bed, like a drowning sailor clutching at a raft, to recruit her strength for whatever was to come, little enough though it might interest her. Only one thing held any meaning for her: three weeks had gone by, three dreadful weeks spent jolting over the endless roads which the bad weather had made more trying even than usual, on a journey rendered hideous by every conceivable kind of unpleasantness, from lost wheels and broken springs to horses that slipped and fell and trees blown across the road. Yet for all this it was three weeks gone from the six months at whose end Jason would be waiting for her.

When she thought of him, which she did every hour, every second of her waking day, it was with a curious feeling of emptiness, like a painful, insatiable hunger which she tried to satisfy by letting her mind dwell constantly on the few, so very few moments when he had been there, close to her, so close that she could touch him, hold his hand, stroke his hair and smell the odour of his skin, the comforting warmth of him and the strength with which, even in his weakened state, he had crushed her to him and pressed that last kiss upon her lips, the kiss whose memory burned her still, and sent a tremor through all her limbs.

They had found Paris deep in snow. The bitter cold froze the water in the gutters, nipping ears and reddening noses. Miniature icebergs floated on the grey, bustling waters of the Seine and there were rumours that people in the poorer districts were dying of cold at nights. Everything was buried under a thick, white blanket which soon became stained and dirty but did not melt, leaving the gardens dressed in a cloak of dazzling white ermine while it transformed the streets into deadly, frozen sewers where it was the easiest thing in the world for anyone to break a leg. Even so, Marianne's horses, frost-nailed, had negotiated the long road from the rue de Lille to Vincennes without mishap.

The ancient fortress of the kings of France had risen suddenly out of the night, grim and uncared-for, its towers demolished now to the level of the walls. Two only remained intact, the village tower bestriding the ancient drawbridge, and the enormous square keep, its dark bulk rising high above the bare trees, flanked by its four corner turrets. Vincennes was an arsenal, its storehouses guarded by veterans no longer fit for active service and a handful of regular troops, but it was also a state prison and the keep itself was strongly fortified.

Yet now it stood, silent within the circle of its curtain wall, cut off on the right hand by the barbican from the wide, white courtyard where the snow-covered piles of ammunition were like odd, conical cream cakes. Opposite was the derelict chapel, beautiful in the frayed lacework of crumbling stone, decaying slowly because no one thought of repairing it, a precious jewel to St Louis but neglected now, in these days of little faith. And Marianne searched her mind in vain for any reason for this audience, held in the secrecy of this rotting fortress with its sinister reputation. Why Vincennes? Why at night?

At a little distance, a noble pair of twin pavilions faced each other, evoking memories of the Grand Siècle of Louis XIV, although they had fared no better than the rest of the buildings. Panes of glass were missing from the windows, the mouldings of the mansard roofs were broken and the walls seamed with cracks. Yet it was towards the left-hand one of these two that Gracchus, acting on Vidocq's instructions, now turned his horses.

There was a faint light showing on the ground floor, behind the blackened windows. The chaise stopped, and Vidocq jumped out.

'Come,' he said. 'You are expected.'

Marianne looked about her in surprise, her eyes taking in the dismal, comfortless dilapidation of her surroundings. Hugging her black, sable-lined cloak more tightly round her, she pulled the furred hood closer round her face as a biting wind whistled across the court, whipping up handfuls of snow and making her eyes water. Marianne made her way slowly into a tiled vestibule which still retained some traces of a former splendour. The first thing that met her eyes was Rustan. Enveloped in a huge, bright red greatcoat with nothing but the top of his white turban showing above the turned-up collar, the Mameluke was striding up and down on the uneven floor, beating his arms together for warmth. At the sight of Marianne, however, he made haste to open for her the door outside which he had been keeping his energetic guard. At last, Marianne found herself face-to-face with Napoleon.

The Emperor was standing beneath the canopy of an immense hearth on which the better part of a large tree trunk was burning briskly. He was staring down at the flames, one booted foot resting on the hearthstone, one hand behind his back, the other thrust into the breast of his long, grey redingote. His shadow, topped by the curved silhouette of his plain, black cocked hat, innocent of any adornment, stretched fantastically, reared up to the carved and caissoned ceiling on which flakes of the old gilding still remained. That shadow alone sufficed to fill the great empty room, bare of all furnishings except for the frayed ends of ancient tapestries on the walls and a few heaps of rubble on the floor.

He watched, thoughtful and expressionless, as Marianne sank into her formal curtsy, then beckoned her to the fire.

'Come and warm yourself,' he said. 'It's horribly cold tonight.'

In silence, Marianne moved forward and held out her ungloved hands to the blaze, jerking her head back as she did so to let the fur hood slide back from her face. The two of them stood for a moment without speaking, looking down at the dancing flames and letting the warmth seep into their bodies. At last, Napoleon glanced quickly at the girl beside him.

'Angry with me?' he asked, his eyes fixed a little uneasily on the delicate, unsmiling profile, with its lowered lashes and straight lips.

Marianne did not look at him as she answered:

'I should not allow myself to be angry with you, Sire. One is not angry with the master of Europe.'

'Yet that is precisely what you are. And I can scarcely find it in me to blame you. You thought you were going, didn't you? You meant to cut the threads binding you to a life you would be done with, wipe out the past, eliminate everything that had been . . .'

The green eyes were turned on him then, the faintest twinkle of laughter in their depths. Really, he was the most extraordinary play actor! It was so like him to try and work himself into a rage when he knew that he was in the wrong.

'You need not try to generate an anger which you do not feel, Sire. I am too well acquainted with . . . Your Majesty. Now that I am here, perhaps Your Majesty will deign to forget whatever it was I meant to do and explain the strange things which have happened in the past months. Dare I admit that I have been very much in the dark, and remain so to this present, indeed?'

'I had not thought you unintelligent?'

'I hope not, Sire. But it would seem that Your Majesty's policies are somewhat too involved for a woman's brain to grasp. And I am not ashamed to admit that I have been able to make nothing of what your judges and your press have been referring to as the "Beaufort affair" . . . unless it is that an innocent man has suffered unjustly and faced death a dozen times merely to give one of your agents the pleasure and the glory of helping him to escape at last, with your blessing and under the supervision of your imperial navy . . . and I myself have nearly died of grief! And now, to crown all, you have me brought here by force . . .'

'Oh ho! Such force!'

'Very well. Against my will, if you prefer. But why?'

Napoleon roused himself from his thoughtful pose and, turning to Marianne, said gravely:

'So that justice may be done, Marianne, and seen to be done by you.'

'Justice?'

'Yes, justice. I have always known that Jason Beaufort was in no way guilty, either of the murder of Nicolas Mallerousse or of anything else. The worst he had done was to take some champagne and burgundy out of France for the delectation of a set of persons whose enjoyment gives me personally no great pleasure. But I had to lay hands on the malefactors – the real malefactors, that is, without destroying the delicate balance of my foreign policies. And in order to achieve that, it was necessary to play the game out to the end.'

'And to risk to the end the possibility that Jason Beaufort might die of his sufferings or the inhuman treatment of your prison guards.'

'I saw to it that he had a guardian angel, and by God! he seems to have done his work well! I had to catch the criminals, I tell you . . . and then there was that matter of the forged English money which forced me to act or else become a laughing-stock, and incidentally reveal too much about the workings of my own secret service.'

By now, curiosity was to some extent overcoming Marianne's first resentment:

'You say, Your Majesty, that it was necessary for you to catch the criminals? May I ask if you have them now?'

Napoleon merely nodded, but Marianne persisted:

'Your Majesty knows who killed Nicolas Mallerousse, who is the coiner?'

'I know who killed Nicolas Mallerousse and I have him fast, as for the coining . . .'

He paused and glanced at Marianne's strained face as though undecided. Thinking it advisable to give him some encouragement, she said: 'Was it not the same man?'

'No. The coiner was . . . myself.'

Marianne could not have been more thoroughly stunned had the ancient ceiling fallen on her head. She stared at the Emperor as if she had begun to doubt his sanity!

'*You*, Sire?'

'I. My idea was to strike a blow at English commerce by producing, in the strictest secrecy, a large amount of English currency and flooding the market with it. I have no idea how the villains who stowed them on Jason Beaufort's vessel managed to get hold of them, but one thing is certain: they were mine . . . though I could equally certainly not proclaim the fact. That is why I allowed suspicion to remain on your friend, while in and out of prisons everywhere in France my agents were working in the dark to unravel the truth. It was for the same reason that I had his reprieve made out in advance and laid the best plans I could for his escape. That could not fail. Vidocq is a clever man . . . and I had no doubt that you would give him a hand.'

'Truly, Sire, we are small things in your hands. I begin to wonder whether a man of genius is a blessing of the gods – or a calamity! But, Sire' – she went on, a note of anxiety in her voice, 'this criminal – or criminals?'

'You are right to say criminals, for there are a number of them, but they have a leader, and this leader – but no – come with me.'

'Where to?'

'To the keep. I have something to show you. But wrap yourself warmly.'

He stooped to pick up Marianne's gloves which she had dropped on the hearth and himself settled the hood once more over her head, his hands reverting instinctively to the old, caressing gestures with which, during those enchanted days they had spent together at the Trianon, he had been used to put on her cloak for her and drape the scarf about her hair. Just as he had done then, he took her arm and led her outside, signing to Rustan to follow as he passed.

Out in the open, the icy wind whirled about them but, leaning close together, they plunged across the vast courtyard, up to their ankles in the snow which crunched beneath their feet. They came to the barbican before the keep and Napoleon made her go before him through the low archway, guarded by two sentries so rigid they might have been frozen stiff. Even their moustaches had icicles on them. On the far side, Napoleon held her back suddenly. In the light of the lantern which hung by an iron bracket from the wall, his blue-grey eyes were very grave, even stern, but there was no hardness in them.

'What you are going to see will be very horrible, Marianne . . . and altogether exceptional. But, let me say it again, justice must be done. Are you ready to look at what I would show you?'

She met his eyes unflinchingly:

'I am ready.'

He took her hand and drew her forward. They passed through another low arch and found themselves at the foot of the keep, standing on a plank bridge spanning the wide, deep moat. There was a wooden staircase going down into the moat and Marianne looked down, automatically, to where some lanterns were moving about below, to draw back almost immediately with a choking gasp of horror. There, in the trampled snow at the foot of the empty moat, with a guard standing on either side of it, was a sinister wooden framework, like a hideous window made of red-painted wood, with a great triangular blade at its upper end. The guillotine.

Marianne stared at the ghastly instrument with eyes dilated with horror. She was trembling so violently that Napoleon pulled her gently within the circle of his arm and held her close.

'It is dreadful, I know. And none can loathe that fearful thing more than I . . .'

'Then why . . .'

'Because it is fitting. In a short while, a man is going to die. He is waiting now in a cell inside the keep and no one, apart from those few who will be present at his execution, will ever know that it took place here tonight, just as no one will ever know how he was condemned. But the fact is that this man is a criminal of an altogether exceptional kind, such a wretch as is rarely found. Last summer, he lured Nicolas Mallerousse into a trap and, with the help of his accomplices, had him carried, gagged and bound to the house at Passy where Jason Beaufort was living at that time, and where he thereafter cold-bloodedly cut his throat. But this killing was only one of his many crimes. Some dozens of my own troops, held captive on the English hulks, have died, torn to pieces by the hounds which this man trained to track them down . . .'

Marianne had known, ever since Napoleon had told her that he held the criminal, that this was what she would hear. For her own part, she had known for so long that it was he who had killed Nicolas. Yet even now, she found it hard to believe that a man of his diabolical cunning could have allowed himself to be caught. Napoleon's last words, however, had thrown a blinding light even on this.

One doubt, stronger than all reason, Marianne had still:

'Sire! Are you sure that this time there is no mistake?'

He stiffened, embracing her in a glance that was suddenly ice-cold:

'You do not mean to ask me to pardon him, now?'

'God forbid, Sire! . . . if it is he, indeed!'

'Come. I will show him to you.'

They entered the keep, passed by the guard-room, its door shut for once, and climbed the fine spiral staircase up to the first floor where they emerged into a gothic chamber, the four bays of the roof supported on a massive central pillar. Here, a warder was on guard, and with him was Vidocq, whose tall figure bent double at the sight of the Emperor. At each corner of the room was a heavy, iron-bound door, leading to the cells which occupied the four corner turrets. Napoleon made a sign to the warder:

'Open the hatch. Try not to make a noise. This lady desires to see the prisoner.'

The man walked over to one of the corner turret doors, opened a small judas window and bowed.

'Go on,' Napoleon told Marianne. 'Look.'

She went, reluctantly, over to the door, both wanting and fearing what she would see, yet fearing most of all to find herself looking at a strange face, the face of some poor wretch who, by one of those sleights of hand at which they were so adept, had somehow been substituted for the real criminal.

The circular cell was lit by a lantern standing on a stool. A fire crackled cheerfully in the conical hearth, but the man who lay at full-length on the bed wore chains on his wrists and ankles. Marianne needed no second look to tell her that this was indeed the man whom she had both hoped and feared to see. It was Francis Cranmere, the man whose name she herself had once borne.

He was sleeping, but it was a restless, fevered sleep which recalled to her mind the little Spanish abbé in La Force. It was the sleep of a man who is afraid and whose fear stalks even in his dreams ... A fine, white hand came down and closed the window before Marianne's wide, horror-stricken eyes.

'Well?' Napoleon asked. 'It is indeed he, this time?'

She nodded, unable to speak, and was forced to lean back against the wall for a moment, overcome by the turmoil of her feelings, made up of a combination of an awful gladness and at the same time a kind of horror, mingled with surprise at seeing the devil who had so nearly destroyed her own life caught at last. When she had recovered herself a little, she looked up and saw the Emperor standing before her, watching her anxiously, while farther off Vidocq stood motionless against the central pillar.

'So,' she said at last, 'it is for him ... the thing I saw below?'

'Yes. And I say to you again: I hate that instrument. I have seen it murder too many innocent people. I am appalled by it and yet that man does not deserve to die, like a soldier, before a firing squad. It is not to you, or even to Nicolas Mallerousse, that I am offering up his head, but to the shades of my own men, slaughtered piecemeal by this butcher.'

'When – when is it to be?'

'Now. See, here comes the priest.'

An old man in a black soutane had emerged from the shadows of the staircase. He held a breviary in his hand. Marianne shook her head:

'He will not want him. He is not a Catholic.'

'I know, but it was not possible to procure a Protestant minister. Besides, what does it matter in the moment of death whose are the lips that speak of God and of the hope of His mercy, so long as the words are spoken?'

The priest gave a little bow and then passed on to the closed door, the warder hurrying before him. Marianne gripped Napoleon's arm nervously:

'Sire! . . . Must we stay here? I—'

'You do not wish to see? I am not surprised. In any case, it was no part of my intention to oblige you to witness such a scene. I only wanted you to be quite sure that this time justice has not miscarried, and that nothing can halt its course now. Let us go down – unless you wish to bid him farewell.'

She shook her head and almost ran towards the stairs. No, she did not wish to see Francis Cranmere again. She would not triumph over him as he went to his death, if only for fear of seeing the last thoughts of the man she had once loved, a man whose name she had borne, turn to hatred at the sight of her. If repentance were possible for such a man as Francis Cranmere, she would not have its blessed course turned aside for any action of hers.

She went down the stairs, the Emperor following, and across the plank bridge without a glance for the dreadful instrument below, and found herself before long in the great, white desert of the courtyard. The wind, buffeting her body, revived her and she turned her burning face to it. It had begun to snow again and a few flakes touched her lips. She put out her tongue and licked them gratefully and then turned and waited until Napoleon, less nimble than herself, caught up with her. He took her arm and they walked back, as they had come but more slowly now, to the Pavillon de la Reine.

'What of the others?' Marianne asked suddenly. 'Have you caught them as well?'

'Old Fanchon and her crew? You need have no fear. They are under lock and key and there is enough evidence against them to hang them a hundred times over, or send them to rot in prison for the remainder of their lives, without so much as mentioning this business. They will stand trial and pay the penalty in the ordinary way. For him, that was not possible. He knew too much and the English might even now have found a way to free him. Secrecy was vital.'

They were back in the empty room where Rustan was stirring up the fire. Napoleon sighed and removed his hat, from which the melting snow was running in thin streams.

'Now it is time to talk of you. When the roads are somewhat

better, you will return to Italy. I must accede to your husband's requests because they are perfectly reasonable. It is not in the Emperor's power to withhold the Prince Sant'Anna's wife from him.'

'But I am not his wife!' Marianne protested wildly. 'You know quite well that I am not, Sire! You know the reason why I married him! The child is no more . . . therefore there is no longer anything to bind me to this – this . . . shadow!'

'You are his wife, even if only in name. I do not understand you, Marianne. It is not like you to turn your back on your duty. I thought you so gallant. You accepted the aid of this poor devil . . . for so he must be in the conditions by which he has chosen to live . . . and now that you can no longer fulfil your part of the contract, you have not even courage enough to face him honestly. I am surprised at you . . .'

'Say disappointed, rather! But I can't help it, Sire. I am afraid! Yes, I am afraid of that house, of what it contains, of that man whom no one ever sees and the evil which hangs about him. All the women of that family have died violent deaths. I want to live, and be with Jason again!'

'There was a time when you wanted to live for me,' Napoleon observed with a touch of sadness. 'How things change! How women change . . . I think, in the end, my love was greater than yours, for all my feelings for you are not yet dead, and if you would . . .'

Marianne lifted her hand quickly to stop what he would have said. 'No, Sire! In a moment you are going to offer me the – the solution to my problem that Fortunée Hamelin suggested to me once. It might satisfy Prince Sant'Anna, but I mean to keep myself now for the man I love . . . whatever risks that may involve.'

'Very well.' Napoleon sighed. 'We will speak no more of it.' From the curtness of his tone, Marianne knew that she had vexed him. Perhaps, in his masculine pride, he had thought that an hour with him might help to soften her longings for Jason and bring her back, chastened and obedient, to the path which he had no doubt designed for her.

After a brief silence, he resumed: 'You must go back, Marianne. Both honour and policy demand it. You must go back to your husband. But do not be afraid. Nothing will happen to you.'

'How do you know?' Marianne said, more bitterly than politely.

'I shall be watching. You shall not go alone. Apart from this curious old fellow who seems to have adopted you, you shall have an escort . . . an armed escort which will remain with you and act as you think fit.'

Marianne's eyes opened wide:

'An escort? For me? But on what pretext?'

'Shall we say . . . as Ambassadress Extraordinary? In fact I am sending you not to Lucca but to Florence, to my sister Elisa. You may easily sort out your differences with your husband without incurring the least danger because I will charge you with messages for the Grand Duchess of Tuscany. I mean my protection to extend to you there, and to have it known.'

'Ambassadress? I? But I am only a woman?'

'I have frequently employed women on other occasions. My sister Pauline knows something of that! And I should not wish to hand you over bound hand and foot to the man you have – yourself – chosen to marry.'

The implication was sufficiently obvious. She was to understand that had she, Marianne, showed more sense, she would have trusted her then lover to provide for her and not gone plunging off into impossible adventures . . . Judging it better to make no reply, she merely bowed and then sank into the ritual curtsy.

'I shall obey, Sire. And I thank Your Majesty for your care of me.'

Mentally, she was calculating that once in Florence it would be easy for her to reach Venice, much easier than she had feared. She had, as yet, no idea how she meant to settle her differences with Prince Corrado, or what form of arrangement he intended to suggest, but one thing was certain: she would never again live in the great, white villa, beautiful and deadly as one of those exotic flowers whose perfume enchanted but whose juice could kill.

Of course, there was still the matter of the escort. That would have to be got rid of...

The door opened suddenly and Vidocq came in. He merely bowed, gravely, without speaking. The Emperor's body stiffened. His eyes turned to Marianne and met hers and she held his gaze steadily, feeling the colour drain from her face in spite of herself.

'Justice is done!' was all he said.

But Marianne knew before he spoke that Francis Cranmere's head had fallen. Slowly, she dropped to her knees on the stone floor, feeling it warm from the fire, and with bowed head and hands clasped together, began to pray for the man who would never again have power to harm her.

Rather than disturb her prayers, Napoleon moved away silently into the shadows.

The cannon were booming through Paris, Marianne listened to the salvos, standing at the window, with Adelaide and Jolival, counting the number.

'Two... three... four...'

She knew what they meant. The Emperor's child was born. Even before this, in the middle of the night, the great bell of Notre-Dame and the bells of every church in Paris had called to every Frenchman to pray to heaven for a happy issue and in the capital there had been no more sleep for anyone, for Marianne least of all for this was the last night she would spend in her own house.

Her trunks were packed and loaded already on to the great travelling carriage and in a little while, when the promised escort arrived, she would take the road for Italy. The letters she was to present to the Grand Duchess of Tuscany lay on the chest, in all the glory of their red seals and ribbons. The furniture of her bedchamber was already clad in its uniform of dust sheets. There were no flowers in the vases. But Marianne's heart had quitted this house long ago.

Jolival, as nervous as she, was counting aloud. 'Seventeen, eighteen, nineteen... If it is a girl, they say she will have the title of Princess of Venice.'

Venice! It was no more than three months now before Jason's ship would drop anchor in the lagoon. The very name, delicate and colourful as the scintillating glassware of the city's own craftsmen, became clothed in all the varied brilliance of hope and love.

'Twenty . . .' Jolival counted, '. . . twenty-one . . .'

There was a pause, brief but so intense that it might have seemed as if the entire Empire were holding its breath. Then the brazen voices resumed their triumphant clamour.

'Twenty-two! Twenty-three!' Jolival shouted. 'There are going to be a hundred and one! It is a boy! Long live the Emperor! Long live the King of Rome!'

His cry was echoed and magnified as though by magic. Everywhere could be heard windows being flung open, doors slamming, and shouting from innumerable throats as the people of Paris poured out into the streets. Only Marianne did not move but stood with eyes closed. So Napoleon had the son he so desired! His pink Austrian brood mare had done what was expected of her. How happy he must be! And proud! She could imagine him making the palace ring with the metallic tones of his voice, the nervous click of his heels . . . The child was born, and it was a boy . . . the King of Rome! A fine name, a name to evoke the mastery of the world! A heavy name, too, to lay on such tiny shoulders.

'Come, Marianne! We must drink to this happy birth!'

Arcadius had already loosed the cork from a bottle of champagne and was filling glasses, handing one to each of the two women. His sparkling gaze went from one to the other as he raised the clear crystal glass with the pale golden liquid foaming within:

'The King of Rome! . . . And to you, too, Marianne. To the day when we shall drink to a son of yours! He will not be a king, but he will be handsome . . . strong and brave like his father.'

'Do you really think so?' Marianne asked. Her eyes moistened even at the thought of so much happiness.

'I do more than think it,' Arcadius said seriously. 'I am certain of it.'

Draining his glass, he sent it spinning over his shoulder in the Russian fashion to shatter against the marble chimney breast.

'As certain as I am that I have broken that glass.'

Intrigued and not a little amused, the two women followed his example. Then Marianne said:

'Assemble the servants, Arcadius, and have them drink champagne also. I want to leave them happy, because I shall come back to this house happy, or else not at all. And now I am going to dress.'

And she left the room to make ready for the long journey ahead of her. Outside, above the joyous clamour of the cheering Parisians, the cannon were still thundering.

It was the twenty-first of March, 1811.